Also by William Westbrook—

The Bermuda Privateer

THE BLACK RING

A NICHOLAS FALLON SEA NOVEL

William Westbrook

McBooks Press, Inc.
www.mcbooks.com
Ithaca, New York

Published by McBooks Press 2018

Copyright © 2018 by William Westbrook

Cover painting: *Coeur de* France © 2017 by Paul Garnett.
Book design by Panda Musgrove.

Library of Congress Cataloging-in-Publication Data

Names: Westbrook, William, 1945- author.
Title: The black ring / William Westbrook.
Description: Ithaca, New York : McBooks Press, Inc, [2018] | Series: The Nicholas Fallon sea novels ; 2.
Identifiers: LCCN 2018024073 (print) | LCCN 2018025138 (ebook) | ISBN 9781590137703 (ePub) | ISBN 9781590137697 (mobipocket) | ISBN 9781590137710 (pdf) | ISBN 9781590137680 (hardcover)
Subjects: LCSH: Privateering--Fiction. | Merchant ships--Fiction. | Treasure troves--Caribbean Area--Fiction. | Pirates--Fiction. | Naval battles--Fiction. | BISAC: FICTION / Sea Stories. | FICTION / War & Military. | GSAFD: Sea stories. | Adventure fiction.
Classification: LCC PS3623.E84753 (ebook) | LCC PS3623.E84753 B53 2018 (print) | DDC 813/.6--dc23
LC record available at https://lccn.loc.gov/2018024073

Visit the McBooks Press website at www.mcbooks.com.

Printed in the United States of America
9 8 7 6 5 4 3 2 1

*In memory of Joe Culligan—
A wonderful storyteller, generous lender of books,
deeply loyal friend, and a good man in a storm.
Cully, in real life.*

Special Thanks

I am grateful to my able crew: Tripp Westbrook, Cabell Westbrook, Bob Westbrook, Kerry Feuerman, and, of course, my own Beauty—my wife, Susan.

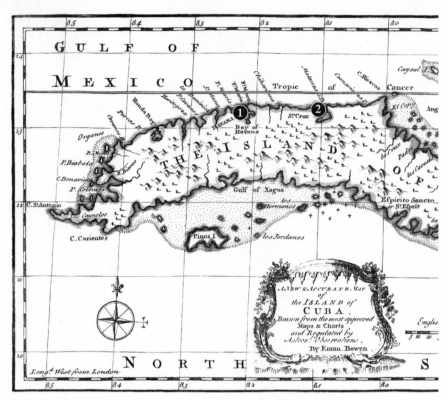

Cuba (above): 1. Havana, 2. Matanzas, 3. Santiago de Cuba, 4. Anvil Hill

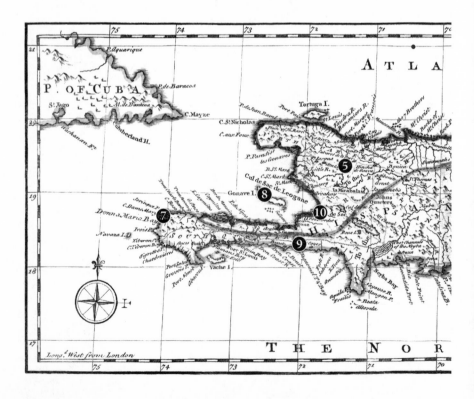

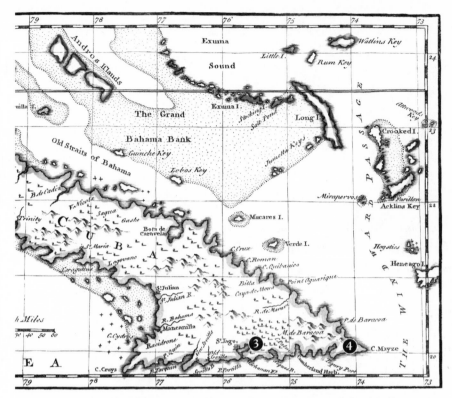

Hispaniola (below): 5. St Domingue, 6. Santo Domingo, 7. Dame Marie,
8. Gonâve Is, 9. Jacmel, 10. Port-au-Prince

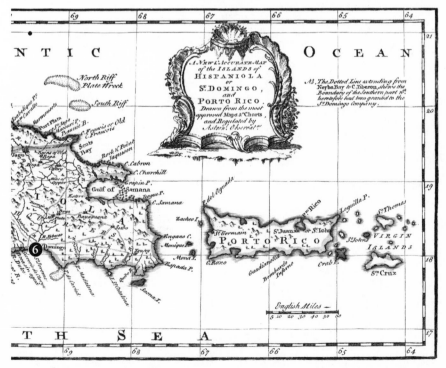

On the island of Martinique is a statue of Marie-Josèphe-Rose Tascher de la Pagerie, once called the Rose of Martinique. When she wed Napoleon Bonaparte, she became Joséphine, Empress of France. The statue is decapitated.

ONE

The Beginning
Senegal, West Africa

*T*HE LONG, *black snake slowly wound its way down from the tree-covered hills and into the tall plains grasses, hidden by the swaying greens and yellows, every bird and animal silenced, every insect suddenly quiet in an eerie, soundless chorus. The spine of the snake undulated as it moved and curved in a lazy S, stretching and constricting a chain attached to a hundred and fifty men at the neck. The slaves choked on the dust and spat out wet dirt until they ran dry of saliva but, to a man, they kept their heads down.*

Behind them, perhaps a quarter of a mile, a long snake of women and children, shackled only at the ankles, moved slower than the men because occasionally the drivers would stop the line to rape one of the women. It happened enough that no one looked up. Anyway, they didn't dare.

This was a business, nothing more. African kings raided other kingdoms and kidnapped their enemies and, rather than kill them, simply sold them as slaves. It was a growing part of the economy of West Africa, where there were many kings. The only nuisance was having to march them from the interior to the island of Gorée, where the European and Caribbean dealers were. But business was good, for every king had many enemies, and kidnapping them had the effect of consolidating a king's power.

Each night found the men and women collapsed on the ground, the only sound being the screams of another assault. There was no thought of escape, only confusion among the slaves about what had happened and where they were going.

And why?

The Seasoning
Gorée Island

THE AFRICAN WARRIOR stood on the auction block, naked. He was tall and strongly built, with a jagged scab on his cheek from a spear tip that could have just as easily killed him as he fought desperately to save his village. He had been a guard when the kidnappers came, and he had obviously failed in his duty because everyone in his village had been either taken prisoner or slaughtered. His failure shamed him. His neck was raw from the constant movement of the tugging chain as he was marched from his village; now the chain had been replaced by manacles on his feet. Around him bidders sized him up; some poked at his arms or legs with sticks to judge his muscularity. They pulled on their beards and gazed at him, evaluating the purchase of a human being like one would a cow or a horse.

The warrior watched as one of the men nodded and pulled out a purse. He did not know he had just been bought by Captain Lebron, an old Frenchman and an independent slaver who bought kidnapped Africans to sell at various slave markets throughout the Caribbean and various U.S. ports. Lebron measured his new slave and noted the scar on his cheek as he wrote a description of his latest purchase on the manifest he kept.

The warrior was taken off the block and led to where Lebron's other slaves stood in bewilderment. He could see his sister in a group of women waiting to be auctioned; the red ribbon in her hair was all she wore. The women were being sold just as the men were, but for far less, for they broke down in the fields under the strain of continuous manual work. Lebron sized up the women carefully, wanting only the strongest and healthiest looking. He bought fifty women, and the warrior's sister was the last chosen. On his manifest, he gave all his purchases English names.

Finally, the bidding and buying were over and all the men, women, and a few older children were divided up. The bidders and bystanders had to endure the wailing of separated families, another nuisance with slaves. But at last the seasoning began. Each slave would now begin to learn how it was going to be, where the lines were, and who the master was, for each slave would wear the brand of the trader or dealer who had bought them. Each was led to a fire where a hot iron waited, glowing red to signal the coming pain, bearing the trader's unique symbol. Men, women, and children would thus become his chattel.

A cow's hide is tough. The branding iron burns only the upper layer of hide, searing off the hair such that it will never grow back. Human skin is different, without a hard hide, so that as the iron touches it, the skin immediately blisters and then starts to bleed. The pain is beyond excruciating and then, as the iron burns farther into layers of blood vessels and tissue, unbearable. The smell of burning human skin is something you never forget, especially if it is your own.

The warrior stood with his back to the branding post, his hands manacled behind it, and stared wide-eyed at the various glowing irons in the fire, each a brand for a different trader. Lebron selected the iron with a small, crude L and banged the ashes off it. He held it in the air and looked at the warrior indifferently; after all, he'd done this thousands of times. Slowly he brought the iron up, hesitated a moment to let the warrior focus his eyes on the iron in fear, and pushed the brand into the flesh of his shoulder. The warrior gasped and screamed despite himself, and tears leapt from his eyes in an involuntary eruption of pain.

Lebron didn't seem to notice. He'd seen this and worse in his years as a slaver, seen men pass out and women throw fits, and children— well, some children died on the spot. Pain was funny that way, he thought, as he put the iron back into the fire to heat up for the next slave. It was all monotonous but it had to be done, else how could you tell the buggers apart?

Lebron's selections were held in a warehouse on the island, chained and shackled. There were lots of thirty men confined in eight-foot square cells with only a slit of a window for outside air. Women were housed separately in the warehouse, naked except for a piece of cloth to tie around their waists. On the floor above the slaves' heads were the dealers' apartments, where nightly festivities and gaiety belied the human misery only a few feet below.

After several days, Lebron was ready to leave. Each of his slaves was rousted and pushed through the "door of no return," a small opening to the outside of the warehouse through which every man, woman, and child walked to the shore and the waiting canoes.

Lebron's ship could hold five hundred slaves, but he had purchased and branded 562. In his business you expected to have waste. How many would die on the Middle Passage across the Atlantic Ocean was not so easy to predict, but you planned as best you could. Satisfied that all his property was accounted for on the shore, Lebron began the process of loading his slaves into the waiting canoes for the short trip out to his ship. The canoes, the water, all of this was terrifying to the slaves, and many had to be whipped into going. The warrior slave stepped into the rocking canoe and held his breath in fear. Finally, the seamen pushed the canoes into the surf and began paddling. Up and down over the waves went the canoes, and general moaning sounded over the water, the slaves' fear becoming audible in their throats. In their panic, two women in the first canoe stood up and caused the canoe to tip enough to throw them into the water, their feet still in manacles. The seamen steadied the canoe and kept paddling, for it was too dangerous and too much trouble to rescue flailing slaves, especially women, who weren't worth nearly as much as men anyway. The warrior watched closely, but by the time his canoe reached the place where the women had gone overboard there were only bubbles on the surface of the sea.

Upon reaching Lebron's ship, the slaves were roughly pushed down into the holds, where there were broad shelves stacked two high, with about two feet of headroom between them. The men were allotted a space of six feet by sixteen inches in which to lie. The women had five feet by thirteen inches and along with the children were quartered separately from the men, which made them easier for the slavers to get to. There was no real air circulation below decks; the only air and sunshine came through two grates on the main deck. For most of the slaves it was dark and suffocating, and they had to breathe air that had already been breathed.

The warrior lay with his body glistening with fear, his heart racing with confusion and concern for his sister. Around him men were crying and jerking at their manacles, the fetid smell of vomit hanging in the air.

And there was more, much more, to come.

TWO

CAPTAIN NICHOLAS FALLON stood up from the desk where he had been working diligently to be someone he wasn't: a record keeper, an accountant, an aspiring manager of the Somers Salt Company of Bermuda. He was lean and tall, with strong shoulders and arms more suited for grappling with drunken sailors than with numbers. His black hair hung loosely about his face, a narrow face punctuated by green eyes that bore a hint of melancholy about the edges, a gift inherited from his mother.

The room in which he was working was the Somers office in St. George Town, and a new desk had been brought in just for him— a partner's desk so he could sit opposite Ezra Somers, the founder of the company. Somers was a gout-ridden old man, wise and blunt, and a crack shot with a pistol despite his age. His wife had died giving birth to Elinore, their only child, and he had struggled to raise her alone without a woman's influence in the house. The last few years had brought father and daughter closer together, however, not least because of their mutual attachment to Fallon.

Somers had built his fortune in the salt business, with Somers's ships regularly making the round trip from Grand Turk, where the salt was harvested, to American ports, where it was sold. Fallon had been a very successful captain for him, protecting his ships and even capturing prizes that were sold to the Admiralty. Now Fallon was trying to learn the *business of the business*, as Somers called it.

It was a business that had always used slaves for labor on Grand

Turk. But Fallon's latent anti-slavery views had been brought out in full force after encountering a derelict slave ship that had been plundered by pirates for the "black gold" it carried. Fallon's crew had searched the ship for survivors but at first had found only the grotesque bodies of slaves and crew who had fought for their lives and died horribly butchered.

Then, a small boy hiding below. A terrified, silent young man who was taken aboard Fallon's schooner and treated so kindly by the crew that, over time, he emerged from his cocoon of fear. He revealed his name as Ajani, meaning *He who wins the struggle,* and over time he became like a son to Fallon. But the experience of finding the slave boy, embracing him, and coaxing him out of his fear had hardened Fallon's opinion of slavery as the abomination it was.

When Somers had asked Fallon to join the Somers Salt Company as a partner, he had accepted under one condition: The slaves on Grand Turk must be set free and paid wages. Somers struggled with that; slaves had been in his family and business since before he was born. But he forced himself to consider Fallon's idea, philosophically and practically. He was an old man, practiced in his ways and thinking, but surely not too old to change. Fallon had asked him to imagine Ajani, to whom Somers had become quite attached, working the salt flats as a slave: boils on his feet from the brine, blinded by the glare of the sun on the salt, ragged and miserable. No, Somers could not imagine that. Could not in a million years imagine that. For the first time in his life, slavery became personal.

Now, having convinced Somers that the salt business could survive, even thrive, paying wages to salt rakers instead of using slave labor, Fallon was trying to prove it. It was an expensive experiment and, of course, salt prices went up accordingly. The American buyers in Boston and elsewhere had complained bitterly, but as Somers had a virtual monopoly on salt production in the Caribbean, and as the United States had no salt production to speak of, the shipments to American ports continued as always. Maybe Fallon was more of a businessman than he thought he was. Why, just now he had been adding up some very important figures on tons of salt shipped at X price to X locations in X number of forty-pound bags and, well, he wanted to put a bullet in his temple.

He decided to walk to the town dock instead. It was not a very long walk and would not take him far, but he wanted a bit of time to work his way out of his melancholy. He stepped out onto Aunt Peggy's Lane, named for a slave woman who often sat at her window and watched over the town, though she was not at her window today.

It was late afternoon, and when Fallon reached the dock he looked out at *Rascal*, moving about slightly in the fickle breeze of the harbor, and tugging on her anchor she rode like a puppy trying to get free of its leash. She was an American-built topsail schooner that he'd captured in an improbable escape from Savannah in 1796. In the two years since, he'd cruised *Rascal* successfully as Somers's captain with a letter of marque to legally fight privateers and pirates on behalf of Great Britain. Her two-month refit had coincided with Fallon's time ashore, and now ship and captain were both ready for sea again.

The crew was mostly ashore in Bermuda; there was only a skeletal watch aboard and Fallon climbed down into *Rascal*'s gig and began rowing out to the ship. The Americans had built her in Maryland along the lines of a Baltimore pilot schooner: She was gaff-rigged and "sharp built," fine at the entry and, owing to her relatively shallow draft, able to move about the coral-strewn Caribbean where larger ships wouldn't dare go.

As he rowed around her lovely stern he looked down the length of her 105 feet. She was built of American oak and elm to balance stiffness with speed. Her gun ports were closed, but behind them were eight 12-pounders each side, plus a long 9-pounder in the bows. The cast iron long nine was considered the most accurate gun in the Royal Navy.

He clapped on and climbed the side easily, to be met by one of the crew at the channel with a salute and a smile. He walked the length and breadth of the ship, taking his time, and then went below decks and inspected the holds and cabins and even the galley. It was all pleasingly familiar to him, every sight and smell. *Rascal* carried all her guns on the weather deck; the crew lived and slept and ate on the lower deck, cramped as it was. As he ascended the companionway he smiled broadly, for he was proud of his command; in all respects, *Rascal* was a fast war machine if handled with alacrity.

As he surveyed the deck of his ship, a ship that had brought him home safely through battles and storms, Fallon fought down the urge to cut the cable and sail out to sea. By any measure he had to admit he had a good life: a beautiful woman who loved him, a father who adored him, a business partner who respected him. A good life, just not the one he wanted.

He rowed back to the dock, keeping his ship in his vision as the sinking sun cast a warm glow on her oiled hull. Tonight, he would visit his father at the White Horse, which, as his father liked to say, was *the oldest pub still leaning in Bermuda.* It had been in the Fallon family for generations and his father would be working there, as he had been every day that Fallon could remember. Tonight, they would share something wet, perhaps a good laugh or two, before Fallon would stumble upstairs to bed.

Tomorrow was another day, he reminded himself. *At the office.*

THREE

Ezra Somers had a truly remarkable library, full of books on astronomy, geography, history, philosophy, and the natural sciences. Fallon and Somers had spent many afternoons after the day's work was done talking about the world outside their windows. Lately, they'd been discussing philosophy and one particular precept that intrigued Fallon: *Everything you needed to solve a problem was within a few feet of where you were standing.*

It had often seemed true in Fallon's life, particularly in his sailing life, when cornered by enemies or besieged by weather. But it hadn't seemed to work on land, at least not until one early afternoon after a packet ship arrived bearing a letter from the Windward Islands, Antigua to be exact, English Harbor to be particularly exact. The letter was delivered to the office by a dock boy, and it seemed to float upon the sea of papers on Fallon's desk. He looked at it carefully, somehow knowing it was going to change everything but not knowing how. Surprisingly, he was fearful to open it, for it bore the official seal of the Royal Navy. It sat there only two feet from his nose. Slowly, Fallon picked up the letter, held it a moment, and tore it open.

His good friend Rear Admiral Harry Davies, in charge of the Leeward Islands station at English Harbor, was asking a favor. And he was willing to pay handsomely for it.

+ + +

THE MOON low and silvering in a light fog.

The narrow streets of St. George Town, barely wide enough to handle a buggy, were almost deserted of traffic. The only faces were the gossips at the windows. In November, the evenings came sooner, descending on the little town with a speed that made lingering summer nights a memory. By ten o'clock every alley was blacker than black.

In an old fisherman's shack at the edge of the marsh, Fallon and Elinore Somers lay on the bed and whispered. She was beautiful in the moonlight that filtered through the window by the bed, her blonde hair tumbling out on the pillow, and her face, half illuminated and half hidden in shadow, revealing both excitement and contentment. This, of all places, was her favorite. The shack had belonged to her uncle, who built it to get away from the women in his house when he wanted to be by himself. A small, simple building with a bed, a few shelves for books, a woodstove on the edge of a circle of rug, a table with one chair. This shack was where Fallon and Elinore had first discovered each other, all angles and dark spaces and secret signals, not this but that, more there, yes. *There.*

Tonight, they'd taken their time, not rushing the moment, lingering over a *this* or a *that* they might have missed. At last they were glistening and spent, each wondering if the feast was over or were seconds still available. The only sound was their breathing, unless Fallon's mind made a *thinking* sound, which he prayed it didn't.

Actually, it did. Or it must have because Elinore knew something was circling around in his head, in a wrestling match perhaps, two sides moving warily, seeking advantage before making a move. She had felt it at dinner, felt it more on the walk to the shack, but had put it aside to be close to him, one with him, knowing whatever it was would declare itself in good time and could certainly wait until—well, until now.

"Talk to me, love," she whispered.

My God, she's a mind reader, Fallon thought. He always believed he was so damned clever, when in fact he was as transparent as glass. Elinore saw right through him. He began to form a lie in his throat, but it would not do. *Wound me with the truth,* Elinore had always told him, *not lies.* He shifted his weight and placed his hand on her belly, as if he could send his thoughts through her skin and not have to say them out loud.

"Ahem," was the beginning. A long pause. "Ahem."

Elinore refused to help him, wanting him to deal with it. Really, how could a man who could fight pirates and face broadsides without flinching be unable to say a hard thing to the woman he loved? Clearly, it was something important that needed saying and needed talking about.

Come on, Nico.

"Ahem," he began again, "I'm not . . . ahem . . . fit to be tied to an office, Elinore. I am trying to be *interested,* but I'm not doing a good job of it. I have learned so much about trading and balancing books and tonnages of salt, and I want very much to like it all and be a good manager but . . . I promised I'd try it for several months, and I have. Please tell me you understand."

A pause. Made longer by a deep breath.

"Yes," said Elinore bravely. But Fallon thought he could hear her spirits sink in her voice.

"I belong at sea," Fallon said simply. "I *need* to be at sea."

Elinore squirmed next to him. Bermuda men went to sea. That's what they did, what they'd done for hundreds of years. And somewhere in the ancient script of her genes it was written that brave women knew when to let their men go.

"I received a letter from Harry today," said Fallon, plowing on but trying to keep the excitement out of his voice. "He's asking me to undertake a special assignment for the Admiralty. It seems I'm to take a senior intelligence agent to Cuba. I'm to pick up this agent off Port-au-Prince, where Harry is evacuating British troops from Saint-Domingue. I shouldn't be gone long, Elinore."

That was *sort of* a lie, for at sea nothing was certain. But at least the whole of it was out in the open, not burning a hole in his heart anymore. Fallon was glad it was pitch black in the little shack, for his face was wincing, hating to do this, to say it all out loud and hurt Elinore, afraid she would see it as Harry versus her, and losing.

Elinore reached deep, wise beyond her years. Knowing that if she won she would only lose, eventually.

"I know you would rather be at sea than in an office," she said softly. "But here I have you, so I want to be selfish. But . . ."

Another long pause. The sweat drying on their bodies now. A moment when the night could grow colder.

"But," she continued in a whisper, very close to his ear now. "I will still love you at sea. Just not like this." And she trailed a fingernail down his chest, slowly giving him a good reason to reconsider going anywhere.

FOUR

THE NEXT MORNING Fallon came to the office on Aunt Peggy's Lane knowing he must tell Ezra Somers he was ready for sea again, and not knowing at all how it would go. Somers was at work early, as usual, energetically managing the affairs of the Somers Salt enterprise like the skilled businessman he was. The thought occurred to Fallon that Somers didn't need him; what he did was completely superfluous. Somers had offered him the job for the future, against the time when Somers would die, wanting the business to go on without him.

Giving Fallon a running start.

But Somers looked too young to die. And Fallon *felt* too young to die, at least in an office. The idea was simply ahead of its time. Now, how to say that to Somers and not get shot.

Fallon went through the letter from Davies, even showing it to the old man, suggesting he was needed more *there* than he was *here*. It was a good job, but not good enough to fool Ezra Somers.

"The other thing, Nico," Somers said with a grin, "is that you can't add two and two. Hell, you've barely got the patience for one plus one."

And he laughed. Laughed a big Ezra Somers laugh that was probably heard at the harbor. In a second Fallon joined in, and they both laughed until Somers gave Fallon every assurance that the partnership would continue no matter where he went as long as he fought the company's enemies, which were also Great Britain's enemies. They shook hands, then hugged, then shook hands again. Somers being a man you could count on.

Now there was one visit left. Fallon walked briskly down Suffering Lane to Beatrice—Beauty—McFarland's house, a bit wary of coming so early but determined to see the thing through. He desperately wanted Beauty to sail with him, but he was unsure that she would leave Bermuda again. He had seen her so infrequently over the past few months that he wondered if she felt her place had been taken by Elinore, which in a sense it had. But perhaps there was something else, too.

As captain of a privateer, Fallon could choose his crew regardless of gender or experience or penal record. As a result, *Rascal's* crew of ninety came from a collection of former occupations, but all excellent sailors as befitted Bermudians on the whole and Bermuda men in particular, most of whom were at sea at any given time. Beauty and Fallon had grown up together sailing skiffs in close races on St. George's Harbor and, as he would be the first to admit, he often followed her stern across the finish line. He had been there when she'd almost drowned in a sudden storm and had pulled her to safety. And he had been there when her leg had been amputated below the knee after an infection had turned gangrenous when she was in her late teens. He had held her hand tightly when the doctor had raised the saw to do his work. Beauty's bravery had often been tested in the years since and, to no one's surprise who knew her, she'd been found fearless.

They were not lovers and never had been; in fact, Beauty's affections went the other way, that is, not toward men. But they were best friends, and he valued her for a keen mind that knew when to tack and when to bear off.

At last he came to Beauty's door and knocked. He heard her coming down the hall, her wooden leg thumping along until the door opened.

"Yes." A statement, not a question.

"Yes, what?" Fallon said, the bewilderment showing on his face.

"Yes, I'm ready to go to sea again."

"How in God's name do you know why I came here?" Fallon looked at his best friend like he'd seen a witch.

"Simple, Nico. I watched you walking up the lane and you were positively floating. You've been poxed working in that office for months and I know it. I hear things in town. When I saw you coming you were smiling ear to ear, so my little brain figured something was up to make you so happy."

"By God, you scare me sometimes, Beauty." And he looked at his friend with a huge grin. "May I come in?"

They sat by the fire in the living room, Fallon watching Beauty as she added a new log, easy with him as always. He told her about Davies' letter, a simple request to land a secret agent in Cuba; he didn't need to add that *Rascal* would also be available for *opportunities* that might come sailing by. That went with the territory if you were a privateer, particularly a privateer in the Caribbean. The French were about, as were the Spanish, uneasy allies at war with Great Britain. Both countries were intent on protecting and attempting to expand their business interests, which largely consisted of trade and agriculture, which meant the Caribbean was a veritable feast of potential prizes for a determined privateer.

But the possibility of prizes could not be the sole motivation for Beauty to leave Bermuda, Fallon reasoned. So, an unanswered question hung in the air, and Fallon debated asking it.

Finally, *what the hell*.

"Tell me, Beauty, are you sure you're ready to leave again? You certainly don't need the money after our last cruise. I'm not trying to pry, but I've barely seen you about for some time and I . . . I mean, I'm curious."

Beauty stabbed at the fire with the poker, sending sparks flying up the chimney and a little belch of smoke into the room. Then she made a few more unnecessary pokes before turning to face her friend, her back to the fire.

"Nico, you know a lot about me," Beauty said tentatively. "More than any other person in the world." She was thinking of a lot of things, a lot of times, not least the time Fallon had seen her with another woman, which he'd never brought up to her, respecting her right to be who she was.

"I may be in love, Nico, I don't know," she said. "But my friend wants to sort out how *she* feels, to understand what it means to be in love with another woman on this tiny island. She isn't strong like I am; she cares what people think. I'm afraid for her, honestly. And by leaving I can give us both time apart to decide if this is what we want. Can we live with the island, and can the island live with us?"

It was quite a confidence, and Fallon stared into the fire a moment, appreciating his friendship with this remarkable woman.

"Thank you for trusting me with that, Beauty," he said softly.

"Tuck it away deep inside, Nico. And let's go to sea."

FIVE

The Middle Passage

SOLEDAD WAS *a square-rigged, wormy, and ill-used slaver with three 6-pound cannons per side and a swivel gun in her bows loaded with grapeshot and aimed inboard to put down any rebellion in short order. On deck were great kettles for cooking, mostly yams and beans. The stench from the holds was overwhelming as more than five hundred souls were forced to lie in their own excrement in ninety-degree heat. It would take most of a month to get to Martinique, where the ship would wood and water, before heading northwest to the market at Charleston. The dead or insane would be thrown overboard each day, while the stench would only grow stronger, able to be smelled a mile away if the wind was right.*

The warrior lay in his space and listened to the moans of the men and women mix with the sound of water moving past the hull. There was no night and no day, only darkness. His shoulder still burned horribly from the branding and his mind, rabid with confusion and humiliation, struggled to understand what had happened to him. The man next to him was older and had grown quiet after screaming for hours. The warrior wondered if he had died, and indeed nudged him in the ribs but got no response.

On the ship plunged across the ocean, plowing a furrow that countless slavers had plowed before her. These were just a handful of slaves compared with the millions who had made the Middle Passage to the

West Indies, ripped from families and friends and a world they under-stood to sail into the dark, unfathomably cruel life that lay ahead. Each day they were fed one meal with a small bit of water, but were rarely let above decks, for they had a 10-1 advantage over their wardens who feared rebellion above all else. Hence the swivel gun. Women stopped menstruating, children stopped talking, and men stopped hoping to es-cape; they were broken both physically and mentally.

Oddly, after a week someone in the hell below decks began singing. At first, the warrior thought it was the ranting of another slave going insane. But it was beautiful, not frantic, and there was enough similarity to his own language that he understood some of the lyrics. The song asked the question: Where are we bound in this world? Someone, a woman he thought, answered with a sing-song voice: We are going to a new land. Another sang out: We will all die. And after a pause, the woman sang again: Keep Africa in your hearts.

The guards above them were oblivious to this singular form of com-munication; it puzzled them but, really, slaves were crazy anyway. And so the singing continued off and on, day after day, the slaves singing to each other and answering. They sang of their homeland, of their families, of sun and fields and times remembered. And when each day more slaves were thrown overboard, the survivors sang of the departed.

And then one day a man sang out: Can we be free? It became very quiet below decks, no one moved, and no one sang back.

The Blue Above

Soledad sailed for day after monotonous day along the route from Africa to the West Indies. At last she reached Martinique, but not even that port provided respite for the slaves, who were only briefly allowed on deck while the ship was resupplied. Then it was back down below to the black and closed world of the lower decks. With her water casks filled and wood stored, Soledad set off for the final push to the U.S. coast, Lebron already counting his money.

The ship had a favorable slant of wind and sailed to the northwest past Montserrat, eventually leaving Porto Rico well to the east as she clawed her way north of Spanish Santo Domingo which, along with the French Saint-Domingue to the west, formed the island of Hispaniola. By now the singing below decks had ceased. A general lethargy possessed the weakened and dissipated bodies lying there.

And then came the terror.

The sound was like nothing the slaves had ever heard: loud like thunder but somehow sharper. The ship shook and they could hear the crew shouting above them on the upper deck. The ship shook again, and this time the thunder was louder and directly over their heads. Again and again the thunder roared, and suddenly an iron ball came through the side of the ship and killed a slave where he lay, smashing his head to red pulp.

All the slaves began wailing in fear and confusion, but the warrior's shouts rose above the din as he urged the slaves to escape up the ladder to the deck. Some of the slaves were quick to understand what he wanted them to do, then slowly they all seemed to understand and began hobbling in their manacles to the ladder. The warrior was now their leader, and he climbed first, but the grate was bolted and locked from the outside.

On the upper deck, Lebron's crew was firing their 6-pound cannons as fast as they could at two attacking sloops that were closing quickly. The battle was a hopeless mismatch with an inevitable outcome, and Lebron knew it.

Suddenly, a broadside from one of the sloops ripped into Soledad and one of the slaver's cannons was upended just at the moment the dying crewman touched the match to the touch-hole. The upended cannon exploded, sending its shot straight down through three decks of humanity and out the bottom of the ship.

A cable's length away a small brig lay hove-to and rode easily on the swells. Its hull was a dull black, with nine gun ports to each side, behind which were 12-pound cannons. The brig's gun crews were at the ready, but they were usually not needed against more or less defenseless prizes like the slaver.

After a particularly devastating broadside of grapeshot across her decks, the slaver went silent. Boats were lowered from both sloops, and crews armed with cutlasses and pistols began pulling for Soledad. But there was to be no hand-to-hand fighting; Lebron's crew was mangled and dying, with Lebron himself draped over the hot swivel gun, hands and mouth dripping blood onto the deck. The last broadside had finished him.

Down below decks, the slaves knew only that the terrible thunder had stopped, but on the lowest deck appeared a new terror: water gurgling up through the floor! The wailing grew louder and held a new note of panic as screams drifted up through the decks and out through the shot holes in the hull. One of the sloop's captains went below to Lebron's cabin to gather up the ship's slave manifest and also to check for any remaining crew who might be hiding. Then, finding no one, he went to check the holds. At the lowest level in the ship he found the seawater rushing in.

Quickly, slaves were put on the pumps and they pumped as if their lives depended on it, which was the case, of course. But Soledad already had almost five feet of water in the well, and the pumps were old, partially clogged with debris, and one soon stopped working. The slaves panicked and would not pump, and instead scrambled up the ladder to reach the next deck. Two were shot, but no threat would bring the others back. The sloop captains soon realized there was nothing for it. The ship couldn't be saved and the thing to do was to get all the slaves they could into the boats quickly.

The sloops' crews broke open the hatches, and the slaves came pouring up, terror in their eyes. They tumbled into the boats and huddled in fear, a sloop captain shouting at them in words they could not understand. The warrior stayed below, calling out for his sister, but in the pandemonium her voice could not be heard. Finally, he was forced up the ladder and onto the deck. In the sloops' boats the slaves wailed in confusion. But the warrior guessed at the truth: They would be trading one hell for another.

Soledad was getting lower in the water; the screaming from the

slaves still trapped below was growing more pronounced. The sloop captains looked helplessly across the water at the brig, aware that this was
not supposed to happen and wondering what would now happen to
them.

On board the black brig, meanwhile, the pirate they called the Holy
One was not happy. He watched the boats pulling for his ship with far
fewer slaves than he had expected. He stood on his quarterdeck in dark
vestments, fingering a rosary and staring at the sinking slaver. Perhaps
he was just too angry to contemplate the fickle world at that moment.
One never knew with the Holy One, and one did not ask too many
questions.

He was tall, with lank gray hair and an aquiline face. A thin scar
ran from his left eye down his cheek to a thin mustache that quivered
slightly over a cruel mouth. He stood completely erect and immobile on
the quarterdeck; now his arms reached upward, his eyes closed in prayer,
the sun flaring off the large silver cross that hung from his neck.

Finally, the slaver began its descent into the ocean, sliding silently
beneath the waves, with dead slaves on the lower decks floating off their
pallets. Globs of air bubbles rose and clung to the underside of the decks
before rolling forward toward the dark bows as the ship purged the air
from the slaves' lungs and the boxes, drawers, chests, barrels, and can-
isters below decks. The slave ship's eventual velocity reached 25 knots
through darker and colder water until it finally crashed with surprising
force onto the lightless bottom of the sea and broke in half. Incredibly, the
trip down took almost ten minutes.

Meanwhile, the Holy One came out of his trance. He had reached a
calmer place. It was unfortunate about the drowned slaves, of course, but
his God would never put a good soul into a black body, so the world lost
very little.

With the captured slaves safely in the holds, the Holy One gave the
order to raise the boats and resume hunting for other opportunities to fill
his holds before turning for Cuba, where the slave markets offered the
best prices in the Caribbean.

Not long after Soledad settled on the seabed, the pirate ships set sail.

SIX

RASCAL BOUNDED across the great blue of the Atlantic Ocean, unleashed from the constraints of her anchorage in St. George's Harbor, free of the incessant tug and pull of her heavy anchor, and once again a living thing. Her crew reveled in her—and their—freedom, none more so than Nicholas Fallon, her enigmatic captain who, at that moment, was high up in the larboard ratlines feeling like the king of the world. The melancholy of life ashore in St. George Town had left his face, and his green eyes were bright again. He hung in the ratlines like an old tar and looked at miles of sky above the impossibly blue ocean and smiled a secret smile to himself. It was a wonderful day, a brilliant day, in fact; indeed, it was a day when anything could happen.

Below him he could see Beauty's roundish, foreshortened body standing next to the helmsman, her short black hair blowing about her face, her peg leg anchored firmly in a ring bolt on the deck against the heel of the ship. Fallon had thoughtfully placed ring bolts in strategic positions about the deck for his first mate.

Fallon could see Ajani on deck—*Aja* as he liked to be called. The boy was learning the art of navigation under the tutelage of Barclay, the sailing master. Barclay was a good instructor and Aja had made remarkable progress.

Since his rescue, Aja had become quite attached to Fallon, becoming his coxswain and erstwhile protector as well as Beauty's right hand. She had taught him to read English; he could already

speak and understand it from working in an English household in
Africa before his family was kidnapped and sold. Certainly, reading had opened up the world to him and contributed to his innate
wisdom, for all on board agreed he was not only older but wiser
than his years. He was only fourteen, but he was well on his way to
becoming a man.

Cully had the ship's youngsters huddled around him and was
reviewing the intricacies of sighting a long nine on a heaving ship,
the younger boys smiling in anticipation of action, not knowing
that death and horror were often consequences. Cully was a white-
haired Irishman with a quick smile and leather face and one eye
that could sight the great guns with uncanny accuracy. He was the
best gunner Fallon had ever known, and Fallon had placed him
over all the other gun captains aboard *Rascal*. Cully's gun crews
could load and run out and unleash their deadly broadsides in two
minutes. It was doubtful many gun crews in the Royal Navy could
match that time.

Rascal was several days out of Bermuda, on the watch for pirates, privateers, and any ship otherwise the King's enemy, French
or Spanish, there being many to choose from. The war with France
had cast a dark shadow over the sunny Caribbean just as it had
over the rest of the world. For the war had many fronts due to
France's ambition to dominate the known surface of the earth.
France's navy, privateers, agents, and armies were active throughout Europe and the Med, India, the Baltic, and the Caribbean,
with Napoleon Bonaparte himself leading his army in Egypt
in an attempt to wipe out British trade routes with India. His
army, while successful against the Egyptian military, had been
left stranded after his navy's disastrous showing at the Battle of
Aboukir in August. But he was hardly finished.

Bonaparte had always been an energetic warrior throughout his
military career. Somehow, he'd found time to marry the beautiful
and seductive Marie-Josèphe-Rose Tascher de la Pagerie, whom he
renamed Joséphine. That in itself linked Bonaparte more closely to

the Caribbean, for she was born to a wealthy plantation family on Martinique. Like most of the plantations on the island, the Tascher plantation raised sugarcane and, until France abolished slavery in her colonies in 1794, had kept hundreds of slaves; indeed, most of the population of every island in the West Indies was composed of kidnapped African slaves.

As he hung on the ratlines, Fallon thought of his friend Davies and the secret mission he'd given him. The rear admiral's letter had been brief and to the point, a favor between friends and allies. Fallon wondered at the responsibilities on Davies' shoulders, for much was required of him besides managing His Majesty's ships in the Caribbean, not least of which was the ability to understand the shifting nature of world politics and its implications for the British Empire, and to act on his understanding in ways that pleased the Admiralty. It made Fallon very happy to be in his little corner of the world, a minor cog in the grand scheme of things. And yet he had to admit to his secret self that he took an interest in affairs in Europe and, truth be known, felt he was capable of playing a bigger role in them one day.

But not today. Today he was Nicholas Fallon, *King of the World*.

Satisfied that all was well in the King's world, he descended to the deck and joined Beauty and Barclay at the binnacle just as Barclay finished noting the ship's position on the slate.

"Did you enjoy looking over your domain, your Highness?" asked Beauty, correctly reading Fallon's mind and mood and, once again, knowing him at least as well as he knew himself.

"I did," replied Fallon. "I think I may punish every other person in the realm for insolence. Starting with sharp-tongued women!"

"Next it will be sailing masters," Barclay said as he shuffled off. Beauty was just about to comment when the hail came from the lookout.

"Deck there! Something in the water dead ahead! *A lot of something!*"

Fallon snatched his telescope from the rack near the binnacle

and moved to the larboard railing to look forward, aghast that the
lookout had spotted something he'd missed only moments ago.
Maybe the King's eyesight was failing.

"Beauty, let's get closer and then heave-to. Then I'll want my gig
lowered, please," he said, a sense of foreboding in his voice. "And
get Colquist on deck. I don't know what we'll find."

Colquist was a young surgeon lent by a merchantman whose
ship was laid up at the dockyard on Bermuda and would be for a
while. Fallon had taken an immediate liking to the man, not least
because he was sober and meticulous in his habits. But he had yet
to be tested with casualties.

Rascal sailed on for a half mile before Beauty brought her to a
standstill with practiced ease, the schooner's sails balanced just so
in the moderate breeze so that the ship would go neither here nor
there.

As Fallon stepped down into the gig and Aja ordered the crew
to push off, he had a premonition, for wreckage floating in the water usually meant one thing: a ship was down. A ship that sank,
any ship—enemy or not—brought a natural sadness to sailors
who knew how fragile their existence was on the ocean.

They rowed a short distance before Aja ordered "oars" and the
gig drifted into the floating debris: wooden boxes, odd timbers,
bits of clothing, and air-tight tins—whatever could work its way
out of a sinking ship and float to the surface. Fallon noticed several
of the tins had French writing on them, but he let them be. There
were no bodies; no doubt the sharks had seen to that. Even now,
ominous dorsal fins cut the water nearby. The crew sat silently,
their oars dripping, unable or unwilling to speak. At last, satisfied
there were no survivors, and in fact having no idea how long the
wreckage had even been floating, Fallon ordered the gig back to
the ship. But, as he did so, Aja reached over the side and plucked a
red ribbon from a tangle of cordage floating on the surface of the
sea. A red ribbon that perhaps had belonged to a woman or child,
a wife or mother or daughter; here was a clue to a life, a story that

would never be known. The gig's crew stared at the ribbon in silence, until Fallon finally ordered them to pull back to the ship. It was a somber little journey and a morose captain who stepped onto the deck.

"Beauty, let's be away from this place," Fallon said as the gig was hoisted aboard.

Beauty ordered the helmsman to bring the ship back on course and soon enough *Rascal* was making her best speed through the water. But the mood aboard ship had altered, and the hands went about their tasks with a lowness.

"What do you think happened back there, Nico?" Beauty asked after *Rascal* was well away from the wreckage and Fallon seemed approachable.

Fallon had been wondering the same thing but could come to no real conclusions based on what he had seen.

"Maybe privateers or pirates and a capture that went wrong," he mused aloud. "Could have been a packet or trader of some kind. Or maybe a slaver that sprang a plank and sank accidentally. Many of those ships are in bad shape, and the slaves are at the pumps constantly. Even a small storm could overwhelm one."

"I wonder if she was British," Beauty said.

"I think French," Fallon responded. "But if she was a slaver she could have been from anywhere, bound for anywhere, of course." Both knew that French, British, and Spanish slavers were opportunistic, selling to the highest bidders regardless of political boundaries on a map.

"I'm going below, Beauty," Fallon announced suddenly. "Call me with any other surprises."

He made his way to his cabin and poured himself a glass of wine. The cabin was not spacious, but stern windows swept dramatically across the rear and there was room for his swinging cot, a writing table, and a small secretary to hold his papers. And his writing. The lines were scribbles, really, a poor attempt at poetry, for nothing rhymed. He moved to his writing table now and took

out a sheet of paper, quill pen, and ink and let the words flow to
Elinore.

> *The gray built up on the day*
> *Until there was no light I believed*
> *Was real. And the only heat in the air*
> *Was from my own breath and the only*
> *Sound the still cry in my throat asking*
> *For you.*

Finished, he folded the paper and put it in his secretary. God
knew when it would get to Elinore. But he felt better for having
written it, and having thought of her instead of lingering on the sad
ribbon floating on the sea.

SEVEN

THERE IS a look to a sea making up for a storm. The ocean begins to move beneath the ship in a different way as it gathers itself, its mood graying and hardening. Old tars can feel it deep within their memories, and throw looks to one another in acknowledgment.

Rascal was now less than four hundred miles from Saint-Domingue, and Barclay, the sailing master, studied the sea the way he studied food before him at mess—intently and reverentially. His eyes narrowed as he stood at the starboard railing and looked into the distance, seeing nothing absolute but feeling that events were coming. It was hard to tell Barclay's age; he was somehow born the way he was, had been that way since anyone had known him on Bermuda. He was gray, stooped, and unremarkable to look at. But he knew his navigation.

Farther up the starboard railing, Beauty and Aja conferred about the weather as well. Rain had begun, and as the glass had been dropping for the past two hours the question wasn't, is there going to be a storm but, rather, how much of a storm? November gales were not unusual in the Atlantic, and certainly the wind was getting up. Always cautious, Beauty ordered the topsails furled, and Aja went below to inform Fallon.

"Deck there, two sail astern!" the lookout shouted.

This was open ocean, and the strange sail could be coming from anywhere, could be anything from any country. As Fallon ascended the companionway and received his telescope from Aja, he turned his attention quickly to the distant ships, which were just visible from the deck: one sail off the starboard quarter and one off the larboard, effectively on *Rascal's* flanks.

"Deck there," came the call from the lookout again. "Now *three* sail."

Fallon could not make out the third sail from the deck, but it certainly made him curious about what he might be facing. He scanned the horizon carefully but saw nothing else. The ships were miles away, but *still*.

The best part of an hour passed. Beauty had ordered the courses reefed in the growing easterly, and yet the distance from the strange sails to the north remained the same.

"What do you think, Nico?" she asked, appearing at Fallon's side with a small note of concern in her voice. *Rascal* was a fast ship but, as every seaman knew, anything could happen at sea. The storm was beginning in earnest and a spar could be carried away or a stay could part or any of a hundred calamitous things could put the ship in harm's way. It was always good to have a plan if the worst thing you could imagine happened.

"Curious, Beauty. They seem to be keeping pace, just watching. And maybe waiting," said Fallon pensively. *Rascal* had no flag up so the strange sails could not be sure of her loyalty. "Let's hold course for the time being and do some watching of our own. We'll wait a bit longer to see if things change."

The afternoon grew darker under a low horizon and, though the rain had stopped, the increased wind made the rigging moan in its ominous way. Beauty had a second reef taken in the main and foresail, for though Barclay forecast that the storm would blow itself out, *who knew?*

The crew went about their tasks obediently, looking over their shoulders often, not overly concerned, but . . . *still*. The strange sails could not be seen in the gloom, but that didn't mean they weren't there. Beauty sent the hands to their dinner, and Fallon went below to have his own after leaving orders to be called if the situation changed.

When less than an hour later Fallon returned to the deck the situation had moderately improved; the horizon had lifted a bit so that visibility was better. The wind and sea were still pitching *Rascal* this way and that, with the waves hissing as they passed beneath the ship. Aja was at the taffrail with the telescope waiting for him.

"They are still following us, Captain, sir," the boy said ominously, motioning with his head to the ships just visible under the low sky astern. "Like *little wolves.*"

"Yes," Fallon replied. "Hunting."

"Who are they?" asked Aja.

"I think they're pirates," replied Fallon. "Maybe privateers, probably Spanish because the French don't usually work together. But who knows? Whoever they are they're probably crammed with men and every one of them smells blood. But . . . they bide their time."

"Maybe waiting for darkness, Captain, sir," replied Aja. "Maybe they attack at night."

They both studied the little wolves carefully. It was hard to see in the dimming light, but they appeared to be still under easy sail, in no real hurry to catch up. Fallon raised his telescope for another look. Two of the ships appeared to be sloops, with the third one in the rear too far away to tell. At this rate, the chase would go on all night unless . . . unless there was a way to force the action.

Fallon called Beauty to join him at the taffrail. Together they studied the distant ships without speaking. It would be dark soon, with every prospect of a moonless night.

"What are you thinking, Nico?" Beauty asked.

"Tell you what, Beauty," Fallon said with a grin. "Let's set a little snare and see what we catch."

The day's curtain at last came down and evening was aboard. The crew changed watches silently, each man looking over his shoulder astern, but there was only black night beyond the ship. Barclay roughly estimated *Rascal*'s speed and distance from the little wolves and worked out calculations for when to heave-to. Three hours passed; the ships were still out of sight, and the time was right.

Rascal struggled to gain way with opposing sails, settling down in an easy bob and dip and essentially staying put in the weakening breeze. The rain had not returned but no lanterns were burning at any rate so the ship was entirely dark. Two lookouts were posted to report any sightings, though they were not to shout down to the deck, as usual, but rather to slide down a stay like old tars to report. The little wolves should pass *Rascal* by sunrise, Fallon figured, if indeed they held their course and speed, faster if they set more sail. They, too, burned no lights that Fallon could see. Cat and mouse, wolves and rabbit. Fallon took the deck while Beauty went below to sleep. There was nothing for it now but to wait.

Time crawled by with no reports from the lookouts, and Fallon pondered possible outcomes as he paced the deck. One wolf had been off his larboard quarter at dusk, and Fallon made up his mind to have the weather gauge to windward of the sloop should she be about when daylight came. An hour passed. Then three. Beauty came on deck but Fallon could not bring himself to go below. A cloudy, starless night engulfed them on the wide expanse of ocean. Fallon strained to see something in the darkness, or to hear a sound, but nothing. Finally, he sank down against the mainmast and dozed fitfully.

An hour before sunrise, Fallon awoke. All was quiet as before, but he gave the order to head up to the east, and Beauty quietly called the hands to stations. Fallon ordered both batteries loaded but not run out, not yet. Shot and powder and slow match were brought up from below. The men went about their tasks quietly, their bare feet padding on the deck.

A slight lightening under the clouds to the east. There was no word from either lookout, but it was still quite dark with no prospect of an actual sunrise. When Fallon felt they had made enough easting, Beauty shook out the reefs and settled the ship down on their old course to await events. The hands went to breakfast while there was still waiting to be done. Fallon stood at the binnacle and stared to the west, wondering if he'd mistimed the thing or perhaps exaggerated the threat. The mysterious ships could have changed course and sailed away anywhere.

Suddenly here was a lookout on the deck next to him. "Deck there," the lookout whispered, though he was standing two feet away. "Sail off the starboard bow." Fallon smothered a laugh at the lookout's discipline. He'd never heard *"Deck there!"* in a whisper.

Fallon immediately raised his telescope and scanned the horizon. Perhaps a faint white mark was visible, just *there*. "Beauty," he ordered in his own whisper, "head down toward that sail. We'll see what this *lobo* is about."

The sloop was ahead, farther south, and *Rascal* sailed down to her with the wind on her larboard quarter. There was no sign of the other ships, but it was not light enough to really see much and might not be for another half hour. The big schooner carried the freshening breeze in her sails and bore down on the sloop, the rabbit after the wolf now, and all hands relished the reversal of roles. *Rascal* drew closer with every plunge of her bow, and the world grew slightly lighter, and when at last the sloop discovered she was no longer the hunter but the prey she ran out her larboard guns and sent up signals to her hunting companions, though it was not light enough to see them at any distance. *Rascal* was a mere half mile away now, and Fallon ordered Cully to man the long nine in the bows. He wanted a couple of shots at long range before engaging the starboard battery. A moment later *Rascal's* British ensign went up, snapping smartly to attention, and the sloop fired her larboard broadside. Though the shot fell well short, that was all the excuse Fallon needed.

"Cully, fire as you bear!" he yelled, and the long nine sent its ball across less than a half mile of dark water, though just wide of the mark. Quickly the gun crew swabbed and reloaded, Cully making a slight adjustment, but only slight, as *Rascal* was eating up the distance between the two ships. Within two minutes the long nine was ready again.

"*Fire*, Cully!" yelled Fallon, and this time the ball crashed through the sloop's larboard railing, sending a chunk of wood like a spear into a man's belly nearby. Fallon thought he could see the man's startled face in his telescope before he disappeared.

"Good shooting, Cully!" yelled Fallon. "Ready the starboard battery now!"

Slowly *Rascal* dropped down on a parallel course with the sloop, behind but closing the gap. Fallon could read the sloop's name on her stern: *Bella*.

Rascal lunged forward to close the distance, finally gaining an overlap on *Bella* as Fallon looked toward Cully and nodded.

"Fire as you bear!" ordered Fallon, and the starboard guns roared one by one in perfectly sequenced, deafening reports that sent deadly iron into *Bella*'s hull and across her deck. Fallon could see her side explode in splinters and her crew tumble—one man seemed literally to be blown over the side and into the darker sky to the west. Quickly, *Rascal*'s gun crews loaded and ran out again. Now two broadsides seemed to fire at once, for the sloop had gotten over her surprise and was showing her teeth. Fallon felt the impact of *Bella*'s broadside on *Rascal*'s hull and watched helplessly as the crew at Number Four gun were knocked backward by an upended cannon; the men were thrown to the deck and the gun captain's head twisted awkwardly, his neck broken.

But *Rascal*'s second broadside into *Bella* multiplied the damage of the first. The sloop's larboard quarter was shattered, sending splinters like darts into the soft flesh of her crew, some of whom died with their eyes open in astonishment. But more! *Bella* had slewed around as the sloop's big boom had been shot clean off the mast to trail over the side.

"You men, get the wounded below quickly!" yelled Fallon. He surveyed the damage to the ship and then called for Aja to summon the carpenter to sound the well in case *Rascal* had been holed below the waterline. The mainsail had two shot holes, and there was a shallow furrow across the deck from the hull to the foremast where a 6-pound ball had come to a stop and was now rolling around. It was a remarkable sight but before Fallon could fully appreciate it, the lookout called.

"*Deck there, here comes the other sloop!*"

Quickly, Fallon looked to his right to see the other sloop sailing out of the morning gloom, to the west of *Bella*, her bowsprit pointed at *Rascal*. The sloop was on a close reach with the wind heeling her over as she rushed into action.

"Beauty!" called Fallon in a snap decision. "Fall off on a broad reach! We'll fire the starboard battery and then wear ship on my command!"

Rascal dropped down with the wind on her larboard quarter to get a better firing angle on the sloop, which was beating against the wind and fighting to hold her line and cross *Rascal*'s stern.

"Fire as you bear!" yelled Fallon, and Cully went gun to gun to be sure every shot told. The sloop seemed to shudder with the impact of *Rascal*'s cannon fire, with shot holes appearing in both mainsail and foresail, but now her larboard gun ports came open and her battery was being run out.

"Wear ship!" ordered Fallon and Beauty brought *Rascal*'s stern through the eye of the wind carefully, the foremast boom and the main boom swinging across the centerline of the schooner as slowly as she could allow and still keep the ship moving. Suddenly, it was done, with nothing carried away, and now the situation with the second sloop had changed dramatically. The sloop was heeled over on a starboard tack, and now she could not come up into the wind close enough to fire her larboard guns. If she fell off the wind, she would have to quickly load her starboard battery and run out. But there was no time.

"Cully!" called Fallon, exhilarated at the change in the tactical situation. "Rake her bows!"

Cully exhorted the gun crews, who loaded and ran out with

anger after what had happened to Number Four's crew. This was a little war all their own now.

"*Fire!*" yelled Fallon with excitement, and the larboard battery thundered its 12-pound balls across very few feet of water into the fragile bows of the sloop. The broadside tore away the sloop's bow railings, bowsprit, and all the attendant rigging supporting the jib and fore staysail. *Rascal* shot past her, and when the smoke had blown away, the scene revealed the total devastation of the sloop's bows. Sails were over the side, and the bowsprit had simply evaporated. Without the pressure of the wind on the headsails, the sloop bore off to the south, revealing her name board: *Estrella Azul*—Blue Star—which Fallon was thinking was a lovely name when suddenly his attention was pulled back to earth.

"Deck there!" called the lookout. "Brig to the west!"

Jesus! Fallon looked up quickly and there, less than a half mile away, a black-hulled brig was slowing, tacking through the eye of the wind. Here was the bigger, stronger wolf coming down on the scene and meaning trouble. Fallon looked at the brig, dark and menacing, settling on her new course and just running out her larboard guns. He looked at *Estrella Azul*, now attempting to tack toward the brig for protection, weighed the odds and decided his business was done. His ship was battered and the wounded were still being carried below.

"Beauty!" he called. "Wear ship again and bring her onto a beam reach. Let's show them our heels. I don't think they'll be following us anymore." And with that, *Rascal* came due south and began sailing out of range of further danger, the distance from the black brig now almost a quarter mile.

Here was Aja with the carpenter's message: only a foot of water in the well. Fallon decided to go below to get Colquist's report in person and to check on the wounded. Some had died, some were dying, and some might wish they were dead already.

Aboard the black brig, a man in the dark vestments of a priest stood on the quarterdeck and turned his face to the sky, raised his arms and closed his eyes, going into a prayer trance. Aja looked at him through his telescope and shivered. What strange man was this who thought God would favor him with an answer to his evil prayers?

EIGHT

In less than two days they would be in Port-au-Prince—assuming good weather—and *Rascal* sailed into the afternoon with a bone in her teeth, tossing off spray with every plunge of her bows. Fallon felt good about his ship, and the ship felt good about its captain. Only one man had died when Number Four gun had overturned, which was considered a miracle by the other gun crews. The wounded would live, though some with disfigured bodies. War collected its fees in obvious and less obvious ways.

No other sails had been sighted since the battle with the little wolves. The routine of the ship had been re-established; the watches rotated on and off, and the distant horizon defined the boundaries of the crew's life. Day and night they were alone in the universe of sea and stars.

Fallon was below, and Beauty and Aja walked round the ship together, two easy shipmates in a small, wooden world. Aja wore the red ribbon he'd plucked from the sea around his wrist.

"You haven't forgotten the wreckage we found, have you?" asked Beauty.

"I am afraid of what happened to the ship," replied Aja. "I even dream about it some nights. I don't know why, because I have seen many men die before. But, in my dream I can hear voices calling from the ship. They wake me up."

"Because you want to help them?" asked Beauty.

"Yes, I want to help them," said Aja. "The voices are African."

Beauty looked at Aja, not for the first time with surprise on her face. Could he be clairvoyant as well as brave? Had the wreckage belonged to a slaver and somehow Aja *knew*?

Sailors were superstitious, Beauty among them, and communication with the spirits was believed to be possible. In Beauty's mind it made Aja all the more remarkable, even powerful, and somehow more than a mere boy.

"Deck there!" called the lookout. "Sail in sight!"

The sudden call snapped Beauty's head back to the business of the ship.

"Where away?" she called.

"To larboard!" called the lookout. "Running before the wind!"

THE CALL startled Fallon, who had been about to write to Elinore, and sent him bounding from his cabin and up the companionway ladder. He joined Beauty by the binnacle, where she stood with a telescope, just calling all hands. Better to be prepared when a strange sail was sighted.

Fallon could see the ship in his own telescope now, though it was hard to keep it in view with *Rascal* rolling in beam seas. He could not yet tell her size or armament, or confirm that she was Spanish or French or British, for that matter. The ship was square-rigged and ran clumsily before the east wind, however, and would cross *Rascal*'s bows if she stayed on her present course. *But would she?*

The ship was not behaving aggressively, or at least Fallon could see no guns protruding from her sides. And on she came, innocent of ill intent, to all accounts. Fallon had a sixth sense that this ship wanted no fight, which at once relieved him and intrigued him, for as it grew larger in his telescope he could see it was a brig yawing toward them, her guns still inboard. Why would an enemy brig refuse a fight with a mere schooner? Perhaps it was no enemy.

"Hoist the colors, Beauty," Fallon said quietly. "Let's see what we see."

Up went the British ensign with the strange ship still perhaps two miles away. There was no response, no flag of any kind, which convinced Fallon even more that something odd was afoot. Aja appeared at Fallon's side with his sword.

"Thank you," said Fallon, and smiled a conspiratorial smile that told the youngster his captain was enjoying this little game.

"The hands are curious, Captain, sir," said Aja. "What do you make of it?"

"I don't know just yet," answered Fallon. "She looks Spanish to me. But we will all know very soon."

On came the brig, now altering course ever so slightly to pass astern of *Rascal* instead of across her bows. That made up Fallon's mind for him.

"Beauty," he said, "let's harden up and sail as close as possible toward the brig. Something feels strange."

Beauty gave the orders that would set the ship more or less parallel to the brig's course; that is, if the strange ship did not bear off farther to the north. On the brig plunged and twisted in the following seas, and she did in fact bear off more to the north. That forced Beauty to tack through the eye of the wind and bring *Rascal* onto a broad reach on a starboard tack about a half mile astern of the brig. Fallon could read her name in his telescope now: *Luna Nueva*—Spanish for New Moon. Now both ships had the wind on her quarter, but *Luna* had the advantage in press of sail, although *Rascal* was sailing higher and gaining slowly, her helmsman steering small at Beauty's command. And, too, the brig's bottom was no doubt foul if she had sailed across the Atlantic from Spain.

"Calm bugger," Barclay said to no one in particular, though Beauty and Fallon both nodded. "Out for a Sunday sail with no worries."

Through his telescope Fallon could just see the officers on the quarterdeck huddled in conversation—*and now what?* Both the Spanish flag and a white flag were going up to the gaff! *Good God,* thought Fallon, *what the hell did that mean?*

"Obviously, that Spanish fucker has heard of Nicholas Fallon," said Beauty under her breath.

Ah, Beauty.

Fallon considered what to do, for they were drawing closer to the brig with every minute. They were within range of the long nine now, and Beauty had ordered the starboard guns loaded. Cully and his gun crews were standing by. Was it a trick? No, there would be no honor in a trick with a white flag. Perhaps the Spanish capitán wanted to talk? It was the only viable conclusion.

As if in confirmation, the brig hove-to.

Beauty let *Rascal* come closer before executing the same maneuver, and the ships settled down a mere half a cable apart. Fallon called for his gig, and with a last glance to Beauty that said *I have no idea,* he was over the side.

As the gig's crew rowed across one hundred yards of sea, Fallon could see the Spanish sailors in their red barretina caps lining the rail. He counted ten gun ports on the larboard side, which meant a 20-gun brig with plenty of muscle. At Aja's urging, the gig's crew pulled solidly over to the Spanish ship, and when at last they'd clapped onto *Luna,* Fallon took a deep breath. *Now we'll see.*

He was met on deck by a bowing officer who introduced himself as Capitán Cabarone, smiling an oily sort of smile that put Fallon on edge immediately. He led the way below decks to his great cabin, which was tastefully furnished above a captain's pay, at least a British captain's. Rich woods and a plush, patterned carpet made the cabin feel quite like a drawing room. Cabarone was of medium height, on the lighter side of dark skinned, and had small, delicate hands that had likely never done manual work.

"So, Captain Fallon, thank you for not firing on my ship. You obviously took my intent to have this talk."

"I guessed as much, Capitán Cabarone," Fallon said in Spanish. "And I am intrigued that we should meet like this. Our two countries rarely talk since Spain allied with France."

Here Fallon was in danger of insulting the man, of being seen as rude in pointing out the betrayal of Spain's Godoy in suddenly aligning with England's mortal enemy, but he didn't care. It *had* been a betrayal, so the hell with being nice about it.

"Yes, exactly," replied Cabarone, either refusing to take insult or missing it entirely. He poured them each a glass of wine and settled himself behind his desk. "To get to business, Captain, I asked to talk so that we might avoid fighting each other and causing unnecessary bloodshed. I am not on a mission of war, but rather an act of diplomacy, for I am carrying two Cuban emissaries back to their home who have been to Spain to meet His Most Catholic Majesty Charles IV. One of these supernumeraries is a woman, and it seems she is with child. As I have been entrusted with their protection by His Most Catholic Majesty, I decided not to risk their injury by attacking your ship."

Which meant to Fallon that Cabarone had no intention of fighting *anyone* if he could avoid it.

"I see. A wise decision, sir," said Fallon, letting the question of which side would win such a battle hang in the air. Again, the arrow missed Cabarone. "I would like very much to meet these emissaries, if it would not be too much trouble. As a simple captain, I know nothing of politics, of course."

Cabarone studied Fallon carefully, sniffing for anything suspicious in the request, deciding it was only to verify the truth of what he had said, which seemed reasonable. He asked the sentry at the door to summon the Cubans, meanwhile pouring himself another glass of wine, satisfied at the way things were going with this rather dull British captain.

In a few moments two somber people entered the cabin, and Cabarone introduced them as Doctor and Señora Garón. Fallon bowed instinctively but never took his eyes off the pair.

"I am very pleased to meet you," he said in Spanish, studying the emissaries closely. "I trust your mission to Spain was successful?"

Cabarone shot a warning look to the Garóns. Instead of

answering, Doctor Garón only smiled weakly and nodded ever so slightly. His wife stood with one hand on her belly and would not be intimidated by Cabarone's gaze.

"As you may know, Captain Fallon," she said quietly, "Cuba is a proud country. However, we were always controlled by Spain, until Great Britain seized Havana. Then you traded us back to Spain for Florida."

Fallon knew this was true, of course, the trade coming in the Treaty of Paris. Many in England thought the British had gotten the worst of the deal. He could feel the emotion in the *señora*'s voice at the thought of being "traded."

Cabarone coughed, as if to put an end to the conversation, but Señora Garón continued, the color creeping up her neck as she spoke.

"We want our independence back, Captain. Independent of England or Spain or anyone, we want our country back. We went to Spain to make our feelings known, speaking for all Cubans, but we were never allowed to meet with the king. Apparently, he was gone *hunting*. We were not allowed to meet with Godoy, either. He was too *busy*. Instead, we met with some lower officials who smiled and introduced us to other officials who introduced us downward until we were meeting with servants and maids."

Here Cabarone had had enough. "Thank you very much for agreeing to meet Captain Fallon," he said as he bowed to the emissaries. "But I fear he will want to return to his ship now. Where did you say you were going, Captain?"

"I didn't say, Capitán Cabarone. But I am delighted to meet you all and I wish you every success in the future."

He bowed to Doctor Garón, who looked at him curiously, and made to bow to his wife, but instead she extended her hand.

"I hope I didn't offend you in any way, Captain," she said. "It is not easy to be Cuban these days."

Fallon took her hand and looked into her deep brown eyes, read something like a novella, bowed deeply, and preceded Cabarone up the stairs. He held the note that Señora Garón had slipped him tightly in his hand as he joined Aja at the side and climbed down into the gig.

The gig's crew made short work rowing to *Rascal*. Fallon was up the side in an instant, not wanting to waste a moment until he could go below to read the *señora's* note away from Cabarone's eyes, passed as it was with great risk to herself. He uncurled his fingers and flattened the torn piece of paper.

Somos prisioneros.

They're prisoners, by God! thought Fallon. He bounded up the companionway and ordered Beauty to make sail, for *Luna Nueva* was already underway. Beauty didn't question the order, only urged the hands to quickly get the ship underway and very soon they were sailing before the wind some quarter of a mile behind *Luna. Rascal* sought an advantage as Beauty spread every inch of canvas aboard, hoping to effectively blanket most of *Luna's* wind, and with every yard sailed the schooner seemed to minutely close the gap. Fallon judged the wind to be close to fifteen knots, and he could clearly see Cabarone standing on the quarterdeck, aware that his advantage in distance and canvas was being challenged. Still, he had the firepower to overwhelm *Rascal* if he chose to fight and, really, it was that or surrender.

Fallon stood next to the binnacle, Beauty at his side, and weighed his motivation for chasing Cabarone and risking his ship. *Luna* would be carrying some two hundred men, more than twice *Rascal's* complement, and she had aboard two political prisoners of dubious importance. But Cabarone had lied, and somehow that made all the difference. Because if his diplomatic mission was a lie, what else was a lie? What else, or who else, was aboard his ship? Why fly the white flag in the first place with *Luna* having such an advantage in men and firepower?

On *Rascal* sailed to press her foe, and as she drew closer still, Fallon weighed his options.

"Beauty, please call Cully aft," he ordered, and in moments Cully was beside him. They both eyed the closing distance to *Luna*.

"If I bear off below *Luna*, how long until you can put a shot across her bows, Cully?" asked Fallon.

The old gunner rubbed his chin and smiled at the thought of action. "Bear off and I can lay the forward guns almost immediately, Nico," he said.

"Beauty, wait until Cully gives the signal and then bear off," Fallon ordered. "Cully, send one shot off her bows, but be ready for a broadside if I give the command."

In moments, Cully waved to Beauty, and she bore off southward slightly to open the angle of fire.

"Fire when ready!" yelled Fallon, and a forward gun roared out, sending its iron ball some fifty yards in front of *Luna*. For a moment, nothing happened; Fallon could see Cabarone studying *Rascal* through his telescope, perhaps wondering if his tormentor was really serious. Then, apparently, Cabarone decided he was. Down came the brig's colors. She had surrendered.

Luna hove-to once again, as did *Rascal*, and Fallon was rowed across to the Spaniard. He brought with him a crew to take charge of the vessel, which would only be possible if Cabarone gave his word of honor not to try to escape. Fallon was met on deck by the capitán, who presented his sword with something like relief or embarrassment on his face. After the formalities of surrender were agreed to, and Fallon was persuaded of Cabarone's honor, Fallon ordered the Spanish officers and crew below decks and put under guard, with the exception of Cabarone, who was confined to his cabin. The Spanish sailors were remarkably docile, which surprised and intrigued Fallon. With the situation in hand, he sent Aja back to *Rascal* with the order for Beauty to transfer to *Luna*, and then went below to interview Cabarone in the great cabin, where he sat looking like the ruined man he was.

Fallon poured them both a glass of wine, for the bottle was still upon the desk from their earlier meeting. The two men sat for a moment eyeing one another, and just as Fallon formed a question in his mind for Cabarone, the capitán answered it for him.

"Gunpowder, Señor. We are carrying enough gunpowder to blow us to the moon. I could not engage your ship and risk killing all my men."

Here Fallon's eyebrows shot up. *Gunpowder, by God!* That would explain Cabarone's reluctance to fight! And the docility of the crew. Cabarone drank some more of his wine and seemed to sink lower in his chair and in his spirits.

"The powder is for the Spanish army in Cuba," he said suddenly, perhaps eager to further explain what appeared to have been cowardice on his part. "The army requires the gunpowder to protect the country from rebellion."

"Then I am doubly glad to relieve you of your cargo," said Fallon with a tight jaw. "Speaking of which, what of the Garóns, Capitán Cabarone? Are they really emissaries?"

Cabarone seemed not to hear the question.

"Come, Cabarone," said Fallon soothingly. "I will be speaking with both Garóns, as you must know."

"They are diplomatic . . . prisoners, Captain," said Cabarone. "I was to take them to El Morro, the fort on Havana's harbor that is also a prison. Godoy invited them to Spain to hear their grievances as a show of goodwill to Cuba, because they are known there to be patriots, but he ignored them. They were to be my, how do you say in English? . . . *sheep's clothing* to get the gunpowder through to Cuba." Cabarone spat these last words out bitterly, for clearly the ruse had failed spectacularly.

"Capitán, we will talk more later. I am going to confine you to this cabin; is that understood?"

"Yes, Captain Fallon. I'm afraid it is." And Cabarone looked around his beautiful cabin with a long, sad gaze.

"One last thing, Capitán," asked Fallon casually. "When are you expected in Havana?"

Here Cabarone hesitated, suddenly aware that he had perhaps

over-talked, but finally he spoke. "The officials there are expecting the powder when it comes, for they are desperate for it. But as to when it is coming . . ." He shrugged the shrug of a thousand Spanish officers and petty officials. *Who can tell?*

NINE

REAR ADMIRAL Harry Davies stood at the stern windows aboard his flagship, *Avenger*, 74, and looked toward Port-au-Prince on the western end of Saint-Domingue. The close of day was turning the windows black; in his reflected image he looked older than he ought—or perhaps he really looked that old, he thought darkly. He was tall at least, with long, light hair tied in an old-fashioned club. Only thirty-nine years old, he felt like he'd been in the service forever, in wars forever, with little to show for it except his rank, which admittedly had come quickly, though whether because of luck or ability he wasn't sure. His parents were deceased and he had no siblings. He also had no wife, not even close. He'd even given up his mistress in Antigua—well, she'd given up on him, truth be told.

Davies went on deck to walk off his mutton dinner. He looked across the Gulf of Gonâve at his two frigates at anchor. HMS *Brilliant* was on the small side, a fifth-rate of 36 guns with a clean bottom and able crew. Her captain, Josiah Peabody, was certainly capable if unimaginative, having fought in a string of conflicts that never earned him distinction. But he was as loyal as a retriever, essentially fearless, and could be relied upon in a fight.

The bigger frigate, *Renegade*, had been sold into the service by Ezra Somers as a prize captured by Nicholas Fallon, the inestimable privateer from Bermuda. The Admiralty had sent Davies a new captain for *Renegade* several months ago, Sir Charles Charles, and he was as big a fop as his ridiculous name suggested. *My God,* Davies thought, *where does this endless supply of incompetence come from?* Davies had immediately put Samuel Jones II into *Renegade* as first lieutenant, so entered in the ship's books because there was another Samuel Jones in the service. Jones had served nobly as Fallon's first lieutenant years ago when Davies had pressed Fallon into service on a different mission. He kept the ship running well, despite Sir Charles's lack of command presence, which was putting it generously. The trouble for Davies was that Sir Charles was senior to Peabody on the Captains List, so any coordinated action involving the two frigates was cumbersome at best and fraught with weakness. Davies' own flag captain, Kinis, was a by-the-book sort of man, with a punctual mind and barman's memory. He was in the right job running a flagship.

All three British ships rode easily in the lee of Gonâve Island, with Port-au-Prince just visible up the bay to the east. Davies could see what looked to be fires burning in the hills, and he could well imagine groups of runaway slaves, or *maroons,* still hiding in the hills, dancing around the flames and practicing their Vodou. Their *houngans,* or priests, wielded great influence over the African slaves. In fact, the Saint-Domingue slave rebellion of 1791 was said to have originated at a Vodou ceremony because of a rumor: A spoiled young white plantation hostess was said to have given a grand dinner party on the island and, distressed that a particular dish wasn't prepared to her satisfaction, had ordered the offending black cook to be thrown into the still hot oven. Rumor in the islands was a powerful force and, in the absence of real news, *became* the news. The slaves of Saint-Domingue worked themselves into a rage and fields were set on fire, white masters murdered, and the sugarcane burned where it stood before harvest. After firing the fields, most of the slaves became maroons and retreated to the hills, living in colonies and continuing to attack white plantation owners.

In the chaos of attacks and reprisals, a rebel leader gradually emerged to organize the rebellion and give it focus. His name was

Toussaint Louverture, a charismatic and complex man: former slave, freeman, slave owner himself, and, finally, rebel general ruling Saint-Domingue.

One of Louverture's earliest and most consistent targets was the garrison of British troops who stubbornly refused to leave Saint-Domingue after having been sent there to protect British planters. With Louverture's rise to power, the planters were generally spared violence, but the presence of British military on Saint-Domingue was a thorn in the side of the French-leaning general. At last, after countless attacks and reprisals, the British officer in charge of the troops, General Thomas Maitland, had negotiated their safe withdrawal and sent word to the Admiralty for ships to remove them. Davies and his little armada had come out to do just that.

But there was more to Davies' mission, for he had also been sent an intelligence agent by the Admiralty with orders to be secreted into Cuba at the earliest opportunity. This proposition was difficult for a British ship, not least because Spain controlled Cuba and was Great Britain's enemy just as France was. And, the task required a ship that was smaller than a frigate and quick in stays, for she could come under the guns of harbor forts. Davies had immediately thought of Fallon, whose American-built schooner might slip in and out of Cuba without arousing suspicion.

James Wharton, the intelligence agent, was a likable fellow, but on the voyage from English Harbor he had been indisposed much of the time and kept to his cabin. Davies suspected sea sickness. In a rare moment on deck, Wharton had revealed that his orders were to explore ways to weaken Spain's relationship with Cuba and to draw Spanish resources away from the war. Wharton hoped to find a nascent independence movement or political discontent that could be fed and nurtured. Even a slave rebellion would be a start. Clearly, thought Davies, London missed the irony of embracing slavery at home and supporting slave rebellions elsewhere.

Well, war itself was ironical, Davies decided. Hated enemies became allies at the stroke of a pen. Prisoners were exchanged only to be captured and exchanged again. God was invoked on all sides, making each side right in the eyes of the Almighty.

Davies reached for the London *Gazette*, which he had brought from English Harbor because it had an article on Louverture. The writer was all praise for the slave leader: "Toussaint is a Negro and in the jargon of war has been called a brigand. But according to all accounts he is a Negro born to vindicate the claims of this species and to show that the character of men is independent of color."

Good lord, Davies thought, now the character of men is independent of color! What would they think of next?

TEN

BEAUTY VERY SENSIBLY waited until dawn to attempt the entrance to the Gulf of Gonâve, though it was not difficult, for she did not want *Luna* to be fired upon by the Royal Navy in poor light. *Luna* flew a British ensign, but a suspicious British captain might have taken that as a ruse from a Spanish brig intent on mischief and blown them to bits. The Gulf of Gonâve was quite large, with Gonâve Island dominating its center. Beauty rounded up and let go well to the west, preferring that the gig's crew row a bit farther in return for having the gunpowder a safe distance away from the flagship, which even now was signaling for *Luna*'s captain to report on board.

The gig's crew made smart work of rowing across the azure water to where *Avenger* lay anchored, and in no time the bosun's chair was lowered and Beauty was raised up over the side.

"Beauty McFarland! It is wonderful to see you again," Kinis exclaimed with unusual emotion, for they had a shared history fighting the French and Spanish, and he respected her courage and seamanship. "I thought that brig was handled exceptionally well when she came in. Now I know why!"

"Thank you, Captain Kinis," said Beauty. "I am very glad to have the anchor down, I can assure you!"

"Come below and see Admiral Davies," said Kinis. "He will want your report, I know."

Davies enthusiastically welcomed Beauty into his cabin, which was furnished traditionally in heavy oak cabinets and cupboards. The stern gallery was massive and threw its light on the cabin and the enormous desk, behind which the admiral had just been finishing coffee and reviewing the embarkation plans for the British soldiers on Saint-Domingue. Even now the soldiers were massing on the shore, and soon Peabody, Sir Charles, and Kinis would be sending boats to begin taking them off. After asking his flag captain to stay and hear Beauty's report with him, Davies bade her begin.

And so the story of the taking of *Luna* tumbled out; the treachery of Cabarone and the courage of the emissaries and, of course, the gunpowder floating barely three cable lengths away. At this Davies' eyebrows shot up and Kinis shifted nervously. But there was more, of course, for some two hundred Spanish seamen and officers were locked below decks on *Luna*, guarded by twenty English sailors, and something must be done with them soon.

Davies' mind instantly sprang into action. "Captain Kinis, please send a detachment of marines to *Luna* immediately to secure the ship against any foolishness. I will make arrangements with General Maitland on shore to receive the Spaniards and turn them over to Louverture, for he has relations with Spanish Santo Domingo on the eastern side of the island. They can be his damned problem."

"There are two Cuban top men among the prisoners," said Beauty. "One of my men can identify them for you. They've volunteered to join *Rascal's* crew, Admiral, and Nico will be glad to have them. Pray leave them but be sure to take Capitán Cabarone, who is guarded in his cabin."

Kinis immediately left to organize the marines, and Davies now asked a very obvious question. "And what of Captain Fallon, Beauty? When can we expect him?"

"He sent me on with the gunpowder and prisoners as quickly as possible while he took off the emissaries and endeavored to make them comfortable. He was particularly worried about the *señora*, as she looked distressed by the excitement and he wanted Colquist, the surgeon, nearby. She's pregnant, you see."

IN THE EVENT, it was early afternoon when *Rascal* hove into view and dropped anchor just as the last of the Spanish sailors and officers had been taken off *Luna* and rowed to shore. In short order, Fallon joined Beauty in Davies' cabin and, after the warmest of greetings from the admiral, Fallon reported on his voyage thus far. He began with the battle against the little wolves, as Aja had called them, and the odd captain in a cleric's vestments. Davies only smiled knowingly. Then Fallon moved on to his interviews with Cabarone and, most important, the Garóns. Davies was all attention, occasionally rubbing his chin and asking a clarifying question.

"Allow me to familiarize you with the situation in the rest of the Caribbean relative to Cuba," Davies said after Fallon had finished. "Your mission will involve you in these affairs in a limited aspect, but I know you both well enough to know that you follow events where they may lead. So better to lay it all out as best I can."

Fallon and Beauty leaned forward in their chairs, all attention now that their "intelligence" mission was to be put in a broader context.

"You know, of course, that Saint-Domingue has been called the Pearl of the Antilles because it has always been the wealthiest of all the colonies. Sugarcane is France's cash crop, and it puts clothes on the backs of her soldiers and food in the bellies of her sailors. But since the successful slave rebellion in '91, led by Toussaint Louverture, the sugarcane production on the island has dropped dramatically. The freed slaves are choosing subsistence farming over the hardships of working in the cane fields, even for wages, and France is losing millions of francs annually. It is rumored that Bonaparte, who is growing more powerful than ever in France, may push to re-establish slavery in the colonies!"

"*Good God!*" exclaimed Fallon, for that would be a dramatic reversal of *Liberté, Égalité, Fraternité!* that could well set off slave rebellions throughout the French colonies in the Caribbean.

"Meanwhile," Davies continued, "Spain has moved to bolster its own sugarcane production in Cuba and take up the slack left by Saint-Domingue. Consequently, Spain's importation of Africans into Cuba has grown by the *thousands*. In some Cuban ports the average price for a strong male is over thirty-five pounds sterling!"

Fallon and Beauty gasped. No wonder the slavers were jammed with kidnapped Africans, and no wonder their ships were being preyed upon. Only gold, silver, or guns would be more valuable cargo.

"I believe the little wolves, as Aja called them, are pirates taking slavers; they are not the only ones, of course, but they are the best organized and likely the most successful because they are voracious," said Davies. "And the most far ranging. They are commanded by a rogue priest known as the Holy One, a man who defiles his religion. He is Spanish but attacks Spanish slavers, as well as any other, from here to Bermuda and west to Cuba's doorstep. Wharton brought intelligence from London that Spain was dispatching at least one frigate, maybe two, to bring the situation under control and to protect Spanish slavers and Cuban ports. That's the commitment Spain has to slavery and sugarcane, by God!"

Davies was thus reminded of the intelligence agent, likely still below deck in his cabin. "Here, steward!" he called. The steward opened the cabin door immediately, ready as always for just such a summons. "Please give my compliments to Mr. Wharton and, if he is not still indisposed, ask him to join us for dinner."

When the steward had left, Davies asked Fallon to invite the Garóns to dinner as well. Aja left to fetch the emissaries in the gig and, meanwhile, Davies summoned the cook to lay on something special for dinner. And to open wine, lots of wine, for this was their last night together for a long time.

ELEVEN

JAMES WHARTON was certainly a remarkable looking fellow, tall with a shock of brilliant white hair. The hair was the only thing that gave his age away; his bright blue eyes had the look of a younger man, as did his lean build and erect posture. In fact, Wharton was at least fifty but, with a hat, could have passed for much younger.

After some perfunctory small talk and Davies' lovely toast to the Garóns' good health, and their child's, the steward brought out several fresh fowl that he'd purchased ashore as well as potatoes, a lamb stew, and various cheeses. The meal went well enough, helped by the Garóns' ability to speak English quite well and, by the time they'd arrived at pudding and port, they had shared their story with the table. Wharton, in particular, had listened raptly.

"And you are a doctor of physic, Señor, I believe?" said Wharton to Doctor Garón. Doctors were several rungs above mere surgeons in skill and medical knowledge, though they often practiced surgery.

"Yes, trained in Spain. My wife is a dressmaker in Havana. Or *was*," said Garón.

"If I may be so bold," Señora Garón asked Wharton, "can you tell us anything of your mission to our country?"

"Yes, of course, Señora," answered Wharton. "First, let me assure you on one point: Great Britain's interest in Cuba is to promote independence from Spain, not to occupy the country again.

Granted, promoting Cuba's independence is in Great Britain's self-interest, for it would weaken one of our enemies. And, in truth, the Admiralty feels that an independent Cuba could also be a valuable trading partner. But my mission is to find a group or an individual we might support in a quest for independence. Nothing more."

There was a noticeable pause at the table, and Fallon looked at Señora Garón closely, trying to judge whether she believed Wharton. The *señora* looked at Wharton a long moment before replying.

"Thank you, Mr. Wharton," she said quietly. "I appreciate your candor and directness. Self-interest can be tolerated when it's in the open. In fact, it would seem our interests might be aligned. We want to see a free and independent Cuba as well. But our visit to Spain has convinced us that diplomacy will do little to make independence a reality. We are amateurs at this and, as we have no army and no weapons, I fear we have no chance."

That logic was certainly hard to argue with, and no one tried. The steward swept the dishes away silently, and more port was poured. Fallon had listened to the exchange between Señora Garón and Wharton and was simultaneously trying to nurture an idea into something comprehensible.

"A question, if I may, Doctor and Señora Garón," he began tentatively. "And I do not mean to be impolite or impolitic in asking it, but it may have some bearing on our conversation. Do you have a position, moral or political, on Cuban slavery?"

Doctor Garón, who had been silent for some time, burst forth animatedly. "It is abominable, sir! I have been called upon to attempt to save the lives of many slaves, slaves who have been tortured and used wretchedly by their owners, so I know firsthand the cruelty of this curse on humankind. Hundreds come to Cuba daily from Africa, but hundreds must surely die daily as well."

"Slavery is a thief that steals dreams," said Señora Garón softly. "I can think of nothing else to say."

"There *is* nothing else to say, Señora," said Fallon in barely a whisper. And then he looked around the table as he spoke. "There may be an army in Cuba that we are not considering. An army that thirsts for liberation as badly as any Cuban alive. To date, I believe the slave rebellion on Saint-Domingue is the only successful such uprising in the Caribbean. No doubt there are many reasons for that success, but surely one would be a passionate and determined leader in Toussaint Louverture. Could such a person be in Cuba now? For surely word of the Saint-Domingue success has spread among the slaves there and may be inspiration for the minor rebellions we have heard of."

"You are very perceptive, Captain Fallon," said Wharton, his blue eyes twinkling. "Indeed, a massive slave rebellion would be capital! But we must remember that Spain maintains something of an army in Cuba, however ragtag it might be, and however short of gunpowder it might now be, thanks to you, sir! The army would be called upon to put down any slave rebellion that might be seen as threatening. Still, it is an interesting thought."

Davies rose to retrieve a chart from his desk and unrolled it upon the table, anchoring the corners with port glasses. "Perhaps, as you imply, Captain Fallon, freedom is contagious; see on the chart how Saint-Domingue reaches her arm out to Cuba, as if to lead the way. A successful slave rebellion in Cuba could be the first step in independence from Spain."

"Why do you say that, Admiral?" asked Señora Garón, alert for anything that would open the door to independence.

"I only have the example of Saint-Domingue, Señora," answered Davies. "I believe Louverture must be at least *considering* declaring Saint-Domingue's independence from France, for he is certainly acting independently."

Here Wharton chimed in. "And I have it on good authority that Louverture intends to sign trade treaties with both the United States and Great Britain." He said this confidentially, even conspiratorially, and all at the table felt a whiff of intrigue.

Fallon was astounded. If a French colony openly traded with

England, it would make France *apoplectic!* And it was doubtful the French government would stand for it. Louverture would have to be very careful how he played his cards, or he would wake up one morning to find a French squadron leveling its guns at his little island.

Fallon looked around the cabin and saw the Garóns deep in thought; well, much had happened to them in a very short period of time. And their eyes had been opened to the nefarious ways of secret agents and revolutionary ideas and strategies. No doubt they were at a loss as to what would become of their country. Or themselves.

"Tell me, Doctor and Señora Garón," Fallon offered, "assuming it is not safe to go home to Havana, at least at the moment, where do you want to go? I can attempt to land you anywhere you desire."

"That is very kind of you, Captain Fallon," said Doctor Garón. "My wife and I have been discussing whether it is safe for us anywhere in Cuba at this time. With the baby coming, we cannot take a chance. Admiral Davies, may we presume to accompany you to Antigua? It might be best for us to be out of Cuba until the birth of our child."

Davies, of course, readily agreed, even offering to help Doctor Garón secure a position at the naval hospital at English Harbor. Suffice it to say, the Garóns were overwhelmed at this unexpected kindness.

"And tell me, Mr. Wharton," Fallon said, "where would you like to be landed in Cuba?"

"I have been talking to Admiral Davies, and, while I had intended to land in Santiago, I should prefer instead to be set ashore in Matanzas and make my way to Havana and back, to be picked up in one month, if convenient." Fallon responded that it would be quite convenient, and the dinner party began to break up.

The Garóns were to shift their things to the flagship in the morning, as the little fleet intended to sail for Antigua with the British soldiers before noon. That settled, Davies called for Fallon's gig to take his dinner party back to *Rascal*.

As they were rowed across the harbor, Fallon looked at the sad-eyed and erstwhile diplomats whose only crime was loyalty to Cuba. And for that they might never go home. He looked beyond the Garóns to *Luna,* her outline visible against the sky, and considered the store of gunpowder in her holds. Suddenly, there was the familiar tingle on his arm, the hair getting up, anticipating the idea that was just now forming in his mind. It might be possible. *Might.*

Fallon's plan was to act against the Spanish, first and foremost, more or less within the context of his mission for Davies. But perhaps the plan might also help the Garóns return to Cuba after their baby was born, without fear of arrest.

But to do that, he would have to kill them first.

TWELVE

AT DAWN the next morning, Beauty and Fallon came aboard *Avenger* to say good-bye to Davies—and to present the idea Fallon had been mulling all night. They were shown to the great cabin, where the admiral and Kinis were reviewing their own plans to get underway. The last of the British soldiers on Saint-Domingue had all been taken off and were aboard the three British ships in the harbor.

Fallon laid out his idea to strike a blow for Great Britain and to help the Garóns in the bargain. It was a typical Fallon plan, long on daring and surprise but short on details. Well, at sea you never knew. Davies listened to the idea with a mix of respect and amusement. Respect, because it really was a very good idea to show Spain that Britain's reach extended to Havana. Amusement, because Fallon cared so little for profit that he was willing to sacrifice a perfectly good and valuable prize to do it.

It was true that Davies was employing Fallon and his crew—paying them handsomely—to transport Wharton to Matanzas and back. And Havana was no great way past Matanzas. But Davies also knew it was Fallon's particular joy to beard the enemy, and he was only acting in character.

By noon most of the gunpowder had been transferred from *Luna* to *Avenger,* leaving ten barrels aboard the Spanish brig. Kinis and Davies waved to *Rascal* while leaving the harbor, and slowly the three stout Royal Navy ships sailed west, eventually to tack south and then east for English Harbor. The Garóns stood near the fore-mast on *Avenger*, bound for a new life.

Soon after the navy ships had sailed, *Luna* and *Rascal* were both off to the northwest. It was a sparkling day, the sun high and warm, and there was a humble breeze from the east. Fallon stood at the taffrail on *Luna* with James Wharton, who had asked to be con-veyed to Cuba on the brig because of its less lively motion.

"Tell me, sir," asked Fallon, "how does one become an intelli-gence agent, if that is what you are called?"

"Well, I have been called many things," laughed Wharton in re-sponse, his blue eyes twinkling. "The service is simply something I fell into by chance. I knew someone who, it turned out, was an agent for the British government, and he more or less recruited me. I think he saw an unremarkable face that could come and go with-out being remembered!"

Now it was Fallon's turn to laugh. He liked this man, his un-assuming way, his quiet intelligence.

"I would think, rather, he saw a keen mind that was clever in the extreme," said Fallon. "But tell me something of yourself; that is, if you're allowed to."

"Certainly," replied Wharton without a trace of hesitation, as if eager to reveal things he could confide in someone who could be-come a friend as a result. "I was born in London, actually, but my mother was unwed, at least at the time. And I was put in an or-phanage. I only found out about all this much later, of course. I vaguely remember being unhappy there, was never adopted, and I ran off before I was ten. I lived on the streets, begging and stealing food and doing what I had to do to keep my little tummy full. I was in and out of trouble with the man on the beat from time to time as well."

"It sounds like a recipe for becoming a clever intelligence man, I must say."

"Yes, I suppose it does. My fortunes turned when a very kind woman caught me pinching her purse. Rather than turn me in, she took me in. She gave me dinner and a good talking to and made me promise to give up my street ways. She, in turn, would take care of me and send me to school. I didn't have to think long about that, I can tell you. It was winter in London and snowing outside and she had a very warm house!"

"A warm heart, as well, I collect."

"Yes, a warm heart," replied Wharton, with a distant look in his eyes. "Anyway, I lived in her house and went to school like a normal boy for once in my life. I did chores for her, house cleaning and the like, and at night we would read together until I could read on my own."

"Is she still alive, then?"

"No, no, she passed away before I turned eighteen. Consumption. It nearly killed me, and I was very prepared to go back to living by my wits when a magistrate said I now owned the house, everything in it, and a small annuity to keep the wolf from the door. I had no idea, of course, no idea at all. But she had always treated me as her own, like a mum."

There was a silence between them now, Fallon not knowing what to say. Wharton's childhood had been so different from his own, and yet here they were, placed by fate on the stern of the same ship.

"A few months later," Wharton continued, "the magistrate brought by some documents to sign to clean up things. He'd gone to the trouble to go through her private papers and found a letter that she'd left for me before she died. You can imagine I was heartbroken to hold it in my hands, for she really had been my savior. I read the letter, which told of her own childhood, growing up poor like me, but pretty enough that the lads took notice. She'd become pregnant by one of them, who promptly ran off on her. She panicked, and when the baby came she gave the child up for adoption and ran off herself. She met a man in Ireland, someone kind, and they married. In a few years, he moved them to London for his job. Something to do with textiles, I believe. When he died he left her well off and there it would have ended except I came along and tried to lift her purse. She said she knew immediately who I was, the way a mother bear knows her cub, but was too humiliated because of what she'd done to ever tell me. So, she took me in instead and treated me as if I were her own—which, of course, I was."

Fallon stood at the rail, stunned speechless.

"Life is a funny thing, Captain, is it not?" Wharton said softly. "And now here we are."

The ship's bell rang and the glass was turned and Barclay called to Fallon about the course. When Fallon returned to the taffrail Wharton had just left to walk round the ship. Fallon watched him amble away, carrying the rest of his secrets with him.

BEHIND *LUNA*, less than a quarter mile astern, *Rascal* sailed peacefully along in the afternoon light, the sun blazing off her sails. Fallon lingered at *Luna*'s taffrail, mulling his conversation with Wharton, but at last his attention shifted to an appreciation of *Rascal*'s lines. He marveled again at how lovely she was under a full press of sail. Since capturing the schooner from the French in Savannah he had grown deeply attached to her, not least because she was the finest sailing ship he'd ever commanded. This was a view of her he rarely had and he savored it.

It was more than seven hundred miles to Havana, where Fallon intended to deliver the gunpowder as Cabarone intended. Well, not *exactly* as he intended. The voyage would take them along the length of Cuba's northern coast, past Matanzas, where Wharton had asked to be landed. But after hearing Fallon's plan to deliver the gunpowder to Havana, Wharton asked to be dropped off in Matanzas on the return trip instead. For once, he could be part of something *overt*, not covert, and he was looking forward to it.

Like Wharton, Fallon had listened thoughtfully as Davies described Matanzas, the port where *Avenger* had sheltered after suffering horribly in the hurricane of '96. Davies had been effusive in his praise of the Matanzas women for their willingness to prod their men to help repair a desperate English ship, a ship that was the nominal enemy of Cuba's ruling country. Apparently, many of the Matanzas women had cut their hair short in open defiance of Spain's cultural influence on Cuba. It was a public and brave show of loyalty, and if an uprising in Cuba were to happen, thought Fallon, Matanzas was a likely place.

The days and nights spent sailing along Cuba's coast were uneventful, with no ships sighted other than coastal fishing vessels. *Luna*'s crew went about their duties as if they had not a care in the world; such was their confidence in their captain that the kegs of gunpowder sitting only feet beneath the deck didn't seem to concern them.

On the morning of the fourth day, *Luna* and *Rascal* hove-to about fifty miles from Havana, and Fallon, Aja, and Wharton were rowed across less than half a cable's distance to confer with Beauty about the plan to sail the gunpowder into Havana Harbor. Their leisurely sailing was over; it was time for action.

In *Rascal*'s great cabin, Fallon unrolled a chart of Havana Harbor for Beauty and James Wharton to study with him. It was an elongated harbor with a narrow entrance off Havana Bay. On the eastern headland stood El Morro, a large fort that was also a prison where the Garóns might have spent the rest of their lives, or at least the rest of the war. On the western shore stood another fort, the Castle of San Salvador de la Punta.

"I presume you know, of course," said Wharton matter-of-factly, "of the possibility of a chain across the harbor entrance?"

Both Fallon and Beauty jerked their heads around to the intelligence agent.

"What did you say, sir?" asked Fallon incredulously.

"Oh, I see you are unaware," said Wharton, aghast. "I was practicing my Spanish with one of the Cuban top men who happened to mention it to me. He said the Spanish fear an invasion by sea and have constructed a chain across the harbor that can be raised in times of imminent danger to keep enemy ships out. He said it was raised and lowered by each fort working in tandem."

"Let's hope," said Beauty looking at Fallon, "that the Spaniards would never suspect a captured ship full of gunpowder to come sailing into Havana Harbor. Do you think they'd consider that *imminent danger?* I think the answer is *fuck yes.*"

Ah, Beauty.

"I only learned of the chain this morning and I assumed you knew," said Wharton. "Obviously, the top man did not know of your plans or he would have brought it forward himself."

They all stared at the chart in silence, *Rascal* rocking gently on the swells, with the ship's noises, the creaks and groans of timbers, so normal as not to be noticed. Fallon hung his head, for he had come a great way to strike a blow for Great Britain against Spain and to free the Garóns from future persecution, but that damned chain could well be up and would put paid to his little scheme. Now he was not so clever, not so cunning. He felt, in fact, like a fool in the eyes of Beauty and Wharton. And worse, a fool in his own eyes.

While Fallon stared at the floor, Beauty turned to walk to the stern windows, deep in thought. The day was still young, with plenty of daylight left, and shafts of it fell about her shoulders as she stared out to sea. Wharton had quietly excused himself from the cabin, no doubt feeling bad that he had dashed Fallon's plan. Indeed, Fallon was in despair. He was on the verge of ordering, what? That *Luna* sail to Antigua and *Rascal* to Matanzas to drop off Wharton? Was there another choice?

Fallon raised his head and stared at Beauty by the stern windows, she who always seemed to know the best course to the finish, and he wondered what she was thinking. He couldn't see her face, of course, but she was smiling.

THIRTEEN

THE SENIOR OFFICER on station at La Punta was Teniente González, and he was very tired. His swarthy good looks sagged a little, for he'd had too much wine the night before, indulging himself a little too much in the delights of Havana. He'd only gotten back to the barracks an hour before dawn and now, fortified by coffee and the memory of a certain señorita, he faced a long day at his post. He stepped out of his office onto the parapet and swept the sea with his telescope. Not much to see. Perhaps the smudge of a sail in the distance, or perhaps not.

González looked across the harbor entrance at El Morro. No signal flags were flying. The chain had been up all night to prevent surprises, which was a new precaution since a privateer had tried to cut out a ship weeks before. It would be lowered later in the morning. For now, things were as they should be—quiet.

RASCAL AND LUNA stood off Havana Harbor about fifteen miles, too far for a telescope from the forts to see them. Fallon and Barclay were on board *Luna*, along with Cully and Aja and a crew of twelve. Just enough to sail the brig in the light conditions of the day.

"Now, Barclay," began Fallon, "lay a course for the middle of the entrance to the harbor, taking into account wind and current, a course that will require no trimming of the sails whatsoever."

Barclay's eyes widened in surprise. "No sail trimming?" he asked.

"This will be a ghost ship steering herself for much of the way," said Fallon. "And, Barclay, we must know how long it will take *Luna* to cross the plane of the forts and gain the entrance to the harbor."

Barclay gulped air.

"Simple, my good man," said Fallon with a wink, and with that he walked away, smiling, to find Cully.

"Cully, you will be below with the slow match," said Fallon to his gun captain. "You are generally aware of how fast slow match burns, of course, but you must be precise. Figure exactly how many seconds to the foot it takes. Aja will come below with the time we need to allot from Barclay. Count out your length carefully—it won't do to have the fire meet the gunpowder too soon. Or too late, come to that. So, Cully, it must be perfect, you see." With that, Fallon resumed smiling. It felt good to give the responsibility for success or failure to someone else for a change.

Beauty's plan was a good one, thought Fallon, and he had heard it out with relief and not a little gratitude. It was really quite a clever idea, plus it had the added benefit of being the only idea they had. *Luna* sailed toward the entrance to Havana for perhaps a mile so that Barclay could get his bearings and record the ship's speed through the water. Conditions near the shore might alter the speed, of course, and there was always the current to consider, all of which Barclay must guess at. When they had sailed as far as they dared, Fallon wore ship and sailed back the way they had come, hopefully undetected.

At last, it was time. *Rascal* had taken station a quarter mile to windward and, once Barclay told him that he had the necessary calculations in hand, Fallon ordered Aja to dip the Spanish colors, signaling they were ready to begin. Beauty dipped the British colors in reply, and both ships began sailing a parallel course toward Havana's harbor, with *Luna* slightly ahead. One of *Luna*'s boats trailed astern the brig, sliding off the face of the waves and shooting ahead, only to be brought up short again by its tow rope to start the dance over again. It was doubtful the small boat could be seen from the fort and, anyway, it was not all that unusual to trail a small boat inshore.

Ten miles from the harbor, Beauty opened fire, a solid broadside that sailed high and wide.

TENIENTE GONZÁLEZ sat up straight in his chair, where he might have been dozing, and was instantly awake. *That was gunfire!*

Again, he stepped out onto the parapet and swept the sea with his telescope. The smudge he'd seen before was now a ship sailing for the harbor, and there was another, smaller ship firing at her.

¡Santa Madre de Dios!

Quickly he looked across the harbor and saw signals going up from El Morro: *What are your orders?*

So, Colonel García was not at the fort—yes, González remembered the colonel was away for two days—*Ai!* That made González the senior officer in charge. He swung his telescope back to the approaching ships, still some miles away, but the situation was slowly coming into focus. The closest ship appeared to be a brig, obviously Spanish, and perhaps the very ship they'd been expecting for weeks from Spain. If so, *Luna Nueva* was carrying gunpowder and, Colonel García had said, political prisoners.

"Send this signal to El Morro," he ordered the *guardavía*, or signalman: "*Prepare to lower the chain.*"

ABOARD *LUNA*, Cully responded to *Rascal*'s perfect broadside with a somewhat ragged broadside of his own, there being fewer hands to man the guns. The shot was low and wide of the mark, the water erupting to mark the shots so the eyes of the forts could believe the battle was real. Both ships continued loading and firing, Beauty letting *Luna* slip ahead by a good two cables when they were perhaps five miles from the harbor. Fallon could see the forts through his telescope now, and could see the signal flags going up and down. *Good*, he thought, *keep talking.*

After another broadside from Cully, Beauty luffed the

foresail as if a brace had parted, and *Rascal* swung up into the wind momentarily—just enough to fall behind *Luna* and effectively close off the angle for another broadside. At least, that's what Beauty hoped the forts' lookouts would think.

Fallon, of course, had no idea how long it would take to lower the chain, assuming the chain was even up and the forts had bought into the little theater unfolding in their telescopes. He could see ships at anchor inside the mouth of the harbor, none of which seemed concerned. Well, why should they be? The forts' guns would protect them from any threat.

GONZÁLEZ WAS SWEATING now, the collar of his uniform sticking to his neck. *Should he lower the chain or not?* Certainly, the country needed the gunpowder, but could he be sure this was *Luna Nueva* he was seeing?

Here was El Morro signaling again—they were ready to lower the chain on his command. *His command!* He studied the oncoming ships again. Both were firing continuously, but to what effect was hard to tell. The brig stood gamely on for the harbor entrance, while the schooner dogged her relentlessly. If that schooner only knew of the gunpowder! *¡Madre de Dios!* She would not be sailing so close.

That more than anything convinced him to lower the chain. He gave the signal to El Morro, and then he ordered the forts to open fire on the schooner.

FALLON HEARD the cannon fire from La Punta, on one side of Havana Harbor, followed by the same from El Morro, on the other side. Though neither shot put them in danger yet, it was good to know he had their attention. He conferred with Barclay, who double-checked course, speed, and distance. *Luna* was well up to windward of El Morro, Barclay having accounted for the wind pushing the brig down toward the entrance to the harbor as she sailed. Finally, Barclay finished his calculations and arrived at the length of slow match Cully should allow, guessing at what the wind and current would be like closer to land, and off went Aja below decks to inform the gunnery captain. At Fallon's order, some of the crew fired off one last broadside, just to show fighting spirit, and then massed at the gangway and began climbing down into the trailing boat. With the sails balanced as perfectly as possible, Fallon gave a quick look to Barclay and lashed the wheel in position. Next, Cully was up the companionway and, after Barclay descended, was soon over the side with the remainder of the crew. A last look around, a wave to Beauty, who was still charging behind in *Rascal*, and then Fallon went down into the boat as well.

"Cast off," Fallon ordered, and the gig's crew pushed off and immediately found themselves in *Luna's* wake. It was eerie watching the ship sail away without a person aboard, *Luna* going about her business as if guided by a mysterious, magical hand.

As he watched *Luna's* stern recede, Fallon thought briefly of the Garóns, and how they had eagerly embraced the idea of appearing to die in order to get a fresh start in Cuba when they returned. Now if only the commanding officers in the forts were fooled. They were expecting a brig from Spain loaded with gunpowder. *Well*, thought Fallon, recalling a Chinese proverb from one of Somers's books: *Be careful what you wish for.*

The shots from the forts soared over *Luna* and landed harmlessly well short of *Rascal*, which had reached the small boat and hove-to to pick up the crew. Even if the lookouts now read the trick, it would hopefully take some time to raise the chain, assuming it had been lowered in the first place, for the action had to be coordinated between both forts, discussions held, gestures made, arms waved frantically, and signals sent and confirmed.

Luna sailed on, a tendril of smoke from the burning slow match drifting up from her hold as the small crew rowed toward *Rascal*, and Barclay counted the minutes.

THE CHAIN dropped slowly; it was not at all clear if it would be lowered enough for *Luna Nueva* to sail into the harbor. González watched through his telescope as La Punta's cannon shot landed close by the schooner and she seemed to bear away. That was excellent.

Now what was this? González looked through his telescope again and saw some of *Luna's* crew going over the side of the ship! Why would they . . . what was going on? Quickly, he focused on *Luna*, but he could see no other crewmen aboard. *But who was sailing the ship?*

A knot was forming in his stomach, a very bad knot that almost doubled González over.

"Guardavía! Signal El Morro to *raise* the chain! Quickly!"

"How LONG, Barclay?" Fallon asked.

"I would say under two minutes now," Barclay answered. And he seemed unconcerned.

One minute. Two minutes. Just as the small boat reached *Rascal's* side, a massive explosion rent the sky and thundered over the water. The very air seemed to detonate as a pillar of black smoke shot skyward, carrying bits and pieces of wood and metal and rope and sailcloth and copper and compass and everything that had made *Luna* a ship. Even from the drifting boats the crew could feel the whoosh of air as the explosion sent its energy outward. Fallon reached the deck and immediately trained his telescope on the harbor—*by God!* It looked like *Luna* had made it inside! Not only had the brig disappeared, but several smaller ships were dismasted and one might well be sinking.

Wharton was dancing around the binnacle like an Irishman. Beauty herself was smiling broadly, and Barclay and Cully were slapping each other on the back. All in all, blowing up a ship in an enemy harbor was a glorious thing, Fallon decided. And all he had to do was mostly stay out of the way and let it all happen.

All hands agreed the explosion was first rate, though Fallon knew the damage inflicted on Spain was more psychological than physical. If Havana officials believed their much-needed gunpowder was aboard *Luna*, along with two political prisoners, then the ruse was a success indeed. Even if they didn't believe it, blowing up shipping in Havana's harbor counted for something.

He was smiling as he went below to his cabin, having given the orders that would take them back to Matanzas. He intended to land Wharton tomorrow and, of course, he wanted to see the women with short hair for himself.

FOURTEEN

RASCAL HOVE-TO off the entrance to Matanzas the next afternoon, Beauty setting two lookouts as a precaution against surprise so close to an enemy shore. It suited Wharton's purposes to be landed at dusk, whereupon he would go his own way in darkness. No doubt he had his own methods of gaining intelligence, which he kept to himself.

Beauty and Barclay joined Fallon in his cabin to study the chart for Bahía de Matanzas over a glass of wine. The bay was shaped like a boot, with a generous entrance at the leg to the north before cutting into the island and swinging right, or west. The town of Matanzas lay near the toe of the boot.

Of particular interest was the fort—Castillo de San Severino— built only sixty years ago to guard the town against pirates and plunderers, which were rampant and quite bold. It was situated on the western side of the bay with a good view of the best anchorage. They could only hope the fort's lookout didn't raise an alarm, but Fallon had a plan for entering the harbor.

"Beauty, we'll go in as an American schooner on a private cruise," he said. "If we're asked, I will be an American investor looking at plantations, and Aja will pose as my servant. I don't expect to be ashore long—just to get Wharton on his way and have a glass of Cuban rum. You never know what you'll hear in a waterfront bar!"

◆　◆　◆

RASCAL, AN AMERICAN SCHOONER to all appearances, glided into the Bay of Matanzas on a faint and dying breeze, the Stars and Stripes hanging at her gaff. It was just sunset, with enough light for Barclay to confirm the coral heads in the center of the bay and keep them to the right of the ship, on starboard. Fallon and Beauty watched the fort carefully for any signs of activity but saw none. Still, they held their breath until they were safely past the guns. Beauty anchored in ten fathoms of water within an easy row to the beach, and Fallon called for his gig. In very little time the boat slid up onto the beach, and he and Wharton shook hands with a promise to meet again at that very spot in one month's time. Fallon felt close to Wharton, a new friend who had told him perhaps the biggest secret of his secretive life. Wharton clasped his shoulder and then the intelligence agent disappeared into the warm blackness of the night.

Fallon and Aja walked up the beach toward the sound of laughter. The few cafés open along the waterfront of the town were busy with customers; there were lanterns and candles glowing inside, beckoning all to enter. Fallon stepped into the first one and hoped for a chatty barkeep. In fact, the barkeep, who glanced at him expectantly, was a woman—a *woman with short hair*. Women who ran shops or other businesses were commonplace in the Caribbean, because their men were often away at sea. Or dead from war. Fallon knew it was true on Bermuda, as well.

The café was a rustic affair, with candles burning along the bar and on each of the few tables. The floor was wooden and worn smooth by the sand tracked in or from dancing. Or both. Fallon had always heard that Cubans loved music. It was not a large space, but the wall boards were freshly painted white and the place was clean. Flowers on the ends of the bar showed a woman's touch.

He ordered rum for himself, but nothing for Aja, who chose to wait by the door, such as it was, it being merely a large opening at the front of the small building, with rough wooden posts holding up the roof. After the barkeep had brought his rum and exchanged some general pleasantries, Fallon stated his interest in investing in plantations as his reason for being in Cuba.

"Tell me, Señora," he asked, "were you here when the hurricane struck in '96? I would not think hurricanes and sugarcane would get along!" Fallon, being the American with more money than sense.

"Sí, Señor," she replied, "it was very bad here but the cane had been cut early that year and most of it was in the mills."

"We heard a rumor in Charleston," Fallon continued, getting well into his persona now, "that there was a big battle in the Straits near here during the worst of the storm. Something about a Spanish treasure fleet?" He was trying to make conversation, of course, but also curious about what she knew.

"Sí, sí, we heard the same," said the woman. "I think it was true because a British warship came here after the hurricane with holes in its sails and sides! I think from the battle!"

"Really!" said Fallon. "A British warship, you say? What happened then?"

"Why, we helped them, Señor," said the woman matter-of-factly. "The men of the town brought their tools and the things the admiral needed to fix his ship."

"An admiral, you say! A British admiral was here in Matanzas!" exclaimed Fallon, hearing Davies' story in his mind. "What did the Spanish authorities do when you helped an enemy ship?"

"The Spanish army wasn't as strong then, Señor. And even now there is no garrison of soldiers at the fort anymore. It is too expensive for the government. Now the fort is used as the treasury and the slave market and to keep political prisoners locked up. It's protected by *guardias* who live inside."

"The treasury, you say?" asked Fallon as casually as he could, his heart jumping.

"Sí, Señor. The taxes for Spain. The money is under lock and key in the fort." And with that she smiled and moved down the bar.

Fallon watched her walk away to help another customer and considered how to proceed. He shifted all thoughts of the treasury from his mind for the moment, for it would not do to be too inquisitive. He was merely an American investor looking at plantations in Matanzas—that was going to attract enough attention as it was without his appearing too interested in the fort's treasury.

He lingered a few moments more, looking around the café, and then left a peso on the bar to pay for his rum and turned to leave when, from seemingly out of nowhere, a woman stood beside him. A beautiful woman with short hair herself, bold and confident in her bearing, her dark eyes alive with interest. She looked at Fallon a moment, as if to size up an adversary. Or a friend. Her entire face seemed to be *thinking*.

"I am Paloma Campos, Señor," she said in English. "I understand from my sister that you are looking at plantations in Matanzas."

"Nicholas Fallon, Señora," said Fallon, "and may I say your English is very good. If you prefer we can speak in Spanish, however."

"No, I prefer English, so I can practice," said Paloma. "I learned it when the British took Cuba."

Fallon searched her eyes for bitterness at the thought of British occupation, and he thought he saw it momentarily. But best to press on, he decided.

"I am looking to invest in a plantation," he said. "My schooner sailed in tonight from Charleston. I was just speaking with the barkeep, if that is your sister, Señora."

"Please call me Paloma. Yes, this is my sister's cafe. So, I know everything." She laughed and put her hand to her mouth and rolled her eyes. Then she grew serious. "Of course, there are many foreign plantation owners in Cuba. We have many French planters who came from Saint-Domingue, for instance, when France abolished slavery. And to the east I believe there are American planters, as well. But you must know that Spain charges taxes on our sugar, Señor. Spain needs money to fight her wars."

"Yes, I understand," said Fallon. "Your sister said the taxes were kept in the treasury in the fort. But tell me, are Spain's taxes so high that ownership would not be worth it to me?"

"I don't know, Señor. But there may be a better reason not to buy a plantation in Cuba."

"And what is that, if I may ask?"

"Meet me here tomorrow morning, Señor Fallon," Paloma said. "I will bring horses and I will show you."

Now Fallon was trapped. He had played at being an intelligence agent *of a sort* and was already in over his head. *Hell and damn,* he thought.

But, "I'd like nothing more" was what came out of his mouth.

FIFTEEN

THE NEXT MORNING began with clouds moving in from the west and a subdued light over the little harbor. Fallon had arisen early, in part due to nervousness and in part to sort through his clothing to find something that would approximate the riding attire of an American investor, whatever that might be. His choices were necessarily limited, but he pulled together the best he had and examined himself by the weak light that came in through the stern windows. Well, he thought critically, a man with no options is a man with no problems. He shrugged his shoulders and called for breakfast.

In truth, he did not feel convincing as an American investor and doubted he could pull off the game. By his second cup of coffee he concluded he was on a fool's errand, one that he had set out for himself. Why? Partly, he had been trapped into it by Paloma's invitation and his dim-witted response. But partly, he admitted silently, it was hubris. For a moment, he had seen himself aiding Wharton in some way, perhaps playing a part in the great events of the day. It was a romantic and totally unrealistic notion, and he cursed himself for it. He was a privateer, he chided himself, and nothing more.

On time, Fallon and Aja were rowed to shore in the gig and found their way to the café they had visited the night before. In the dim daylight, the place looked a little lonely and forlorn, but standing in front was Paloma Campos in riding attire, holding three horses by the reins. Soon they were all mounted and riding east, across gently rolling hills and plains that were covered in sugarcane as far as the eye could see. Aja had likely never sat a horse before and bumped along, thankful they were not galloping. His eyes seemed to miss nothing of the landscape, but if he had thoughts or apprehensions about the day he kept them to himself.

"The cane here grows twelve to sixteen months before it is harvested," Paloma said to Fallon as they rode, with the sun just making its appearance and shining in their eyes. "It can grow to be ten feet high and is very tough. No doubt we will see some of it being harvested today." A pause. "It is brutal work, if you've never seen it."

Fallon knew very little about sugarcane, which Señora Campos was no doubt coming to figure out already.

"Tell me more," he said with genuine interest. "I am not a planter, of course, just a businessman."

Paloma looked at Fallon with curiosity, and he squirmed in his saddle under her gaze.

"Planters organize slaves into gangs, Señor," Paloma continued. "The hardest work goes to the strongest gang—the planting, manuring, and cane-cutting. The weaker gang handles the less physically demanding work, such as loading the cane or working in the mill doing menial jobs. The days are long during harvest; no slave works less than twenty hours."

"Good God!" exclaimed Fallon before he could stop it.

"The leaves of the cane are like tiny knives," Paloma continued, as they turned the horses through a bend in the road. "A thousand cuts on the legs fill with dirt and perspiration and it is like fire. And then there are ants that live in the roots of the cane that bite your feet."

Fallon wondered if Aja, riding behind, could hear what the *señora* was saying. That could well describe his life if his slave ship had reached the market and he'd been sold to a plantation owner. Unable to resist, he turned around in his saddle to see the young man's eyes wide with, *what?* Interest or fear?

They came over a low rise and before them were burned fields on either side of the road. Paloma pulled her horse up, and Fallon and Aja followed suit. "This is what I wanted to show you, Señor Fallon. Runaway slaves set fire to this plantation last week. It is the way they rebel against their lives. When they are caught they will be severely punished. Their owner will probably amputate an arm and brand them as runaways."

"Jesus! Does that happen often?" Fallon asked with an involuntary wince. On Bermuda, runaway slaves were rare because the sea surrounded the island. There was literally nowhere to run.

"This is not uncommon in the country around Matanzas, where there are many plantations," answered Paloma. "Cuba was not so cruel like this before thousands of slaves were brought to grow the sugarcane. There are so many more slaves to control, and the planters believe examples must be made."

Fallon looked over the blackened fields, wondering if this was the time to probe further about the chances of rebellion. Instead, he lost confidence and stayed quiet.

A sadness seemed to come across Paloma's beautiful face. Fallon saw it and felt she had perhaps sought a sympathetic ear, and he had been found deaf. Without a word, Paloma urged her horse forward, and Fallon and Aja followed.

They rode for perhaps a half hour more and then turned down a long lane, at the end of which was a large white house and a very large sugar mill, along with a few barns and sheds. On all sides were fields of sugarcane, and there were slaves in the fields harvesting it with machetes. The newly emerged sun glistened off their blades.

As Fallon and the others rode down the lane, he saw several buildings off to the side of the mill behind a hedge.

"What are those buildings, Paloma?" he asked, trying to reengage her in conversation.

"The white house to the rear is the overseer's house, and no doubt those are his dogs you hear barking in the pen next to it.

The low buildings you see, the ones without windows, are where the slaves sleep, Señor," she answered, nodding to the barracoons and barely hiding her disgust. "They have only the one small opening in the door for ventilation and light. At night, the slaves are locked inside and sleep on dirt, or straw if the overseer feels generous. And see the smallest barracoon, there behind the others? That is where they put the strongest men and healthiest women and force them to couple. They are trying to breed the best slaves for the fields so they will not have to buy all the time. The average slave working the cane lives only three years, you see."

Fallon was still trying to absorb what life in a barracoon must be like and wondering what Aja must be thinking. He wanted to turn in his saddle again but Paloma cut into his thoughts.

"I believe this plantation is for sale," she said without emotion. "The owner is an old man named Serles. I don't know where he is from, but he speaks English and Spanish well. I think I see him in the yard with his overseer now."

Indeed, a short, fat, old man in a white shirt was talking to a much larger man with a bald head who was tying a slave to a whipping post in the yard. The slave was obedient, yet stoic.

All three riders dismounted and Aja took the horses' reins, all the while keeping a wary eye on Serles's overseer, who was just then taking a long whip out of a burlap bag. After brief introductions, Fallon expressed a casual interest in finding a plantation investment, maybe a full purchase. He tried to appear nonchalant, interested but not overly so.

"We can talk," said Serles in English, his wrinkled face showing a small smile. "But I got to punish Young David first, you see. Boss here says he's been malingering. Thinks too much and works too little, he says."

"Young David?" Fallon asked absently, watching Aja watch Boss, who was shaking out the curls of the whip.

"On the slaver's manifest, he was listed as *Young, David*—they give 'em names when they buy 'em on Gorée, you know. And Boss here can't read so good and just called him Young David. Kind of stuck with him."

Boss turned his back to Young David and began to slowly walk away, the whip trailing behind him. The slave's eyes followed the whip, which looked like a black snake uncurling. Fallon looked at the slave closely. He was a large man, perhaps in his late twenties, well-muscled, with a jagged scar on his cheek. A small L had been burned into his shoulder. And encircling his left breast, burned into the skin, was a large black ring.

"Is that your brand, Mr. Serles?" Fallon asked.

Serles followed Fallon's gaze. "Ah, the black ring. Like a manacle, it is," he said with obvious pride. "To remind 'em they can't escape. Thought of it myself, if I must say. Never lost a slave either." And then: "Boss, show Young David what happens when you break rules."

The first lash came with a snap that made Fallon, Paloma, and Aja jump. Young David winced with the pain, and a welt appeared across his neck and chest that slowly began to weep blood.

"We can go up to the house soon," Serles said. "This is going to get boring. Boss likes to take it slow, give 'em something to think about between lashes. He'll be at it for most of an hour. And then we rub a little pepper in the cuts to finish the job. Young David won't be forgetting the pepper anytime soon."

Paloma inadvertently let out a gasp and covered her mouth and, for a moment, Fallon thought she would be sick. He wondered about Aja as well, but the boy was staring hard at Young David, who was staring back, their eyes locked in wordless communication.

Snap! The whip laid another bloody stripe across Young David's chest.

"Ahem," Fallon croaked, clearing his throat. "Mr. Serles, I must come back when we can talk further. For now, I am getting the lay of the land, so to speak, and I fear I have another appointment.

Thank you for your time. It has been . . . valuable indeed."

Serles tried to object, but Fallon mounted his horse quickly, as did Paloma and Aja. In very little time they were well along the lane and then down the road without looking back.

SIXTEEN

THEY RODE BACK along a river they had not seen before; Paloma said it was a shorter distance to town. For a long time, they rode without speaking; what they had seen on the plantation had deeply affected them all. After a while, Paloma stopped and dismounted to water her horse, and Fallon did the same. They handed their reins to Aja, and Fallon asked her to walk to a copse of trees nearby.

"Paloma," Fallon began, "I fear this has been a trying morning for you. I did not expect—that is, I had no way of knowing . . ."

"Do not think to apologize," she replied firmly. "I saw your reaction to the lash. It is inhuman, no? Slavery is a living death, Señor. I had hoped when you saw the burned fields that you would be so concerned with losing money that you would abandon your idea. It is I who must apologize for trying to change your mind. I led you here under false pretenses."

Fallon looked at her closely and could not tell her another lie.

"I fear I have not been honest with you, either, Paloma. I am not a businessman at all, but a simple sea captain acting on behalf of Great Britain against the Spanish government. I was hoping to find sentiment in Cuba for a rebellion that Great Britain could support. Perhaps a slave rebellion such as that on Saint-Domingue. I'm afraid I have used you badly. Please forgive me."

Señora Campos took a moment to absorb Fallon's admission. The day was growing cloudy again and there was the smell of a shower in the air. She looked at the sky and then toward Aja with the horses. She didn't appear *angry*, exactly.

"Why did you choose Matanzas?" she asked.

And then Fallon told her about Admiral Davies and *Avenger* and his story about the rebellious Matanzas women with their short hair. He made no mention of Wharton, fearing to compromise the man. Fallon watched her face in the telling, and unless he was very much mistaken her eyes grew moist.

"I remember Harry," she said.

THEY FOLLOWED the river all the way back to town, and along the way Fallon listened to Paloma on the topic of Cuban independence. This was not a woman who could live happily under anyone's thumb, and clearly Spain made the rules and dictated them to her country. Even Cuba's economy was in large part what Spain decreed it would be. In Paloma's mind, the Cuban people were economic slaves of Spain.

It was the first dogwatch when they reached the town, and Fallon said good-bye to Paloma. And it *was* good-bye, for he planned to sail on the morning tide. He'd overstayed his value, as it were. Paloma had asked him to give Davies a message when he saw the admiral again though, which Fallon said he would do. At the beach, they all dismounted and Paloma tied their horses to a post. She then headed to her sister's café, asking Aja to follow her and wait on the message. Aja had not spoken a word on their journey into the country, or back, and Fallon believed the day had scarred him badly.

The café was beginning to do business, and a few customers wandered in and out. Fallon stood outside near the horses, but he could see Aja talking to Paloma animatedly. After she had written her message for Davies and sealed it with wax from a bar candle, she gave it to him. Standing up, she waved good-bye to Fallon and disappeared into the cafe.

It was but a few moments more when Fallon and Aja climbed

into the gig, which Beauty had thoughtfully sent to the beach. Fallon was somber as the crew pulled for the ship. Aja was silent, and still.

Back on board, Aja went immediately below while Beauty sat with Fallon in the great cabin as he ate cold mutton and peas and drank a glass of wine. The ship was silent above him, as if it had caught his somber mood. The image of Young David whipped at the punishment post stayed with Fallon and, as he described the barracoons and the breeding program for slaves, Beauty seemed to pale.

"It's bigger than we are, Nico," she said. "We can fight bigger ships with more guns and try to think our way out of situations, but slavery is different. It's not a *situation*. It's the way the world works. This is a long game and whole countries are invested up to their necks in it."

"Yes, but it's not a very pretty picture of humanity, all the same," he said. "You should have seen Aja's face when Young David was whipped. I've never seen that look before. It actually scared me a little."

"Why, Nico?"

"I've been trying to figure that out," he said. "I don't have it yet."

SEVENTEEN

HE SWUNG the machete with the force of ten thousand swings against the cane, up from the ground in a murderous arc, his powerful arm snapping out just before the blade cleaved Boss's head in half like a coconut, his two eyes staring at each other in disbelief as the halves of his head fell away. Then Young David stripped Boss's pants from him and cut off his manhood. As he walked past the giant dogs who were frantic in their pen he tossed the entire genital package over the fence, where they fell upon it ravenously, for they hadn't yet had their dinner that night.

Young David went to each barracoon and pried open the locks with Aja's dirk, quietly telling the slaves that if they wanted to escape they could come with him. He didn't tell them where he was going or what he was going to do, which was to burn every plantation he could find until someone killed him.

Some slaves cowered in the corner of their barracoons, afraid to come out. But the rest rushed the doors and ran to the shadows of the mill. Young David motioned to them to be quiet and stepped out of the group to stand before Aja. In the moonlight, the lashes on his chest were dark with dried blood and pepper.

"Thank you for coming back," Young David said in a mix of his native language and the elementary English he'd learned on the plantation. "I did not know who was prying the lock off the door. But I could guess. Tell me your name."

"My name is Ajani," he said, using his given name.

"Ajani, you are my brother," said Young David, clasping the boy's shoulders in his big hands. "Even if I never see you again I will never forget you. Now go quickly, for soon the sky will light up with fire."

Aja hesitated, unsure that he had heard Young David correctly. And then he knew he had, and he began running back the way he had come, back along the river toward Matanzas, running faster and faster to get to the beach before daylight. Then he would have to swim out to the ship without drowning. And then he would have to get aboard without anyone noticing.

Just keep running, he told himself. And don't look back at the sky.

EIGHTEEN

FALLON CAME on deck before dawn the next morning feeling troubled and alone. Between what he had seen at the Serles plantation and the feeling that he'd made a hash out of play-acting as an intelligence agent, he was ready to be away. For now, he'd forgotten about the treasury lying just across the water. The tide would begin making in an hour and already *Rascal* was preparing to leave Matanzas.

He looked around the ship, though it was still shrouded in darkness, and then looked to the east to a glowing sky. At first, he thought it was the beginning of a glorious sunrise but he soon smelled the drift of smoke. He could imagine the story: burning sugarcane fields, runaway slaves who were desperate for freedom, the hiding and running and terror of being caught, an arm amputated and, if that didn't kill you, back to work in the fields. Fallon watched the eastern sky grow brighter with the fires and shuddered. Yesterday he'd been right there.

Suddenly, Aja was beside him, rubbing his eyes and looking to the east as well.

"What do you think?" Fallon asked.

Aja looked at the sky's glow and knew what he was seeing. "I think we had better leave here soon, Captain, sir," he answered. "It is too dangerous to be black."

Beauty had *Rascal* underway in short order and the ship eased out of Matanzas Bay, first around the heel and then north up the leg of the boot. Fallon gave orders to sail generally southeast along Cuba's coast, which meant tacking against the trade winds for more than five hundred miles until—*what?* He had a month before he was due to be back to pick up Wharton and fulfill his obligation to Admiral Davies. In the meantime, he would look for *opportunities*.

On deck, Beauty posted a lookout and took a turn around the ship. *Rascal* seemed to delight in sailing hard on the wind, first on starboard and then larboard, the spray kicking up and over the bowsprit, soaking the hands forward, who didn't mind in the least.

If you took away the imminent threat of an enemy just over the horizon, it was really a glorious day to be sailing. In spite of Fallon's dark mood, *Rascal* was a happy ship, the men going about their business with very few discipline issues, each man believing fame and fortune, or at least fortune, were just over the horizon.

On the second day out of Matanzas, it appeared to be true.

RAIN WAS SHEETING across the deck when Fallon reached the top step of the companionway, but Aja was behind him with his cloak and hat. The rain had flattened the seas, and visibility was poor, barely a mile when the rain was pouring its hardest. A dull grayness seemed to engulf the world.

They were just passing into the narrow band of deepest water between Cuba and the Great Bahama Bank, and Beauty had her hands full tacking through such a confined space in relatively shallow water. The Mucarias shoals were off their larboard side at the southern edge of the bank, a string of coral islands off Cuba on their starboard side, and the hands were busy between the two dangers.

"Deck there," came the hail from the lookout. "Sail ahead!"

Fallon found the image in his telescope, although it was difficult to see in the rain and mist. It looked to be a sloop sailing wing on wing, the mainsail hanging over the larboard side and the jib out to starboard. With the wind behind her it was difficult to see her flag, if she even flew one, but something about her design said *French* to Fallon. Of course, she could be a captured French ship.

Fallon wondered briefly where the sloop was bound, Havana presumably, but there was no real way to know. The poor visibility meant the two ships were already quite close when they had sighted each other, leaving both captains with very little time to react. In the narrow chute between Cuba and the Bahama Bank the sloop would either have to pass close aboard or wear and sail back the way she'd come. It was not a good tactical situation either way if it came to a fight, and no doubt her captain knew it.

The sloop's dirty copper was just visible at the bow, a sign of a ship long at sea. Her sails were patched in places and appeared the worse for wear. Perhaps she had come from France, or was in the vanguard of a French squadron just over the horizon. The question was: *How to know?*

Certainly, her orders would make all known, but any captain worth his rank would throw his orders overboard immediately if faced with capture. There was no question the sloop could be taken in battle, but perhaps there was another way. An idea began to form in Fallon's mind, and he quickly ran through the reasons that it wouldn't work, all the arguments against it. But what if it *did* work?

Now the rain was heavier, visibility again reduced, and Fallon made up his mind.

"Quickly, Beauty," he ordered. "Have Cully load both batteries but not run them out. And then, Beauty, tack across the sloop's course and heave-to."

Beauty gave the orders and the crew jumped to their tasks, the ship swinging slowly into the wind as she began her tack. The powder boys ran to bring up shot and powder and slow match, and the gun crews prepared to swab the barrels of each 12-pound cannon. The men went about their duties efficiently and quickly, for each task had been practiced hundreds of times with unquestioning obedience. Except just now Beauty's face revealed she wasn't at all clear what Fallon could possibly be thinking.

"We're going to put the hay down where the goats can get it,"

Fallon explained, remembering a saying of his father's. "After we heave-to, I want my gig lowered over the side, in plain sight of the sloop. And order the men to stand easy, not a care in the world, mind you. No gawking at the sloop. I want the captain's curiosity to overcome his suspicion."

"I get that," said Beauty. "And if suspicion wins?"

"If he wants to fight, or tries to escape, we still have a tactical advantage," Fallon said. "We'll get underway quickly and be prepared to fight either side of the ship. It would be a foolish captain who couldn't count the odds in our favor."

As *Rascal* was now about to cross the sloop's course, Beauty ordered the ship to heave-to and, when the sails had been adjusted and the schooner had settled, Fallon saw the crew assume relaxed postures as he'd ordered. He was counting on the sloop being far from home and her captain hungry for any information of the war, for news and gossip were always at a premium at sea. But for the trick to work, *Rascal* would have to appear both friendly and vulnerable, like a dog rolling over on his back.

On the sloop came, less than a mile away now, and Cully leaned casually against the larboard railing, his back to the sloop, and his gun crews hidden against the railing next to their guns. Aja appeared with Fallon's sword and stood behind him; Fallon noticed he had apparently forgotten his dirk, a gift from the crew. He must remember to ask Aja about it later—if there was a later, he thought ruefully.

Fallon took off his cloak and hat, revealing that he wore no uniform, which he hoped would give the sloop's captain comfort as he looked through his telescope. On the sloop came, and Fallon wondered briefly who was fooling whom. Perhaps the Frenchman, if that's what he was, had not bought the ruse and was even now bearing down on the defenseless schooner who had her gun ports closed and her crew ambling about as if an impending battle that could blow them all to pieces was part of their routine.

There was still time for the sloop's captain to wear ship and he might be considering doing that even now. Unless . . . unless Fallon could think of a coup de grâce. Something that underlined *Rascal*'s intent to parley. Something so out of the ordinary that it would beggar explanation.

"Aja!" he called. "Into the gig quickly with the crew!"

"And what is this about, Nico?" asked Beauty, with real concern in her voice.

"I want to convince the captain to come closer if I can," said Fallon with a smile. "Then it's up to my powers of persuasion. If that's not enough, I may need *extra* persuasion. So, if you see me wave, run up the colors and run out *Rascal*'s guns."

"But Nico," Beauty objected, "why . . ."

"Remember George Danton's famous words, Beauty," said Fallon with a grin as he went over the side. Beauty would know that Danton was a leader of the French Revolution. "We need audacity, and yet more audacity, and always audacity!"

"Nico, Danton went to the guillotine, remember?"

"Oh," Fallon yelled as the gig pushed off. "I forgot about that!"

Then the gig's crew began to row toward the oncoming sloop. The little boat bobbed over the ocean, pulling away from safety and advancing on an enemy ship whose officers were no doubt suspiciously studying the developing situation through telescopes and who must even now be wondering what the devil was going on with this gig rowing toward them—*to do what?* It had to be to talk, or to deliver a message of some sort, they must be thinking. At least, that's what Fallon hoped they were thinking.

At a cable's distance from *Rascal*, Fallon nudged Aja, who ordered "oars" and the gig drifted on the placid sea. On instinct, Fallon stood up in the stern, as if impatiently waiting for the sloop to arrive. It must have made an incongruous sight aboard the sloop, and Fallon hoped it completed the picture of a man who wanted only to talk, which in its way was true. Indeed, on the sloop came, though it appeared more menacing with every yard. Fear crept up into Fallon's throat like bile, and he was on the verge of sitting down quickly and ordering the crew to get underway and row back to *Rascal* when the sloop abruptly hove-to, not one hundred yards from the gig. This was as close as the *capitaine* wanted to go and, indeed, she ran out her guns as an extra precaution. Fallon could clearly see the French tricolor now. The next move was up to him.

"Aja, we will row to the sloop and clap on," said Fallon calmly, as if it were to be a friendly visit. "I want to talk to *Monsieur le Capitaine.*"

The gig was now very close to the sloop, which looked very big from sea level. As they approached the sloop's quarter, Fallon stood up again. He could see the *capitaine* and his officers looking at him curiously.

"*Bonjour, Monsieur,*" he called as the gig drifted even closer. His French was better than passable and might stall a precipitate move by the *capitaine.* "You have a fine ship, Monsieur!"

"What is it you want, Monsieur?" called the *capitaine,* obviously suspicious. "State your name and your business."

Fallon could see muskets leveled at his head and gun crews standing by their cannons. The French sloop was eerily quiet as he seemed to have everyone's attention.

"I am Captain Nicholas Fallon and I have come to offer you a trade, *Capitaine,*" said Fallon.

"And what is the trade, Monsieur?" retorted the *capitaine,* seeming to grow irritated. He was an older man in a shabby uniform but held his head at a certain angle that suggested self-importance.

Now the gig clapped on.

"No, Monsieur! State your—" demanded the *capitaine,* looking over the side of his ship. "Stand off!" he fairly screamed. The metallic sound of cocking muskets and pistols punctuated the air. "I will have you shot, Monsieur!"

"That would be unfortunate for both of us. But if I am to be shot," said Fallon coolly, "allow me to wave good-bye to my ship and crew."

Without waiting for permission, Fallon looked toward *Rascal* and raised his hat in the air. Instantly the British colors went up to *Rascal*'s gaff and twelve black muzzles pushed out of her side, cold and all business. Fallon turned back to the *capitaine*, whose mouth had come open.

"Kill me and you kill yourselves, *Capitaine*. Is that a trade you want to make?"

Fallon watched the emotions play out on the officer's face, rage and wounded pride in succession. Now was the moment to force resignation.

"Monsieur," Fallon said loudly, looking directly at the *capitaine* but wanting every man to hear. "Your 6-pounders will do little damage at this range, but I have a very good one-eyed gunner aboard my ship who can sight the guns perfectly with his good eye. I have never seen the like! The first broadside will kill half of your men. Within two minutes the second broadside will kill the rest." He let his words hang in the air.

"I have another trade in mind, if you would allow me to present it," said Fallon, offering his olive branch. "I will trade your ship for your lives. Why not surrender now and save useless dying?"

The sputtering *capitaine* looked at Fallon, at *Rascal*, and back to Fallon again. The crew kept their guns on Fallon but looked out of the corners of their eyes at the 12-pounders pointing at them. And then Fallon leaned closer to the sloop and looked directly up to the *capitaine* and lowered his voice.

"I will put you and your men ashore on Saint-Domingue and you can live to fight another day," said Fallon. "There is no dishonor in saving your men's lives, sir. Worse would be sacrificing them for false pride."

For a moment, nothing.

Every face turned to the *capitaine*, whose own face was rigid, pained, and pale. Even his waxed mustache seemed to droop slightly as he looked down to Fallon's upturned face. His entire career was at stake, his reputation, his honor. After months at sea, fighting wind and sea and perhaps glorious battles, it came down to this moment, and he had to make a decision—a near-instant, life or death, decision.

He chose life.

Softly, the *capitaine* gave the order for the French colors to come down. Then he stepped back, and Fallon and the gig's crew climbed up through the channel. The *capitaine* stiffly handed his sword to Fallon. He had made the only decision a wise man could make, saving his crew's lives in the bargain; there had been no better option.

The French sailors threw down their cutlasses, pistols, and muskets and backed against the railing as Aja and the prize crew took charge.

"Here there," ordered Fallon to the French crew. "Run those guns back inboard!" No sooner had the last of the 6-pounders been pulled inboard than *Rascal* got underway and began tacking over to the sloop. Fallon ordered the French junior officers and crew to lie down on deck, guarded by Aja and the gig's crew. The *capitaine* was ordered to stand off to the side, for Fallon did not want him near his own cabin.

With Beauty alongside at last, the prisoners could be transferred to *Rascal* to be locked below decks. Now Fallon was free to search the *capitaine*'s tiny cabin, where he found the last meal sitting half-eaten on the table with a glass of wine nearby. Fallon quickly turned his attention to the writing desk, which was locked. Looking around, he found the *capitaine*'s dirk, a beautiful and bejeweled dagger, and forced the lock. Inside the desk he found the log book and a weighted packet wrapped in a waxy canvas sheath bearing the official seal of the French Revolutionary Government. It was addressed to Marqués de Someruelos, Salvador de Muro y Salazar, Governor of Cuba, and it was marked: *Confidentiel*.

Quickly, Fallon gathered up what he'd found and went on deck where the last of the prisoners were being securely locked in *Rascal*'s hold.

The first order of business was to select a prize crew for the sloop, for Fallon intended to send her to Bermuda and the prize agent there. He had what he needed from the ship, and he wondered what message fate had delivered into his hands.

NINETEEN

THE SLOOP—*Petite Bouton,* or Little Button—had enough food and water aboard to sail to Bermuda, and Fallon planned to sail *Rascal* to Port-au-Prince and land the prisoners there as he had promised. What was it Beauty had said about Davies' plan for *Luna's* prisoners? *Make them Louverture's damned problem.*

Fallon had not opened the confidential dispatch he'd found aboard *Petite Bouton,* thinking to get it into Davies' hands for a more informed assessment of its importance. But now he was reconsidering his decision. A French message to the Governor of Cuba was certainly intriguing, and he was consumed with curiosity about what it could be.

It was past dusk when *Rascal* and *Petite Bouton* parted ways, the French sloop carrying Fallon's letters to Elinore as well as a quick note to his father. Fallon was necessarily vague about his activities since leaving Bermuda, fearing to give too much away should *Petite Bouton* fall into enemy hands on her journey north.

Rascal hove-to off the Gulf of Gonâve for the night; it made no sense to enter the bay not knowing what ship might be anchored there. The schooner was quiet as Fallon asked Beauty to his cabin and, by the light of candles reflecting off their wine glasses, he opened the secret packet.

Inside was a letter from the French government to Cuba's governor. "*Good God!*" he exclaimed when he was finished reading it.

"The French government is asking the Marqués to use Santiago de Cuba as a staging area should France need to attack Saint-Domingue! It would be a massive invasion if France needed another country to stage it!"

"Jesus, Nico! Anything else in the letter?" asked Beauty, for she was as stunned as he.

"Only what isn't said."

"What's that?" asked Beauty.

"Louverture's days are numbered."

AT DAWN the lookout reported that the gulf was clear of ships, and *Rascal* weighed to begin the slow creep toward Port-au-Prince. In her hold were thirty French prisoners whom Fallon hoped to land ashore. He was still wondering how that would be received several hours later when *Rascal* dropped anchor in eight fathoms of water.

The prisoners were bustled into the boats, and Fallon and twenty Rascals led the party to shore under a white flag. Once there, they were met by a large black man in a uniform who identified himself as Louis Lacroix, head of militia for Port-au-Prince. Lacroix was not confrontational in his manner, although he fronted thirty militiamen with muskets. Fallon spoke French to him easily and offered him thirty prime French seamen as volunteers for his force. Lacroix accepted gleefully, as most of the soldiers on the island were fighting to the south with Louverture and his own unit was undermanned.

"Who is the general fighting?" asked Fallon casually.

"Rigaud, I'm afraid," answered Lacroix with a shrug. "He is a good man, and a free man like Toussaint, but they are rivals. Rigaud will lose, of course, but he is very clever and the war goes on longer than it should. We call it the *War of Knives* on Saint-Domingue because the people know of Rigaud's skill with the sword." Lacroix winced as he said this, feigning the cut of a blade to his throat.

"Where are they fighting at this moment?" asked Fallon.

"Jacmel, Captain. On the southern coast," answered Lacroix. "Rigaud controls the eastern end of the town. Toussaint has the western end, and they are at a temporary truce to help the wounded. A runner has just brought word from there."

Fallon bade Lacroix good-bye, and he and his crew boarded the boats and very soon were back aboard *Rascal*, eager to raise the anchor and be away. It wouldn't do to be caught by an enemy ship in the gulf. Ideas were moving quickly in Fallon's mind, and after the boats were aboard and Barclay had set a course to take them out, Fallon asked Beauty to join him in his cabin.

"I have been wondering what to do about this," said Fallon as he stood by his desk staring at the letter. "Whether to act on it in some way. Perhaps get it to Louverture."

"To accomplish what?" asked Beauty.

"Perhaps this letter could drive a deeper wedge between the general and the French government. It might push Louverture further toward independence."

"Yes, and it might also keep Louverture alive. Which means his rebellion might live a little longer."

Fallon nodded, and it was then that Beauty's eyes lit up with a flicker of understanding.

"Does getting this letter into Louverture's hands have anything to do with what you saw in Matanzas? At the plantation?" asked Beauty, cutting to the chase.

"It has everything to do with that," said Fallon softly.

Beauty studied her good friend's face, sensing somehow that he wanted her agreement to proceed, because going to Jacmel was not part of their mission for Davies. What Fallon had seen on the Serles plantation had changed him and would now change the mission.

"I'll have Barclay set a course for Jacmel," said Beauty. "You better figure out what you're going to say to Toussaint Louverture— assuming you can find him!"

TWENTY

THE FRENCH government had tried to encourage, even force, Jacmel's farmers to grow sugarcane, but the *advice* didn't take. Coffee was in the farmers' veins, and they knew their soil and climate better than anyone in Paris; as a result, the area had grown to become a coffee-trading center. André Rigaud was making a stand there, facing death or exile to France, and the famous swordsman's small army was being hacked to pieces.

Rascal entered Baie de Jacmel on a late afternoon breeze, and Fallon could see smoke rising from fires in the hills beyond the shoreline. A large river flowed into the bay from the north, and the village of Jacmel lay on its right bank.

Fallon and Aja and a crew of ten seamen rowed to shore in the gig, Fallon with a white flag on a spare oar held up high. They landed the gig near the mouth of the river, slightly west of the village, in hopes the situation was still unchanged and both sides were at a truce. After a half hour walking through shrub and marsh, they found a road of sorts that seemed to meander eastward toward Jacmel. They took it, Fallon and Aja walking in the lead with the flag. Another hour and they were on the outskirts of a village, presumably Jacmel, which was pitch black and ominously quiet. Fallon could see large buildings and smaller shops but no signs of movement. He was not attempting stealth, but rather wanted to make his presence known, and he hoped the white flag of truce would be his protection. If there was trouble, his crew was armed with enough pistols and cutlasses for a small war.

The road ran through the center of town, with a spur off to the left, and Fallon led the crew that way, whistling. Surely, he reasoned, no one would think an enemy planning mischief would so obviously announce themselves. The question was who would discover them first, Louverture or Rigaud?

They had not gone fifty yards when a forceful voice ordered: "Stop that damned whistling."

A short, slight man stepped out of the shadows behind a warehouse that smelled faintly of coffee. Behind him was a detail of many soldiers, perhaps fifty all together, making the prospect of a fight moot. They held mostly machetes, though some had muskets with bayonets. Where they got those Fallon had no idea; perhaps from dead British soldiers.

The short man appeared to be bowlegged and somewhat oddly put together, yet he walked up to Fallon with an air of confidence such as Fallon had rarely felt himself. He wore a military uniform festooned with many medals, and on his somewhat disproportionately large head he had a French officer's plumed hat with a gold cockade. His skin was dark, made darker and more mysterious by the night.

"I am Toussaint Louverture," he said to Fallon in French leavened with a rich island patois. "Whom do I have the honor of welcoming to Saint-Domingue?"

"I am Nicholas Fallon, captain of His Majesty's privateer *Rascal*, General Louverture," Fallon responded in French. "I was at Port-au-Prince weeks ago when the British troops were evacuated. But I've come back to give you a message."

Louverture studied Fallon carefully. "A message from General Maitland or Admiral Davies?" he asked.

"Neither," said Fallon. "The message is from the French Revolutionary Government."

Louverture took a moment to recover from the shock, no doubt weighing whether Fallon was crazy, for he *had* been whistling on a dark road in the middle of a war.

"Come," he said at last. "Step into this warehouse. Your men can wait outside."

Louverture led Fallon and Aja, who snuck behind his captain like his shadow, into a warehouse full of bulging burlap bags and the delicious smell of coffee beans. To the side of the main room was an office of sorts, and it was here that Louverture must have been making his headquarters, for there were lit candles that brightened the windowless room. In the center was a rough table with a map of Saint-Domingue on it.

The two men sat opposite each other, and Louverture removed his elegant hat and plumage.

"May I offer you some wine, Captain Fallon?"

"Thank you, sir. A glass would be welcome," answered Fallon. Clearly the general travelled in a certain style.

As Louverture's aide poured the wine, Fallon studied the general more closely. His skin was less dark by the light, and he had a pronounced separation between his front teeth. Was it a coincidence that the French word for opening was *ouverture?*

"Now, Captain Fallon," the general began, "you have my undivided attention. Clearly, you've come some way to deliver a message of some kind and have wandered about in the dark in a strange country—whistling—to do it, so pray let me hear what you have to say." There was a certain twinkle in his eye as if he expected to at least be amused.

"Days ago," said Fallon, "I intercepted and took a French sloop off the Great Bahama Bank, sir. The ship was the *Petite Bouton*, and her log revealed she was on her way from France to Havana, which is curious in the first instance. But in the *capitaine's* desk I found this." Here Fallon removed the waxed packet from inside his shirt and laid it on the table in front of the general, who whistled through the *ouverture* in his teeth.

"And you've opened this and presumably read it, I see?" asked Louverture.

"Yes," answered Fallon.

Louverture opened the letter and Fallon watched his eyes fall on the signature at the bottom, then the Marqués' name at the top, and then he began reading. When he had finished, he read it once more, his face immobile.

"May I ask why you risked your life to bring me this?" asked Louverture evenly.

It was the question Beauty had asked him. The answer was simple and yet somehow complicated.

"Great Britain would like Saint-Domingue to be an independent country, not a French colony," said Fallon. "I doubt that surprises you. If that is your wish then I have been of service to both you and my country, and I am very happy."

"But there is more, I perceive," said Louverture. "You do not seem like a political agent or provocateur."

Fallon studied the rebel general's face carefully. He *was* perceptive, and perhaps that was his power. It was a more useful skill in war than was Rigaud's sword.

"You are the leader that slaves the world over have been waiting for," said Fallon earnestly. "You are the only hope for them, sir. If you are lost, France will likely bring back slavery in the colonies soon after. And then hope is lost. What I have done is little enough. What you have done, and what you will do in the future, is history."

There was silence in the room. Fallon had done no more than tell the truth. He knew nothing of Louverture's plans or strategies, of course. But a man facing a massive invasion of his country might do well to make adjustments to his thinking.

"I must thank you for bringing me this," said Louverture, tapping the letter with his forefinger. "You give me hope for the British."

Fallon smiled, and Louverture reached across the table to shake his hand. "My men will see you safely back to your ship, Captain. I will never forget what you've done."

Fallon and Aja were led back outside the warehouse to where the crew still stood, and Louverture designated several guards to see them back the way they'd come. Within two hours they were all at the beach and aboard the gig, and when at last they were through the gangway and aboard *Rascal*, Fallon could relax.

He found Beauty waiting for him, of course. She would not quit the deck until he was back safely. Once they'd gone below to his cabin, Fallon gave her the full report of his visit to Jacmel, including the gist of his conversation with Louverture and the general's inscrutable reaction to the letter.

"I think he wasn't surprised, Nico," she said at last. "You can't go that far out on a limb and not expect someone to try to cut it off. He's put his thumb in France's eye, and France doesn't like it."

"I think you're right," replied Fallon. "Louverture is nobody's fool, and he would know France will not suffer a challenge to its power, even in so far away a colony as Saint-Domingue. Time will tell us if Louverture heeds the warning."

Suddenly, Fallon was very tired and he longed for the beckoning embrace of his cot. Beauty took notice and left to go on deck for one last turn around the ship to check the watch. They were still anchored in an enemy harbor, after all, and it wouldn't do to be less than vigilant.

As Beauty left, Aja slipped into the cabin and asked if he could have a word. And he said it in a way that made the tiredness in Fallon's mind and body disappear.

"Certainly. What's bothering you?" asked Fallon, assuming something *was*. He expected it to be about the meeting with Louverture.

"Captain, sir," began Aja, obviously struggling, "there is something I need to tell you. Something that I did."

Fallon was at full attention now; the day's and night's events fell away as he looked at the pain on his young friend's face.

"I . . . I helped Young David escape that last night in Matanzas," Aja blurted out. "I went back to help him."

Fallon was astonished. How in God's name had the boy pulled that off? And why . . . well, of course he knew *why*. He looked at the young man standing before him, obviously afraid Fallon would be angry or hurt by his deception.

"Aja," Fallon said, gathering his thoughts on the fly. "That was such a dangerous thing to do! And a brave thing to do!"

And as he thought about it: *such the right thing to do.*

Fallon put his hands on Aja's shoulders and looked at his face a long moment. He wasn't angry, of course. Nor was he disappointed in the least that Aja had set Young David free. In fact, his only disappointment was that he hadn't done it himself.

TWENTY-ONE

THE PORT of Santo Domingo was fed by the Rio Ozama, a slow-moving river on Santo Domingo's southern coast. Its mouth was fairly wide, but still not easily navigable by damaged vessels, their wings clipped, sides shot through, and crews depleted by battle. It was remarkable the sloops made it to the river at all; in fact, the sloop captains considered it a miracle that the Holy One hadn't simply sailed away and left them helpless after the surprise attack by the British schooner.

The Holy One had, of course, considered doing just that. Good sense intervened, however, and the problem of replacing the sloops and crews seemed bigger than nursing what he already had to safety and the promise of repair. It had been a slow and dangerous voyage; holding the sloops together had required constant vigilance and threats of death or abandonment or worse. Often, one of the sloops would have to be towed by the brig, which put the Holy One in a foul temper. Well, fouler than usual.

At last, the three ships sailed through the strait between Porto Rico and Santo Domingo, with the sloops' crews at the pumps constantly and the jury-rigged spars barely functional. Once through, they sailed around the southeast point of Santo Domingo and downwind into the generous bay into which the Rio Ozama flowed. The Holy One knew the river well and had careened his ships there before for repairs and replenishment at the settlement of Santo Domingo. It was, in fact, his only base, because most of the time his ships were afloat.

It was frustrating and tedious to careen the sloops, patch the shot holes above and below the waterline, and search the forest for trees that could be fashioned into spars. Green wood wasn't ideal, but beggars couldn't be choosers. The Holy One fretted constantly at the loss of time and profits. And of particular concern was the news he'd received from the alcalde of the nearby Spanish settlement that Spain had sent two frigates to protect the trade in slaves to Cuba. One had sailed to the mouth of this very river!

This was something that needed praying over. It also meant paying the settlement's fishermen to keep watch over the river's entrance and to report any ship that entered the bay. It would not do to be surprised by the returning frigate, and he would want early notice in order to escape. In that case, he would leave the sloops. That wasn't even a question.

Days went by, then weeks, and the repairs dragged on. The Holy One's mood turned darker and darker; dark on the edge of explosion. The only calming effect was when he raised his arms to the sky and went into his trance-like meditation, praying to God that he be allowed to quickly resume the good work he was doing for the Almighty.

It was during an evening prayer that a fisherman hailed the Holy One's brig with word that a schooner had been sighted entering the bay that afternoon, but she had tacked away to the south.

THE DISTANCE from Jacmel to English Harbor was seven hundred miles as the crow flies, but of course the crow wasn't heading straight into the brisk trade winds and neither was *Rascal*. Still, the sailing was exhilarating and the crew urged every ounce of speed out of the ship. Tack on tack, *Rascal* responded with her shoulder buried in the sea; though the larboard tacks were favored, Beauty kept close to Santo Domingo on short tacks so as to follow a shorter course to Antigua. The only sails sighted belonged to local fisherman in small boats.

The brief stop in Jacmel hadn't bothered the crew; the sale of *Petite Bouton* in Bermuda would add substantially to their purses, and their belief in Fallon was such that they would essentially follow him anywhere, on any adventure. Theirs was a dangerous occupation and they knew it. Secretly, most relished the danger as much as the money.

Fallon had made a fair copy of the letter he'd given to Louverture to give to Davies and was eager to hear the admiral's thoughts about the possibility of a French invasion of Saint-Domingue. How would Davies respond to that kind of enemy force in the Caribbean? How *could* he respond?

They were two days out of Jacmel under a cloudy sky showing only a patch of blue—*enough blue sky to make a Dutchman a pair of trousers*, as old Bermudians would say. But that opening in the clouds was behind them and, indeed, Fallon thought he could hear thunder in the distance ahead.

The sea had been remarkably free of sailing vessels these last days, and thus there was no temptation to take a prize. Barclay and Beauty conferred before each tack; the wind was out of the east northeast and the larboard tacks continued to be preferred.

Fallon felt light of spirit; he was by no means a decent intelligence agent but he did have *intelligence* to share with Admiral Davies, so that was something. He was about to ask Aja to fetch his cloak, for the thunder was growing louder, when it struck him that he was hearing the boom and echo of great guns.

"Lookout there," he called, "what do you see to the south?"

"A low horizon, sir," called the lookout. "Nothing that I can see!"

There it was again. A low rumble punctuated by an echo retort.

"Beauty," said Fallon. "Let's fall off and sail down to the southeast. Call all hands."

"Southeast it is, Nico," answered Beauty and then, in response to another rumble: "I think that's cannon fire, by God!"

Rascal slowly bore off, sailing lower and a little flatter and faster now that the wind was more off the beam. All hands strained to see into the distance as the minutes crept by. Cully had sand and shot brought up, and the gun crews stood at the ready.

"Deck there! Two ships off the starboard bow! Frigates!"

Fallon's telescope now picked out the situation as the images grew bigger. Two frigates were on parallel courses sailing to the west and indeed exchanging broadsides; the frigate closest to *Rascal* was certainly Spanish and had the wind on her starboard quarter. Smoke obscured the other ship.

"What do you think, Beauty?" Fallon asked, lowering his telescope. She was watching the battle as well, and continued watching for a moment through her telescope before answering. The smoke was just clearing a little as they drew within a mile of the ships.

"I have some news for you, Nico," she said.

Fallon raised his telescope again and, yes, even as an upside down image the ship fighting the Spanish frigate was clearly of Spanish build herself and looked familiar: *Renegade!*

"*Good God!*" Fallon exclaimed. "*What the hell?*"

The ships were barely a cable's distance apart—two hundred yards or so—and to Fallon's eye, *Renegade* was getting the worst of it. Her sails were shot through, and her broadsides weren't coming regularly. And there! The fore-topgallant mast was going over!

"My guess is that's one of the Spanish frigates Davies told us about, Beauty," said Fallon as he watched the battle through his telescope. "She was sent to protect the slavers going to Cuba. But *Renegade*'s found her!"

Rascal was perhaps a mile away from the scene now, sailing down to the ships on a converging course. Beauty and Barclay were looking at Fallon expectantly, waiting for orders. Certainly, there was no point in engaging a frigate on equal terms. But *Renegade* was clearly in trouble and, unless she broke off and managed to sail away, she could well be taken. The Spanish capitán knew his business and continued to fire well-timed broadsides, mauling *Renegade*'s starboard hull piteously and opening more daylight in her sails.

It was doubtful anyone on either ship was watching *Rascal*

approach the battle, so engaged were they in mutual destruction. But that wouldn't last.

"Beauty, up with the French colors quickly!" Fallon ordered, making what seemed like a snap decision when, actually, to his mind there was no other course of action. He had to get closer if there was any chance to help *Renegade* and avoid accidentally firing into her. He hoped the French flag would buy him time. He watched helplessly as the Spanish frigate edged closer to *Renegade*, obviously preparing to board.

The Spanish capitán's attention had either not been called to *Rascal* yet or, more likely, he had seen *Rascal* and was unconcerned. A schooner was not going to give his frigate any trouble. Well, not an *ordinary* schooner.

"Beauty, have Cully load the starboard guns with grape," ordered Fallon. "But don't run out yet. Tell Cully to fire when I give the order, and tell him I don't want to see a living Spaniard on deck!"

Rascal was edging closer to the scene now, Fallon anxious about how close they could get before being discovered. Then a counter-intuitive thought struck him: *Get the Spaniard's attention.* Maybe that would buy them more time!

"Beauty!" he called. "Have the men start cheering as loudly as ever they can! Cheer on the Spaniards, Beauty! Hats in the air, men! We're French and we're on their side!"

Rascal erupted in cheers, and as the ship edged closer to the battle the yelling began carrying across the water between broadsides. Spanish crewmen looked over their shoulders and saw an approaching *French* schooner, and Fallon could imagine the capitán's moment of confusion and doubt at this cheering intruder arriving just at the moment he was boarding a British frigate.

The Spanish frigate's starboard guns were still behind their gun ports, which was encouraging, but any moment that could change. *Rascal* was perhaps a cable's length away, the men still cheering. Fallon could see the capitán looking through his telescope at *Rascal* just as his own ship drove against *Renegade*'s starboard hull and the grappling hooks were thrown out to secure the two ships together. In those few seconds, Fallon ordered the French flag hauled down and the British ensign went up. *Rascal*'s guns rolled out and the capitán's mouth came open.

"*Fire!*" yelled Fallon.

A fusillade of iron balls flew across the Spaniard's decks, cutting down men just as they rose on the railings to board *Renegade*. Some fell forward; others turned in surprise, already dying, wondering why a French ship would fire on them.

"Beauty, luff her there! Spill your wind!" called Fallon. "Cully, give it to her again, by God!"

The Spanish capitán recovered his wits, and his starboard gun crews were quickly called into action. But as the gun ports came open, here was *Rascal*'s second broadside roaring out, tearing the Spanish gun crews to pieces where they stood. The Spanish ship mounted sixteen guns to the side and several smaller guns on the quarterdeck, and it was one of these that got into the action first and fired on *Rascal*.

"Beauty!" called Fallon. "Harden up quickly and let's—"

But the Spaniard's quarterdeck gun had exploded *Rascal*'s binnacle near where Beauty stood, and she was down, a jagged splinter in her chest and her blood running onto the deck.

"Beauty!" Fallon called. "My God, I—"

Precious moments passed as Fallon struggled with whether to remain at his post or to forget the ship and rush to his friend's side where she lay writhing in pain.

"Aja!" he called. "Beauty is hurt! Quickly!"

Then the world seemed to shut its doors to light and air as the Spaniard's broadside thundered into *Rascal*, blasting her starboard railing and ripping apart men who a moment before had been alive and cheering. Now their arms and legs were shattered and their guts blown open. *Rascal*'s ship's boats simply *disintegrated*, sending splinters out in every direction to find soft, fleshy targets.

Fallon lay on the deck and stared at the sky, unable to move. He

felt heavy, crushed into the deck, and there was warm blood cover-
ing his chest. His mind fought to come back to reality, but it would
not focus. He thought he could hear voices he recognized, *but not
Beauty, because she was lying over there. He had to get to her, pull her to
shore before she drowned . . . He—*

And then Fallon lost consciousness.

Aja was at Beauty's side screaming for someone to fetch
Colquist, but he knew the ship must get underway quickly before
the Spaniard fired another broadside. He looked around frantically
for Fallon but could not see him, then searched for Barclay to give
the orders that would set them sailing, but the sailing master had
already been carried below, knocked insensible by a falling block.
The crew left standing were waiting for orders, *any* orders, and Aja
knew he must do something. He yelled at full voice to head up close
to the wind, and the crew rushed to the sheets to haul the sails
in tight. Slowly *Rascal* gathered way. She put her starboard bow
into the sea as she hardened up and began drawing away from the
Spanish frigate. Men were bleeding and many others were staring
stupidly at the deck as the shock of the last broadside still gripped
them.

Colquist at last came on deck and rushed to Beauty just as Aja
found Fallon and rolled a dead seaman off his chest.

"Captain, sir!" he called frantically. "Wake up, please! Can you
please wake up?"

Fallon could hear a voice he knew, the one that had given orders
to get the ship moving. He opened his eyes and blinked and finally
focused on Aja's terrified face looking down at him.

"Aja, are you all right?" he asked with a slur.

"Yes, Captain, sir. But Beauty is hurt very badly. And the ship is
hurt but we have sailed away."

"Here, help me up," said Fallon. And Aja and two of the crew got
him to his feet. He was unsteady from his collision with the dead
sailor, the force of which had driven his head into the deck, and he
was soaked in the sailor's blood. His whole head and face hurt but

he had to see the ship put to rights.

Now he could see Colquist bending over Beauty, a pained look on his face.

"You men!" Colquist called to two confused but unwounded men who had simply sat down in a daze. "Get her below now! Do you hear me? Get up and get her below!"

My God, thought Fallon, *Beauty . . .*

But there was no time to linger on his friend, for the crew must make the wounded comfortable and sort them out from the dead and dying. The Spaniard's broadside had been low, so most of the rigging was spared, but there were shot holes in *Rascal's* starboard side, and large chunks of the railing were gone. The binnacle was destroyed, a piece of which was now in Beauty's chest.

Fallon looked over his shoulder and saw the Spanish frigate, *Doncella Española*—Spanish Maiden—already throwing her dead overboard. Her foremast seemed to be teetering precariously, and the battle seemed to be over, for beyond her Fallon could see *Renegade,* which had apparently broken away after *Rascal's* attack, drifting away to the southwest.

Fallon's attention was called back to the ship and the need to see the wounded below. Like so many battles at sea, this one had no winners, only losers. Men were dead, Beauty was critically wounded, and nothing had been accomplished by anybody.

TWENTY-TWO

HOLD THE LIGHT steady!" ordered Colquist, and Jenkins, the loblolly boy, trembled as he moved the light closer to Beauty's chest. He had likely never seen a woman's breasts before, and this was not what he was expecting, at any rate.

Beauty lay on the table, drifting in and out of consciousness, Fallon holding her hand and talking softly to her. Colquist gently moved the splinter this way and that to test her body's grip on it. The splinter protruded about two inches above her left breast, the wound oozing blood steadily.

"The splinter has to come out, of course," Colquist said to Fallon in a trembling voice. "These kinds of wounds, as you know . . ." and his voice trailed off.

Fallon nodded that he understood and watched as Colquist dribbled laudanum generously into Beauty's mouth. She opened her eyes briefly and looked at Fallon, showing him fear and determination in equal measure. And then she seemed to set her jaw, as if her body were preparing for the worst.

Slowly and carefully Colquist pulled on the splinter, first gently and then with more force, until at last it was free. Jenkins's eyes grew wide and his face was pale, and as Fallon looked at him he thought the boy would topple over. Beauty seemed to have lost consciousness.

"Hold the damn light, son!" demanded a nervous Colquist, and the boy steadied.

Blood was flowing freely now and Beauty's chest ran with rivulets of it. She was still unconscious as Colquist washed the wound as best he could and hoped the blood would purge any dirt or whatever it was that caused infection. In his heart, Colquist feared for her survival.

"Not good, is it?" Fallon asked.

"No, not good. But we both know Beauty's the toughest sailor on board. Maybe she'll find a way. She needs to see a real doctor, Captain. How long until we reach Antigua?"

"A few days more. Keep her alive until then, Colquist," said Fallon gravely. "A few days more."

THE NEXT several days went by in a grim lunge east, a sense of dread over the ship and her crew and especially her captain. *Rascal* beat to weather as fast as ever she could, a special urgency in each tack and sail adjustment. Seven men had died or would soon be dead from *Doncella*'s broadside—a high price to pay for no real gain, by Fallon's reckoning. *Renegade* may have escaped, but why had she fought so poorly in the first place? And Beauty! Losing her was inconceivable, and he refused to think about it. She was in and out of consciousness, not speaking coherently, her eyes telling Fallon she knew she was in trouble. According to Colquist, her chest was dramatically inflamed.

Rascal was battered and the carpenter and his mates went about making repairs, pride driving them to make the ship presentable when they entered English Harbor. The days dragged on, Fallon rousing himself to absorb Beauty's duties as Barclay was still recovering. Aja helped around the edges as well. Fallon resolved to make him second mate sooner rather than later, because *Rascal* had none and, though he was young for the role, Aja wasn't *too* young. Besides, Fallon had no one else who could do the job better. Aja was a better than average navigator, having studied under Barclay. He understood the great guns, firing sequence, range, elevation, and something of the strategy of battle. He had proven to be a quick study since coming aboard two years ago.

Tomorrow would see them in English Harbor, and not a minute too soon. Colquist reported that Beauty's condition had worsened and the infection had driven her to fever and delirium. He bathed her in cool water in an attempt to bring the fever down, but it did little good. Colquist was preparing Fallon for her possible if not probable death, but Fallon remained steadfast in denying it. The crew knew the situation, of course, and knew that but for the quarterdeck gun on *Doncella* they could have freed *Renegade* without the loss of a single person. But plans rarely worked perfectly at sea; Fallon was not to blame, fate was.

The night before they were to reach English Harbor was a long night, indeed. Fallon had the deck for most of it, and when Aja came up to relieve him he found he wasn't tired in the least. Going below to his cabin, he settled at his desk to write to Elinore, describing the events since he'd written last and concluding with Beauty's condition, which he admitted was dire. She and her father were almost as close to Beauty as he was, and the news would be hard to hear. Yet Elinore always said *wound me with the truth*, and it was a comfort to share his anguish. It went without saying that he would not leave Beauty's side until she was either on the road to recovery or . . . no, *on the road to recovery*, insisted Fallon to his doubts.

ENGLISH HARBOR was chock-a-block with ships of all sizes and descriptions either going about their business or at anchor. The harbor was the most active of all Caribbean ports, being home to His Majesty's Caribbean fleet, small though it was, and all the ships that supported it. The harbor was relatively wide at the entrance, with good holding near both the western and eastern shores. As an extra precaution against hurricanes, there were arresting cables laid across the harbor so that ships could drag grappling hooks in the hopes of catching one to prevent them from running ashore. Farther on, the head of the harbor lay north, divided into two large bays, surrounded by government buildings and shops of all kinds.

Barclay, his forehead swollen and his eyes blackened from the falling block, brought *Rascal* easily toward the headland that jutted out into the harbor. Farther on was where the dockyard was situated; Horatio Nelson had built it up significantly as commander-in-chief until he left his posting in 1787. Fallon could see many buildings and docks, a guardhouse, and a saw-pit shed. The whole dockyard was surrounded by a low stone wall, and just beyond the wall was a naval hospital.

It called for finesse to bring *Rascal* in under sail to the wharf, as opposed to having her warped in, but Fallon knew it would be easier and faster to lower Beauty to the dock than to call for a boat from shore, for *Rascal*'s own boats had to be completely rebuilt after *Doncella*'s broadside. Fallon took the wheel and ordered the sails furled in sequence so that the ship lost way just as she approached the wharf. It was a deft maneuver, and shore-side sailors and merchants all stopped their business to watch it with admiration, not knowing that it was dictated by necessity. Quickly, the ship was secured and Colquist supervised the hands who moved Beauty up to the deck and over the side of the ship to the dock as gently as carrying eggs in a basket. It was a short walk to the hospital. Fallon led the way, Aja by his side, with Barclay left in charge of the ship.

Once inside the hospital building, Fallon immediately found the administrator in charge, who announced his name as Kibbleman, and demanded to see the best doctor at the hospital. Kibbleman informed him it was a *naval* hospital for officers and men of the Royal Navy and, unless she was one or the other, Beauty couldn't be admitted. He was quite clear on the point and didn't deign to look at the fevered body on the stretcher, still held by *Rascal*'s men. Colquist made to intervene but was cut off immediately.

"Let me tell you something," said a barely-in-control Fallon. "This brave woman is dying for Great Britain, and you will find a bed for her this instant! I want the best doctor in the hospital or on the whole goddamned island to see her immediately, or I swear on my mother's eyes that Admiral Davies will hang you for treason! Or I will! Or we both will!"

Kibbleman paled and made to argue, but something in Fallon's face told him his life was quite literally in danger. He directed the Rascals to carry the stretcher down the hall—*gently now*—suddenly worried about Beauty's health. After locating an empty room outside the ward, something he felt Fallon would demand anyway, Kibbleman hastily left to find a doctor. Colquist had the men transfer Beauty to the bed as carefully as possible, though she was quite clearly unconscious.

The room was spare and smelled of lye. One bed, a small table next to it, and a wooden chair against a plaster wall that needed painting.

In short order, Kibbleman led the physician into the room, introducing Doctor Garón, who exclaimed, "Captain Fallon!" Both Fallon and Aja were shocked, but before either could respond Garón recognized the patient and bent over Beauty, examining her wound and conferring with Colquist in low tones as everyone else backed away into the hall. Fallon preceded Kibbleman, who by this time was wringing his hands that Doctor Garón knew these people, and perhaps Captain Fallon was *somebody*, and the threat of hanging wasn't an idle one.

"Is Doctor Garón your best physician?" asked Fallon as he rounded on Kibbleman in the hallway. "Answer me truthfully." The *or else* was implied.

"Yes, sir," replied Kibbleman, swallowing heavily. "He is relatively new here, but he has some inventive techniques that most of our naval surgeons don't have. He even insists we wash the sheets and all of the rooms every day. This patient has her best chance with him."

Fallon looked through the door at Garón and Colquist, serious and concerned looks on their faces, and finally they motioned him into the room.

"Here is the situation as I see it, Captain," began Garón. "I believe there is part of the splinter still in Beauty's chest that is causing the infection. Señor Colquist took out all that he could see, but this splinter is likely imbedded in the tissue around the breast. It must be removed if she is to have any chance to live."

"Can you do it, Doctor Garón? Can you save her life?" asked Fallon, a plea in his eyes.

"I am going to try, Captain. But I may have to remove her breast to do it. It is very infected, as you know. I . . . I must tell you I have never removed a breast before. I have done many kinds of surgeries, of course, but this . . . never." Clearly, he seemed worried. Unsure, not of his diagnosis, but of what it required.

"You're her only chance, sir," Fallon said. "Do what you have to do to save her life." He thought of Beauty then, her pragmatism and common sense in tough situations. "She would understand, believe me," he added.

Garón took a deep breath, looked at Beauty lying on the bed, her chest red and inflamed, and nodded to Colquist.

"Let's get her into the operating room where the light is better," he said. "You men bring her and, Captain Fallon, please come with us. I will want you to hold her hand and talk to her. She may hear you somehow, and it may give her strength."

After Beauty was moved, Aja led the men back to the ship and, after conferring with Barclay and spying an untended dockyard boat tied to the wharf, left in it with a small crew to find *Avenger*, Admiral Davies' flagship. The two bays at the head of the harbor were about equal in size, though not visible from the dockyard. Aja ordered the bow of the boat pointed toward the bay on the left, the one more populated with buildings on the shore, and in very little time he could see *Avenger* swinging to her anchor, a massive shape compared with the other ships and vessels nearby. Aja urged the men to row faster, for, as he'd heard Fallon say many times before, there was not a moment to lose.

TWENTY-THREE

ADMIRAL DAVIES and Captain Kinis had been ashore at Government House when *Rascal* reached the wharf at the dockyard. They'd been summoned by the governor to explain yet another drunken incident involving British sailors and a bawdy house. Well, it was a simple explanation: *They were sailors.*

After Kinis promised for what seemed like the hundredth time that it would never happen again, the sailors were released from confinement and a detachment of marines marched them to the admiral's barge tied at the wharf. The sailors kept their eyes on the bottom of the boat, not wanting to see Davies' face.

Once aboard, the now-very-sober sailors were turned over to First Lieutenant Brooks for punishment. Brooks reported that while the officers were away *Rascal* had sailed into the harbor and was even now tied up at the dockyard wharf. A visibly surprised and elated Davies grabbed a telescope and, indeed, here was Aja—not Fallon—and a small crew rowing for all they were worth to *Avenger*. Suddenly, Davies had a feeling that something was wrong. Perhaps very wrong.

In very little time, Aja was welcomed aboard and quickly blurted out the news of Beauty's wounding, omitting the details of the battle in his haste to convey the most urgent news. Immediately, Davies called for his gig and left for the dockyard wharf, followed by Aja in the dockyard's boat.

As his gig's crew rowed, Davies looked toward the hospital.

Before he had installed Doctor Garón there, it had been a mephitic institution where sailors went to die, not to get well. The smart ones chose to stay aboard their ships, if they could, for their chances of recovery were better there, even under the care of ships' surgeons, who were an uneven lot. But Garón had changed the level of care at the naval hospital, over that idiot Kibbleman's objections, and Davies had backed him every step of the way. Now the hospital was spotless, the English doctors were learning from the Cuban doctor, and wounded sailors actually walked out instead of being carried out.

They were drawing closer to the wharf, and Davies looked around the harbor. His two frigates were away and his several sloops were out to intercept privateers preying on slavers and merchant ships. His flagship was the sum total of his fleet in the harbor today.

For Davies, English Harbor was his prison as much as his home, for he rarely left. The flagship was his command post, and His Majesty's ships and sailors in the Caribbean came and went and returned home to *Avenger* like a touchstone. He envied Fallon; perhaps not at this very moment, of course, faced with the possible loss of his best friend. But at least Fallon was free, and if a ball or sword should find him, at least he would die at sea.

FALLON STEPPED out of the hospital room, hope and fear in equal parts written on his face. He had talked softly to Beauty throughout the operation; her eyes fluttered once, but that was all. Whatever Garón had given her for pain had either done its work or she had simply given in to unconsciousness. She was sleeping now, her breathing labored and her chest rattling. Colquist had assisted Garón, the two of them working well together, saying little during the operation beyond what needed to be said.

At last, Beauty had been sewn up and Garón stepped from the room to join Fallon. It was at that moment that Davies appeared, followed by Aja. Garón could give his report to all of them at once.

"It was a very bad situation, and it still is," said Garón, obviously very tired from performing the surgery. "The infection covers her chest and is in her whole body by this time. I did not take her breast and can only hope that was the right decision. I have done all I can do for her; she is in God's hands now."

"How long until we . . . know?" asked Davies, looking at Fallon and reading the question on his face.

"Usually an infection this bad must begin to resolve within a few days for the patient to have a chance," answered Garón. "If it doesn't begin to retreat by then, I'm afraid she is lost. She will be too weak for another operation. I will be with her night and day, have no fear on that point. My wife will join me here; she is very good at prayer."

With that, Fallon, Davies, and Aja left the hospital and walked to the wharf and the waiting boats. Fallon was beyond spent and could barely think. But he did have a question for Davies, and he was determined to ask.

"Is *Renegade* in port, Admiral?" he asked.

"No, she's been out for two weeks," answered Davies. "Why do you ask?"

"We found her heavily engaged with one of the Spanish frigates, *Doncella Española*, three days ago. She was just on the point of being taken when we happened upon the battle. I believe she escaped but the Spaniards may have pursued. Beauty was hurt by a chance shot to our binnacle, and I was temporarily out of action, so I don't know what happened next."

"I see," said Davies, clearly concerned. "Had she hauled down her colors then?" Surrender was much frowned upon in the Royal Navy and had ended many captains' careers. Particularly if it was *premature*.

"I don't know," Fallon said without emotion. "I was knocked to the deck and couldn't see. The last thing I remember was the Spaniard preparing to board *Renegade*."

He asked to give his full report to Davies in the morning, and Davies agreed, knowing there was much more for Fallon to report, not least about landing Wharton in Matanzas. He invited Fallon for a late breakfast, knowing he would want to check on Beauty first thing in the morning.

When Fallon climbed through *Rascal*'s gangway it was almost time for dinner, but he had no thought for food. He asked Aja to let the hands know Beauty's condition and gave him his letter for Elinore with instructions to find the next packet to Bermuda and get it aboard. That done, Fallon collapsed in his cot and was immediately asleep, the soft bumping of *Rascal* against the wharf like a metronome, marching him to a deep dream world.

TWENTY-FOUR

Fallon awoke abruptly at two bells in the morning watch and hastily dressed. It was still quite dark, but he knew the path to the hospital and made his way there quickly. The air was humid, with a light breeze doing little to keep the moisture at bay. A faint light shone on the east side of the hospital, and Fallon knew it came from Beauty's room. He took heart that a candle still burned.

When he entered her room, he found Doctor Garón and his very pregnant wife at Beauty's bedside—Señora Garón knitting something and the doctor dozing in a chair. They both looked up with a start as Fallon joined them, but he went immediately to Beauty. She was still sleeping, perhaps a trifle more comfortably, but was feverish to the touch. Her face was the color of the muslin sheet that covered her body.

"She was delirious most of the night, Captain," said Garón, now quite awake. "She talked a little and called to you several times. Something about swimming to shore in a storm. Perhaps an hour ago I gave her something to relax her and help her sleep. She has a fever, as you felt. But that's to be expected."

Fallon relaxed a little himself, his confidence in the doctor having grown exponentially since watching him operate. Señora Garón was standing off to the side, and Fallon turned to embrace her.

"Thank you for coming and praying, Señora," he said. "It is wonderful to see you again, but I wish it was a happier circumstance."

"Yes, Captain," she replied. "But God has a plan for each of us. Beauty is in His hands now. I'm just trying to convince Him to let her stay with us."

"I hope He is listening to you, Señora," Fallon said with a weak smile.

A last look at Beauty, a few words spoken quietly and privately, and Fallon left to return to the ship. He needed to get his thoughts in order before breakfast with Davies. And he needed to shave and put on his best clothes. Though Davies was a good friend, he was still an admiral.

DAVIES HAD thoughtfully sent his gig to bring Fallon to breakfast. Fallon and Aja sat in the stern sheets, unspeaking, consumed with worry for Beauty, and oblivious to the lovely day unfolding around them. As Fallon climbed through Avenger's gangway, Kinis was there to welcome him and to show him below to the great cabin. Davies bid them both to sit for breakfast and, after asking about Beauty's condition, asked Fallon to begin his report.

Fallon described Luna's explosion in Havana Harbor—"Beauty's idea," he told Davies—with the apparent loss of several ships within the harbor. Then James Wharton's landing in Matanzas, uneventful really, and a promise to retrieve him in a month, now three weeks' time. At Fallon's mention of Paloma Campos, Davies' mouth came open in surprise, but he did not interrupt to ask questions. Fallon described their trip to see sugarcane plantations and the meeting with Serles, the punishment of Young David, and Aja's secret and successful effort to free him. At this, both Davies and Kinis slapped the desk in astonishment, surprised but not surprised, for both held very high opinions of Aja and could imagine him taking matters into his own hands.

In fact, in the way of things aboard ship, Rascal's crew had learned of Aja's late-night escapade and viewed him with awe as a result. Most of the men had no real position on slavery one way or the other; rather, they accepted it as a way of life. But in their hearts

the crew loved a good rescue, a daring kind of rescue, and Aja's reputation as an enterprising and courageous fellow elevated him to
heroic status in their eyes. No doubt that respect compelled them
to follow Aja's orders in the heat of the battle against *Doncella*.

"Before I forget, sir," said Fallon, remembering his duty. "I was
asked to give you this message." He slid the note from Paloma
across the desk to Davies, who looked at it like a thirsty man
would a cup of water. That is to say, with longing in his eyes. But
he let the note sit there, deciding to read it later, privately. If Kinis
was surprised, or even interested, he didn't show it.

"Pray continue, Captain Fallon," Davies said quietly. "Your report is absorbing."

The breakfast came and with it hot coffee, bread, and real but-
ter. Fallon found he was ravenously hungry, having had no supper
the night before. Between mouthfuls he described the taking
of *Petite Bouton* off the Mucarias shoals without a shot. Davies'
eyebrows went up, but Fallon merely attributed the capture to
luck and an aged *capitaine* who made a wise decision. Then, with
some little drama, he drew his fair copy of the letter found in
the *capitaine*'s cabin from his breast pocket and pushed it across
the desk to sit next to Paloma's note. This one Davies picked up
eagerly.

"That was locked in the *capitaine*'s desk aboard *Petite*," said
Fallon. "Do you read French, sir?"

"I do somewhat, thank you," replied Davies, and opened the
letter and began reading. When he was finished he looked up in
astonishment and said to Kinis: "The French government is asking the governor of Cuba to use Santiago as a staging ground in the
event France decides to invade Saint-Domingue!"

It took a moment for Davies and Kinis to absorb the importance of the letter, how the balance of power in the Caribbean
would be affected by a French fleet action and the certainty of
Louverture's defeat. What then? Davies' attention focused on the
letter, and he looked up at Fallon with a question.

"I see this is a fair copy, Captain. What happened to the original?"

"I gave the original to Toussaint Louverture, sir," said Fallon, holding his breath lest the admiral find fault with his decision.

"*Good God!* You met with Louverture!" exclaimed Davies. "But how did you do that? What did he say? Good Lord!"

Fallon told them of his journey to Jacmel and finding Louverture, omitting the whistling, and Louverture's inscrutable reaction to the letter. And then Beauty's observation that Louverture wasn't surprised at the French government's intentions.

"Truly, you have acted in the best interests of Great Britain in this matter," proclaimed Davies to a visibly relieved Fallon. "In fact, going to Jacmel was beyond the call of duty. Whatever in the world convinced you to do that? Really, I am astounded—and I thought your intrepidness could never astound me again!"

In fact, Davies proclaimed himself astounded *again* as Fallon described the battle between *Doncella* and *Renegade*, and *Rascal's* attempt to prevent *Renegade* being boarded.

"You said earlier that *Renegade* escaped once you engaged, Captain Fallon. Was she crippled at all? I am trying to understand why she left you in such a precarious position after you put your ship in such danger to help her."

Fallon sat uncomfortably, unable to answer beyond noting that *Renegade* had lost her fore-topgallant mast and *Doncella's* own foremast seemed to be teetering and about to go over. Davies sat quietly, as well, thinking of Sir Charles Charles on *Renegade's* deck under heavy fire. He was a captain due to influence, not ability, but influence did not stop a cannonball or keep fear at bay. He was about to ask another question when his steward knocked on the cabin door with the news that *Renegade* was just entering the anchorage. And her ensign was lowered to make room for the invisible Flag of Death.

TWENTY-FIVE

FALLON, DAVIES, and Kinis rushed on deck to get a glimpse of *Renegade* as she dropped her anchor. She was badly battered on her starboard side, and her sails were pockmarked with daylight. Even without a telescope Fallon could see her bowsprit was jury-rigged and her fore-topgallant mast had not been replaced. Her ensign indeed flew one flag's height below the gaff, leaving room for what old tars called the invisible Flag of Death. It meant an officer was missing or dead.

Davies ordered the signal *Captain repair on board* to be hoisted, and a ship's boat was slowly lowered from *Renegade's* deck. It took several minutes for the crew to board and push off from the side. Davies raised his telescope and saw that Lieutenant Samuel Jones II was in the stern sheets. As the boat drew closer, Davies could see that Jones's shoulder and arm were in a sling and his head was bandaged, and he asked Kinis to order a bosun's chair to be made ready.

At last, *Renegade's* boat clapped on, and the bosun's chair went over the side and brought back up the pale and seriously wounded first lieutenant, who immediately fell into Kinis's arms while attempting to stand. Quickly, the flagship's surgeon was sent for, and Jones was carried below without having said a word.

"Sir, I might be of use aboard *Renegade* just now," said Fallon. "If you'd like me—"

"Of course, Captain. Thank you," interrupted Davies. "I would ask you to accompany Lieutenant Brooks and, if he is required to stay aboard, bring back a report on the situation. And any word of Sir Charles."

Fallon left in *Avenger's* gig with First Lieutenant Brooks and, of course, the ever-present Aja, and soon was alongside *Renegade's* starboard quarter, which was holed in several places. Climbing through the channel, they were met with a grim scene of destruction. Guns were overturned, half the spokes were shot off the wheel, the mainmast was damaged, and the deck was turned up in furrows like a freshly plowed field. Blood painted every surface black where it had dried, and the men they saw were either bandaged, or stupid with exhaustion, or both. It appeared that whatever repairs had been made were just enough to get the ship sailing.

At last, Brooks and Fallon were met by Second Lieutenant Ashby, who looked in rather poor shape himself with a bloody bandage around his arm. After the briefest of introductions, Brooks asked after the wounded and learned the surgeon was badly taxed, possibly drunk, and definitely overwhelmed. The pumps were at work, and what men were able were manning them every three hours.

"And the captain, Ashby?" asked Brooks. "What of Sir Charles?"

"I'm afraid he died, sir," answered Ashby, his eyes lowered. "He was standing in the waist with his sword out and was shot in the throat."

Fallon wondered where Sir Charles had seen that romantic image before: a captain with his sword out challenging the enemy. *No doubt it made a good painting,* thought Fallon. But it was no good to think ill of the dead, and Fallon turned instead to what it would take to set the ship to rights. In his opinion, it would need the dockyard, and the hospital, and a month at the least.

Fallon watched Brooks's face as it seemed to reflect his disappointment in the ship's condition, then turn to empathy for Ashby's predicament at the loss of his captain and severe wounding of his first lieutenant, not to mention his own injury.

"Ashby, we must get the ship to the dockyard that you passed as you came into the harbor," said Brooks. "Once you get close I will have you warped in the rest of the way. There is a naval hospital there with an excellent doctor, and your men will receive the best of care, on my word."

"Thank you, sir, yes sir," was all Ashby could mumble, though he was visibly relieved to relinquish command. Brooks began shouting orders and asked Fallon to row to the dockyard to re-quest boats to warp *Renegade* into the wharf and tie off behind *Rascal*. There the wounded could be off-loaded before the dock-yard received the ship for repairs.

FROM *AVENGER'S* DECK, Davies watched Fallon being rowed to the dockyard and *Renegade* simultaneously weighing anchor, and he could guess the story. *It must be hell on that ship,* he thought, as he went below decks satisfied that Brooks had taken charge. There would be questions aplenty for Jones, assuming he recovered, and for Sir Charles, assuming he wasn't dead. But, for now, there was the note from Paloma to read, and it waited on his desk.

In his cabin at last, he closed the door and sat heavily in his chair, the weight of the world on his shoulders, but the weight of that note seemed heavier still. He tore it open and began to read:

> *Harry,*
>
> *By the time you read this I will either be in prison or disappeared, for I intend to act on my desire to rebel against Spain. Enough talk! What I intend to do is unimportant to you, for you have your own war to fight. But here it may make a small difference, and that is enough.*
>
> *Please remember me as we were that last night on*

the beach. I think of that night often, and it will comfort
me in the days and weeks ahead.

Paloma

"Good God!" Davies exclaimed as he jumped up from his desk. What was Paloma going to do that could get her killed or imprisoned? Where was she now? Questions flew through his mind and, like a dagger, his own powerlessness stabbed him in the heart. She was clearly in danger, or would be, and he could do nothing. *Nothing.*

He thought of that last night on the beach in Matanzas before *Avenger* weighed the next morning. He'd hosted a party for everyone in the village who'd worked so hard to repair his ship. Later, he'd asked Paloma to go for a walk, and he'd finally found the courage to kiss her and she'd kissed him back. *What a kiss!* His hand trembled a moment as he thought of it, the letter falling to his desk. That night she'd asked him to come back. *Was she asking him again?*

No, he decided. She wouldn't do that. But what in God's name was he to do?

TWENTY-SIX

Young David never intended to kill anyone; well, not after killing Boss, anyway. He was not a murderous man, nor an ignorant one, though he had no formal education. But he knew enough to know that without sugarcane there would be no economic reason for slaves in Cuba. So, he intended to burn every sugarcane crop to the ground.

He got off to a good start outside Matanzas and gradually worked his way east. To his surprise, several white Cubans joined him in support or helped him with food and shelter, and as he burned fields and freed slaves his band of rebels grew to more than one hundred. Unknown to Young David, it was the white Cubans helping him that spurred the governor to action. That wouldn't do; in fact, it was a dangerous idea that might spread among the general population. If many more whites joined the rebellion it might be very hard to stop. So, the governor called upon the Spanish army to find Young David, either capture or kill him, and put a stop to that nonsense.

His orders: Kill any slave with a black ring around his breast.

By the end of his first week of freedom, Young David had reached the cane fields near Santa Clara, staying along the northern coast of Cuba, and as he freed more and more slaves he began to lose control over them, such that white planters were sometimes murdered, usually burned alive in their own homes. The rebellion moved quickly, staying ahead of its own news, and most planters were unaware of the danger *until they awoke to the smell of smoke.*

Young David finally broke off from the band when it reached two hundred runaways. It was too large to feed and manage, and new voices arose to challenge his leadership. He left with twenty former slaves and a white Cuban—the woman he'd seen with Ajani when he'd been whipped by Boss. Young David's band went their own way, making faster time and not killing anyone.

Meanwhile, the fields burned night and day.

Paloma Campos came to accept Young David's strategy as a sound one; well, it was basically the only strategy that unarmed rebels could employ that produced tangible results in the form of burned fields and freed slaves. For her, though, it had the added benefit of action against Spain. It might not create a rebellion that could overturn Spanish control; in fact, it likely would not succeed. But it was something a Cuban patriot could do.

One night the rebel group camped by a copse of trees in a ravine—a good hiding place away from roads and, hopefully, anyone after them by now. Young David sat off to himself, as he usually did, and Paloma approached him timidly. Her role in the rebellion was as a guide to plantations owned by Europeans, for she would not condone burning Cuban fields.

"Young David," she said as she knelt down beside him, "perhaps we should not burn for a while. It tells anyone hunting us where we are and where we are headed. Perhaps we should take another direction and hide and make a new plan."

Young David looked at her with expressionless eyes. At once, Paloma felt very aware she was not a slave and had never suffered for her color or race. She wanted to pull her words back into her mouth and swallow them lest Young David question her intentions in joining his rebellion.

"This is all I can do," he said softly. "It is all I know how to do."

Paloma studied his face intently and saw that he was only telling the truth. He was not the rebel leader who would lead slaves, and Cuba, to freedom. He was no Louverture, the black leader she had heard of on Saint-Domingue. He would not draw people to his side or make himself head of an army.

She slipped away quietly. Young David would fight his private war his way, burning one field at a time and, in the end, he would die for it. They all would.

TWENTY-SEVEN

J UST BEFORE DAWN, on the fourth day after surgery, Beauty's lips
trembled. Fallon didn't see it, though he was at her bedside, because his face was buried in his hands. But Doctor Garón saw it,
and he leaned closer to hear if she was trying to speak.

She stirred. Her eyes fluttered and then squinted open.

"Am I . . . *lopsided?*" she asked in a voice barely above a whisper.

Fallon raised up with a start and tears leapt from his eyes.
Beauty! Oh, my God!

"No, you're all there," he said, wiping his eyes and laughing for,
apparently, she'd been more aware of her situation than anyone
knew. "You're missing enough parts as it is!"

"I agree," said Beauty weakly, and drifted back to sleep.

Doctor Garón motioned for Fallon to leave the room while he
examined Beauty. The swelling in her chest had gone down somewhat and the stitches looked healthy enough. He felt her face and
took her pulse and, satisfied, joined Fallon outside the doorway.

"She'll be in and out of consciousness for a while," he said, visibly
relieved. "But I believe she will come through this. It's a miracle."

"Yes, Doctor Garón," said a very relieved Fallon. "But, if not for
you, there would be no miracle. I thank God, but I also thank you,
sir. Thank you." And he shook Garón's hand vigorously.

As Fallon left the hospital he started to jump for joy but, fearing it would look undignified, he half walked, half ran to where
Rascal was tied against the wharf and immediately called all hands.

Barclay and Aja gathered the men together, and Fallon told them the good news about Beauty. To a man they cheered.

"Louder, men! She can't hear you," yelled Fallon.

And, indeed, they cheered very loudly, and then louder still, for every man jack respected Beauty's courage and leadership and, not least, her seamanship. She could make *Rascal* do things that Fallon couldn't, and he was a very good seaman, indeed.

Inside the hospital, Doctor Garón had just finished changing Beauty's dressing when he heard the cheers through the open window. He stopped momentarily and looked at her face. Her lips trembled as if she were trying to speak again, or smile.

FALLON DASHED off a quick note to Davies with the good news about Beauty and asked Aja to take the gig, now rebuilt, to *Avenger* to deliver it. Just as Aja was about to depart, however, Davies' own gig hailed *Rascal* and the admiral stepped aboard. Fallon met him at the side and saw the distress written on his face. Anticipating that his concern was about Beauty, Fallon quickly told him she had spoken, and Garón believed she was through the worst of it. Davies was obviously delighted, and he pumped Fallon's hand in congratulations.

But the distress didn't leave his face. He asked if he and Fallon could talk privately, and Fallon led him below to his cabin. Shutting the door, Fallon turned to see the admiral standing at the stern windows staring out to the harbor.

"I need to share something with you," Davies said to the glass. "As a friend, for you are certainly not my subordinate in the Royal Navy. But I find I have no one to talk to about this and, to be honest, no real friend in this world save you."

Fallon was surprised and touched, but fearful about what he was about to hear. Maybe he was also a trifle embarrassed for Davies. What he was about to do would admit weakness of some sort, which was very unusual for an admiral.

"You know the story of *Avenger*'s time in Matanzas, how we

limped into the harbor years ago for repairs after the hurricane and battle with the Spanish fleet. What I left out was Paloma Campos. I was smitten from the first time I saw her, and doubly smitten by the time we sailed. I have lived with her memory since then; wondering how *she* felt, of course, and despairing that this interminable war would prevent me ever going back to Cuba. Her note brought news that she felt the same as I, but that she was going into danger to stand against Spain, somehow. She expected that the authorities or the army would kill her or perhaps imprison her for what she was about to do. The note was to tell me good-bye. She may very well be dead now, Nicholas, and I will never know."

Davies turned around from the glass, and Fallon could see his eyes were full of emotion. The fact that Davies could reveal the depth of his feelings made Fallon respect and admire him all the more, for it made him less an admiral and more a man. But, clearly, a man in pain.

"There is no action I can take," continued Davies, "for I am bound to the Royal Navy and stationed here. But when you return to Matanzas to pick up Wharton could you . . . that is, if you could inquire discreetly about Paloma I would appreciate it. I couldn't ask you to do that without telling you everything."

"Of course, sir," answered Fallon without a thought. "If there is anything to find out I will find it out, believe me." He was thinking of Paloma's sister at the café, the café where everything was known.

"Thank you, Nicholas," Davies said. "I am deeply appreciative of your kindness. I can't think of another soul on earth I could have talked to about this."

"You don't need anyone else . . . Harry," said Fallon, calling him by his first name for the first time, at least to his face. "You have a good friend right here."

As the two men shook hands, Aja knocked on the cabin door to report that Mr. Kibbleman was standing on the wharf next to the ship with a message. Both Fallon and Davies hurried up the companionway steps to hear what he had to say. Kibbleman was indeed on the wharf, and at the sight of Fallon and Davies together his throat seemed to constrict, or at least his voice came out as a squeak.

"Sirs, I have news about both officers!" said Kibbleman. "Doctor Garón sends his respects and says that the woman is awake and has eaten some thin soup and is resting comfortably. And, Admiral Davies, Mr. Jones will recover, though he has a broken arm and clavicle and possibly a fractured skull."

"Thank you, Kibbleman," said Fallon, "that is indeed good news all around."

Whereupon both officers climbed down to the wharf to visit the hospital. Davies to visit Jones to ascertain when the first lieutenant would be well enough for a full interview, and Fallon to check on Beauty while still absorbing everything his friend had said, and everything he'd asked him to do.

TWENTY-EIGHT

*T*HE SUN *rose glowing before them each morning, and the sky glowed with fire behind them each night. As Young David and his followers pushed into the interior of the country, the cane fields stretched as far as could be seen. They scrounged for food during the day and set their fires at night, freeing every slave they found. Sometimes they were discovered and had to run off; several times they were shot at or dogs were set upon them. The dogs they killed with cane knives—it had to be done.*

Paloma Campos trudged along with Young David's small band of rebels, who were joined by several other runaways who came and went. Most of the slaves they freed scattered into the countryside to fend for themselves, drunk with the feeling of freedom and frightened of the consequences of being caught.

Neither Young David nor Paloma knew of the Spanish troops sent from Havana, marching relentlessly at the governor's orders to capture Young David and the rebels or kill them outright. The soldiers thought they had them once, but it turned out to be a group of slaves that had been freed the day before.

A rebel's life is equal parts fear and exhaustion, and it happened that Young David's rebels stayed in one place too long. They were all tired of moving so quickly and spent one entire day sleeping in an abandoned barn. When they awoke the next day they were not alone.

A group of Spanish soldiers surrounded the barn.

Young David had been a free man almost three weeks when he was captured and put in chains along with the other rebels, Paloma included. The soldiers and their prisoners began the long march back to Matanzas and Castillo de San Severino, which, like all such forts, housed a stone prison.

Young David was stoic, as was his usual mien. All the other slaves marched with their heads down, but not Young David. This was not lost on the soldiers, who regarded him with respect and curiosity. Well, they thought, let's see how proud he is in front of a firing squad.

TWENTY-NINE

WHEN AT LAST the sloops were ready for sea, the Holy One could resume his business. The time ashore had given him pause about his strategy, however, and whether it needed to change with the report of Spanish frigates sent to protect slavers from, well, *him*.

He had searched his mind for opportunity, and he found it on land. The plantations on Caribbean islands often swept down to the harbors and bays, and the barracoons could easily be seen from the water. Hundreds if not thousands of slaves were asleep each night within reach, and no frigate could defend them.

His plans were executed first on St. Kitts, where he took off 75 slaves; and then perfected on Martinique, where he took off almost one hundred. His sloops would enter the harbor at dusk, and his captains would lead their crews ashore to the barracoons. Any resistance from the planter or his overseer was easily dealt with, usually with knives. The slaves were led obediently to the ships' boats, and the entire operation was completed before dawn. He sold these slaves at a market in Santo Domingo, though the prices were far less than what he could get in Cuba. But this was just the beginning, and when the holds were full and bulging with black gold it would be worth the long sail to Cuba, where the price for a sound slave was the best in the Caribbean.

Really, this new strategy was brilliant, and the Holy One was surprised that he hadn't thought of it before.

He'd always been clever, even as a boy in Cadiz. But *different*, his parents had said. They'd tried to discipline him when he'd done *different* things, such as torturing animals or stealing from shops. So, he decided to simply leave. Well, not *simply* leave, for first he'd set fire to his room to erase any trace that he'd ever been there. Later, he learned the entire house had burned down, his parents within it. It hadn't troubled him.

He'd taken refuge at a monastery in the port city of Alicante, pretending to be interested in Jesus. The monks had allowed him to stay and worship with them, hoping to save a wayward soul. In fact, he stayed almost a year but, in his cell-like room at night, he created a vengeful image of God, merciless and all-powerful. It was a God he could pray to for guidance.

He left Alicante with a robe and a cross, using them to secure free passage on a small trader bound for West Africa. He absorbed the lessons of sailing and ship handling easily. Once in Africa, he watched in fascination the endless procession of black Africans loaded onto slave ships, and he knew he'd found his calling. Later, he secured free passage on a slaver as a priest in return for ministering to the needs of the slaves and the crew and, two days out of Senegal, he'd murdered the captain and impressed his will upon the small crew by displaying the captain's mutilated body on the bow of the ship. His career, such as it was, was launched.

Cruelty builds a reputation faster than goodness, and stories of the Holy One's sadistic behavior soon became legend and legion. Not only did he attack his victims, slave or merchant, with impunity but they were punished for resisting. In some cases, captains were tortured for hours and then set adrift in a ship's boat, flayed and bleeding, to drift to their deaths under a relentless sun. To resist the Holy One was to resist the will of God, in his mind.

His God did not forgive. Or forget.

THIRTY

FOR THE BEST part of the next week, Fallon visited with Beauty every day, and every day he saw her condition improve slightly, her spirits and strength grow incrementally. It was a tribute to the human body that he'd witnessed with injury and illness before: the body wanted to be well. Soon Fallon would need to leave to pick up Wharton in Matanzas, and he wanted to leave knowing Beauty was well on her way to a full recovery. Thanks to the Garóns, she seemed to be.

Unbeknownst to Fallon, Lieutenant Brooks had approached Captain Kinis with an unusual request. Knowing Fallon was due to sail soon, and knowing he would leave without a second in command, Brooks had volunteered to sail with *Rascal*. He was a young man aboard a flagship usually confined to English Harbor and, as much as he tried to avoid saying it directly, he wanted more real sailing experience and, frankly, excitement. Kinis read between the lines as Brooks stammered out his request, and he remembered his own service as a first lieutenant. He could understand and did not take offense at such an unusual idea. In fact, he secretly wished for a little more adventure himself.

Davies had very generously agreed with Brooks's request when Kinis confided it. Fallon was very appreciative, even overwhelmed, having already taken a liking to Brooks. Nonetheless, the young man would have to dress down into ship's slops so as not to advertise himself as a British officer.

Soon enough, Brooks was aboard *Rascal* and was supervising her provisioning, with Aja in close attendance. Certainly, the ship could have anything it needed with Admiral Davies' blessing.

Lieutenant Jones was making progress from his injuries but was not yet able to take the full load of restoring *Renegade* to fighting trim. He was, however, ready for his interview with Davies as to the battle with *Doncella Española*, and the admiral had asked Fallon to be in attendance since he'd played so integral a role in the outcome. Fallon admired Jones and knew him to be an excellent officer whose account could be believed.

It was early in the first dogwatch when the meeting convened aboard the flagship, with Kinis present as well. Although it was not a formal inquiry, it might lead to one, and Davies would want corroboration of what was said.

Jones looked uncomfortable sitting at the table, either from his injuries, or the report he was to give, or both. Certainly, the battle with *Doncella* had been a disaster for the Royal Navy, a blot on Jones's career, and already word of the battle's outcome would be on the waterfronts and in the harbors throughout the Caribbean.

"Tell us, Lieutenant Jones," said Davies to open the meeting, "of the events leading up to and including the battle with *Doncella*. I realize you were injured during some part of the affair, but tell us what you can."

Jones swallowed hard and looked at each of the captains in the room, gathering his thoughts, for his story was not an easy one to tell.

"On the morning of the twenty-first we came upon a Spanish frigate—*Doncella Española*—sailing northwest, and Sir Charles ordered *Beat to quarters*. As we were also sailing northwest but coming from the south, *Doncella* had the weather gauge."

"How was your supply of powder and shot, sir?" asked Davies, cutting to the chase.

"Excellent," replied Jones, but a downward glance confirmed what Davies suspected.

"Specifically," asked Davies, "had you practiced the men at the great guns with live ammunition since leaving Antigua the month before?"

It was a direct question from an admiral, and Jones could only give a direct answer.

"No, sir," he said. And everyone in the room knew that Sir Charles, like too many British officers, hoarded powder and shot at the expense of practice at the great guns.

"Go on, Jones," said Davies, beginning to form a picture of Sir Charles's command.

"We engaged *Doncella* on starboard and the men bent to their guns with a will," said Jones, intentionally defending the crew's actions. "And—"

Here Davies interrupted, knowing well that what wasn't being said could be more important that what was. He was determined to get the full story, just as much as Jones was determined to avoid impugning his commanding officer, dead though he was.

"Mr. Jones, was *Renegade* a disciplined ship?" asked Davies. "Was she in all respects ready for a fight?"

This was the crux of it, the moment Jones had dreaded in the interview. As first lieutenant, it was Jones's responsibility to see to it that the ship was indeed ready for battle. Ready, in fact, for *anything*. Fallon watched Davies carefully, for he had been through a similar interview and knew that Davies would continue to probe for a deeper narrative until he felt he had not only the facts but also the underlying story behind them.

"Let me make this easier for you, Mr. Jones," said Davies. "Answer the following questions with a simple *yes* or *no*, please."

Jones nodded, and Fallon thought he could detect a sense of relief on the man's face.

"Did you attempt to persuade Sir Charles of the need for practice with live ammunition?"

"Yes."

"And he did not agree?"

"No."

"Did Sir Charles agree with your handling of the men?"

"No."

"Did he think you were too soft?"

"*Hardly!* I mean, no."

"Did Sir Charles countermand your efforts to discipline the crew then?"

"Yes." Jones was barely speaking above a whisper now, looking at the floor, equal parts humiliation and embarrassment. Davies had known other captains who tried to curry popularity with their crews by being lenient. It never worked.

"So, you went into battle with *Doncella* with a poorly disciplined crew who had no practice with live ammunition. Is that correct?"

"Yes, sir."

"And would you like to add anything further?"

"No, sir."

"Describe the battle now, if you please," said Davies.

Fallon listened to Jones review the tactical situation again, knowing well the scream of shot and picturing the chaos and loss of life aboard *Renegade* with each incoming broadside—*Doncella* had fired two complete broadsides to every one of *Renegade*'s.

"Did Sir Charles take active command of the ship, Mr. Jones?"

"He . . . he tried to, sir. But I don't think he . . ."

"He what, Mr. Jones?"

"He lacked experience, sir. He didn't really understand how to fight the ship. He had his sword pointing to *Doncella* and was yelling *Fire! Fire!* before the guns were even reloaded."

"*Good God*, man!" exclaimed Davies. It was clear that Sir Charles had a very romantic and ultimately tragic notion of what a British captain should be: He was long on show and short on competence.

"He was shot in the throat early on, sir," continued Jones. "A Spanish sharpshooter was in the tops, I believe. As I tried to rally the men we lost our fore-topgallant mast, which somehow managed to find me as it fell to the deck, and I don't remember anything afterwards. But I believe the second lieutenant, Ashby, took charge of *Renegade* just as Captain Fallon arrived on the scene to draw *Doncella*'s fire. The rest you probably know, sir. And may I say thank you, Captain Fallon. I am sure the ship would have been lost without you. I'm very sorry Beauty was so seriously wounded, but as I am in the ward next to her, I can confirm that she is mending well."

"Thank you, Mr. Jones," said Davies. "And may I say your account is wholly believable and I pray will do you no lasting disservice. I will have to petition the Admiralty for a new captain, of course, but as you are the senior lieutenant on station, *Renegade* will be under your command until the new captain arrives. As soon as you are able, pray get her ready for sea as fast as ever you can."

Fair to say, Jones was caught flat-footed by Davies' approbation of his conduct as first lieutenant under Sir Charles. He was being given a second chance to reclaim his reputation, for Davies could quite rightly have placed Brooks in command of *Renegade* and Jones knew it. He left *Avenger*'s great cabin in a daze, shaking Fallon's hand at the gangway, who was himself descending to visit Beauty at the hospital. *Rascal* would leave for Cuba in a few days, and he had yet to tell her.

IT WAS NEVER going to be easy. Though Beauty was feeling as well as could be expected after surgery, she was in no condition to go to sea, and she and Fallon both knew it. But she refused to accept that he would leave without her.

"If you sail without me you'll likely get lost," she said as she sat up in bed, wincing at the pain but trying hard not to show it. "Someone else should go get Wharton."

"There really is no one else to go, Beauty," said Fallon soothingly. "Besides, Davies wants me to inquire in Matanzas about a particular person who may have gone missing. I promised him I would. There's more to the story, as you can probably guess."

Beauty shifted her pillows a bit. It obviously was a woman they were talking about.

"Nico, I think the salt air would do me a world of good. And

Colquist could look after me if there was any problem. Look, I'm getting stronger by the day—Garón has me walking up and down the halls so much I'm wearing a groove in the floor. Can't this wait a few more days?"

But, of course, it couldn't. Brooks would do fine as *Rascal's* first lieutenant, though Fallon had to admit it wouldn't be the same. Brooks was no Beauty, as it were. But the ship and crew were ready and, in truth, so was Fallon. Getting to Matanzas a few days early should give him time to find Paloma if she was to be found.

"So, tell me, Beauty," said Fallon, hoping to change the subject, "how are you feeling? I know on the outside you look like you're coming along, but a wound like you had, you know, you could have died. Maybe you ought to reconsider, well . . . your job."

"Sailing with you is dangerous, Nico," Beauty said with a smile. "But listen to me. I know you're trying to change the subject, but since you asked, I'll tell you. I've had my dark moments, I admit. I'm human. I'm a woman. You might not know it but I have my own vanity. And I still have to go home and face someone else with a big scar across my chest. I'm not really worried about how she'll react, but you leave one way and come back another and, well, I guess you're never sure. Doctor Garón was pretty clear about what I faced. He told me you gave him permission to remove my breast if it would save my life. Thank you. By the way, I would have done the same for you. Cut off your breast, I mean."

Ah, Beauty.

"But, let me ask you something, Nico," said Beauty, turning serious. "Were you with me for the surgery?"

"Yes, I was," answered Fallon.

Beauty took a moment, her face turning red from embarrassment as she pictured the scene, Fallon by the bed holding her hand while Garón and Colquist did their work, her body naked to the waist.

"And what did you see?" she asked softly.

"I saw a sailor with a chest wound," Fallon answered immediately.

"That was the right answer, Nico," Beauty replied.

THIRTY-ONE

FALLON WAITED until Saturday to leave English Harbor, for every sailor knew it was bad luck to sail on Friday. He said good-bye to Beauty on Friday, though, both of them stoic and resigned that he had to leave without her. Beauty was making real progress and was out of bed as much as she was in it. Doctor Garón was due the credit for that.

Admiral Davies came to the wharf to see *Rascal* away and to thank Fallon again for inquiring about Paloma Campos in Matanzas. He still had anxiety in his face, Fallon noted, and he hoped he could bring back good news that would put his friend's mind at ease.

It was more than thirteen hundred miles to Matanzas, and Barclay laid a course taking them above the islands of Porto Rico and Hispaniola before reaching the north shore of Cuba. Fallon's mind lingered on Cuba for a moment, wondering whether Wharton's mission had been successful.

Fallon and Barclay kept a vigilant eye as they neared Porto Rico. The area between Santo Domingo and the Lesser Antilles was the deepest part of the Atlantic Ocean, a trench more than five miles deep, and old sailors recounted tales of giant waves seemingly coming out of nowhere to capsize ships and drown crews. The islands would shake, coconuts would fall to the ground, and huts would collapse. No one knew why, of course, but these were the stories sailors told.

Rascal cruised through the area without incident, all sails set and drawing, the wind just on her starboard quarter. Brooks very wisely rigged preventers on the big booms to keep them out to larboard lest the ship should slip down a wave and accidentally attempt to wear. Fallon liked Brooks, who was a tall, genial officer given to humor and self-deprecation, a rarity in the Royal Navy. He knew his business well, and the men responded quickly to his every order. In all respects, he was an excellent first lieutenant. Fallon noticed that Aja observed him keenly.

Even sharp-eyed lookouts failed to turn up anything on the horizon, and *Rascal* dipped and rolled past Porto Rico and on toward Santo Domingo. Louverture had begun his rebellious activities there, rallying the slaves against Spanish planters and developing the leadership qualities that would serve him so well when he turned his attention to Saint-Domingue to the west.

Aja walked to the larboard railing, where Fallon and Brooks were standing, and followed their gaze out to Hispaniola. From sea, the country was lush and verdant, with forested hillsides sloping down to fields and meadows that seemed to run to the beaches. The bloodshed of thousands of slaves couldn't be seen from the sea; indeed, it could barely be imagined from the land.

"Aja, one day you will be able to tell your grandchildren that you met Toussaint Louverture, a famous man in history," said Fallon. Aja looked at the shoreline deep in thought.

"Do you think France will allow the rebellion to continue, sir?" asked Brooks, a dubious tone in his voice. "If France invades Saint-Domingue, the world may never remember Louverture, I'm afraid."

"There is an old saying we learned as children," Aja said. "*Until the lions tell their tale, the story of the hunt will always glorify the hunter.*"

"Well, let's hope Louverture will live to tell his tale," said Fallon. "France doesn't need more glory, much as Bonaparte might want it."

Brooks left to supervise the changing of the watch, still getting used to a privateer's casual ways versus those of the Royal Navy.

The watch turned up, the lead was cast, and the ship sailed toward Saint-Domingue and into the early evening, making only fair speed, for running before the wind was not *Rascal's* best point of sail. Cuba lay in the dark distance, and Fallon wondered what he might find of Paloma Campos. Davies' feelings for her seemed deep, and it put him in mind of his own feelings for Elinore and how they always seemed magnified when he was at sea.

Retreating to his cabin for the evening, Fallon poured a glass of wine and sat on the stern seat with pen and paper. The light was dim, but he wanted to write Elinore a letter. Instead, a verse of a sort began to appear on the paper, as if written by its own hand.

> *Tonight, I breathe your love*
> *into my lungs and your lips*
> *part over mine*
> *and your smell*
> *reaches*
> *into the secret parts of*
> *my body*
> *until, exhausted from*
> *holding you inside,*
> *I exhale.*

As always, he thought little of his own writing, though Elinore seemed to appreciate his efforts. Lovers can be forgiven for almost anything, he thought. Even bad poetry.

FALLON AWOKE before dawn, stiff and cramped from a night on the stern cushions, his paper and pen on the deck of the cabin where they'd fallen. His wine was untouched on the desk, as was the dinner his steward had quietly set out on the chance that he'd awake and be hungry. He was now, indeed, fabulously hungry and called for coffee and toasted cheese immediately while he shaved and shifted his clothes.

By the time he arrived on deck it was to a lightening sky behind

him and a grayish bow wave forward. Cuba was out there somewhere, and even now James Wharton might be making his way to
Matanzas for the rendezvous in a little over a week's time. Fallon
wondered idly whether Cuba was indeed ready to challenge Spain.

"Good morning, Captain," said Brooks, approaching Fallon
from behind to snap him back to the present. "We're about ten
miles off the east coast of Cuba, sir. Within the hour we should be
off Cayo Guillermo on the larboard bow." Brooks, ready with the
answer before the question—like a good first lieutenant.

"Thank you, Mr. Brooks," said Fallon. "Have you ever been to
Cuba?"

"I have not, sir. But I've heard the wom—that is, I've heard it is
very beautiful."

"Yes, they are, Mr. Brooks," said Fallon with a grin to a visibly
embarrassed first lieutenant.

"Deck there!" called the lookout. "Sail to the west!"

Here was Aja with Fallon's telescope, though nothing could
be seen from the deck. Barclay appeared at the binnacle, as well,
and all eyes looked ahead to the west. But the morning would not
be rushed, and so the light took its time coming. Minutes passed
slowly, until finally the lookout called.

"Deck there! She's ship rigged. Tacking toward us."

Fallon now found himself in the same uncomfortable position
Petite Bouton had been in: a narrow strait with not much room to
maneuver, though he certainly had better visibility and thus more
time to decide a course of action than the French *capitaine* had.

"Lookout! What is she?" he yelled.

"She's just tacked again, sir!" called the lookout. "I make her a
packet of some kind!"

Well, that took the pressure off, thought Fallon. He decided to
have the colors sent up and see how the packet responded. He also
asked Brooks to call all hands as a precaution.

The British ensign went up and almost immediately the lookout
called.

"Deck there! She's flying British colors!"

"Heave-to, Mr. Brooks," said Fallon. "But have the gun crews stand ready. Let's see what this fellow has to say."

On the packet came, tacking this way and that while Fallon paced the deck with his chin in his chest, catching a glimpse of the slowly approaching packet out of the corner of his eye. It was a ponderous thing, unhandy and clumsy in tacks, but after the best part of an hour she hove-to within hailing distance of *Rascal* and the captain spoke through cupped hands.

"I am Captain Stipes, and this is the slaver *Plymouth* just back from Havana."

"His Majesty's privateer *Rascal*, Captain Fallon in command, sir," yelled Fallon back. "What news of Havana, pray?"

"None, sir. But very difficult to get in nowadays with the chain. Took me the better part of the day! They finally sent a boat out to check my papers. And the slaves were bellowing like cows!"

Fallon could see Stipes laughing even as his own stomach tightened. And then Stipes added something else.

"I was hailed by a Spanish frigate this morning, sir! *Doncella Española*, she was! On patrol for pirates attacking slavers, by God. I was empty by then but the capitán, Diaz, would have protected me if I'd been full! He said Cuba wants all the slaves it can get no matter who brings 'em to her!"

"Which way was *Doncella* bound?" yelled Fallon, for it wouldn't do to run afoul of the frigate again.

"Toward Havana, I make!" called Stipes. "No hurry, mind, sailing easy under plain sail."

A few more pleasantries and Fallon had all the information he was going to get. He bid Stipes good day and castigated himself for not sinking the slaver on the spot. But that wouldn't be legal, and wouldn't end slavery; in fact, it wouldn't make any difference at all. Still, once *Plymouth* was away upwind and the slaver's scent blew down on *Rascal*, Fallon almost reconsidered.

Brooks brought *Rascal* back on her old course as Fallon went back to pacing. As things stood, there was no danger of *Rascal* over-taking *Doncella* and finding herself in an unpromising situation. As a precaution, Fallon was about to ask Brooks to reef the foresail and slow the ship down when the most extraordinary idea came to him. It was in his mind and fully formed and was so counterintuitive that he forced himself to pause before he gave the order to do the opposite of what any sane schooner captain would do.

He was going after a frigate.

THIRTY-TWO

"MR. BROOKS!" yelled Fallon over his shoulder. "We have a ship to catch!"

Immediately *Rascal* came alive; all hands thrilled to the chase as the topsails were set and drawing. *Rascal's* bottom was fairly clean and Fallon could only hope that *Doncella*, so far from home, had a foul bottom to compensate for her greater press of sail.

"Mr. Barclay and Mr. Brooks," said Fallon excitedly, "*Doncella* is moving up the coast toward Havana and we must do everything in our power to catch her!" Both men looked surprised, Brooks especially, since he had no experience with Fallon and did not know his ways. For his part, Barclay knew an idea was afoot.

"Mr. Brooks, coax whatever speed you can from the ship! Put Kirby on the helm—he will know to steer small, but instruct him to head up on each lift to get everything he can out of it. By dawn tomorrow I want to be in range for the long nine. A half mile or less, just enough to pray for a lucky shot!"

It was not in Fallon's mind to engage *Doncella* in a battle of broadsides, for that would be suicidal. Rather, he intended to harass and generally annoy the Spaniard from the safety of a rear action. Unless *Doncella* had a stern-chaser, *Rascal* would be in no danger and he could nip at the frigate's heels until Havana. And then, if conditions warranted, he could spring his little surprise.

Kirby was a Welsh ex-miner who had stepped off a coal packet in Bermuda and never went home. For a rough man he had a light steering touch and was Beauty's favorite helmsman. He steered small, in the sailor's language, making minute adjustments instead of sweeping reactions to wind and wave with the wheel. The result was a ship that sailed faster through the water. Each time the wind veered, for it never stayed *exactly* the same direction, Kirby made small adjustments to keep the breeze on the starboard quarter. This was a faster point of sail than dead downwind, and the ship's speed increased with each lift.

Barclay cast the log regularly to keep track of *Rascal*'s speed through the water, and he continually called for adjustments to either add more twist to the sails or less. The hands were watching a master at work, with tweaks aplenty, and with each cast of the log they nodded in agreement that Barclay and Brooks were getting the most out of the ship.

All day it went on like that, a quarter of a knot gained here, half a knot there. The hands changed watches and looked to the west but saw only an unblemished horizon. And when, at last, evening came and Barclay was sure of their position, Fallon went below to have his dinner knowing that everything was being done that could be done to close the gap with *Doncella*. Morning would tell the tale.

At two bells in the morning watch, Aja crept into Fallon's cabin and lightly touched his shoulder.

"Daylight soon, Captain, sir," he said softly. "Mr. Barclay estimates we are past Cay Sal Bank and in the Florida Straits."

"Thank you, Aja," said Fallon, instantly awake. "I'll be on deck shortly."

Within minutes Fallon appeared in the gloom of early morning and peered ahead to the west, seeing nothing. He sent for coffee and settled in on the windward railing, feeling the wind on his neck as he watched the bright green disturbed water flow down *Rascal*'s starboard side. Why it glowed so he had no idea, but every sailor knew the Caribbean's waters glowed green when disturbed at night. The incandescent green globs seemed to roll down the sides of the ship and spin off in her wake to disappear, slowly, in the black water left behind.

At all costs, Fallon intended to keep his ship safe and to pick up Wharton in Matanzas. But he had a day to spare for mischief, and he thought of Beauty, wishing she were with him, knowing how much she loved a good chase. This was her kind of day: a race to the finish line, a come-from-behind, all-or-nothing flyer. A day when anything could happen.

It was after Fallon had had his breakfast and come back on deck that the lookout spotted *Doncella* in the distance, several miles ahead. She was indeed under all plain sail, lumbering along on patrol, no doubt, without a thought of being challenged. Fallon approached Brooks at the binnacle just as he'd finished reproaching the helmsman to steer small, Brooks getting into the chase with both feet now. Fallon looked through his telescope at the frigate's stern. He could just make out figures looking back at him. Not surprisingly, Capitán Diaz seemed unconcerned. No doubt he recognized *Rascal* from the battle with *Renegade* and perhaps felt humiliated at being tricked, but he would not act stupidly. He had the superior firepower, and thus nothing to fear from this nuisance astern.

Within three hours *Rascal* had eaten up the distance to *Doncella* to less than a mile. It was time to start the dance.

"Mr. Brooks," said Fallon, "please ask Cully to load and run out the long nine. We're going to try a ranging shot on the up-roll."

"Ranging shot on the up-roll it is, sir," said Brooks, hurrying forward to confer with the master gunner.

Fallon had no illusions about hitting anything, but it would do the men good and get the barrel hot to try a few shots. A hot barrel shot a truer ball than a cold one. In his telescope, he could see no stern chaser on the frigate, which was a comfort. Always good when the enemy couldn't shoot back.

Cully's crew worked in harmony to get the long gun primed and ready to fire. First, the barrel was swabbed with water to remove

salt or any debris that had found its way inside. Then a flannel cartridge containing packed gunpowder was loaded into the barrel,
followed by a wad of cloth, and a crewman rammed both home
with a wooden rammer. Next, the gun captain poked a small wire
down through the touch-hole to prick the cartridge open, shouting
"*Home!*" once he'd done so. Cully then ordered the 9-pound ball to
be loaded into the barrel and yet another cloth wad was rammed in
behind it to keep the ball from rolling out. The gun was then run
out, priming powder applied to the touch-hole, and it was ready to
fire.

Rascal's bow was moving up and down, rising onto the tops of
waves and falling into troughs, and Cully would have his hands
full sighting the gun. But he knew his business and stood patiently
looking at the frigate, watching her motion and feeling *Rascal's*
own, and then he bent to sight the gun. On the up-roll, he fired.

All hands looked forward to see the fall of the shot. Short and
left, but they were still more than a half mile from *Doncella* and,
undiscouraged, the gun crew went through the drill again. They
would repeat the process, exactly replicating each movement, again
and again, Cully nodding and making minor adjustments, still getting the sense of the ship and his timing, still missing.

But getting closer with each shot.

After an hour, Capitán Diaz had had enough and Barclay noted
that *Doncella's* topgallants were now set and were full and drawing.
There would be no catching her, and even now she was pulling away
from *Rascal*. They were off Matanzas on a broad reach and Fallon
called Barclay and Brooks together. Aja hovered nearby, within ear-
shot, as always.

"Gentlemen, you are no doubt wondering what your crazy captain is up to with this chase, so let me tell you what I plan. First, a
question: Have either of you ever raced skiffs?" And as they looked
at him curiously, Fallon explained small boat racing and tactics
when sailing behind the leader.

After Fallon had laid out the idea, Barclay brought the bow

northward and *Rascal* sailed off on a 45-degree angle away from *Doncella*, picking up a great deal of speed as she came onto a beam reach. Fallon wondered what Diaz was thinking; hopefully he had never raced skiffs as a boy and thought that *Rascal* had given up and was sailing away.

Fallon ran the calculations in his head, wind and tide and speed, his racing instincts in full play. Barclay was below at the charts, running his own calculations to compare. *Doncella* was well out of range now, far to larboard on her way past Matanzas toward Havana, rolling and yawing with the wind on her stern. Fallon was all attention, for left too late the game was over. If he tacked too early he might come under El Morro's and La Punta's guns, and they would likely remember *Rascal*. In fact, he was counting on it.

Within an hour they had lost sight of *Doncella* from the deck, but Fallon was sure she was soon to wear ship and make her turn for Havana Harbor.

"I say we wear in thirty minutes, Mr. Barclay," said Fallon. "What say you?"

Barclay had been bent over his notes and figures—well, he was always bent, in truth—and raised up with a smile on his face.

"That is exactly what I would suggest, Captain!" he said with surprise and more than a hint of admiration in his voice. "Really, most extraordinary that we should agree like that!"

"Mr. Brooks! Wear ship in thirty minutes, if you please," said Fallon. "Then, Mr. Barclay, pray lay a course for Havana Harbor. And call me when you've found *Doncella*. Now we shall see what we see!"

Fallon went below to have a very late breakfast, for he realized he had quite forgotten to eat in the excitement of the morning. In very little time events would be upon them, and he intended to face them with a full belly.

Before he had finished his meal he heard Brooks's order to wear ship, and he could feel *Rascal* come about on her new course. Slowly, she picked up speed and was once again on a beam reach, this time on the larboard tack, dashing for Havana Bay. It took all his resolve to remain below decks, but he wanted Brooks to be seen executing the plan if it should succeed. If it should fail, the failure would belong to Fallon, of course.

"Deck there! Frigate off the larboard bow!"

The lookout's call did for his breakfast and Fallon bounded up the companionway, almost running Aja over in the process. Gaining the deck, he could indeed see *Doncella* off to his left, just where she was supposed to be. By sailing on a faster point of sail, even slightly away from Havana Bay, *Rascal* had head reached on Doncella and made up the distance between them to the harbor—a fact that doubtless had just been revealed to Diaz.

"Mr. Brooks, have Cully go back to the long nine," said Fallon coolly. "He is to commence firing on my order. And Mr. Brooks, I want us as close to *Doncella's* stern as you can get us until I give the order to come about."

"Aye, aye, sir," answered Brooks, who could barely tear his eyes away from the converging ships. El Morro and La Punta could both be seen easily at this point, guarding the entrance to Havana Harbor at the southern end of the bay. *Doncella* had completed her turn for the harbor and was even now signaling the forts, announcing her arrival. But *Rascal* was coming up very fast.

COLONEL GARCÍA was called from his office, where in truth he had been dozing, as soon as the big frigate made its turn for the harbor. He could see she was Spanish through his telescope, and he could also see a British schooner sailing close behind her. This was *exactly* the scene that bumbling Gonzalez had described at his trial, before he'd been led away to the bowels of the prison at El Morro.

What was this? The schooner was firing a bow chaser at the frigate. And now the frigate was signaling. First the ship's number—García quickly referred to his list of ships to identify it as *Doncella Española*.

Then the signal: *Lower the chain.*

The colonel had a moment of doubt. But events were overtaking him as *Doncella's* signal was still up and the schooner was still firing, or *appeared to be!* This is what that fool Gonzalez had described, and he had fallen for the British trick and lowered the chain and the whole harbor had blown up.

¡Madre de Dios!

Two miles from the harbor entrance was usually the point of no return, when the chain would have to begin lowering to a depth sufficient for a large ship to pass over safely. García could feel the sweat suddenly pooling in his armpits beneath his uniform, belying the calm he was trying to show the *guardavía* who was awaiting his order.

García took in a slow breath. The ships were in a line for the harbor, the schooner was still firing, and *Doncella* was still signaling.

"Guardavía!" said Colonel García resolutely. "Signal: *Chain is lowered.*"

"But, sir," said the trembling signalman, "the chain is up!"

"Yes," said García, "but two can play this game."

FALLON COULD quite easily see *Doncella's* stern with his naked eye and, more, could see the stern windows blow out at Cully's last shot. God knew what destruction the long nine was causing inside the frigate, but he could envision quite a bit. Men might well be dead and bleeding themselves out, and Diaz could do very little about it. If he hauled his wind to turn and fight, *Rascal* would simply sail away. Besides, Diaz would know *Rascal* would not dare enter the harbor under the guns of two forts.

By sailing so close to the Spanish frigate, Fallon had prevented the forts from firing, or thought he had, until a flurry of signals from the ramparts and the boom of cannon convinced him otherwise. The shot landed close enough that he ordered Brooks to come about, for *Doncella* was almost to the harbor entrance anyway. The thing was going to work or it wasn't.

The forts' guns continued to fire—not at *Rascal*, but at *Doncella!*

Diaz signaled furiously and kept signaling right up until the time the ship lurched to a stop and all her masts snapped forward and overboard, taking her pleading signals with them. The force of a wooden ship displacing twelve hundred tons travelling at fourteen knots meeting a three-foot diameter iron chain hanging beneath the surface of the sea cannot be exaggerated. The bow of the ship attempted to ride over the chain, but the leading edge of the keel was literally sliced off as the chain sawed its way into the ship.

As *Rascal* sailed away to the northeast, Fallon thought he could hear a massive grind and for a moment he thought *Doncella* was over, but then the frigate settled and slowly began to sink. The ship was in shambles, with rigging and masts floating about, and men clinging to the ship's boats in desperation.

Brooks and Barclay were all smiles as Fallon ordered spirits piped up, with an extra tot for Cully's gun crew. Barclay laid a course for Matanzas, and for a moment Fallon's mind leapt ahead to what he would find there. But here was Aja grinning broadly and shaking his hand, pulling him back from the future to a very happy present that only a fool of a captain would ignore.

THIRTY-THREE

THE PACKET ship *Ariana* glided into St. George's Harbor carrying mercantile goods, one hundred bolts of West Indies cloth, all manner of farm utensils, and a letter for Elinore Somers. Elinore was not feeling at all well that day and, indeed, had been ill for several days. Ezra Somers had no problem handling the office while his daughter recuperated, and when the letter arrived he recognized Fallon's handwriting and immediately took it home to Elinore himself. He hoped it would lift her out of her malaise and do her some good.

Instead, it sunk both their spirits, for as Elinore read the letter aloud and the nature of Beauty's wound was revealed they both felt powerless. Elinore knew Nico would never have written if Beauty's situation weren't serious, even dire. Was he secretly hoping she would come at once? Nico could be obtuse like that. And if she went to Antigua, would it be to help her good friend get well, or to bury her?

"What is it we can do, Father?" Elinore asked, holding the letter to her breast as tears formed in her eyes. "Is it just to be prayers? Surely not." She had forgotten all about her own discomfort now, and thought only of Beauty's struggle to live and Fallon's burden in caring for her with his other duties and responsibilities weighing on him.

"I will get us there, Elinore," said Somers. "But the only ship I have is *Petite Bouton*. I decided not to sell her into the service, but buy her myself for some light carrying trade. So, I had her careened and her bottom cleaned. New sails have been ordered but they'll be awhile coming. What I need is a captain and a full crew to supplement the Rascals who brought her in—but leave that to me. You get yourself strong enough for sea, and I'll get the ship ready to go."

MOST OF BERMUDA's men were to be found at sea, but Somers would not sail without enough men to work the guns and an experienced man to lead them. There was simply too much danger in the Caribbean. He decided to ask around at the White Horse that night and get something wet in the bargain.

In the event, Somers arrived at the White Horse in the early evening after seeing that Elinore was settled for the night—still and always a father. Elinore was improved, but anxious about Beauty. The island doctor had been around to see her, and after the examination she seemed to feel better, or rather *less sick*, but she hadn't confided in Somers the source of her discomfort. *A woman thing*, he figured.

When he walked through the door of the White Horse, Somers saw the usual crowd, a mixed bag of Royal Navy, farmers, merchantmen, and shopkeepers. He knew or recognized many of those he saw, and the senior Fallon welcomed him warmly to a seat at the bar.

While he was waiting for his ale, a giant of a man walked in, ducking under the low doorway, and made his way to the stool next to Somers. He had the unmistakable gait of a sailor, a little sway side to side, balancing on an invisible but remembered deck. His face was scarlet and weathered, his eyes were rheumy, and his hands were gnarled and arthritic from years of pulling ropes in all weathers. He sat down heavily at the bar, ordered his wet, and turned to Somers.

"Name is Stuyvesant," he said in a gravelly voice. "Captain of the barky *Drummond*. And who might you be, sir?"

"I'm Ezra Somers, a trader in salt, sir. Pleased to make your acquaintance. You are new to Bermuda, I collect?"

Stuyvesant looked at Somers with liquid eyes, as if in appraisal, and nodded.

"I brought the barky in with a sprung plank. On my way to Gibraltar from Boston with dried cod, and she started leaking in a gale of wind. It took two days to blow itself out, hands at the pumps watch on watch. We was off course by then and closer to Bermuda than Boston, so here I am. Old *Drummond* needs her whole bottom refastened, in truth, but I want another trip out of her."

Somers knew the tendency to push for a few more cruises before tending to ship maintenance, for he was guilty of it himself with his own ships. Stuyvesant seemed a bit on the rough side, and Somers guessed he'd worked himself up from the lower deck. A Dutchman by name, and perhaps by character, for the Dutch believed in going to sea to trade their way to prosperity. In Somers's experience, they were also staunchly individualistic, even stubborn.

"So, you're at the dockyard, I take it?" asked Somers.

"*In line* is more like it. Don't know when *Drummond* will get on the ways. I could be on the beach a month or better." Stuyvesant lifted his glass and drank half the contents in a series of long swallows. "Pumping every three hours to keep *Drummond* floating, we are."

Somers stared at his own glass, the contents of which he'd barely touched, and considered Captain Stuyvesant. Perhaps, just perhaps, here was the captain he needed, but was he the captain he wanted? Stuyvesant might be interested in a cruise south, for he could sail to Antigua and back before his ship was likely to get on the ways. And he certainly looked the part of a captain, but that was very little to go on. His thoughts were interrupted by Stuyvesant ordering another ale and then turning to him with a question.

"A salt trader, you say?" asked Stuyvesant. "Would you be needing a short carry anywhere then? And maybe a captain for it?"

His question caught Somers off guard, surprised they'd both been thinking along the same lines. Somers was anxious to get to Antigua, feeling instinctively that he and Elinore were needed, given Fallon's letter, and he abhorred being in the dark about Beauty's condition. Maybe Stuyvesant was a gift from above just when he needed one.

"Maybe a short carry, Captain," said Somers. "Let me think on it. Tell you what. You come 'round here tomorrow night and we can talk some more."

With that, Somers paid for his ale and waved to the senior Fallon and left the White Horse to tell Elinore their problems getting to Antigua might be solved. Tomorrow he'd visit the dockyard and check out Stuyvesant's story. Maybe get a look at his ship and crew while he was at it.

Maybe things were looking up.

THIRTY-FOUR

THE SPECTER of Castillo de San Severino loomed over the entrance to Matanzas, an impressive and forbidding presence. Water lapped at the stone stairs leading to the main entrance, and the quay was large and long to accommodate slave ships. The fort had been built in the 1600s but, when the British took Havana in 1762, the fort's commander, García Solís, had attempted to blow it up rather than see it fall into British hands. Thereafter it was in a continuous state of disrepair, for the explosives had severely weakened the foundation and battlements. Still, it housed the treasury and the slave market where *calimbo*, or branding, took place. The fort also served to house special prisoners; in fact, Spanish firing squads occasionally executed Cuban pro-independence patriots there.

Rascal once again entered the harbor as an American schooner to all intents, creeping in peacefully. Her sails had been shortened and the hands stood by to furl them completely when ordered. Matanzas looked just as Fallon had left it, locked in amber, sleepy and quiet. *Rascal* sailed up the long boot of the harbor and anchored very near where she'd anchored the first time. Only it was Brooks who ordered *"Let go!"* and not Beauty.

It was late afternoon when they arrived and, after seeing the ship settled and the hands given their duties by Brooks, Fallon and Aja were rowed to shore. Fallon did not expect to see James Wharton on the beach, for they had time to spare before he was due to show up. In the meantime, Fallon intended to learn something of Paloma Campos. Her sister's café seemed like a good place to start.

The café was not yet full when Fallon and Aja entered; the earliest customers were just trickling in and the candles hadn't even been lit.

In a moment, the barkeep made her appearance, and Fallon recognized her as Paloma's sister. Instead of cheerful, she looked tired and worried, and Fallon was immediately put on guard for bad news.

"Señora, you may remember me as a businessman looking at plantations some small time ago," he began tentatively. "I am wondering if Paloma is about, for she was very helpful to me."

"No, Señor," she said, tears welling in her eyes, "she left to help the rebels! It was madness to go, and this very day I learned the soldiers captured them all! The slave rebellion is crushed and the soldiers are bringing the prisoners to San Severino. They should be here tomorrow!" So distraught was she that Fallon thought she would faint at the bar. He heard Aja gasp at the news; he would of course be concerned not only for Paloma but for Young David as well.

"*Good God!* Señora, can you be sure of this?" asked Fallon, his mind already seeing Davies' face upon hearing the news. "What can be done, then?"

"I don't know," she said. "Nothing can be done. The authorities will lock them in the fort and . . . and they say they will shoot them all! It is what the governor decreed!" The *señora* was clasping and unclasping her hands, which Fallon noticed were shaking badly.

Fallon felt shocked and powerless. Paloma was even now being marched across the country to prison. The anguish on her sister's face was more than he could bear, and he left her with a promise to think of something to help, which he knew was a lie.

THE SOLDIERS *took their time, for they had what they'd come for and, besides, their prisoners were tied in a line and could move only so fast.*

They had been marching for almost two weeks and tomorrow would reach Matanzas at last. Colonel Munoz rode his gelding at the head of the column with practiced horsemanship, his back straight and his eyes forward. A proud soldier, he never questioned orders and served Spain obediently. Yet this hadn't been an honorable expedition, he felt, and his sympathies lay with the scared and bedraggled band of rebels limping behind him. And the woman! How beautiful she was to be going to San Severino, which was a wretched place. No doubt the rebels were criminals, murderers even, but he could not see the woman murdering anyone. Perhaps her sympathies were simply misplaced. Well, like his own, he admitted.

Colonel Munoz kept his eyes forward, but his thoughts were behind him.

FALLON AND AJA were rowed back to the ship, each lost in his own thoughts, silent as strangers. As Fallon reached the deck he was met by Brooks with the news that the lookout had reported a brig and two sloops sailing into the harbor on the last of the sea breeze. Even now the wind brought the smell of human cargo to Fallon's nose, and as he brought his telescope to his eye he recognized *Negro Sol* just making the turn toward the toe of the harbor's boot, leading her wolf pups. Indeed, he could see the Holy One standing on the quarterdeck looking through his telescope at *Rascal*.

As Fallon watched the progress of *Sol* to the fort's quay, he wondered what the Holy One was thinking, for he must recognize the schooner that had set a trap for his sloops. And he obviously saw it flew an American flag. Fallon could feel Brooks and Barclay and the rest of the crew waiting expectantly for orders to up anchor and attack. Or at least to run out the guns. Or *something*.

But it was not so easy. Fallon quickly considered his options, but as quickly as he considered attacking *Sol* he reconsidered, for an attack on Spanish ships in a Cuban port would likely draw the fort's guns or, at the very least, local militia into the fray. Yet it was a standoff, for Fallon also knew the Holy One would not attack an American ship in a Cuban port for fear of incurring the wrath of Spain, and perhaps even the United States. Fallon felt powerless as he stood gaping at *Negro Sol* and the sloops, now landing at the quay, those evil ships that caused or abetted so much human misery.

But he fought to put the Holy One and the little wolves aside and out of his mind, for there was nothing he could do. Ezra Somers always said that a man with no options was a man with no problems and, in this case, it was true.

"There is nothing for it, Brooks," said Fallon bitterly, not deigning to explain further. "Have the men go about their duties."

For the better part of two hours the black brig and sloops unloaded their trembling cargoes and the slaves huddled in naked groups while prospective buyers prodded and poked them to assess their value. One by one or in small groups the buyers led them away to be branded after presumably paying a small fortune for them, though the transactions could not be seen from *Rascal's* deck.

Fallon's frustration was compounded by ironical thoughts that he could not shake: Young David rampaged through Cuba freeing slaves, which no doubt created a slave shortage on plantations around Matanzas, which drove up demand and, presumably, prices for slaves in the market, which attracted slavers and pirates all the more to the trade. And the irony of ironies: Fallon had sunk *Doncella Española*, a frigate sent by Spain to hunt the little wolves and their ilk! So, Fallon's mind reached a twisted but inescapable conclusion: He was at least partially responsible for the Holy One counting his money right now.

The thought sunk his spirits, and he savaged himself for a fool.

His mood did not lighten when, in the early evening, *Negro Sol* and the sloops eased away from the quay. Fallon watched dejectedly as the Holy One ascended his quarterdeck and raised his arms to heaven, as if in prayerful thanksgiving for his good fortune in selling his slaves. Oddly, the Holy One seemed to have lost all interest in *Rascal* and may have even had his eyes closed as his ship disappeared into the night. A further testament to how lightly he regarded his adversary across the harbor.

LATER THAT EVENING the stars made a full showing over Cuba. Every constellation that could be seen in that early winter sky was showing brightly. Fallon stood at *Rascal's* stern deep in thought, for his mind fought to forget the humiliation of the day, to put it in the past, and to think of something to do to help Paloma. And Young David, come to that. But, whether due to his black mood or the capriciousness of fate, for once an idea didn't come, a daring plan didn't form, and the longer he stared at the lover's sky the more forlorn he felt. He had failed today, and he would fail tomorrow. The enormity of the problem pressed on him, like the enormity of the sky, and even conjuring lovely thoughts of Elinore failed to bring up his spirits. He imagined Davies this very night, looking at this very sky, wishing to the stars that Fallon would return with good news about Paloma. Finally, he went to his cabin, not to sleep, but to lie awake until dawn.

THIRTY-FIVE

THE NEXT MORNING found *Rascal* moving about her anchor in a small, indecisive breeze and Fallon on deck with his black coffee, a darkness on his face. He looked up to the Stars and Stripes flying rather proudly and would have smiled to himself at the deception had his spirits allowed. His gaze came down to the shoreline, deserted at this time of morning except for a beggar who'd apparently slept on the beach. Fallon reached for his telescope. He swept the town and looked up the road leading from the east. He was looking for dust from the approaching soldiers, but saw nothing. Finally, returning his focus to the beach and then onto the beggar, who was awake by then, he saw James Wharton smiling at him.

In very little time, Aja left in the gig to retrieve Wharton, who was soon aboard and shedding his disguise, the ragged coat and hat and walking stick cast aside. He seemed as fit as the day he'd been set ashore.

"Come, sir, join me for breakfast below while I hear of your derring-do," said Fallon, trying to escape his low spirits. "And I might have a few things you may find of interest as well."

Leaving instructions with Brooks to be alerted if the Spanish soldiers approached, Fallon led Wharton below to his cabin. Wharton bade Fallon speak first, curious about what he would report and whether it would corroborate what he had learned in the last month.

Fallon began by telling Wharton of Young David, his escape from slavery thanks to Aja, and of his apparent success in burning sugarcane from Matanzas to Santa Clara, setting slaves free along the way. Wharton nodded in appreciation, and nodded more vigorously when told that white Cubans had aided and abetted Young David and that some, like Paloma Campos, had even joined him.

"That's what we're looking for!" exclaimed Wharton. "Pray continue."

"It has all gone bad, I'm afraid," said Fallon. "The governor sent Spanish soldiers to capture Young David and the rebels and soon, today perhaps, the soldiers will bring them to the fort. I fear they will all be executed."

"I have no doubt of it, I'm afraid," Wharton sighed. "Spain is worried, truly, and is tightening its grip on Cuba. I have confirmed that now two Spanish frigates are in the Caribbean: *Doncella Española* and *Tigre* are their names. Ostensibly, they are here to protect Spanish slavers and Cuban harbors. It seems a Spanish ship blew up in Havana Harbor recently, if you can imagine!"

"I *can* imagine," said Fallon, remembering that glorious explosion. "I can also imagine *Doncella Española* running into the chain across that very harbor and tearing her bottom out." He let that sentence hang in the air, and Wharton smiled broadly and shook his head.

"Really, my friend, you never rest, do you?" he said. "Is there no end to your ideas for mischief?"

Fallon did not smile, for he was in no mood to accept compliments.

"Tell me, sir, is there any hope for Cuba?" he asked instead. "Was this so-called rebellion doomed to fail?" He was afraid he knew the answer.

"Very probably," said Wharton, shaking his head sadly. "The governor has become quite active in prosecuting Cuban loyalists, and ferreting out rebel slaves from their *palengues,* or hiding holes. And there is no opposition leader stepping out of the shadows.

Young David was perhaps on his way to becoming a folk hero but now he will be shot for his trouble. I have been in and out of Havana, spoken with diplomats and American agents and a wealthy loyalist or two, and can find no basis for optimism, sadly. Spain rules Cuba and will do so until a war separates them again. These two frigates she sent are a strong signal that Spain will not be denied its colony. Or its slaves."

Their conversation was interrupted by a hail from Brooks, and then Aja knocked on the cabin door with the news that there was a great deal of dust to the east. After taking his leave from Wharton, Fallon called for his gig. He and Aja climbed down into it quickly and in very little time they were rowed to the beach, from where they could see a crowd was gathering alongside the road.

Here came the soldiers, on foot and dusty, led by a decorated colonel mounting a fine horse. The soldiers marched in two columns, inside of which trudged the prisoners. There were 22 in total, all rebel slaves except one white Cuban—Paloma Campos walked behind Young David, who was in the lead.

Fallon and Aja stood next to the road as the soldiers approached. Many of the bystanders cried, including Paloma's sister, who was wailing with grief. Paloma smiled weakly at her, trying to be stoic, and then as she walked farther her eyes fell upon Fallon and Aja. Young David had seen them as well. Both Fallon and Aja nodded slightly in recognition, with Paloma and Young David nodding back with curiosity in their eyes. No doubt they're wondering why we're here, thought Fallon. He had the answer to that if he could have spoken to them: *We're here to set you free.*

He just didn't know how yet.

ALL AFTERNOON Fallon paced the deck deep in thought. He had watched as the prisoners were escorted along the beach and then up the steep stairs into the fort. Presumably, they were locked in their cells now, unaware of their fate. The rumor in Matanzas was that, indeed, they would be shot the next morning. Fallon stared at the fort through his telescope once more. It was certainly a formidable structure, with levels of battlements and, from what he could see, a courtyard surrounded by the prison walls. It seemed impregnable by anything but an all-out military assault.

As he watched, the work detail assigned to the continuing reconstruction on the walls and foundation began packing up their tools and leaving for the day. Their supervisor, no doubt the engineer for the project, waited patiently for the last workman to gather his things before stepping back and taking a last look at their day's work.

Suddenly, an old, almost forgotten surge of excitement shot through Fallon's body.

"Cully! Mr. Brooks!" called Fallon excitedly. "Come here quickly!"

Both men hurried to where Fallon was standing and followed his gaze to the fort. Brooks raised his telescope just as the engineer was making to leave.

"Mr. Brooks!" said Fallon, pointing at the engineer. "I want that man brought here. However you do it, even if you have to knock him on the head! But I want that man!"

Without a moment's hesitation Brooks answered, "Aye, aye, sir!" without having a clue how he was going to follow Fallon's orders. He motioned for Cully to come with him in the gig along with four crewmen and they were off within a minute. The crew rowed with deliberate speed to the quay by the fort, Brooks hailing the engineer before he could walk away. Cully stood in the bow of the gig and waved for the man to come down the quay, which he did, seeing no reason not to. There was no one else about, for the day was ending and there were no militia on the ramparts; presumably, the *guardias* stayed inside the fort as Paloma's sister had said.

The engineer walked casually down the quay, his papers and plans under his arm, and was met by Brooks and Cully, who persuaded him, or rather Cully's knife in his ribs persuaded him, to step down into the gig. The engineer was surprised into panic and sat with his papers trembling. In very little time he was tentatively climbing up the side of *Rascal*, Cully with his knife in his teeth climbing behind him for added terror, to be met by a beaming Fallon. The first part of a plan he didn't have was falling into place.

The engineer was led below to Fallon's cabin, where Wharton waited with two glasses of wine and a kindly smile. Fallon had just finished telling him what he needed and why, and the intelligence agent was going to work. Fallon left them to it and went back on deck.

The sun was going low and already the harbor was graying. Barclay was at the binnacle with Brooks as Fallon approached with an odd but remembered gleam in his eye. Here was the old Fallon back from the dead.

"Gentlemen," Fallon began, Aja by his side as ever. "Tonight's plan will unfold as we go. Best be prepared for anything."

THIRTY-SIX

S LOWLY, RASCAL was warped by the ship's boats to the fort's quay, her bow pointing out to sea. The fort was quiet, and no light was visible from the deck of the ship. It was slack tide, with no breeze, and *Rascal* didn't move at the dock.

Below decks, James Wharton and a quite-drunk engineer were laughing like the best of friends, the plans of the fort laid out before them on the desk held down by several empty wine bottles. The engineer was quite proud of his work on the fort, though he admitted the walls were still weak from the shock of the gunpowder years before. Under Wharton's gentle prodding, he revealed the location of the prisoner's cells, the head jailer's office, and where the Spanish *guardias* were billeted. Most important, he described the exact location of the treasury, which Fallon had specifically asked Wharton to find out. That would get the crew excited for what lay ahead.

The only way into the fort was through a massive gate, which was guarded day and night by several armed *guardias*. Worse, because the execution tomorrow involved a local and popular woman, a 6-pound cannon had been positioned inside the courtyard, thirty feet away from the gate, with a tub of slow match next to it. Clearly, the guards were taking no chances on an armed uprising. All of this Wharton revealed to Fallon while the engineer snored softly on the stern cushions in the captain's cabin.

All that was compounded, Fallon also learned from Wharton, who had learned it from the engineer, by the Spanish troops camped nearby. Tomorrow, after the execution, they would decamp for Havana. It wouldn't do to have the soldiers intercede in any rescue plan.

Out of respect for Paloma's grieving sister, Fallon felt he should disclose to her his intention to attempt a rescue, although just how was not completely clear to him. The problem was that, if he was successful, Paloma would have to leave Cuba to be safe from the soldiers' pursuit. That meant the two sisters might well never see each other again. Well, first things first, he decided. Paloma certainly wasn't free yet. Fallon called for Aja to accompany him to the café, and they left in the gig.

The café was partially full of local patrons, all talking in subdued voices, looking furtively at the end of the bar where a group of three Spanish army officers huddled with their drinks. Fallon looked for Paloma's sister and saw her in the far corner talking to several women, all of whom were crying and wringing their hands.

All had short hair, he noticed, unafraid to show their loyalty to Cuba, even with Spanish soldiers about. No doubt the local authorities were used to it.

Not wanting to intrude, Fallon and Aja waited until Paloma's sister looked up and motioned them over. Her face was red and swollen and her voice cracked with gasps of anguish as she tried to speak.

"Oh, Señor, you must help us!" she whispered urgently. "My dear sister is to be shot tomorrow, and I cannot even see her to tell her I love her and to be brave! Oh, Señor! What will I do?"

Fallon looked at the women and saw they were all looking at him expectantly.

"Where are the soldiers camped, Señora?" he asked, stalling for time to think.

"They are to the south on the edge of town in a grove of trees," one of the women whispered. "The officers left a sergeant in charge while they came into town to drink to their success in capturing Paloma and the runaway slaves, *los cimarrones*."

"How do you know this?" Fallon asked. It really was the café where all was known.

"There are the Spanish officers," Paloma's sister fairly spat out, nodding to the three officers at the end of the bar. "Colonel Munoz is the one in charge, the big man with the medals."

Aja studied the officers carefully, watched them laugh and drink and talk in loud voices, though he couldn't hear what they said. Fallon was quiet, his mind trying to sort through the obstacles to success in getting the rebels and Paloma out of prison. Then Aja tugged on Fallon's sleeve.

"Captain, sir," he said quietly. "There is something I learned as a boy: *Without a leader, black ants are confused.* I know this to be true, for I have seen it many times."

Aja nodded in the direction of the Spanish officers, and Fallon smiled, Aja once again surprising him with his wisdom. It was time for action.

"Aja, back to the ship quickly, and tell Colquist I want something strong enough to put three men to sleep for a week! Hurry now!" Aja smiled a broad smile, aware that events were going to move fast and that he was playing some part in them.

Fallon turned his attention back to the short-haired women.

"Ladies, we are going to attempt to rescue Paloma and the *cimarrones* tonight," he whispered. He had their attention now, their eyes drying, their mouths coming open at this turn of events. "But we need your help."

"Anything, Señor!" said Paloma's sister, and all the women nodded vigorously. "Ask us to do anything!"

COLONEL MUNOZ and his junior officers were quite happy with themselves. Their unit had been efficient and relentless, unlike many units in the Spanish army, and upon their return to Havana they were hoping for medals, or promotions, or both. Capturing the rebel Young David had put paid to a dangerous movement in Cuba, and they knew it. And they knew the Spanish authorities knew it.

The officers were not popular in the café, of course. They had one end of the bar to themselves, in fact. The barkeep had served them perfunctorily, without welcome or comment, but Munoz expected no less because the beautiful woman he'd captured with Young David was from Matanzas. Well, he thought, she brought it on herself.

His junior officers were becoming quite drunk, and Munoz was feeling the effects of the drinks himself. He was on the verge of calling it a night when the barkeep returned to their end of the bar with a decidedly friendlier manner. She was actually smiling! Perhaps she'd finally noticed him!

Well, he thought, *one more round wouldn't hurt.*

BACK ABOARD *RASCAL*, Fallon paced the deck deep in apprehension. That damn cannon wouldn't give them a chance coming through the gate, even if they could knock it down. It would be a slaughter, not a rescue.

He plunged back below decks to his cabin to study the layout of the fort again. Wharton had left the cabin and the engineer was still fast asleep on the stern cushions as Fallon lit several candles and moved them close to illuminate the plans of the fort on his desk. It appeared the *guardias* were billeted to the back of the courtyard from the gate, putting them on the right side of the fort from where *Rascal* was tied. The prisoner cells, then, were directly opposite *Rascal* on the far side of the square.

So many times in Fallon's experience, the counterintuitive thought was the bolder course; the less predictable the better. So it was now. The sane approach would be to attempt to breach the gate in some way and kill the guards. But that was suicidal. That left the only alternative: Go through the walls. They were still weak from the explosions years before; maybe they were just weak enough.

Fallon called Barclay, Brooks, and Wharton together to review the plan that was forming even as he described it. He would do what he could to rescue as many as he could, but he had to protect the ship above all else.

"Mr. Barclay," Fallon said, "when will the tide ebb?"

"It will begin the ebb at five bells in the middle watch, sir." So, about 2:30 AM *Rascal* would begin to feel the gentle tug of the tide pulling her against her lines toward the harbor entrance.

"Very good," said Fallon. "Then at six bells we will launch an all-out assault on the fort. I am allowing us fifteen minutes at the most before the soldiers get organized and reach the fort to counter-attack. By then I want to be on our way to sea."

No doubt it would take longer for the sergeant in charge to mo-bilize his troops, but it might also take even longer than that to get into the fort and extricate the prisoners, not to mention the treasury. Fallon wanted time on his side.

"In the meantime, Mr. Brooks," Fallon said, "please have this engineer carried to shore and laid upon the beach. I believe he has served his purpose aboard this ship. Now, as to the plan . . ."

THE SPANISH OFFICERS moved to a table to finish their drinks, feeling too tired or drunk to stand at the bar. The café became no-ticeably quieter, the few locals having left for the evening and the only remaining patrons the husbands of the short-haired women. They stood at the bar nursing their drinks and keeping a wary eye on the officers.

Slowly, their words slurring, the officers began going to sleep at the table. First, the junior officers put their heads down and, finally, Colonel Munoz himself was overcome by tiredness. At the last, he tried to wake his junior officers but found he hadn't the energy to even shake them. Sleep seemed so welcoming, calling to him to re-lax just for a moment, for tomorrow would come soon enough.

THE RASCALS were to get charcoal from the cook's stove and rub their faces black, then strip to their waists and rub everything black that was white. Fallon had detailed thirty men for the assault and divided them up for specific duties once inside the fort.

Brooks would stay with the ship, over his objections, of course. He was to have hands ready to slip the lines and set the sails as soon as the crew was out of the fort and back aboard, hopefully with the prisoners and the town's treasury.

Just before four bells, Fallon called Brooks and Cully together— so black was Cully's face that his white hair seemed radiant in contrast.

"Cully, from the engineer's plans it looks like most of the weakness in the walls is on this side of the fort, right in front of us. That's where the explosives did their worst in '62. I want you to put a broadside into an imaginary circle on the wall six feet in diameter. Double shot the guns. We are at point blank range, and unless I am very much mistaken, we could lead a parade through that hole!"

"Mr. Brooks," Fallon continued. "Have the men armed with cutlasses and pistols and, once Cully has done his work, I will lead the crew through the wall. Each man knows his duty once inside. Are you clear, Cully?"

"Very clear, Nico!" responded Cully, showing his white teeth through his smile.

Aja stood nearby waiting for his orders, for he would be with the attack as well. Fallon had a special assignment for him.

"Aja, you are to get the jailer's keys as soon as he is down, hopefully by my hand. Get his keys and run like the wind across the courtyard to each cell, as many as you can, anyway, and free the prisoners. Be sure to find Paloma! Get everyone to stay together until my command, then get them quickly back to the ship. Understood?"

"Yes, Captain, sir!" said Aja with enthusiasm, relishing such an important role in the assault.

And, finally, a word with James Wharton. The agent had been hovering nearby, not anxious to go ashore with the crew but certainly wanting to be part of the attack.

"Mr. Wharton, would you be so good as to carefully count each man who comes back? We are sending thirty into the fort, and I want thirty back on board. No one is to be left behind."

"I will, Captain. You will have your men accounted for."

Now Fallon was at last satisfied that everything was planned that could be planned. He left to blacken his own face and body, for it was four bells in the middle watch, and there was not a moment to lose.

THIRTY-SEVEN

THE VILLAGE of Matanzas was asleep; the torches outside the cafés had all gone out and the clouds hid the moon. On board *Rascal*, those going ashore massed behind the gun crews and waited patiently for the attack on the fort to begin. For incentive, every man had been told about the Matanzas treasury just inside the walls.

Fallon stood behind Cully, his face and body black from charcoal, his sword in his hand. The ship moved slightly beneath his feet, tugging at her lines like a Thoroughbred ready to race, drawn by the ebb toward the sea. Slow match burned in a tub by each of the eight larboard guns, which were primed and double-shotted as Fallon had ordered. Cully had personally sighted each one with his good eye.

Fallon looked around at the blackened faces, the white eyes and teeth, and gripped the handle of his sword tightly.

"*Fire!*" he yelled, and *Rascal's* broadside roared out across the quay and into the side wall of the fort with a tremendous explosion that deafened the ears and temporarily blinded the crew. And the wall! Already weak, the wall seemed to shatter at the impact of sixteen cannon balls from short range in a concentrated spot. Stone blew back into the fort and the sill collapsed, leaving a hole the size of coach and four!

Immediately, Rascals poured through the opening and into the courtyard, pistols at the ready. The stunned *guardias* at the front gate turned to meet a spray of bullets that killed them instantly. Cully and his crew ran for the cannon, attacking the gunners who stood to their duty there. None was armed beyond swords—the cannon was their gun—and they went down quickly.

But here came the rest of the guards, even as the Rascals screamed and charged. The militia found it hard to aim at the blackened figures, and the screaming disoriented them. The Rascals dashed into the confusion, swinging their cutlasses like deadly scythes at anyone they didn't know.

Aja and Fallon moved quickly to the head jailer's room, and the moment the man opened the door Fallon brought his sword down on his arm, nearly severing it. The jailer made to scream but Aja had already raised his pistol and brought it down on the man's head, knocking him out. In a flash Aja began searching for the cell keys while Fallon stood guard. All the drawers of the desk were pulled out and the contents dumped on the bed next to the nightstand candle. Nothing. Aja held up the candle and quickly walked around the room, moving the light up and down, and finally the keys revealed themselves on a hook by the door. Grabbing them, Aja ran from the room and across the courtyard.

The fighting was intense outside the *guardias'* cells, but the surprise and ferocity of the attack had given the Rascals the upper hand. No quarter was given on either side, however, and the dust of the courtyard absorbed the blood of the wounded and dying. Fallon jumped into the fighting and rallied the crew against the *guardias*, who were half naked and losing ground, though they fought valiantly enough.

"Clear the courtyard!" Cully yelled, and his gun crew turned the courtyard cannon around to face the far wall and ran the gun toward the treasury. He brought the muzzle of the 6-pounder very close to the massive lock on the treasury door and ordered his men to stand back for fear of exploding splinters.

"*Fire!*" yelled Cully, and the cannon hurled its 6-pound ball at the lock. The *guardias* who were still fighting were momentarily stunned and distracted by the explosion, and the Rascals swung their cutlasses in murderous arcs, decapitating some and horribly wounding the rest.

Now it was a mad dash to the treasury room, where the shattered door stood open and the town of Matanzas' coffers were revealed. Strongboxes were stacked against the side walls halfway to the ceiling, and the Rascals fell on them quickly. Then something like a reception line was formed to get the heavy boxes out and to the ship. Time was running out, and at any moment the soldiers or even other militia would be upon them.

Aja opened each cell door and called for the prisoner to step out and get down. When Young David emerged, he grasped Aja's shoulders and smiled at him, Aja smiling back in the darkness. At the last of the cells, Paloma Campos stepped out cautiously. She had watched the fighting in fascination—all the prisoners had— but it was not until Aja opened her cell door that she knew who was *doing* the fighting. She was led to the group of prisoners, all the rebels, including Young David, and told to kneel down. It wouldn't do for a stray bullet to kill one of them after so much effort and bloodshed had been expended.

But the fighting was almost over. At a yell from Fallon, Aja moved the prisoners quickly across the courtyard just behind the last of the crew helping the wounded and carrying the strongboxes. In a moment, everyone was through the hole in the wall and running down the quay toward *Rascal*.

All except Young David.

"I am not going, my brother," he said to Aja, pulling him aside.

"What?" Aja exclaimed. "You can't stay here! They will catch you and kill you!" Aja was beside himself, for surely all this hadn't been for nothing!

"Yes, probably," said Young David calmly. "But my life, however humble, is here. My purpose is here. Go, my little brother. You will always have my thanks for saving me yet again."

With that, Young David turned and ran in the direction of the beach, past a crowd that was already forming but warily staying back. Aja stared after him, anguish in his chest, trying to comprehend his decision but there was no time to think it out. In the distance he could see the torches of the soldiers, who were moving rapidly toward the fort.

"Aja!" ordered Fallon in exasperation. "Hurry!"

Rascal had slipped her bow line and was about to slip her stern line when Aja leapt aboard. When he rose to face a clearly agitated captain, there were tears in his eyes, and Fallon wisely put his arm around his shoulders instead of berating him for holding up the ship.

"Mr. Wharton," Fallon called. "All aboard?"

"All aboard, sir! Mostly in one piece!" answered Wharton.

Brooks ordered the fore-staysail sheeted home, and Barclay edged *Rascal* away from the quay and out of the harbor on the ebb tide and a small land breeze. Fallon could see the soldiers were just arriving at the fort to sort through the situation, but he hoped that by the time they figured it out, *Rascal* would be well out of musket range. And, besides, the early morning was still very dark.

There was much to do. Colquist was tending to the wounded, of which there were twelve with serious lacerations or other wounds. Thankfully, none of the Rascals had been killed. Surprise had been on their side, for a guard half asleep bursting from his quarters with his trousers around his ankles will always be a poor shot. Paloma Campos had been invited to rest below in Fallon's cabin but she elected to stay on deck, standing at the taffrail, watching her home and family recede into the blackness. Aja stood next to her, two conspirators in freeing Young David, bonded together forever.

Fallon gathered the prisoners and offered them the choice of joining the ship or being put ashore in Antigua as free men. He spoke English and Spanish and French to them, and then Aja spoke his own native language to them in hopes they could understand what was being offered. Surprisingly, they all opted to join the ship, though no one knew exactly what that meant. The prospect

of freedom was wonderful, but freedom in a strange place with nowhere to work and earn a living, when all they'd ever known was
servitude, was confusing and overwhelming. What they *did* understand was that they were no longer slaves and no longer prisoners,
and it was because of these wild men painted black. So, gratitude
played a part in their decision to stay aboard. Brooks would begin
forming them into something like sailors tomorrow.

The strongboxes were arrayed on the deck to be opened in daylight in front of all hands. Who knew what was inside? But as heavy
as they were, it was good odds that the men would be very happy.
It had certainly been an easier way to make money than facing
broadsides.

Fallon approached Paloma quietly, and Aja thought it best to
move away. Fallon could well imagine she would wonder where they
were bound, and her options had to be discussed.

"Paloma," he began, "I trust you were not harmed in the
fighting?"

She turned to face him and almost gasped at his black face and
skin, now streaked with sweat and grime.

"No, I am fine. I am just trying to absorb what's happened,
Captain Fallon. Aja said I was due to be shot in a very few hours,
and now I am aboard your ship! I am very, very grateful to you and
your men, sir. I can honestly say that when Aja opened my cell door
it was the biggest shock of my life!"

"I can well imagine, Señora," replied Fallon. "You should know
that your sister and several of her friends made it possible for us to
rescue you. They drugged the Spanish army officers and put them
to sleep. I'm hopeful the women can disappear for a while into the
hills until the soldiers leave, or there will be repercussions. But once
the officers were asleep, all we had to do was get into the fort and
get you out."

"I see," said Paloma, knowing there was more to it than just getting into the fort and rescuing a few prisoners. "I thought I saw my
sister in the crowd on the beach as we left. Of course, it was very

dark. But she will know I am safe, and that's what matters. But, Captain, *why?* Why did you rescue all of us? I can't imagine the reason to risk your life like that!"

"We have hurt Spain by blowing up her fort and taking her money," he replied matter-of-factly. "And we have done it under the military's nose." He paused. "And I have kept my word to a friend."

"May I ask who was the friend?" she said, holding her breath for the answer.

"I believe you know, Paloma. And we should talk about whether you want to go to Antigua."

THIRTY-EIGHT

THREE DAYS out of Bermuda, Somers was still not sure about Stuyvesant or the wisdom of having hired him as captain of *Petite Bouton*. He was a rough sort and given to drink, but it hadn't seemed to interfere with running the ship. There were a few men from *Petite*'s prize crew, and the rest were from *Drummond* or off other packets. At Somers's insistence, Stuyvesant practiced them at the guns for the first few days.

Petite Bouton was a fine sailor on her clean bottom. The sails were old and patched, but they still drew well and the miles seemed to roll by day and night. Somers noticed the men seemed happy enough; well, he was paying them very well. But each day Stuyvesant came on deck later, and each evening turned in earlier. And there was something disquieting in the way he looked at Elinore. She first reported it to Somers when they were coming aboard. It wasn't a leer, exactly, but its close cousin. Somers took to carrying a small pistol in his belt, hidden from view.

The weather was cloudy and portentous all week, but perhaps it had all been a bluff, for nothing hazardous or troubling had beset them. The ship was steady on a beam reach, and would be all the way to Antigua. Somers wanted speed, and he was getting it from the French-built sloop. Stuyvesant knew how to sail fast, give him that.

Ahead was the unknown, but Somers and Elinore were going to help their friend Beauty through whatever had befallen her, and the prospect of seeing Fallon again brought Elinore joy. The fresh salt air had improved her health wonderfully, and she reveled in the wind and spray, not caring if she got soaked to the skin.

The ship was still sailing under patchy clouds when the sun finally broke out and bathed the world in warm, yellow light. Somers dozed in his chair at the stern and Elinore came on deck to a blue sea of whitecaps and a glorious breeze. Stuyvesant was at the binnacle, sipping from his flask as he had been all day, and he watched Elinore on the windward rail embracing the weather. Her hair was wild in the wind, blowing around her face, unmanageable and free. Spray rose up from the bow, creating rainbows in the air, and flying fish seemed to race over the tops of the waves to keep pace with the ship.

Finally, Elinore was soaked through and, as the sun had gone behind a white cloud again and the air had turned cooler, she went below to change. Stuyvesant looked over his shoulder at Somers, asleep in his chair, his head on his chest. Taking another nip from his flask, then another, he made for the companionway and went below.

Elinore had just slipped off her wet dress in her small cabin when Stuyvesant opened the door and stepped inside.

"Get out!" she ordered. "Get out this instant or I'll scream!"

He pulled a knife from his trousers and waved it at her face.

"You wouldn't want to do that, Missy," he sneered. "Your captain friend wouldn't like you so much without a nose!" And he moved to her quickly, holding the knife to her startled eyes with one hand, tearing at her undergarments with the other. Elinore backed away, screaming, and kicked at him, but he ripped her bodice and pushed her down on her small cot. His weight was smothering, and he fumbled with the buttons on his trousers with his free hand. Elinore made to scream again but he pushed the knife blade's tip against her throat.

"Shut up, you bitch!" he hissed. "You're going to like this!"

Suddenly there was the cold steel click of a pistol's hammer being cocked.

"Mr. Stuyvesant," said Somers, the rage hissing from his lips even as he tried to remain completely under control. "Rise up slowly and drop your knife. Don't hesitate. *Do it now.*"

Stuyvesant took a moment to decide, for his alcohol-riddled mind was having trouble sorting through options. Finally, he pushed himself up off Elinore, dropped his knife to the floor, and started to turn toward Somers. His penis was still hanging out of his trousers, and he made to put it back in.

"Don't, Stuyvesant," said Somers in barely contained fury as he moved to one side of the cabin. "Keep your hands up. Walk to the door and up the companionway steps, if you please."

Elinore was trembling in fear and anger, but as Stuyvesant turned to walk past her father she reached for a coat to cover herself and followed Somers up the steps. Stuyvesant stumbled and lurched a little at the top of the companionway from the roll of the ship, then stepped into the sunshine with Somers behind him holding the small pistol.

"Walk to the leeward railing," Somers ordered. And Stuyvesant did as he was told, though he was looking furtively side to side at the crew, hoping for intervention. But the crew saw the situation clearly; saw Stuyvesant's member hanging out the front of his trousers; saw Elinore's terrified face; saw Somers at a boil. No one moved.

At the railing, Somers ordered Stuyvesant to turn around and, as he did so, Somers raised the short barrel of the pistol to point at his face. Stuyvesant's eyes widened and his jaw went slack. Elinore walked up to Somers's side, her eyes locked on Stuyvesant.

"Do you know Heraclitus, sir?" asked Somers, trying to keep his voice calm and steady, but appearing *interested* in the answer.

Stuyvesant looked at Somers with wild, bloodshot eyes, his greasy hair blowing about his face.

"Can't say that we ever met, your honor," he said, speaking out of both sides of his sneer.

"Heraclitus believed a man's character was his fate," said Somers, his voice low and dark. "Which means you're fucked."

Stuyvesant's eyes blinked and focused on the barrel of the gun pointed at his head. He was consequently slow to see Elinore's roundhouse swing on the way, her arm arcing from her toes, her fist bunched and carrying rage and fury and rough justice when it met his soft, fleshy face. Stuyvesant staggered momentarily, his head snapping back, throwing his weight outboard just as the ship fell off a wave. His arms flailed in the air for an imaginary hold but it was too late.

He was over and gone, lost in the tossing seas, and Somers had no intention of turning back.

THIRTY-NINE

IF THERE WAS a more fortunate ship afloat than *Rascal*, Fallon could not imagine it. When the Matanzas treasure had been opened for all to see, it was a veritable fortune. Brooks had taken charge of counting it out, slowly and carefully, and then twice to be sure. Every man would have more gold and silver than he'd ever seen at one time, or *imagined* seeing at one time. Perhaps this accounted for the crisp sail handling and smooth tacks as the schooner made her way against the building seas and wind down the coast of Cuba. Even the dousing spray could not dampen the crew's spirits.

Fallon's spirits were not immune to success, either. His lowness was gone, replaced by the old optimism with which he usually greeted each morning. The sky was infinitely blue, the sun warming. Indeed, he thought, today was a day when anything could happen.

When the treasure had been securely stored in the holds at last, *Rascal* was well past the tip of Cuba with Anvil Hill far astern, a table-topped mountain with scarped sides rising more than two thousand feet into the air. Barclay called for a long larboard tack to take them below Hispaniola into the Caribbean Sea.

"Deck there!" came the call from the lookout. "Sail to the northeast!"

Aja appeared with Fallon's telescope, but he could see nothing from the deck. The sail could be anything, of course. But it could also be *something*.

"Deck there!" the lookout yelled. "It's a ship-of-the-line, sir! Turning north for Saint-Domingue. I see a French tricolor!"

Now that was something, thought Fallon. Why would a French ship be calling at Port-au-Prince? Particularly a ship-of-the-line? An emissary? A signal from France, flexing her muscle? Of course, he thought of Louverture, and the secret letter portending a French invasion, and the first cloud of the day came over his face. It was troubling; no, it was more than troubling. And Davies would want to know about it. Barclay looked at him as if asking whether to change course, but Fallon shook his head, *no*. He would learn nothing by chasing a French ship into Port-au-Prince; better to return to English Harbor with the news.

It was then that Paloma Campos came on deck looking wonderfully refreshed and radiant. No wonder Davies was smitten, thought Fallon. She was dressed in ship's slops, which had never looked that good on anyone else, and her hair was blowing about her tanned face. She waved to Aja on the larboard railing and then approached Fallon with a smile on her face.

"You are looking very well, Paloma," he said, returning her smile. "We have left Cuba astern and are making a long board to Antigua and English Harbor, where, if I am not mistaken, a certain admiral is even now pacing the deck of his flagship."

"I hope you are right, Captain," she said, blushing through her tan. "Because you have gone to a very lot of trouble if he isn't!"

THE EASTERLY WIND had increased dramatically and was gusting to forty knots. The waves opened like mouths, their upper lips curled with menace, the white froth trailing like spit behind them. *Petite Bouton* struggled to hold the course that was Somers's best guess for Antigua. Sails had been reefed, of course, and the little sloop had tacked against the strong wind bravely. Somers knew little about running a ship, though he owned many of them, but he knew they were making much too much leeway. The navigational problem was that cloudy skies had precluded noon sights, which one of the crew knew how to do, or even steering by the stars, for that matter. So, their exact position was a mystery, and becoming more so. Though they had plenty of sea room, Somers grew concerned, having lost confidence in his dead reckoning. Well, perhaps tonight or tomorrow would give them something to steer by.

Elinore had not recovered from the shock of finding Stuyvesant in her cabin bent on rape, and spent her afternoons standing in the cleansing spray of the ship, shivering. Somers wisely let her be. They were still six hundred miles—a guess—from English Harbor and, if she was not herself by the time they got there, he hoped caring for Beauty would set her to rights. He'd taken everything of Stuyvesant's and thrown it overboard, but the bastard's memory was still aboard.

The responsibility for hiring Stuyvesant weighed on him. He'd been too eager to leave Bermuda and had imprudently jumped at the chance to be away. He thought he could manage any situation that Stuyvesant might create, rough as he was, and perhaps he had *managed* it. But at what cost to Elinore?

It was two days since Stuyvesant had fallen overboard, and Elinore still had not spoken of it. That afternoon he'd asked her to have dinner with him, and she'd demurred. He'd pressed, and she'd finally relented. His intention was to bring comfort if she'd accept it.

The meal was in *Petite Bouton*'s captain's cabin, such as it was, for she was only a sloop. Though the ship was thrashing badly in the relentless east wind, Somers's steward had produced something of a meal, and the old man and his daughter braced themselves against the table as best they could. After a brief prayer of thanksgiving delivered by Somers, they began eating in silence. Somers watched his daughter carefully.

"You are wondering if I can go on as before," said Elinore quietly, intuitive as always.

"Yes, I suppose I am," admitted Somers. "What happened was a horrible thing, I know. Unimaginable to a man. How can I make the world safe for you again?"

Elinore stopped eating and looked at her father, that good man whom she'd grown to love and accept over these past years in spite of barely abiding him all the years before. He was doing his best.

"I'm afraid you can't make the world safe for me anymore, Father," she said, reaching for his hand. "I'm not a child and I know too much. But hear me: I love you for trying."

Somers was visibly relieved. First, because she was talking to him. And second, she seemed to be forgiving him for hiring Stuyvesant in the first place. Well, now that he was dead, at any rate.

"I should tell you that I will be fine, but I was never worried for myself. Not even when . . . when . . . you know."

"But who were you worried for?" asked Somers, obviously surprised.

"My baby," Elinore said quietly. "I'm pregnant, Father."

RASCAL MOVED deep into the Caribbean Sea, heeled over in the gusts of the strengthening wind, before tacking north again toward Saint-Domingue and then, later, toward the western boundary of Santo Domingo.

Brooks had the ship well-managed in the blustery conditions. It was doubtful he'd ever sailed so close to the water since he'd joined the Royal Navy. It was real sailing for him, with every rise and fall of the ship telling him something as opposed to the muted movements of a frigate or a ship-of-the-line. Brooks had wisely taken in the top hamper in the rising wind and seas, and had ordered a reef in the courses. *Rascal* was comfortable enough, if wet.

Unfortunately, *Rascal*'s movements were apparently not kind to James Wharton's stomach, and he spent much of his time below decks in distress. Colquist could do nothing for him, for the usual remedies seemed not to apply. By the fourth day out of Matanzas, the surgeon grew concerned, and then quite concerned, for Wharton sank into unconsciousness. Fallon was called below, for Colquist felt something was going on besides seasickness. *What?*

was the question. Colquist suspected something was constricting Wharton's intestines, or perhaps he had a heart ailment, or his lungs were failing. In other words, Colquist had no idea why James Wharton was sick. Well, the man wasn't a doctor of physic, and the intricacies of the human body were largely a mystery to him. Dressing a wound or amputating a limb were more in his line.

Fallon was by Wharton's bedside as much as possible, but his conversation and even his hand-holding seemed to have little effect. So it was, on a long board away from Santo Domingo, that James Wharton quietly died. It was a sad affair to bury him at sea, with only his name and his secrets. His death brought a pall over the ship, for he had become popular with the crew. Still, seamen so used to death mourned him as a right shipmate and let him go, along with his memory.

Fallon grieved as he had rarely grieved for a shipmate. He felt he had made a friend in Wharton, though he had to admit that he actually knew very little about him save his childhood and his bravery. It was how the intelligence agent wanted it, perhaps how he had to have it to be successful and stay alive. But now that he was dead, what had it mattered?

It was the afternoon of the morning burial and Fallon was in his cabin going over charts to keep his melancholy at bay. He heard Barclay order the ship to go about on the starboard tack, which would take them toward Santo Domingo yet again, the ship making slow progress to Antigua. Instinct or boredom led Fallon to set the chart aside and climb the companionway to have a look at the land with his telescope.

"Deck there!" came the lookout's call. "Three sail off the starboard bow! Coming out of port!"

Well, that was to be expected, thought Fallon, remembering the river called Rio Ozama from his chart. Santo Domingo had a large enough port that ships would be coming and going. Still, it was an *enemy* port, and it was best to stay clear of 3-1 odds in case of trouble. They were miles away from the sails, which he could not see from the deck, so he felt no apprehension.

Rascal held her course and Fallon conferred with Barclay on the distance left to sail for Antigua, for he was anxious to deliver the news of the French ship-of-the-line and eager to see Beauty's progress. Seeing Paloma in Davies' arms would be something special as well. It was a romantic thought, and he held onto it right up until the lookout shouted down again.

"Deck there! Out of the port! Two sloops and a black brig!"

Well, well, thought Fallon as he snapped out of his reverie. *The little wolves.*

FORTY

ARCLAY ESTIMATED the little wolves to be six miles ahead, tacking against the strong easterly wind and apparently making for the eastern Caribbean, just as they were. Now the wolves were being followed, at least for the moment, and Barclay looked at Fallon with a quizzical eye, wondering what his captain was thinking.

Fallon was wondering what he was thinking himself. Revenge was a fickle thing, and chasing it was often a fool's errand. He couldn't let his wounded pride make his decisions. And yet . . . it was likely that the Holy One's lookout had seen *Rascal*, but unlikely he could recognize the ship from such a distance bow-on. It was also likely that the ships had been in the port of Santo Domingo for wood and water after the long trip to and from Cuba. Now they were off hunting again. Fallon decided to lie back and keep his identity from being discovered for as long as possible.

Aja stood near Fallon at the windward rail while *Rascal* was on the starboard tack, concern etched on his forehead. He had kept to himself since leaving Matanzas and tempered his joy of rescuing the prisoners with the sadness of seeing Young David refuse to come aboard.

"Captain, sir," he said to Fallon. "Where do you think Young David went when he left us?"

"I think he went back to the country," said Fallon as compassionately as he could. "Back to burn fields and free the slaves he found. God help him."

"He will never be captured alive again, will he?"

"No, Aja, I'm afraid not. He wouldn't let that happen again," answered Fallon. "One day we may hear about a brave and resourceful African slave who refused the life he was kidnapped into and risked everything for freedom. He might be as famous as Louverture."

Aja hung his head.

"Try not to be sad. Young David made his choice and we must agree with it," said Fallon softly. "You gave him the chance to have that choice, and he took it. Respect him now, for God willing we could all be so brave at a moment like that."

The boy looked out to sea, thinking. Fallon let him be, and finally Aja walked away, his head up now, more proud than sad. Aja had pictured his friend afraid and hiding. But Fallon had drawn a different picture, with Young David astride a white horse, waving a sword and calling slaves to freedom. It was a new, sustaining picture that Aja could almost imagine.

THE LOOKOUT aboard *Negro Sol* had reported a sail in the distance and believed it to be a schooner, but it flew no flag he could see. The Holy One was not concerned by a single ship, though he wondered for a moment if it was the American schooner that had mauled his sloops and then appeared in Matanzas. That would be too much of a coincidence, he decided, and even if it were the same schooner she would be no match for the combined firepower of his little fleet, now at full strength. The schooner had run once, she would run again. That possibility addressed, he returned his attention to his good fortune in the sale of hundreds of slaves at the market in Matanzas. It was a long way to take them, but the Cuban prices!

Raiding plantations had now become his new business, and he pointed his ships to Porto Rico for, though the island was controlled by Spain, it was a plentiful source of slaves. The Holy One was ambivalent when it came to which countries he robbed. The lowlands of Porto Rico were covered in sugarcane plantations whose fields sprawled to the sea. That's all that mattered.

The wind was becoming a problem, however, and the sloops had already taken in one reef and were asking for permission to take in another. The Holy One decided to anchor in the Bahia Salinas on the southeastern Porto Rican coast, not only to get his ships out of the wind but because the tall stacks of the sugar mills on shore were like beacons guiding him toward inestimable riches.

PETITE BOUTON was struggling in the worsening conditions of wind and sea, and Somers knew they were far off course. With no land to windward, the seas had a long fetch and had grown so large that tacking was dangerous. And, too, several of the crew were below with injuries from wrestling a cannon whose carriage had come loose. Nothing that wouldn't mend eventually, but they were effectively absent from their duties in handling the ship. With the wind rising to a shriek, the little sloop was pitching and plunging wildly, making considerable leeway to the west with every wave and gust. Somers had done his best to navigate, but he had no real idea of their position until he saw an island in the distance that, after consulting with the chart, he confirmed as Porto Rico. The sloop was far off course, indeed.

FALLON CLIMBED the ratlines to see the little wolves for himself. It was coming on to the second dog and the sun was behind *Rascal*, giving him a good view of the ships far ahead. The little wolves were on the starboard tack, while *Rascal* had gone about on the larboard tack, effectively sailing away from them. Still, the point wasn't to overtake the little wolves but merely to keep them in sight until an opportunity presented itself.

Fallon decided to have a word with his first mate.

"Mr. Brooks, the wind and seas continue to set us farther south on this tack. I would like to keep a loose cover on those ships," he said, pointing to his left in the direction of the little wolves. "Perhaps you can just see them from the deck now."

Brooks looked at the distant ships through his telescope. They were still quite far away and now on a long tack to the north.

"Is that the black brig we saw in Matanzas unloading slaves?" he asked.

"Yes," answered Fallon, "I believe he is a Spanish pirate who usually sails with those two sloops and raids slavers. Aja calls them *the little wolves*, for they hunt in a pack. For now, I want to see where they are going and what they're up to, if possible. At least while there is light."

Brooks instantly called for a starboard tack and *Rascal* slowly came about on her new course, roughly parallel with the brig and sloops but at least three miles astern. Fallon looked down the starboard railing at Paloma and Aja talking, the boy no doubt acquainting the *señora* with the little wolves. Fallon still had no plan to attack, and if they sailed through the strait between Santo Domingo and Porto Rico he would not catch them before night fell, at any rate, though *Rascal* was a better sailer than any of them.

His curiosity was piqued, however. He raised his telescope to scan the distant shoreline of Porto Rico's southern coast. He could see the spires of sugar mill smokestacks but little else save the green, undulating hillsides.

Where are you going? he wondered.

It was a decision Somers hated to make but one he was forced to. He ordered the ship to fall off and sail down toward the western end of Porto Rico. There was no sensible or safe way to continue tacking against the prevailing easterly, strong as it was, with a depleted crew and evening coming on. No, better to get into the lee of Porto Rico and anchor for the night, snug and secure in a quiet cove. Then, in the morning, fresh and rested, they could resume their journey to Antigua. Elinore was down below with morning sickness, or seasickness, or both. She had been sick all day, and Somers had to think of her well-being as well.

The shock of hearing she was with child had quite given way to joy at being a grandfather. He had no care for the scandal her pregnancy might cause on Bermuda. He was only concerned for her happiness and her health, and the gossips on Bermuda could go to hell. Of course, he wasn't the one who would be most affected by gossip, he admitted. But Elinore had enough of his blood in her veins that he doubted she would care either.

He thought briefly of Fallon's reaction, if and when they caught up to him. He was a good man, an honorable man, and he seemed to love Elinore deeply. There would be a wedding, by God! He was as sure of it as he was of his own name.

But first they had to get to shelter and get the damned anchor down.

FORTY-ONE

*P*ETITE BOUTON's crew was able to get the little ship to the western coast of Porto Rico without difficulty, and when they were in the lee of the island the wind and sea were dramatically moderated by the land. Somers had consulted the chart and chosen Bahia Salinas as an anchorage for the night. It was well down the coast and would give them an excellent jumping off place the next day to resume their journey to English Harbor. They sailed comfortably southward, and when they finally arrived at Bahia Salinas the bay was empty and the backdrop of the island was lush and golden in the late afternoon light. When the anchor was finally down and the sails furled, Somers sent the hands to supper. With a last look around he went below to check on Elinore.

THE HOLY One led the way in *Negro Sol* toward the southwestern tip of Porto Rico, and then the sails were eased to round Rojo Cabo to starboard before proceeding up the coast to Bahia Salinas. His ships were sailing quite close to the coast of Porto Rico now and the smokestacks were clearly visible without a telescope. The Holy One never smiled, but his upper lip did curl slightly at the thought of his ships' holds stuffed with black gold by dawn.

It would fall to the two sloops, *Bella* and *Estrella Azul,* to anchor as close to shore in Bahia Salinas as possible, not least because the Holy One wanted many slaves tonight and that would mean rowing back and forth from shore to ship to load them. Typically, each sloop sent fifteen men ashore, moving to the mill smokestacks that were visible against the sky. This led them to the barracoons where the slaves slept. If the overseer appeared while they were stealing the slaves, he was killed. If the planter appeared, he was killed as well. No one had any value except the slaves.

The sloop captains had been aware of the distant sail shadowing them, aware that in all probability it was the schooner that had bedeviled them with a surprise attack at dawn and watched them in Matanzas, but they had no real concern as they were protected by the brig. In very little time they would be anchored for the night close in shore with *Negro Sol* anchored farther seaward, which would prevent any surprises.

The Holy One hated surprises.

Well, he hated them unless they were a gift dropped right into his lap. *What is this?* the Holy One thought as *Negro Sol* entered Bahia Salinas. *A lone sloop anchored for the night? A third sloop for his little fleet!*

He signaled for *Bella* and *Estrella* to do their work.

FALLON WAITED until the little wolves had rounded Rojo Cabo before deciding to follow them. The day was beginning to lose its light, and he worried briefly that his pride made the decision—a reaction to the impotence and humiliation he'd felt in Matanzas. Well, he had to admit that maybe wounded pride was some of the reason. But the rest of the reason had to do with the evil he felt emanating from the Holy One, an evil made more immoral by promoting unspeakable misery while presuming to be a man of God. That *offended* Fallon and called up a sort of righteous indignation he'd never experienced before.

Rascal would be no threat to a brig and two sloops in a straight-up fight, of course, but Fallon had no intention of fighting a straight-up fight. He would simply let events take their course until he lost sight of them, then call off the chase. That was the deal he made with his pride, at any rate.

The wind was still blowing hard, and *Rascal* rolled and plunged in the seas in spite of the best efforts of the helmsman to steer small. Paloma went down below, with a word to Aja that she didn't feel well, and Fallon wasn't surprised. She was a landswoman, though this sea would test anyone's stomach.

"Mr. Brooks," said Fallon to his first lieutenant. "We'll be going around Rojo Cabo soon and I don't want to be caught out if the little wolves are waiting for a fight. Pray have all the guns loaded but not run out. Ask Cully to load the long nine, as well."

"Aye, aye, sir!" said Brooks with relish, for the long day tacking back and forth had made him eager to catch the little wolves in spite of Fallon's orders to shadow them loosely. The chase had sorely tested his patience and the call to load the guns excited him, though 3-1 odds were more than he had ever faced in battle.

Here was Aja at Fallon's side with his captain's sword, anticipating that action could be around the corner, as it were. The little wolves held a special fascination for him, a dark kind of fascination, primarily owing to his last vision of the Holy One on the quarterdeck of *Negro Sol*, the silver cross around his neck, standing with his eyes closed and arms outstretched to the sky, praying. *Praying*—while he sailed away from the miserable wretches he'd sold into a life of unspeakable horror. Aja looked at Fallon, cool as always, and wondered if he, too, was secretly hoping the ships were waiting. But they were about to round Rojo Cabo, and all would become known very soon.

SOMERS WAS CALLED to come on deck immediately. Three ships were entering the bay, and the quiet anchorage he'd chosen was suddenly not quiet. *Petite Bouton* lay with her stern facing the sea, her guns useless against the advancing ships. The black brig and two sloops were coming from the southwest and, if they held course, would pass *Petite* rather too close to be friendly.

"Load the larboard guns, quickly!" he ordered, figuring the guns might bear if the oncoming ships chose not to pass between *Petite* and the shore. "Load and run out!" And then, as an afterthought, "Have the colors run up!"

If these ships were hostile, Somers at least wanted to make a fight of it, although they had no chance as it stood. The ships had no colors up as yet, but he could see them bearing down on *Petite Bouton* now, and it didn't look good. Quickly, he went down below to tell Elinore to stay there.

And to get his pistols.

FORTY-TWO

Lookout there, any sign of the ships?" yelled Fallon with growing anxiety.

"No, sir!" came the shout to the deck.

That meant they'd gone into one of the bays to the north, presumably for the night. It all seemed normal enough, Fallon thought, and he was about to call off the chase. Then he heard the cannons.

"*What the devil?*" blurted from his lips. *Those were broadsides, by God!*

"Mr. Brooks! Up with the colors, if you please," he called. "And call all hands, all hands! And get the boats over the side quickly! Aja, get the freedmen below deck with Paloma, please!" He knew the former rebel slaves would be a nuisance on deck and likely to get hurt if it came to a fight.

Suddenly, all thoughts of a 3-1 disadvantage disappeared. The ship sprang into action, Barclay tweaking the sails to gain an extra half knot of speed. In very little time the gun crews were at the ready with pistols and cutlasses in their belts. The cannon fire thundered louder now, reverberating ominously across the water.

Slowly, *Rascal* rounded into Bahia Salinas and the war before them was beautifully bathed by late afternoon light. Fallon gasped, for there was *Petite Bouton*, the very same sloop he'd captured and sent to Bermuda, under fire from the little wolves! The smoke made it difficult to see but it was clear that *Petite* was all but overwhelmed, though the British ensign still flew. Fallon looked at the situation to try to see a tactical advantage where he could inter-vene, but *Negro Sol* was hove-to and *Bella* and *Estrella* were sailing back and forth firing into *Petite* at will. As he looked, *Petite* got off a ragged broadside, though Fallon couldn't see any damage done. The smoke cleared, and through his telescope Fallon saw a white-haired man limping around behind *Petite's* larboard battery, waving a pistol like a madman and urging his men on.

"Good God!" exclaimed Fallon out loud. *Ezra Somers!*

"Cully! The long nine for *Negro Sol!*" yelled Fallon, desperate to attract the Holy One's attention. *Rascal* was still over a quarter of a mile away from the brig, in quiet water, for the breeze was notice-ably less in the lee of the land. There was still some light—perhaps enough for Cully to get a lucky shot.

The one-eyed master gunner sighted the nine and yelled, *"Fire!"*

The ball was low and into *Sol's* hull, but it quickly got the Holy One's attention—and everyone else's, for that matter. Somers leapt into the air as the sloops broke off their attack on the hapless *Petite Bouton* and turned on this new intruder, a *remembered* ship.

And now *Negro Sol's* starboard battery fired a massive broadside, the shot erupting geysers around *Rascal* like large stones thrown into a pool of water. Only one ball came aboard, but it found the larboard bow and sent a chunk of railing into an unlucky crewman, his glistening guts splattering Cully and the rest of his gun crew.

But Cully calmly called for the man to be dragged below and urged his men to get on with reloading the nine. Within two minutes—a long two minutes—the gun was ready.

"Fire!" he yelled once again, and Fallon jerked his mind from the approaching sloops to see the fall of the shot. The long nine ex-ploded *Sol's* gig and two crewmen cartwheeled backward, speared with black splinters.

The sloops were both sailing toward *Rascal* now; one trailed the other so they effectively blocked another broadside from *Negro Sol* as the brig was still hove-to directly behind them. It was a pretty pickle, but not even a madman like the Holy One would fire on his own ships. Well, *probably* not.

"Mr. Brooks," Fallon said, "I'm going to harden up. You fire into that starboard sloop first, then I'll fall off toward the larboard sloop and you quickly run to the larboard guns! Tell Cully to make every shot count!"

But here was *Bella*, the starboard sloop, her black teeth showing, less than fifty yards ahead and closing fast. Fallon could see her men at the railing, and his last thought before Brooks opened fire with the starboard battery was how dirty they looked.

Rascal's guns fired one at a time, in perfect order, and her 12-pound cannons hurled their iron into *Bella's* hull and deck. Fallon could see some of her crew go down and her captain wave insolently before a ball tore his arm from his body. He looked at Fallon with surprise, his mouth open in a wordless scream before he whirled around and collapsed to the deck. When *Bella's* broadside came in return, it was uneven, but *Rascal's* forward-most gun was upended and two men near the foremast were killed with one ball. Then she was by!

Quickly, Brooks ran to the other side of the ship as *Estrella Azul* was almost to *Rascal* and running out her guns. Fallon ordered the helmsman to let *Rascal* fall off the wind and down toward the oncoming sloop. It was almost completely quiet now, and Fallon quickly looked for *Negro Sol*, fearing he had ignored her and she would be upon them in an instant. *She was weighing, by God!* Soon he would have a brig to fight besides the sloops, a fight Fallon knew he could not win.

"Fire!" came Brooks's order, and *Estrella* seemed to rock back from the hail of 12-pound balls slamming into her side, killing the men at the tiller and exploding the binnacle. *Estrella* veered away with no one steering, and her own broadside carried almost a mile into the Caribbean Sea.

That helped the odds immeasurably in Fallon's mind, but not

enough to save them. For there was *Negro Sol . . . what? . . .* she was
not sailing toward them! She was turning in a circle on her own
axis, *but why?* The brig swung slightly and Fallon had his answer:
Somers had managed to entangle *Petite*'s bowsprit in *Sol*'s foredeck
rigging, by God! The old man must have cut his anchor cable and
raised his mainsail and sailed right into the brig! He was pushing
the black ship in a circle!

The ships were at least a thousand yards away and *Sol*'s crew was
furiously hacking at *Petite*'s bowsprit, for such was the perpendicular angle of the two ships that the brig couldn't fire into the sloop
and the sloop couldn't fire into the brig. But there was Somers, a
crack shot with a pistol, picking off anyone who put their head up
over the rail. All of his crew were hiding and firing, as well, and
Petite Bouton's mainsail was well out to starboard, capturing and
holding the small land breeze and pushing the two ships around.

"Cully!" yelled Fallon, "back to the long nine for the brig!"

"Captain, sir!" called Aja. "*Bella* is coming back!"

Indeed, *Bella* was bearing down from the west demanding a second chance. At least, *Estrella* had drifted away—apparently when
the men at the binnacle had been lost the helm itself had been
blown apart. Her crew was fighting to control the ship with sails
alone.

"Cully! Fire when ready!" ordered Fallon. The words were barely
out of his mouth when the long nine came to life with a single,
thunderous roar and one of *Negro Sol*'s stern windows blew apart.
The 9-pound ball would likely travel the length of the ship, exploding splinters up through the deck and killing anyone in its path. At
the very least, Fallon thought ruefully, the Holy One would have
nowhere to sleep tonight.

Fallon ordered the larboard guns run out and *Rascal* edged up
to the west to meet *Bella*, which was very near now. But Brooks
was ready, and patient. *Bella*'s forward gun barked early, and it took
steely resolve for Brooks to hold fast until every shot could tell.

"*Fire!*" he yelled, and both broadsides fired at once, creating a combined explosion that nearly deafened anyone not killed. But Brooks was down with blood spurting from his neck, and crewmen were writhing around him, the life running out of them. Fallon could see Cully sprawled at the foot of the foremast; it was impossible to tell if he was alive.

Rascal had her larboard guns intact but had lost more men than could be tended to just then. Yet here was Colquist helping drag the wounded below to try to save their lives. Fallon quickly checked to see if the helmsman still steered. He did, white knuckles on the wheel, his eyes forward. Barclay lay nearby, moaning but not moving.

Fallon was unsteady himself. He staggered to the binnacle, blood running into his eyes from a scalp wound. Most of his crew was alive but must be rallied. He saw *Bella* sailing westward, toward *Estrella* far away, her boom dragging in the sea and her battle seemingly over. Fallon wiped the blood away from his eyes and could see that *Negro Sol* and *Petite Bouton* were still in their strange dance, not six hundred yards away, spinning slowly. Now *Sol* had caught the breeze and was pushing *Petite* back around so that the brig's shattered stern was facing *Rascal* again. Fallon could see the Holy One at the taffrail on the quarterdeck, facing the sinking sun, the last rays of daylight on his face. He stood with his arms outstretched to heaven as if asking for spiritual guidance from God. *A madman!*

Fallon knew he must act, and soon, but his mind could not focus. He wanted to close his eyes and rest, anything to escape a decision. He looked at Brooks's lifeless body and started to go to him but there was no time. A yell from a crewman, and Fallon saw that *Negro Sol* was free at last, her crew having hacked *Petite Bouton*'s bowsprit in half. Somers's crew was scrambling to get off a last broadside but the brig was drawing away, ignoring the little sloop and slowly turning to bring the land breeze on her larboard side as she crept toward *Rascal* bow-on. It was virtually dark now, the dusk breathing its last breath of day. But here was Aja, pleading with him for orders.

And then it was clear to him, the only path, an all-or-nothing chance.

"Aja!" Fallon said hoarsely. "Have the larboard guns loaded with chain-shot! Quickly, Aja! But don't run out, do you hear?"

Aja called to the powder boys to run for chain-shot, balls joined with chain that could cut through rigging like a scythe. The ships were drawing closer even in the light air, and Aja quickly took charge of the larboard gun crew. The guns were swabbed as the ship's boys brought the chain-shot on deck to each gun to be loaded and rammed home. It took precious minutes but at last they were ready.

"Aja," yelled Fallon. "Now run out the starboard guns! Don't bother loading them! Run out! Run out!"

Aja hesitated a moment, confused by the order, for he had just loaded the larboard guns. But trust in his captain trumped his confusion, and he ordered the starboard battery run out, unloaded.

Fallon then turned to the helmsman, who was as confused as Aja. "Listen now," Fallon said, suddenly alive with the moment, "I want to fall off just enough to show the brig we intend to pass to leeward. He needs to see our sails and hopefully the starboard guns. Then on my order head up quickly and cross his bows, hard on the wind, do you see?"

Fallon watched the helmsman smile in the dim light and knew he understood and was ready. They would get this one chance to even the odds by a trick, but it had to be executed perfectly. *Rascal* could sail close to the wind because of her fore and aft rig, closer by far than the square-rigged brig. Fallon hoped that by crossing the brig's bows he could surprise the Holy One and cause him to react without thought and head up too close to the wind, hopefully luffing and stopping his momentum. Then the main chance.

"Aja! Come quickly!" Fallon yelled. And when the boy was close he told him the plan. If it worked, there would be no return fire. *If it worked . . .*

ON THE SHIPS CAME, and Fallon ordered the helmsman to fall off to the west, showing her unloaded starboard guns to the Holy One. The ships were now on opposing and parallel courses, and the land breeze felt stronger on Fallon's cheek. It was eerily quiet, this moment before action. Fallon thought he heard the order for *Negro Sol's* starboard battery to run out and then the trucks creaking and groaning under the massive weight of their guns as black muzzles pierced the side of the ship. *So far so good.*

"Steady now," Fallon said to the helmsman as the ships drew closer to passing. Closer, closer . . . "Now! Helmsman, head up! Head up! Aja, run out the larboard battery!"

Rascal's crew hauled the big booms to the centerline, the ship picking up speed, her sails coming in to point the ship's bows as close to the wind as possible. Now she was crossing in front of the brig, which momentarily held course until Fallon heard a cry from her lookout and saw the brig head up herself, trying to cut off *Rascal* before she got to windward.

Rascal's larboard guns trundled out, sticking their noses into the coming fight, the gun crews edgy with excitement, their fear at bay for these next minutes. Each gun was elevated, each gunner clear on his orders.

Negro Sol's foresail shivered as she came up too far, her momentum slowed, and orders were shouted the length of the ship to let her fall off. But it was no good. She was in stays, dead in the water. *Rascal* was by, sailing at an angle toward the shore, away from the brig, which was now attempting to get her larboard guns loaded and run out even as she tried to fall off and gain speed. Fallon judged it was time.

"Let her head fall off now," he said calmly to the helmsman, and the schooner came parallel to the brig, but now to windward.

"Fire as you bear!" he yelled. "Maximum elevation!" And Aja

went gun to gun, as he had seen Cully do so many times, and *Rascal's* 12-pounders roared in measured explosions, each gun sending its deadly charge upward into *Negro Sol's* rigging. The chain-shot snapped ropes so long under tension that the spars shook reflexively.

But two guns found a softer mark.

The whirling black bolas spun across the water, up toward the Holy One, who stood stoically on the quarterdeck. The first chain-shot cut his body cleanly in half at the waist, and his eyes opened briefly in astonishment in the instant before the second bola severed his head from his shoulders. Fallon thought he saw the glint of sunset's last light on the Holy One's silver cross as it flew across the stern of the brig into the sea.

Fallon stared stupefied; they all did. The Holy One, that personification of evil, that impersonator of Godliness, was simply *removed* from life.

The head of the snake had been cut off, and now *Negro Sol* began to drift downwind, partially crippled, away from Bahia Salinas and westward. Aja led a cheer and Fallon was about to call for *Rascal* to wear ship and give chase when he heard a single gun farther inshore. He turned and saw a distant blue light burning, presumably on the stern of *Petite Bouton*, which Fallon had quite forgotten about in the heat of battle.

"Aja!" Fallon yelled, making an instant decision. "We'll sail down to the sloop! Prepare to come alongside!"

Rascal sailed across the bay and the outline of *Petite Bouton* gradually revealed itself. As they approached the sloop a voice suddenly called out across the water.

"Nico, Nico! Come quickly!" Somers called through cupped hands, and something in his voice alarmed Fallon and put every nerve on edge.

Now they were up to the sloop and even in the darkness Fallon could see the little ship was horribly mangled and might well be sinking, for she was low in the water. He ordered the sails furled to take way off as *Rascal* drifted down to *Petite Bouton.*

"Clap on, Ezra!" Fallon yelled anxiously. "Aja! Prepare to anchor!"

"Hurry, Nico! It's Elinore!" yelled Somers.

Elinore! The ships came together and clapped on to one another, and Aja ordered the anchor dropped. Without asking why, or how, or anything at all in the way of explanation, Fallon jumped down to *Petite's* decks as they drifted backward to set the anchor. Somers led the way below and threw open the door of the captain's cabin. There was Elinore lying on the stern cushions. Her eyes were open, but her face was wan and her body was almost translucent—except for the stain of blood that soaked her linens and even now was dripping onto the cabin floor.

FORTY-THREE

PETITE BOUTON'S surviving crew helped move their wounded aboard *Rascal*, with Elinore carried below by Fallon to a busy and bloody Colquist. Paloma was there as well, helping the surgeon with the wounded and dying. As soon as she saw the woman in Fallon's arms she knew who she was. When she saw the blood on Elinore's lower garments she also knew instinctively what had happened and immediately took charge. Elinore was sobbing now, her breath coming in gasps. Fallon moved to comfort her, unsure what had happened and wanting to be with the woman he loved, but Paloma's look said: *you are for later.*

Backing away, bewildered, Fallon stumbled up the companionway with Ezra behind. With Somers's blessing, he ordered the crew to get personal items like clothing off *Petite*, including Elinore's chest, and then he threw off the grappling hooks holding the ships together and let the sloop drift away. She was battered and sinking, and he had no use for her anymore.

It was very dark on deck, and the dead or near dead were lying about, many whimpering for the blessed end. Fallon went to each of them, kneeling down to give what comfort he could, holding their heads or their hands until they died. It was a wretched business, but these were his friends. Barclay had recovered enough to stand and was rubbing the back of his head, but his wits seemed elsewhere. When at last Fallon found Cully, the gunner sat holding his head and swaying back and forth, clearly concussed. Fallon thanked him

for his handling of the long nine, which had diverted the attention of the little wolves away from *Petite Bouton*. But the one-eyed gunner seemed not to understand what had happened.

Somers limped to where Fallon sat on the deck with Cully, but Fallon could barely look up. He suddenly found he was physically and emotionally spent from the death of his men and the discovery of a bleeding Elinore. Not even the death of the Holy One could rouse his spirits. Somers helped him to his feet and led him away to the capstan with his arm around his shoulders.

"Elinore will recover, Nico," said Somers softly. "She will mend."

"What happened, Ezra?" Fallon asked. "Why were you even here?"

"When she got your letter about Beauty, we decided immediately that we had to come to Antigua to be with her. We were gripped with worry. Maybe it was unwise, in retrospect, though our intentions were good. But tell me, how was Beauty when you left her? Tell me she is recovering."

"When I left she was," said Fallon. "But it will go slowly and there is no way to know if infection . . . it could still strike her down. It was a truly horrible wound, Ezra. It would have killed a lesser person."

Somers closed his eyes in thanks.

"But, Ezra," Fallon said anxiously, "tell me about Elinore, please! Was she on deck at all during the fighting?"

"No, Nico. She was below," said Somers. "But you see, there's something you don't know. I didn't know it either before we sailed for Antigua. I think she wanted to surprise you. Elinore was carrying your baby."

Fallon swallowed. *My God*, he thought. *My baby. What have I done?*

Somers read the guilt perfectly, expecting it even. It's how he would have felt receiving the same news. Helpless and guilty. All that.

"No, Nico," he said. "Guilt is useless at a time like this. You both love each other, so there can be no guilt. Not on either side."

"So . . . she lost the baby . . . *our* baby?" Fallon asked incredulously. The full magnitude of Elinore's misery was now apparent to him, and he understood why Paloma had pushed him away until he understood.

"*My God, Ezra.*"

ELINORE WAS ASLEEP in Fallon's cabin thanks to a potion from Colquist, who continued to work into the night tending to the wounded by lantern. Six sailors lay dead on the deck, plus poor Brooks. And four of *Petite's* crew would not see daylight.

Thankfully, Aja had stepped up to take charge of getting the ship to rights and assigning a night watch in case the little wolves returned, which was unlikely given their sudden lack of leadership. The carpenter had his crew patching and fixing anything vital on *Rascal.* He'd sounded the well and reported no apparent shot holes below the waterline.

The moon was just coming up halfway through the middle watch by the time *Rascal* felt secure, the dead crewmen and Brooks having been sewn into canvas weighted with shot and placed by the railing for burial tomorrow.

A weary Fallon went below decks and quietly slipped into his cabin, where he saw Elinore asleep, the moonlight through the stern windows giving her an otherworldly quality. He studied her lovely face, a face he knew so well, and bent to kiss her forehead. She stirred slightly, then settled, her breathing long and slow. He backed away to the stern seat and stretched out in the moonlight. What he cared most about in the world was mere feet away, safe but damaged, and he wondered if things between them would ever be the same.

IT WAS SOMETIME later that Fallon opened his eyes to an angel, and for a moment he imagined he'd died. But Elinore was real and he was alive and she was touching his face and crying silent tears and murmuring, "*I'm sorry.*"

He sat up and pulled her beside him, holding her closely and stroking her hair and telling her he loved her, that one day they'd have their baby again, a lot of babies if she wanted, and they'd be married in the small chapel on Bermuda that faced the sea—in the spring of the year, when the small flowers bloomed among the rocks. She quieted, and held him with an amazing strength, clinging to his body and willing herself to believe everything he said.

The thing is, he meant every word.

FORTY-FOUR

AT FIRST LIGHT, when the horizon could be scanned and pronounced all clear, *Rascal* made her way out of Bahia Salinas. The wind was out of the northeast, and Barclay sailed south along the coast of Porto Rico before turning eastward for a long larboard tack along the southern coast of the island. *Rascal* was under reefed topsails, mainsail, and foresail but still bounded along energetically, plunging and swooping over the white-capped seas like a horse making for the barn.

Aja and Barclay had things well in hand on deck, knowing that Fallon would need to be with Elinore down below. He had been present to bury Brooks and the dead crewmen that morning but had not been seen since. *Rascal*'s decks had been holystoned back to their usual condition, the spilled blood sanded off, but the gouges and furrows remained to tell the tale.

Somers was at the stern, looking over the taffrail as the sea passed underneath the ship. In his mind, the hiring of Stuyvesant had set in motion a chain of events that had led inevitably to the battle in Bahia Salinas and to poor Elinore's miscarriage. Colquist had said the constant pounding of cannon fire had no doubt been the cause. Now, Elinore wasn't going to be a mother, Nico wasn't going to be a father, and he wasn't going to be a grandfather, at least anytime soon. And he found all of it unbearably sad. A child had died because he'd made a bad decision. What was that line from Euripides?

Come back. Even as a shadow, even as a dream.

But nothing would bring the dead child back.

Somers watched as Elinore and Fallon stepped on deck, holding onto each other for mutual support. Elinore had barely spoken to Somers last night and not at all this morning. *Give her time*, Paloma had said. But it was hard, and Elinore's silence made him feel all the guiltier.

Elinore had changed into a simple dress and she had a bit of color back, but her face looked drawn and utterly *sad*.

Somers thought of the battle with the little wolves, as Fallon called them. *Petite* had been all but done for when *Rascal* suddenly appeared, and he shuddered to think what would have become of Elinore and his crew if Fallon hadn't shown up when he did. It had turned out badly enough as it was. Could Stuyvesant have made a better show of fighting? Perhaps, admitted Somers. But Stuyvesant was a cold, dead bastard so it didn't matter now.

What mattered, the only thing that mattered now, was that he thought he'd seen Elinore smile at Aja. *Smile*, by God! That lifted his spirits immeasurably and gave him hope that she would recover. And what was this? Elinore was walking toward him, her arms outstretched, tears streaming down her cheeks. *My God, could he be forgiven?*

FALLON WATCHED as Elinore and Somers embraced, and held their embrace a long while, each apparently not wanting to let go. Somers had no doubt been blaming himself for the miscarriage, somehow, but Elinore didn't. And when Fallon told her of Somers's courage in tangling with *Negro Sol* her eyes grew wide, for without that single act it might all have all ended in death, the Holy One giving no quarter.

Paloma approached with a cup of coffee in each hand and gave Fallon one.

"I'm glad to see Elinore and her father like that," she said, motioning to father and daughter holding hands now and talking at the stern. "It will take her awhile to come back to herself, Nico, but she will find her way."

"Yes," said Fallon. "She is going slowly, even with me. I am not asking questions. Only answering them. Not giving advice, only listening if she wants to talk."

"I see why she loves you, Nico," Paloma said with a smile. "How did you get to be so smart?"

THE SHIP changed watches and Barclay marked their position on the slate with each tack, though Porto Rico was still easily in sight by the first dog. Aja had taken a tolerable noon sight, which got very close to Barclay's own; the young man was actually a navigator of some skill now. Barclay was impressed, doubly so upon learning how Aja had taken charge of the ship when he'd been knocked senseless.

It was late in the second dogwatch when Elinore was ready to speak to Fallon privately. They walked to the starboard railing, and she told him of feeling unwell the past two months and the doctor confirming her pregnancy. Initially she'd been embarrassed and fearful of a scandal, but then shame turned to the possibility of joy as she thought of telling Fallon. He stopped and turned to her and held her tightly as she began crying softly. The crewmen working nearby found something pressing to do elsewhere in the ship.

Then she described Stuyvesant coming into her cabin and Fallon stiffened. He could feel his body going on full alert even as Elinore described Somers coolly coming in behind him with his pistol out and marching him up the companionway and onto the deck. It was a Somers kind of trial: Her father quoted Heraclitus and was about to kill Stuyvesant when Elinore threw her punch and took care of business herself.

Fallon could feel his body calm down, Somers being a man you could count on, and Elinore being a *woman* you could count on. The next part of Elinore's story he could speak to from his vantage point on *Rascal's* deck. She asked how the attack on *Petite Bouton* began, and he described the sloops swooping in, firing again and again. Elinore said her pains had begun with the first broadside. She had grown tense and anxious as the ship shuddered with each hit, and then the pain had grown worse and she had known something was horribly wrong. By the time she'd understood what it was, it was done. And she had fainted, no doubt from loss of blood.

Fallon expected her to break at this point, to crumble and cry, but she stiffened her back and looked out to sea for a long moment.

"Why did those ships attack us?" she asked. "They had no idea who we were or where we were from."

"They're pirates; we called them *the little wolves.* Usually they attacked slavers, overwhelmed them and stole the slaves to sell for profit. But they had attacked us once as well, and we beat them back. No doubt they came into the bay and were just as surprised to see you as you were to see them. But there you were, a prize for the taking, something purely opportunistic. Lucky we were following them."

"And did you fight all three ships?" she asked incredulously.

"Well, yes," answered Fallon. "We really had no choice. But when your father pushed the brig around, the tide turned for us."

Elinore was still absorbing Fallon's explanation when Aja appeared at their side.

"Mr. Barclay's duty, sir, and he'd like to come about on larboard for a long tack," he said.

The afternoon passed like this, tack on tack, and the ship's bell rang out and the watches were changed, and when at last it was time for dinner Fallon asked Somers, Aja, and Paloma to join him and Elinore in his cabin. It would be a tight fit, but it was their last night at sea, for tomorrow would see them in English Harbor. Fallon couldn't hope for a lively evening, but he did hope for a pleasant one where they all could look forward in anticipation rather than backward with sorrow. After all, they would see Beauty tomorrow.

In the event, he was not disappointed. Two bottles of claret during the meal worked wonders on the group dynamic, and Paloma and Elinore especially were becoming friends. Paloma shared her story with Elinore and Somers, noting Aja's daring in setting Young David free, which both embarrassed and pleased the boy. She said little of Davies, but a careful observer could read between the lines. And Elinore, of course, was a careful observer.

When at last the stories were told and all things were known that would ever be known that night, they went off to bed. Fallon took a last turn around the ship with Aja, making sure of the watch rotation and checking the course with Barclay. It was a spectacular night, the kind of night that often moved Fallon to dream of Elinore, or write to her, but now she was below decks, perhaps just slipping off her dress and climbing into his cot.

It was not a night for romance, he knew that. It was a night for holding the woman he loved and making the world safe again.

FORTY-FIVE

YOUNG DAVID made his way westward by night and rested during the day, aware of the danger he faced from soldiers who would stop at nothing to find him. He was sure the soldiers had seen him run along the beach as Rascal had sailed away from Matanzas.

He passed the fields that had been burned at his hands and foraged for food in gardens and drank from streams. He had a knife and flint that he'd stolen from a farm, but he had no real plan except to carry on westward, past where he'd been captured, and continue to burn the cane.

He refused to let others join him, choosing instead to free slaves and move on quickly. He grew thinner and tired, frightened by noises in the night, awakened by noises in the day. In the time since he'd escaped from Matanzas he'd freed more than two hundred slaves, most of whom would eventually be recaptured and punished. He understood that. But he also knew that even a few moments of freedom restored what slavery stole from men and women: dignity.

Cuba's rolling plains stretched almost six hundred miles in front of him, arcing to the south before giving way to mountains in the southeast. Young David walked by the stars, lights without names to him, but small reminders each night that he was moving in the same general direction as the night before. Where that would take him, he had no way of knowing. He was a night explorer, carrying anger and redemption in his heart.

And fire in his hands.

FORTY-SIX

ENGLISH HARBOR in the forenoon.

Rascal glided in on a light breeze and Fallon brought her to rest against the quay at the dockyard in her old spot as if it had been held for the ship. *Renegade* was nearby, apparently still undergoing repairs, but she looked fit to Fallon's eye. And there was Jones waving from the quarterdeck, his hat in the air, one arm in a light sling. Paloma and Elinore and Somers were all on deck, taking in the scene as Fallon pointed out the various buildings. A lone figure sat in a chair under a tree at the water's edge in front of the hospital, a light shawl draped over her shoulders. But now she was up, walking slowly but with determination toward the ship, her peg leg pushing softly into the path next to the harbor.

The entire crew aboard *Rascal* cheered Beauty and tossed their hats in the air; she smiled in return, giving them a low wave as she couldn't raise her arm just yet. The ship docked, and Elinore was the first off and ran to Beauty to gently embrace her, followed by Somers and Fallon gathering around with absolute joy on their faces. Now here was Aja, as well, and Beauty gave him the best hug she could. She was noticeably thinner and weak, but her eyes were clear and the set of her chin said: *I'm back.*

Paloma stood to the side until she was introduced by Fallon; she was part of the little family now. It was a joyous moment, yet tinged with sadness for all of them, for poor Brooks was dead along with many of their shipmates. James Wharton was dead and Young

David might well be, of course. But Beauty was quite alive, and that was to be celebrated.

Fallon asked Aja to carry word to Davies aboard the flagship that he had a special visitor waiting for him, and Aja left in the gig as soon as it could be lowered. Meanwhile, the little party moved aboard *Rascal*, a bosun's chair lowered for Beauty, and in very little time an awning had been rigged under the main boom, and chairs and stools had been produced. Each crew member came by to pay his respects to their first mate, for she was revered as well as beloved. And finally, Colquist appeared, the one who had probably saved her life by removing the splinter that had nearly ended it. In his medical way he asked after her health and, assured it was amazingly good, he beamed proudly.

And when at last the greetings had all been given, there came a hail from Aja as *Rascal's* gig clapped on. In a moment, the admiral's gig clapped on as well, and then the admiral himself climbed over the side and stood face to face with Paloma Campos. Elinore and Fallon watched in anticipation, for these two had not seen each other for several years. Perhaps the fire they once had had died. Or cooled, at least. Perhaps time had . . . but no, Davies held out his hands and Paloma took them in hers. Most of the crew looked away, slightly embarrassed but pleased, for it reminded every sailor of his own sweetheart or wife and the reunion they would have when they returned to Bermuda. Aja, being at a curious age, didn't look away at all and saw Davies embrace Paloma and hold her a long while, tears in their eyes and smiles that seemed permanent on their faces.

Well, it was a *moment*.

The gathering on deck continued all afternoon, fortified by wine and rejuvenated by the Garóns arriving just as it was about to break up, for they would need to be acquainted with all the stories, too. They were particularly interested in Paloma, of course, being fellow Cuban loyalists, and the story of Young David genuinely moved them. Fallon considered pulling Davies aside to tell him about the French ship-of-the-line at Saint-Domingue, but thought better of it. That bad news could wait a bit. The world seemed very complicated just then, or maybe it was always complicated, but at that moment events seemed to overwhelm all their senses. It would not be the first time, or the last, that someone wondered: *What is the world coming to?*

FORTY-SEVEN

FALLON WAS ROWED to the flagship in his gig the next morning to give his full report to Admiral Davies. He intended to fill in the considerable blanks between the major points he'd already given Davies under the awning aboard *Rascal* the day before. Davies greeted him in the enormous great cabin, asked after Elinore's health and, assured all was as well as could be expected, bade Fallon begin.

Much had happened since *Rascal* departed English Harbor to retrieve James Wharton, and Fallon relayed the events in a straightforward manner, beginning with the encounter with the slaver *Plymouth* off the coast of Cuba and the subsequent chase after *Doncella Española*.

"Wait," said Davies. "You ran into *Doncella?*"

"Well, not exactly, sir," said Fallon. "We didn't run into her, but *she* ran into the chain across Havana Harbor and, ahem, she sank."

"*She sank?*"

"Yes, sir," said Fallon matter-of-factly, and proceeded to explain the chase and Brooks's excellent handling of the ship and Cully's remarkable work at the long nine and, finally, the frantic signaling between *Doncella* and the fort right up until she struck the chain.

"You knew the Spanish officials would not lower the chain again, didn't you?" asked Davies, knowing the answer.

"No, sir," objected Fallon. "I'm afraid I'm not clairvoyant. I only hoped."

Davies smiled at such a modest answer. If *Rascal* had been a Royal Navy schooner that sank a Spanish frigate, the *Gazette* would have gushed in praise. The whole of London would be cheering. But as it stood, London would never know of this brave and resourceful privateer captain. And the captain cared not a whit.

Fallon then detailed his arrival in Matanzas, noting the subsequent arrival of the Holy One to unload slaves. He made little of Paloma's escape from Castillo de San Severino, or at least said no more than was necessary. Davies nodded in appreciation, aware that Fallon was playing down his own heroics once again. But he had gotten the picture from Paloma of the fighting and the rush to the ship and Young David's refusal to board. On the matter of the Matanzas treasure, Davies refused to claim any of it for the Crown.

"I didn't hear a word you said about any treasure, sir," said Davies. "I think I may be losing my hearing, you see, either from cannon fire or captains' exaggerations. But tell me about poor James Wharton and what intelligence he conveyed about Cuba before he died."

"There is not much to say, I'm afraid," said Fallon. "Wharton felt most Cubans were not ready for independence. The white Cubans, that is. Although, certainly *some* are. But he could find no real political will for it and could identify no military or political leader to organize a movement."

"I see," said Davies, disappointed. "I was hoping for some good news to report to their Lordships, since it was their idea to send Wharton out. And now the poor bastard is dead."

They sat in silence for a while, the ship's noises going on overhead, and Kinis could be heard calling out to someone.

"Pray carry on with your report, Nicholas," said Davies.

"On our return down the Cuban coast our lookout reported a French ship-of-the-line turning for Port-au-Prince," said Fallon, letting that bit of news hang in the air like a bad odor.

Davies stood up from his desk, his face dark and worried.

"My God, what do you think that's about?" he asked somberly. "A show of force, perhaps?"

"That occurred to me, yes," said Fallon. "Perhaps France sent an emissary to explain to Louverture how things were going to be. Perhaps to kill the trade treaties. Or even to replace the general with a French official."

Again, a long moment of silence as Davies digested the news.

"Now we have a conundrum," he said finally. "A French ship at Saint-Domingue; why, we don't know. *Doncella* is finished, but the other Spanish frigate, which Wharton said was *Tigre*, is somewhere up to something. And we still have the usual scofflaws sailing about. Suddenly the Caribbean is very crowded with the King's enemies." A pause. "But I must say I am most concerned about that damned ship at Port-au-Prince. That could alter the balance of power in the entire region. A bully on the field, as it were. Tell me, is there any good news, Nicholas?"

That prompted Fallon to describe the battle with the little wolves, the valiant Somers in command of *Petite Bouton*, and again the unfortunate death of Brooks, which he'd already made known to Davies when they'd arrived in English Harbor. In deference to Elinore's privacy he left out her miscarriage, though he had no doubt Paloma would share it with Davies later.

"I am very sorry about Brooks, sir," said Fallon quietly. "He was a good man, even a very good man, brave and well-liked. He died facing a broadside."

"Yes, Brooks had a promising career in front of him," agreed Davies sadly. "But he was excited to sail with you, Nicholas. He volunteered, remember? And he died doing what he wanted to do. Not so many men can say that, I guess." Here he was thinking about his own situation, locked in English Harbor aboard the flagship.

"But it seems you have put paid to the little wolves' depredations, and I must say in a rather spectacular manner," Davies continued. "Without the Holy One I believe they could well disband, or at the least they will not be as dangerous. That counts for a lot, and would no doubt satisfy Brooks enormously were he here to know it."

Fallon was about to ask about *Renegade*'s fitting out, but Davies had turned to look out the massive stern windows and was clearly lost in thought. Fallon thought it best to let him get to wherever he was going.

"Nicholas," he began, turning to face Fallon, "on a deeply personal note, I hardly know where to begin to thank you for rescuing Paloma. It was beyond anything I would have expected, for I asked only of news of her. But you could not simply bring me back news of her imprisonment and death, could you? Simply to report back to me would have violated your dignity and duty, and I know that. From the beginning, therefore, it was an unfair request. I see that now. In the midst of my joy and inestimable relief to have her here safe, I must apologize for putting you and the ship in such danger. I should have known you were never going to leave her in anything like a precarious position, if you were going to leave her at all."

Fallon stared at the cabin sole for a moment, that perfectly organized checkerboard of black-and-white painted canvas, and thought for the hundredth time how alike he and Davies were. How similar their minds and even their hearts. Worlds away in rank and station, they were nonetheless bound by something deep and profound that existed only in the fighting brotherhood.

"Harry, you don't owe me anything for doing exactly what you would have done for me," said Fallon simply. "The look on your face when you came on board and saw Paloma was the happiest I've ever seen you. I also saw the look on Paloma's face. Love is a wonderful thing, Harry. I have done more for less in my life."

"It shows on my face then?" asked Davies with an embarrassed smile.

Fallon could only laugh. Apparently, cluelessness was something they shared, as well.

UPON HIS RETURN to *Rascal*, Fallon was greeted by the unexpected sight of Beauty on deck overseeing repairs from the battle in Bahia Salinas. It both surprised and gratified him to see her in her accustomed role, but he wondered at the strain it might cause her.

"Not a word to me, Nico," she said emphatically as he approached her. "I have moved back aboard and don't plan to leave. So, get used to it and let me do my job. Dr. Garón knows all about it and believes a ship is healthier than a hospital."

Well, there wasn't much Fallon could say to that because it really wasn't going to be a discussion, per se. Neither was it at all clear if Garón simply knew about it or actually approved of it. *Right, let her do her job*, he told himself. That might be the best medicine.

Now here was Cully asking permission to restock the ship with ordnance, for shot and powder were low, and of course Fallon sent him off to the magazine with a shore party to secure what he needed. After all, *Rascal* was still in service to the Admiralty until she arrived home in Bermuda, and Davies had encouraged Fallon to leave with a well-stocked ship. Beauty would see to the other stores, as well as wood and water, which would begin coming aboard tomorrow. With everything well in hand, Fallon went below to have a nap—*yes, a nap, by God*—before Somers and Elinore arrived for dinner.

When was the last time he'd done that?

FORTY-EIGHT

*T*HE SOLDIERS *marched over the rolling plains and followed the smoke until there was no more smoke. At this point, Colonel Munoz guessed, they were ahead of Young David.*

Munoz was a patient man. He reasoned that Young David travelled by night and slept by day, hidden in a ravine or tree, and so looking for him by day would do no good. No, his thinking went, better to wait for him at night, hidden in the cane of the next field ahead of Young David.

It was a good plan.

Young David approached the field where the soldiers were hidden just after midnight. He carried dried leaves and a piece of flint in his hands. He knelt next to the cane and made a nest of the leaves, then took out his knife and flint and prepared to start a fire.

But he never got that far.

FORTY-NINE

Admiral Harry Davies climbed down into his gig for the short row to shore, his boat's crew well turned out, as always. It was almost evening in the Caribbean, and the low sun on his face felt wonderfully warm; the strain and worry of command temporarily at bay.

Once ashore, he walked briskly along the path into the village and the inn that Somers, Elinore, and Paloma temporarily called home. The Pegasus Inn had a white exterior picked out in blue trim, and across the front was an expansive porch lined with white wicker chairs. As Davies approached, Paloma Campos rose from one of them.

He gasped at her beauty and the fluid grace of her descent down the steps and into his arms. It occurred to him that this was all any man could want and more than he deserved.

"I have been thinking of you all afternoon, Harry," Paloma said softly. "I have been imagining the story of your life, for I don't really know you well enough to be in love with you."

"And what did you imagine the story of my life to be?" asked Harry in a teasing voice as they began to walk toward the mouth of the harbor.

"I imagined you as a young boy in England. A boy that other boys looked up to who would not be pushed or bullied. At a young age, you joined the Royal Navy to see the world and fight your country's enemies. You were very patriotic. Your parents didn't want you to go. But you had a romantic notion of war then, which you no longer have. You never married; the service was your wife. With promotion and age came wisdom and a more cynical view of the world. Not exactly negative, but also not optimistic. You found too many things to be angry about to be fully happy in your role as admiral. You look at Nicholas Fallon with envy, seeing the Harry Davies that might have been. You have no close friends, no one who is your peer, but he is the closest you have to a brother. And then . . . and then I come along. And the question you must be considering is the question I've been thinking about on the porch all afternoon: Where do I fit in with the story of your life?"

"*Good God!*" Davies exclaimed.

"You even curse like Nicholas," Paloma said with a smile. "It's really quite adorable."

"I just meant . . . that is, I'm so taken aback at your story. I mean *my* story," stammered Davies. "How in God's world did you figure all that out?"

"It wasn't that hard, Harry," Paloma said, laughing. "*Cuando el río suena, agua lleva.*"

"What does that mean, may I ask?"

"When you hear the river make noise, it's carrying water," she replied with a smile.

FALLON STOOD at the stern of his ship awaiting Somers and Elinore for dinner. The sun was ready to throw its golden light on the other side of the world, and the Rascals were at peace and safe as houses. That afternoon he had watched Aja working with the new freedmen, who were practicing knots and splices, for they had all kept their word and signed on as hands as Fallon hoped they would. The crew seemed open-minded about their new shipmates; it was the way of sailors to judge a man by his skill rather than his skin. Fallon smiled to himself as he looked around his happy ship.

It was time to take them all home.

And yet . . .

He wondered about that French ship at Port-au-Prince and what it meant for Davies. And for Louverture. He had met the Frenchman, and he liked him. More than that, he'd meant what he'd said about Louverture being a beacon of hope for slaves throughout the Caribbean. But what if that light went out? Freedom was a tenuous thing, as Louverture would no doubt agree. Fallon thought of the letter to Cuba's governor and what it portended. Could *Rascal* sail away not knowing why that damned ship was sent to Saint-Domingue?

Davies had called a meeting to discuss the situation the next morning, and Fallon wanted to take a turn around the deck to focus on what he could offer. But here were Somers and Elinore close by the ship. It would not do to be otherwise occupied in thought when he was with Elinore. She read him too well.

She might guess he was considering not going directly home to Bermuda.

FIFTY

I'VE ASKED you here because I'd like your opinion on the Caribbean situation before I make a decision about how to proceed," said Davies, looking around the great cabin at Jones, Fallon, and Kinis. "But first, I must say to Captain Fallon that you are here as an advisor only, sir. You have done quite enough to help the Crown, putting yourself and crew in the gravest of dangers again and again. It is tempting to think of *Rascal* as Royal Navy, but, of course, you are not. I fully expect you to return forthwith to Bermuda, but I've asked you here because you see things from a privateer's view, a view that I've personally always found helpful, if often *unexpected*, shall we say."

Fallon nodded slightly. Davies was letting him off the hook, helping him leave with honor. The other officers smiled, knowing full well the esteem in which Davies held Fallon. It was deserved and they knew it.

"To continue," said Davies, "we believe there is a French ship at Port-au-Prince. Why, we don't know, but she is a formidable enemy and is likely not there to pat Louverture on the back. We know *Doncella* is sunk, but we believe Spain also sent another frigate—*Tigre*—perhaps to protect Havana and other Cuban ports, or perhaps for other reasons. The question is: How do we proceed? *Renegade* is coming off the ways soon and, with *Avenger*, we are fully capable of dealing with the situation. But we need a strategy, or we will simply be sailing about looking for an opportunity and perhaps find none. I give you the floor, gentlemen." And Davies sat down at his desk, a chart of the Caribbean in front of them all, and waited.

No one said anything immediately. Jones was the most junior and certainly wasn't going to volunteer an early opinion. Fallon was trying to be a passive observer, but it wasn't working; in truth, he was trying to winkle an idea out of its hiding place in his brain. So, it was left to the stolid Kinis to break the ice by pointing at the chart, as if a plan might appear there.

"The problem, sir, as you've pointed out, is that we have two un-related enemy ships, except that they are allies," Kinis began. "We know where one supposedly is, if she's still *there*; we haven't a clue about the other's whereabouts, or if she's even *here*. So, the question is: Do we wait to learn more and then act, or is there something we can do now?"

"With your permission, sir," said Jones tentatively. "Could we not try a full-on attack on the French ship?"

"I would suspect she is very well positioned against just such a possibility, Jones," said Davies. "The harbor is quite narrow near Port-au-Prince, and if she is indeed a ship-of-the-line it would be heavy going against well-manned guns. It may be our only option in the end, of course. We certainly don't have the ships or the time to blockade the port and make her come out."

Everyone in the room knew Davies was right. But now Fallon was at last focused on the idea he'd been teasing out. He had an elastic mind when it came to solving unsolvable problems; perhaps if he talked it out, it would come.

"I am wondering," he said quietly, "if we might provoke a *situation* and turn this very large negative into something more positive. Something that would confuse these allies to the point of hostil-ity to each other, now and in the future, at least in the Caribbean. Perhaps it would have the benefit of preventing their cooperation against Louverture's rebellion in the bargain. Surely, that would be in Great Britain's interests."

The cabin grew quiet, and all eyes turned to Fallon.

"What is that remarkable mind of yours thinking?" asked Davies, without a hint of sarcasm.

Fallon paused before answering. He had their full attention now, but there were so many points he hadn't had time to think out. It might all sound like so much fantasy.

"*Renegade* is Spanish-built, as we all know," continued Fallon, taking a deep breath. "I am wondering if *Renegade* should become *Tigre*."

Jones gasped as Kinis coughed. Only Davies smiled.

"And then, Nicholas?" he said.

"And then . . . *Renegade*, the new *Tigre*, might provoke an incident of some kind. Perhaps attack French shipping? Or a French base? Or something *bigger*: We know there's a French ship at Port-au-Prince. Could the new *Tigre* strike there? France might not get over that anytime soon. And then whenever French and Spanish ships happened to meet again . . . who knows how they might react?"

"God, you are the very devil, Nicholas!" said Davies, with a wicked grin.

But Jones, who would be commanding *Renegade* as *Tigre*, hadn't gotten over the part where he was to attack a ship-of-the-line.

"But surely, sir," said Jones, excited but cautious, "it would take more than a Spanish flag to fool those French buggers. Begging your pardon, Admiral."

Davies only continued smiling, for he was starting to guess where Fallon was going.

"Yes, Jones, you are very correct," said Fallon. "You would need to rename your ship and outfit yourself and your officers in Spanish naval uniforms. Your crew could even wear barettina caps, I believe they call them."

It took a moment to absorb Fallon's thinking, but then one by one each officer smiled until everyone in the cabin was smiling, Fallon included.

"You have given us a true privateer's perspective, Nicholas!" said

Davies. "Thrust and parry, deceive and attack and sow confusion. The devil is in the details, of course. But let us put our heads together now to flesh out this extraordinary idea."

And so they did. For the best part of the next three hours. And when at last Fallon climbed down into his gig to be rowed back to *Rascal*, it was agreed among the remaining officers and Admiral Davies that they wouldn't want that particular privateer for an enemy.

For Fallon's part, he wasn't about to let this idea go to sea without him.

IT WAS FOUR BELLS in the forenoon watch when Fallon climbed aboard *Rascal* to be met by Beauty, a grin on her face.

"Your majesty," she said with exaggerated deference. "While you've been hobnobbing with royalty on the flagship, Cully has been getting ordnance aboard, and he's made the most amazing discovery. Would you like to see it?"

"Why, yes, I would," said Fallon, mystified.

"It's best seen on deck," Beauty said. "So, let me fetch Cully from below to show you what he's found in the magazine ashore."

Soon Cully appeared carrying a projectile of a kind that Fallon had never seen before. It was a solid iron canister, out of which protruded a short spear with a barbed point. Wrapped around the shaft of the spear was pitch-soaked canvas. Cully was as happy as a child at Christmas holding a new toy.

"And what have we here, Master Gunner?" asked Fallon.

"This they call a fire arrow, Captain," answered Cully proudly. "I found these in the magazine—something new from the Admiralty— and brought some aboard. The idea is that when the gun fires, it ignites the wad around the arrow."

"Really!" exclaimed Fallon. "That is most extraordinary. The barbed tip sticks into the ship's side and the ship hopefully catches fire! By God, I'd hate to see these coming across the water toward my ship!"

"Exactly," said Beauty. "Of course, we don't know for sure that they really work. We're the first to try them out here. But maybe we'll get the chance . . ."

Yes, thought Fallon, as he held the fire arrow in his hands. *Another little trick might be good to have.* He handed the fire arrow back to Cully, who took it gingerly and left to return it below.

"Beauty," said Fallon tentatively, turning his attention to his second mate. "There is a plan afoot to strike a blow against the French and Spanish alliance. A little something to sow mistrust and confusion. I am going to present it to the crew, and anyone who wants to go home instead of sailing with *Rascal* can take the next packet to Bermuda. I wouldn't blame anyone for leaving, and they will lose no favor with me. I know you are especially ready to go home to Bermuda, and I don't blame you, either—you're still recovering. So, I will arrange passage on the next—"

"Well, you can forget that, Nico," interrupted Beauty. "I swear, sometimes I think you are the dumbest smart man in the world. The crew will vote to stay with the ship. This has been a profitable cruise, but there's always more money to be made. And you know I'm not staying here on shore. You sailed off without me once, Nico. It won't happen again."

"Well, I just thought it was best," said Fallon, outmaneuvered. "But we should see what Dr. Garón says."

"Tell me, Nico," said Beauty, ignoring the condition Fallon laid down. "Whose crazy plan is it?"

Fallon looked at her, smiling now, old friends who knew each other so well.

"Right," she said. "Now I know I'm going."

LATER THAT NIGHT, Fallon helped Elinore down into his gig and pushed away from the quay. The gig was not built to be rowed by one person, but he managed to get it out to the center of the harbor with a slow grace born of a lifetime at sea spent in all manner of boats. The moon had not yet made its appearance, and the sky was splashed with a dome of stars that illuminated the world, or at least the English Harbor part of it. He could see the flagship against the sky, her towering masts perfectly still on this windless night. The only sound to be heard was the gurgling water disturbed by the gig's oars.

Elinore sat in the stern, her blonde hair loose about her shoulders, her face at peace. Fallon's fear was that what he had to say would destroy that peace, for he had to tell her he was leaving on yet another mission for Davies. *And it had been his idea.* He was a coward at times like these, weak in the face of disappointing someone he loved.

Elinore trailed a hand overboard; her eyes were closed when she spoke.

"What's on your mind, Nico?" she said softly. "I can sense you are preoccupied." This was to have been a romantic tête-à-tête, their first opportunity to be alone together since returning to Antigua. And already she *knew*. Fallon shipped the oars and let the gig drift.

"Elinore, I know you are ready to go home; in truth, my whole crew is as well. They are wealthy enough to live their whole lives and never go to sea again. And you have been through so much anguish and disappointment that you must long for Bermuda."

"But?" she asked in a small voice, barely above a whisper.

And then she answered her own question.

"But you are a sailor," she said. "And sailors go where the wind blows them. And the wind is blowing you somewhere else instead of Bermuda."

Fallon hung his head to his chest, wondering not for the first time how she could read his mind. But the thing was out and had to be seen through.

"We have a plan to turn Spain and France against each other in the Caribbean. I will be sailing on *Rascal* to help facilitate the plan, not to take part in it, *per se*. That is the truth, Elinore. There is much to do before we can leave, but once we sail I expect to be gone only a few weeks, if that."

If Fallon could have seen Elinore's face better he would have seen her eyes were moist. But she would not cry. Would not, in fact, do anything to keep Fallon from going to sea. It was a pact she'd made with herself when she'd fallen in love with him.

"I have no intention of *not* coming home to you, Elinore," Fallon said quietly. "And in one piece. Remember my promise to you about having lots of babies? I intend to keep that promise!"

He was hoping for a smile. Something to *lighten* her.

And then she did force herself to offer a brave little smile, the kind of smile wives and lovers of sea captains the world over give their men to send them off.

"Well, let's get started then," she whispered.

Elinore unbuttoned her dress and wriggled her way out of it, almost tipping the gig over and causing Fallon to laugh out loud as he steadied the boat. She spread out the blanket she'd brought from his cabin to cover the floorboards of the gig and watched in anticipation as Fallon got undressed. No words were spoken, for what could they say?

Elinore guided Fallon onto his back and she lowered herself to sit astride him. Slowly, carefully, she began running her fingers over his chest, over his various scars and wounds, new and old, getting to know his body again. She took her time, smiling, and when at last she was ready she mounted him and began a slow back and forth dance, torturous in its patience, prolonging the ecstasy of the finish for the delicious agony of expectation. The boat drifted and rocked, the stars kept their quiet vigil overhead, and Elinore's glistening white body pumped faster, desperately faster, and then suddenly— paused. She threw her head back and arched her back and screamed a scream so full of rage and release it was a wonder candles weren't immediately lit in every home in English Harbor.

Well, perhaps they were. But there was nothing to be seen from the houses. Only a small boat adrift in the harbor, and no one appeared to be aboard.

FIFTY-ONE

EVENTS IN ANTIGUA began to take on a certain urgency.
Fallon had volunteered *Rascal* to be the eyes of the fleet,
ranging ahead of *Avenger* and the newly renamed *Renegade*
as they crossed the Caribbean in search of their French or Spanish
enemies. He was not to go into battle under either enemy's guns,
but rather to be the first line of defense—or offense, as the case
might be—scouting ahead and reporting back. Somers understood
and even approved, knowing Fallon was a warrior at his core and
could not simply sail back to Bermuda and leave his plan lying on
the chart in Davies' cabin. He needed a role, if only minor.

Señora Garón volunteered to lead the seamstress contingent
and, based on the uniforms of several captured Spanish officers
currently confined on Antigua, she began gathering material and
braid and flourishes. Fallon cautioned that the uniforms need not
be perfect replicas, only good enough to pass muster when seen
through a telescope on a moving ship.

Aboard *Rascal*, the crew signed on for the new mission without
hesitation; after all, though they were rich they could always be
richer, and no matter *Rascal*'s presumed role, Fallon had a way of
finding *opportunities*. The new hands from Matanzas were drilled
at the great guns by Cully and instructed in sail handling by Beauty
until they were so weary they could drop. Still, they were cheerful
enough. They were free men, free to leave if they chose, and most of
them had never been free to do anything else in their lives.

Beauty had secured Doctor Garón's permission to go, on the condition that she would not take the wheel and would get only modest exercise each day. She readily agreed, but she would have left with or without his permission, and Fallon and Garón both knew it.

Renegade took on stores, and Jones supervised the painting of *Tigre* on the stern, making up the design himself. Fallon gave him a Spanish flag, and Jones had it raised to gauge the effect for himself. His arm was nearly healed now; anyway, he would have concealed any discomfort if it wasn't, and his exuberant spirits were shared by his men, who saw their own redemption in the plan. They knew their role in the coming weeks would be critical.

Davies was particularly enamored of the idea of a quick strike on the French ship-of-the-line at Port-au-Prince. But there were contingencies to work through, for none of his experienced officers expected things to go as smoothly at sea as they were imagined in port. What if the French ship had flown? What if the ruse failed and the French ship attacked *Renegade* instead of vice versa? *What if?*

Davies could leave the fitting out of *Avenger* to Kinis, and this allowed him to spend time with Paloma, at least when she wasn't busy in the Antigua Sewing Circle, as Elinore called Señora Garón's seamstress group. Elinore herself found sewing the barretina caps wonderfully therapeutic, and it allowed her to get to know Paloma on a deeper level as they passed the afternoons together. They could often be seen on the porch of the Pegasus Inn, finished red caps stacked around them, bolts of red cloth nearby. They understood men, and they understood war, and they understood men had to go to war. But neither was the type to wring their hands over it, not if their hands could be doing something useful to the effort.

"Do you ever get used to Nicholas leaving?" Paloma asked Elinore as they sewed. "Does the idea of . . . you know . . . injury or—"

"Death?" interrupted Elinore. "Does it worry me? Of course, but I can't show him. Otherwise, he might decide not to go. He tried that once, working in my father's office a few months, and it changed him. And not for the better."

Paloma nodded, putting herself in Elinore's position in her mind, thinking of Davies about to leave. Already steeling herself to say good-bye.

"When I fell in love with Nico," Elinore continued, "I had to accept that he was who he was and love him *just that way*. And I do. But he's also different from the other captains who leave Bermuda for trading or war. He's very romantic, for one thing. Do you know he writes me verse?"

"Really?" said an obviously surprised Paloma. "What kind of verse?"

"Oh, I can't tell you that," said Elinore, giggling like a schoolgirl. But the flush in her cheeks gave up the answer.

Paloma looked at her new friend affectionately. "Listening to you reminds me of how young Cuban girls describe the perfect man."

"How is that?" asked Elinore with a smile.

"*Café de la parte superior de la taza y chocolate de la parte inferior.* It means: Coffee from the top of the cup and chocolate from the bottom."

"Yes," said a laughing Elinore. "*That* is Nicholas Fallon. He knows the way to a woman's heart is chocolate!"

Their conversation was interrupted by gunshots coming from west of the village where, on a long, flat beach, Ezra Somers was practicing with his pistols. He had no intention of staying in port while *Rascal* went to sea and, as he owned the ship, there wasn't going to be an argument about it. Besides, he was a crack shot and Fallon knew it. He might be old, but he was a man you could count on. Most mornings he could be seen limping along the beach carrying a satchel of pistols and ammunition. His gout still flared from time to time, though he found if he cut down his nightly wine consumption it seemed to subside slightly. Still, he reasoned, that was a steep price to pay.

Evenings found Fallon and Elinore busy with each other, and Paloma and Davies were not to be seen either, so Somers gradually developed a friendship with Doctor Garón and enjoyed their deep and often philosophical discussions. The doctor was well read in the classics and had a passing acquaintance with Descartes's *Meditations*, but he knew nothing of the great Greek philosophers. He was, however, a font of information on Spanish and Cuban *thinkers* of the day. Books and opinion consumed their after-dinner walks.

The days and nights passed thus, until a week and then another were gone. When at last the uniforms and hats were delivered to the newly named *Tigre*, and the shot and stores were aboard all three ships and the contingencies all addressed satisfactorily, Davies called for departure at first light on the morrow to catch the tide.

The last night in port would be a night for lovers, for final embraces and more, for heartfelt promises to wait and earnest pledges to return. Both Fallon and Davies slept out of their ships; Jones and Beauty fidgeted in their respective cots; and Somers slept like a baby.

FIFTY-TWO

THE THREE SHIPS weighed and sheeted home, gradually leaving Elinore, Paloma, and the Garóns waving good-bye in the strengthening light of early morning. They all put on brave faces, but no one could predict the future. That was, no doubt, just as well. At sea anything could happen, and quite a bit of it was bad.

Once clear of the harbor, Fallon turned his attention to Barclay and discussed once again the course that would take them to the open Caribbean. The trades were reliably behind them, and Beauty ordered the helmsman to bear off whenever possible to keep the wind on their quarter so as to stay ahead of *Renegade* and *Avenger*. Meanwhile, there were several islands to navigate, though all of them were colonies of Great Britain, or at least neutral.

Beauty thumped about the ship on her peg leg as if completely healed, although Fallon guessed she hid whatever pain she still felt. She seemed to relish being aboard a ship she knew so well, with a crew she clearly trusted and who trusted her. The color had returned to her cheeks, and she could be seen smiling with Aja and Barclay at the binnacle as the schooner threaded her way through the islands toward the open sea. All was well for now, but tomorrow could be entirely different, of course. Fallon mulled the possibilities as he walked the length of the ship and back, again and again. While *Rascal* was not to have a fighting role against more formidable foes, he knew *needs must when the devil drives.*

At last, they broke into open water and *Rascal* could have her head, with Beauty taking advantage of each slant of wind in the otherwise predictable trades. It was good to exercise the crew and to immerse the new hands in the working of the ship. Cully practiced loading and running out with his gun crews, and Barclay and Aja took their noon sights religiously for comparison each day. Somers watched it all from his chair at the stern of the ship, set up just for him, like a royal personage with gout.

Two days out of English Harbor, *Avenger* and *Renegade* were left behind; *Rascal* was totally, wonderfully alone on the deep blue. The ship was thirty miles south of Bahia Yuma, a small bay on Santo Domingo's southern shore, sailing west with no vessels in sight. Tomorrow would see them at the mouth of the Gulf of Gonâve, looking for a French ship; there was a good chance she was still there, either negotiating with Louverture or provisioning for the long journey back to France. Or, up to something more sinister.

Fallon had conferred with Beauty during the forenoon watch about Aja, and they were both in agreement that it was time. He had proven himself again and again as a natural leader, much respected by the men, with the complete trust of Fallon and Beauty. They made plans to honor him at dinner and, of course, invited Somers, Colquist, Barclay, and Cully to join them.

For the event, the cook prepared a suckling pig with potatoes and leeks and some soft but still serviceable carrots. The claret was passed around, and around again, and by the time the pig arrived on the scene it was a happy party, indeed. Cully, in particular, was in rare form and told jokes with an Irishman's wink, and the table laughed themselves silly.

At last, the dishes were cleared and the duff pudding made a grand entrance, with Barclay making a toast to duff pudding and all puddings in the world, for he was a pudding aficionado.

Then it was time for Fallon to do the honors. He stood and

held his wine glass up and looked around the table, a smile on his beaming face.

"Two years ago, some of you will remember, we were aboard *Sea Dog* heading south toward Grand Turk Island, and we came upon an utterly destroyed and sinking slaver. A pirate had taken off the hands he wanted and slaughtered the rest. But this is not meant to be a sad story. For down below, Cully found a young boy who was still alive, having cleverly hidden behind barrels to escape the pirates. We brought him aboard *Sea Dog*, but he would not speak. Not a word, mind you."

Aja lowered his head, embarrassed, having no idea what was coming but moved because it was coming from Fallon.

"In the time since, we've watched him grow into a capable top man, a fair hand with a sword, and a better than average navigator—watch your back, Barclay! He's a fellow who is always there, in thick or thin, *just when you need him most*. But I must say, more than any of that, he is a *leader*. You all know how the men respect him, how the men follow him."

Now there was banging on the table and *Hear! Hear!*

"So, I want to propose a toast to someone utterly remarkable. Someone wise beyond his years. Someone whose loyalty to the ship and to the crew and to me can never be questioned. Only, I cannot make this toast to *Aja*."

Fallon smiled as Aja's eyes looked up in confusion.

"Instead," said Beauty rising from her chair, "let's raise a glass to our new *second mate, Ajani!*"

Hear! Hear! rang out around the table again as Aja now put his face in his hands with an involuntary cry from the effects of the toast; certainly, it was not from wine, as he'd had none. Suddenly the table shook with a *whunk!* When Aja raised his head and made to dry his cheeks with his sleeve, he saw a beautiful, bejeweled dirk stuck in the table. It was the very dagger Fallon had taken from the *capitaine*'s cabin on *Petite Bouton*. Aja's eyes opened wide and he looked at it a moment and then around the table, and finally at Fallon.

"I believe you lost your other dirk," Fallon said with a wink. "Be careful with this one."

AT DAWN the next morning, First Mate Beauty McFarland and Second Mate Ajani toured the ship to be sure all was well, Aja carrying his new dirk proudly. His uniform hadn't changed; well, there was no real uniform aboard a privateer. But those crew who were on watch saw a confident bearing in his stride and knuckled their foreheads in respect as he passed. All hands agreed the promotion was deserved.

Fallon was on deck as the ship rounded the southwest corner of Saint-Domingue. Several hours should see them at the outer entrance to the Gulf of Gonâve, and he scanned the horizon with his telescope to no avail. There were no sails to be seen.

The wind was on *Rascal's* starboard beam until, at last, they hardened up and began working their way to Port-au-Prince on the far eastern shore. They made their tacks crisply, but as the gulf was quite long it would be several hours before the hail from the lookout came.

Satisfied that all was well for the moment, Fallon returned to his cabin to study the chart for the gulf carefully, noting the small bays and indentations along the shoreline. Who knew how accurate the charts were? Well, it was all he had, and he memorized what he saw before moving his attention to Gonâve Island.

The island had been the inhospitable home to hundreds of runaway slaves who escaped Saint-Domingue before Louverture's revolution. It was arid and made of limestone and scrub. Most of the slaves who reached the island died trying to live there. Fallon stared at it now, a paper image, and tried to imagine the misery of the place. When some time later he had the features of the gulf in his mind, he rolled up the chart and was just leaving to gain the deck again when the lookout's call came.

"Deck there! Ship at anchor. French, I think! She's a first-rate!"

Good God, thought Fallon, that meant three gun decks and at least one hundred guns. If France was delivering a message to Louverture, it was a serious damn message! There was certainly no need to deliver a simple letter with a first-rate.

He climbed the ratlines and raised his telescope to have a look for himself. The French ship was anchored fore and aft between Gonâve Island and the southern shore of the gulf. All fifty guns on her larboard side were behind closed gun ports. But the angle of the ship—athwart the wind with her larboard side facing the entrance to the gulf—told Fallon the *capitaine* knew his business, had set a spring line, and was prepared for any surprise. That would be something for Jones to consider, certainly, and it might change the plan.

"Sir!" said the lookout just as Fallon had started to descend to the deck. "A sloop coming out! She's flying French colors!"

Quickly, Fallon raised his telescope to see a sloop putting her nose out from behind Gonâve Island, apparently to investigate this nosy schooner. The sloop was no doubt acting as the first-rate's sentry while in harbor and, though she was still several miles away, Fallon would need to decide what to do. If he withdrew, would the sloop follow? For how long? If he stayed and fought, would it provoke the first-rate into weighing in order to join the fight?

Fallon hung onto the ratlines to think. He assumed the sloop had preceded the French ship into the gulf and *Rascal*'s lookout couldn't see her when the big ship had been spotted weeks ago. Well, no matter, the sloop was very visible now and Fallon had a decision to make.

He climbed down to the deck and was met by Beauty and Aja, who were looking at the oncoming sloop with their own telescopes.

"What do you think, Beauty?" asked Fallon, mindful of precipitating action that would put the existing plan with Renegade-now-*Tigre* in jeopardy.

"I see the problem, Nico," she said, reading his mind as she so often did. "But what's the opportunity?"

The question caught Fallon off guard, and for a moment he could think of no opportunity, no way to turn this negative into a positive.

"That is a very pretty sloop, Captain, sir," said Aja. "It is a very good size for me, I think." And then he smiled at Fallon.

And, slowly, Fallon smiled back, and then nodded.

"Beauty," he said, "come about and sail off to the west. Not too fast, mind you, we want this Frenchman to follow us and not lose us. We must keep him *encouraged*."

At all costs, Fallon didn't want the eyes of the first-rate on the battle, for it had to be seen that the sloop was driving *Rascal* off. Well, in a sense, it was true, he thought. *For now*.

Rascal came about and steadied on course to the west, back the way she'd come, as if retreating. The French sloop, in turn, gave chase, was almost obligated to give chase as a show for the first-rate, and Beauty sailed just loosely enough to let the sloop keep up with *Rascal*. She wanted the terrier to feel very proud of herself running off a bigger dog. Fallon kept a constant eye on the sloop, the wind, and their relative positions, and when they were well away from Gonâve Island, and the first-rate's lookout, he deemed it time.

"Beauty, I want to wear ship in two minutes and point for her bows," said Fallon with a grin. "We're going to see what this *capitaine* is made of! And then hoist our colors, please. Let's tell him who he's fighting!"

Somers had been watching Fallon as he stared at the sloop and wondered if Fallon had a plan. Well, whatever it was, he planned to do his part, and he went below to get his satchel of pistols. He was limping a little, but not that much, and he wanted to be ready. He looked over his shoulder as he got to the companionway and saw the sloop was noticeably closer, and Beauty would be ordering the ship to wear soon.

FIFTY-THREE

THE SHIPS had a bit more than a mile between them when *Rascal* wore ship smoothly, coming up into the wind close-hauled on the larboard tack and sailing back toward the French sloop. The wind was out of the east-northeast, shifting slightly here and there, and the sloop sensibly had the breeze on her starboard quarter. Her guns were still behind her gun ports.

Fallon and Beauty studied the tactical situation closely. The obvious thing would be to sail low and rake the sloop on her larboard side, for Rascal was being pushed down slightly to the south as it was. But that meant *Rascal* would have to suffer a broadside, and Fallon wanted to protect his men at all costs since they should really be on their way home to Bermuda at this point.

"Beauty, time the lifts," he said with a hint of excitement in his voice. "Like the old days racing on the harbor. The *capitaine* won't notice them but we need to know when the wind comes more north."

Beauty nodded and looked away to study wind and water. The wind never stayed in exactly the same direction, but oscillated through several degrees in a fairly predictable pattern. By timing the lifts they could anticipate them, and catching one would enable *Rascal* to sail closer to the wind than she was sailing now and claw up more to the north.

"Ask Cully to load the guns with grape," said Fallon, an idea turning into a plan. "Then at three cable's distance we'll run out both batteries."

Beauty looked at him quizzically. Here was something new.

"I want the *capitaine* to have that same look on his face!" said Fallon with a smile. "Stay on his bows, and whatever he decides we must be prepared to do the opposite of what he expects. I think he will expect to engage us on his larboard side, believing we can't get up any higher, but he may not. That would be logical, though."

Beauty cackled, for her captain delighted in doing the *illogical* thing whenever possible. She gave the necessary orders; the crew was told off and went to their positions, standing by to execute her commands when they came. The sloop was almost three-quarters of a mile away now, and a cast of the log indicated the two ships were probably closing at a combined speed of almost twenty knots. Fallon did the math in his head: When *Rascal*'s batteries ran out at three cables, the French *capitaine* would have less than a minute to make up his mind what to do.

"Ezra!" Fallon called, "please set up in the bows." And then Fallon yelled out: "A guinea says the *capitaine* falls to his pistol, lads! Who wants the bet?" Fallon could hear several calls from the crew and saw Somers grin. Betting on him was never a bad idea.

Aja was by Fallon's side, his new dirk at the ready, eager to do what was asked.

"Aja," Fallon said. "Organize a boarding party and be ready with grappling hooks. We're going to take that ship!" Fallon was mad with the fight now, his eyes dancing in his face, his mouth set in determination.

Beauty had been timing the lifts, satisfied that they were coming roughly two minutes apart. But that raised an important question.

"Barclay," she said to the sailing master, "how long until we reach the sloop?"

Barclay scratched his head and judged the distance and speed of the two ships. He scribbled on the slate, rubbed his chin, and then looked up.

"I make it almost three minutes, give or take," he said confidently, though trying to hedge a *little*. Beauty nodded, and looked in the distance, searching for any changes in the wind on the water's surface.

"It will be a near thing," she said at last to Fallon, who was watching her face closely. "If you're thinking what I think you're thinking."

At five cable's length, still over a thousand yards, both ships were still sailing straight for each other. Beauty was calm, but Barclay and Aja fidgeted in spite of themselves. The ships came closer still, but the Frenchman still would not commit. Now little more than three cables separated the two ships.

"Run out the batteries!" Fallon ordered, and there came the deep, unmistakable rumbling of a ship preparing for war. Both starboard and larboard batteries ran out, stiff black wings hovering over the waves. Seconds went by. More seconds.

Suddenly, the French sloop's larboard battery ran out; the *capitaine* had made his decision.

"When can we head up, Beauty?" asked Fallon as calmly as he could, but the tension was in his voice.

"A moment, my Captain," she replied, fighting her own nervousness. And then under her breath: *Come on wind!*

There! She both felt the wind shift on her cheek and saw it on the water. She hesitated, one eye on the sloop, which was almost upon them, and one on the foresail.

"Now!" she said as she touched the helmsman's arm. "Come up! Ride her up!" The wind indeed had shifted momentarily, more from the north, and the helmsman carefully guided *Rascal* up to it . . . up, up . . . it wouldn't do to stall . . . a little higher still . . .

Then the lift petered out, the wind came back to its old direction, and *Rascal* had to fall off—but she was heading down the sloop's starboard side!

"Stand by the starboard battery, Cully!" called Fallon. "Rake her!"

The French *capitaine* could do nothing but look on in disbelief. His starboard guns were behind their gun ports, loaded or not, and there was no time to run them out.

Rascal's starboard battery thundered and the startled French crew was cut down, spinning to the deck with arms and legs flailing as a thousand iron balls tore across a very few feet of water. No, a thousand and one, for Ezra Somers was at the starboard bow as Rascal swept out of the smoke, and he took careful aim at the French captain's heart. The capitaine died with surprise on his face, though whether from Fallon's trick or the impact of the ball in his chest would never be known.

"Wear ship, Beauty!" yelled Fallon, for the sloop had rounded into the wind and was going nowhere, her helm deserted and her deck a cemetery of dead bodies. Beauty put Rascal alongside the sloop, and Aja grappled on to lead a boarding party onto her deck. The dead lay in all manner of grotesque postures, Cully's gunners having done their job beyond well, and Aja met little resistance. In a moment, the remaining French crew surrendered, the few officers still alive offered their swords, and the ship was taken. Not a single shot came aboard Rascal, and her crew was deeply grateful, many shaking their heads in disbelief. Colquist would have no British seamen to tend to. French wounded, however, were another story.

Beauty smiled broadly and complimented the helmsman repeatedly, for he had taken Rascal as far as she could go but no farther, which would have stopped the ship in her tracks. Heaven knows what would have been the result of that, but it didn't bear thinking about. Victory was to be celebrated, not questioned.

It was the work of an hour to move the wounded below decks on Rascal. The prisoners were transferred over as well, while the dead crew was thrown overboard with a brief prayer by Fallon. The French officers were stripped of their uniforms, which were given to the cook and ship's boys to wash while the blood was still fresh on them.

The sloop's name was Mistral. While Beauty organized a crew to put the little ship to rights, repairing rigging and such, Fallon rifled the capitaine's cabin. He was looking for a signal book and any clues as to the late *capitaine's* orders or, more important, orders for the first-rate, whose name he discovered was *Coeur de France*—Heart of France.

He read in the ship's log that *Mistral* had sailed from Les Sables-d'Olonne on the Bay of Biscay as *Coeur's* tender and dispatch vessel eight weeks before, arriving in the Caribbean two weeks ago, and proceeded immediately to Port-au-Prince. *Mistral's* orders did not mention what the purpose of the mission was, but Fallon's eyes fell on the last paragraph and his eyes widened reflexively.

"Good God," he said aloud in the empty cabin. "*This changes things!*"

THAT NIGHT *Rascal* was to rendezvous with *Avenger* and *Renegade* off Dame Marie, on the far southwest tip of Saint-Domingue, and it was early evening when Beauty rounded into the wind near the ships and ordered the anchor down. Aja, following behind in command of *Mistral*, did the same. Davies ordered: *Captains repair on board.* The gigs were lowered and the captains were rowed to the flagship; Aja was rowed over as well, for the plan would now change somehow and might well involve *Mistral*.

"You just can't seem to resist taking a prize, can you, Nicholas?" said an amused and impressed Davies as they all settled in his great cabin. "Tell us the story, please, for we are all fascinated to hear it!"

Fallon described the scene in the Gulf of Gonâve and the presence of a first-rate lying athwart the wind. Jones swallowed hard, for that meant the ship was *prepared*. Then Fallon recounted the sudden appearance of *Mistral*. He compressed the story of the chase and gave all credit to Beauty's boat handling, Cully's gunnery and, of course, Somers's marksmanship. He even noted that Aja had led the boarding party, which made the young second mate smile self-consciously. But he was a smart young man, and the manner in which Fallon gave credit to others was not lost on him.

"Excellent!" exclaimed Davies. "For a *noncombatant* on this mission, you've drawn first blood! But surely this might affect our little plan?" This, a statement as much as a question.

"Yes, I believe so, sir," said Fallon. "I found *Mistral*'s orders in the *capitaine*'s desk, which revealed her as a tender for the first-rate, *Coeur de France*. But here is the complication: The orders state that *Mistral* is also to escort *Tigre* into Port-au-Prince!"

The cabin grew quiet as each person attempted to calculate the implications of that bit of news. It was Davies who broke the silence.

"Why should *Tigre* trust *Mistral*? I know they are nominal allies, but unless this has all been arranged beforehand . . ." His voice trailed off as he looked at Fallon.

"Yes, I believe that is so," said Fallon. "I found two signal books aboard *Mistral* containing a common set of signals so the French and Spanish could communicate among themselves. There can be only one reason for that. I believe they intend combined action of some sort, probably against Louverture or Great Britain."

Fallon looked at each of their faces carefully, seeing the shock come to their eyes, for though France and Spain were allies they had never joined forces *literally*. Fallon wondered if they could see what he was seeing as an opportunity.

"Where and when is *Mistral* to rendezvous with *Tigre*?" asked Kinis. "That may alter things for us, I would think."

"Yes, *Mistral* is to meet *Tigre* in Santiago de Cuba, where she is wooding and watering, in four days," Fallon explained. "Thence they are to sail to Port-au-Prince to meet with *Coeur*. The French aren't taking any chances on a surprise. And Spain gets assurance of their frigate's safety by following *Mistral* into the Gulf of Gonâve."

"I see," said Davies. "*Mistral*'s role is to be the go-between between two suspicious allies, one of which has one hundred guns!"

Davies' steward appeared with glasses and several bottles of wine, and one ginger beer for Aja. The group drank the King's health and scratched their chins and pulled their ears deep in thought. It was very dark outside before anyone spoke.

"*Recherche de la faiblesse,*" mused Davies to no one in particular, for his eyes were closed.

"Yes," said Fallon. "*Look for the weakness.* I believe this little French sloop has an important role, for she decides who goes into the Gulf of Gonâve and who doesn't. She was quite fearless in chasing us away! *Mistral* is the only link between two uneasy allies, and both sides must trust her."

"And we have her!" exclaimed Jones.

"I think that is their weakness, gentlemen," said Davies, opening his eyes and looking around the room, and then at the chart with fresh eyes. "And it is our strength."

Everyone nodded, but it was Fallon who spoke.

"Picture *Renegade* as *Tigre,* to all eyes, escorted into the harbor by *Mistral,*" he said quietly, causing the others to lean in closer. "She is arriving, a bit early perhaps, to her meeting with the first-rate's *capitaine.* How far can we take this little deception?"

"Said another way," said Davies, catching where Fallon was going, "can *Renegade* do more damage than just a passing broadside from long range? Is that what you're wondering?"

"Yes, exactly," replied Fallon. "We can do more than poke the bear. We can *enrage* the bear. And then maybe bag a tiger!"

A collective gasp around the cabin. All realized this took the plan in a new direction.

And then Fallon laid out a scenario that was very like a three-act play. A play with a mad privateer directing it. The storyline was really very simple, assuming the French and Spanish actors played their parts exactly as they were supposed to.

Of course, safe to say no one at the meeting believed that would happen.

FIFTY-FOUR

The *capitaine* of *Coeur de France*, Henri Ardoin, awoke the next morning wondering if *Mistral* had sailed in after dark, having successfully chased the schooner away from the gulf. It had been an impudent little schooner—it looked American to his eyes, and though America and France were not officially at war, the two countries were certainly in a *quasi*-war. He had a suspicion the schooner was sent to further ties with Louverture and to promote trade with the fledgling United States, something France was quite against. It was well known in Paris that the U.S. Secretary of State was in contact with Louverture and offered a very convincing point of view in support of Saint-Domingue's independence. As a response, and Louverture knew this quite well, France had issued an *exclusif* prohibiting Saint-Domingue from trading with any country except France. It remained to be seen whether Louverture would be bound by it. Or would be bound by *anything* coming out of France.

Except, that is, the abolition of slavery in France's colonies. Yet, even so, Ardoin knew there was speculation in Paris that, at some point, slavery would be reinstated by decree of the French government. It would be justified as an economic necessity. What would Louverture do then, he wondered? It was believed that Bonaparte, who was rapidly gaining power, was in favor of it. If slavery came back, every black finger in the Caribbean would be pointed to

Joséphine's influence on Bonaparte as the real reason, for her plantation family on Martinique had suffered greatly since slavery was disallowed.

No doubt Ardoin would learn more from Thomas Hedouville when he came aboard in the forenoon. France had sent Hedouville to Saint-Domingue months ago as something of a special agent. His primary mission: Drive a wedge between Louverture and Rigaud. By all accounts he had succeeded, for the country was divided by civil war. But there was more to Hedouville's orders, of course. There was *always* more.

France intended to extend a hand to Spain as an ally against Great Britain, and Hedouville was to meet with the captain of *Tigre*, a Spanish frigate awaiting a rendezvous at Port-au-Prince. They were to establish a basis for coordinated action against the British in the Caribbean, which to Ardoin meant: *You do what we tell you.* He doubted that would go over well, for Spanish officers were proud to the point of arrogance, in his experience, and not to be trusted to hold up their end of a bargain.

Ardoin dressed by the light of several candles, with the aid of his steward, for he had only one arm. A romantic liaison had led to an angry husband's challenge to a duel two years before and, though the husband had been killed, his shot had shattered Ardoin's left arm. He stepped out of his cabin and passed the sentry, breathing in the salt air as he went. As he gained the deck he could see the sky lightening to the east over Port-au-Prince. He looked the length of his massive ship, a wooden behemoth with more than eight hundred officers and men. An enemy ship intent on mischief would face a withering hail of metal if she attempted an action on Port-au-Prince, or on *Coeur* for that matter.

Ardoin was not concerned that *Mistral* had not returned, but if she did not come sailing into the harbor today he had to assume the worst: that she had engaged the schooner and was lost. Then *Tigre* would miss the rendezvous, for *Mistral* was to escort her into the Gulf as a *précaution enter amis*—a precaution between friends. Ardoin did not trust Spain, and no doubt Spain did not trust France, and both sides had their reasons.

"How DO I look, Mr. Barclay?" asked Fallon.

Mistral had sailed first out of Dame Marie late that morning, carrying Fallon and a small crew toward the gulf on a light breeze. She certainly looked like a French sloop that had been in battle. She had a few scars on her hull and deck, but her rigging had been set to rights and the decks holystoned to remove the blood, which had been considerable, and her officers and crew were *apparently* all still aboard. The *capitaine's* coat was a bit short on Fallon, and the bullet hole over his heart was disconcerting, but he was comfortable enough. Barclay was playing the role of first lieutenant, his gray hair tucked up under his hat, and the crew from *Avenger* were all enjoying the little theatre of sailing as a French sloop.

"You look tolerably French, sir!" replied Barclay. "I see the bullet to your heart didn't faze you, however. So surely you are actually British!"

That was the morning's first laugh, and Fallon was still smiling as he walked to the stern of the little sloop. Behind *Mistral* came *Renegade,* her Spanish flag flying proudly, her officers in their new Spanish uniforms, and the crew in barretina caps, courtesy of the Antigua Sewing Circle. Fallon wondered if Jones was feeling awkward in the capitán's uniform cluttered with medals and plumage, having never impersonated an enemy officer before.

Well, he thought, *welcome to a privateer's life.*

COEUR'S CABIN was spectacular and lavishly appointed. No expense had been spared in the selection of exotic woods and inlays, and the rich patina of the paneling warmed the room even on the cloudiest of days in the dead of winter. Ardoin felt blessed to have his position, for it was surely the finest housing he would ever enjoy. The steward was just finishing dusting it all when Thomas Hedouville was announced.

"I take it your meeting with Louverture went as expected?" began Ardoin, beckoning the diplomat to take a seat near the gallery of windows, which covered the entire width of the stern.

Hedouville sat down heavily and sighed the sigh of the impatient.

"No, for the great general was still in the country fighting Rigaud, I was told. He plays at his little war while France tolerates it, which may not be much longer. I will go ashore yet again this afternoon when, it is to be hoped, he returns to Port-au-Prince. I want the full situation in hand before meeting with the captain of *Tigre*. And then I intend to leave this damned island!"

In truth, Ardoin himself was in no real hurry to leave for France, as his frequent trips ashore had familiarized him with the beauty of not only the island but also the women of Saint-Domingue. One planter's daughter in particular had been quite forward with her glances, and he had accepted her invitation to dinner that evening. Her parents would be in attendance, of course, along with other French planters, but perhaps an opportunity might present itself . . .

"On the topic of *Tigre*," continued Hedouville. "We must treat the captain like royalty itself. Salutes and everything are due, of course. The Spanish are very thin-skinned with their pride, you know. I trust you will receive him accordingly. If we are to work together as allies to defeat Great Britain, he must feel we are equals."

"Even though we are not," said Ardoin with a sniff.

Hedouville only smiled.

FIFTY-FIVE

THE SUN had almost disappeared when the hail came from *Coeur*'s lookout that *Mistral* was in the offing. And she was leading a Spanish frigate into the harbor!

Capitaine Ardoin had been dressing for dinner and had just had his left sleeve pinned up by his steward when he heard the hail, and he quickly came on deck, his anxiety provoked by such an unexpected turn of events. The dimming light made the images in his telescope faint, but he could see the little sloop and her crewmen aboard and, less than two cables behind, a Spanish frigate with her officers on the quarterdeck looking through their telescopes at *Coeur*.

Both *Mistral* and the Spanish frigate made the private signal, so Ardoin relaxed. Yet he tried to piece together a likely scenario that would fit the facts before his eyes. Apparently, *Mistral* had successfully chased off the American schooner—that much seemed obvious, for here she was—and then perhaps she'd encountered *Tigre* sailing on her way to or from Santiago and decided to escort her to the rendezvous in the gulf. A little early, but why not?

Well, thought Ardoin, that explanation would do for now until he had more information in hand. He ordered a signal be hoisted from the signal book especially created so the French and Spanish could communicate—*Captains repair on board*—and went below to finish dressing. It would be awhile until the ships had their anchors down.

Little did he know.

An hour later the Spanish frigate had still not settled, having tried unsuccessfully to anchor directly off *Coeur*'s larboard side before apparently being ordered away by *Mistral* so that *Coeur* could maintain a clear view of the harbor. What a fool this capitán was, thought Ardoin. At this rate he would be late for dinner.

A full cloud cover blocked the moon and stars, and Ardoin could barely see the frigate attempting to set her anchor to the north of *Coeur*, between the first-rate's bow and Gonâve Island, with *Mistral* hove-to nearby until the task was done. Again and again the frigate tried to get the anchor down but apparently the coral around the island extended outward to the south, for the holding appeared to be uncertain.

It was now very dark, and Ardoin was very late for dinner, even *rudely* late. Duty said to send apologies to shore and wait for the damned frigate to anchor, no matter how long it took. But he felt secure enough in the harbor, perhaps a bit too comfortable, yes, but the planter's daughter was so beautiful . . .

At last, Ardoin picked up the speaking trumpet with his right hand and ordered the *capitaine* of *Mistral* to report in the morning, bringing along the Spanish capitán. Who knew when the damned frigate would anchor? Someone aboard *Mistral* acknowledged the order, perhaps Lieutenant What's-his-name.

Ardoin carefully climbed down into his gig for the short row to shore, shaking his head at the unpredictability of war and the strange bedmates it made.

AFTER HE had answered the hail from *Coeur*, Fallon burned a shaded light briefly from his bow to signal Jones to get his anchor down. This task was accomplished easily enough as the holding was really very good. The light breeze out of the east meant that the newly named *Tigre* was lying athwart *Coeur*'s bows, just as Fallon had predicted, about a cable away. That done, *Mistral* turned her

own bow for Santiago, sailing off as a lightless shape on the gulf's
black water.

CAPITAINE ARDOIN was back aboard *Coeur* by midnight, slightly
drunk but deeply satisfied. His decision to go ashore had been the
right one, as a late-night stroll in the garden with the planter's beautiful daughter proved. At the end of a long, winding path among
fragrant flowers there was a little-used garden shed and, by moving
a few rakes and shovels, something of a bed was created atop several
loose bales of hay. Nature, or at least *human* nature, took care of the
rest.

Once back aboard *Coeur* he was met by his first lieutenant.

"*Tigre* has settled at last, *Capitaine*," he said. "Just after you left
she got her anchor down."

Ardoin nodded, looking out into the darkness at the bare outline
of the frigate off *Coeur*'s bow.

"And *Mistral?*" he asked.

"I believe she anchored on the other side of her," said the lieutenant. "I could not be sure because of the darkness, of course. But
everything is quiet now."

Well, thought Ardoin, it would be an embarrassed capitán who
showed up tomorrow morning. Or, at least, he should be. It just
proved you couldn't trust the Spanish, even with the simplest of
things.

Ardoin went below without another thought. He got undressed
and into his cot, mindless of the straw that fell off his coat and
breeches to the cabin floor. In a moment, he was in contented sleep.

MEANWHILE, *MISTRAL*'s tired crew sailed for Santiago de Cuba,
at least two hundred miles to the northwest. The clouds scud-
ded across the sky to reveal stars aplenty to guide them, while the
trades were their constant friend, pushing the little sloop easily
along through the early morning. Fallon tried to sleep in his cabin

but dozed fitfully, imagining the scene in the gulf in a matter of hours and wishing he were there. But his little play needed a director, a leader who had the ability to speak both French and Spanish convincingly. Perhaps the hardest part would be the next part. For in Santiago he must go back into secret agent mode, which meant impersonating someone, and he remembered all too well his past experience in Matanzas as an erstwhile investor.

When, at last, sleep claimed him he dreamt of home. In his dream, his father was dressed in a waistcoat, and it surprised him because he couldn't remember his father ever *being* in a waistcoat before. And everyone was at church, all of his past and present crewmen. Flowers were everywhere and music was playing. He saw Ezra Somers, also formally dressed, sitting in a pew with Aja and Beauty and Elinore, with their heads down. He, the omniscient he, thought for a moment he was at a wedding, perhaps his own. The music stopped, and a priest stood at the altar and uttered a prayer for everlasting life. Everyone was praying now; no one looked up. And then it occurred to Fallon that perhaps it wasn't his wedding. And he woke up suddenly.

FIFTY-SIX

*C*APITAINE! CAPITAINE! Wake up!"

Who was that insistent voice and why wouldn't he stop? thought Ardoin, who wanted nothing more than to turn over in his cot and find the dream he seemed to have misplaced. The one with the planter's daughter, who was just now stepping out of her dress—

"*Capitaine!* There is a British frigate in the harbor!" yelled Ardoin's steward in his ear.

Instantly, Ardoin was awake with his feet on the deck. Not waiting to dress, he sprang for the companionway in his nightshirt and grabbed his telescope, but quickly saw it was not needed.

There, not a cable's distance away sitting across his bows was the Spanish frigate that had come in last night and had had trouble anchoring. Even in the gray light Ardoin could see she had her guns out, pointing directly at *Coeur de France*, and she now flew a British flag.

Merde!

"FIRE!" YELLED JONES.

Renegade's broadside exploded in a thunderous cacophony that reverberated off the hillsides surrounding the harbor and echoed off the limestone hump of Gonâve Island in the millisecond before it tore through the bows and forward rigging of *Coeur*. Anyone in the heads would have been smashed to red jam where they sat. *Coeur's* lovely figurehead, a golden maiden with one hand over her heart, was unfortunately decapitated and the arm lost. Quickly, Jones ordered the guns swabbed and reloaded.

Aboard *Coeur*, pandemonium spread like fire. Jones assumed he was dealing with a capable captain who would act quickly, leaving the mystery of a Spanish frigate becoming a British frigate *overnight* for later. *Coeur*'s predicament was clear: To get her guns to bear, the stern spring line would need to be cast off so the massive ship could swing round into the wind and become parallel to *Tigre*. Then the fifty larboard guns would bear. In fact, at the precise moment that Ardoin's spring line was cast off, *Renegade*'s second broadside ripped through his ship, cutting down men who were rushing to man the first-rate's larboard battery.

"Give it to 'em, lads!" screamed Jones, ecstatic as every shot told, and wood and rigging blew over *Coeur*'s sides. The smoke cleared away quickly, revealing dead French sailors strewn about the deck. It was a glorious thing to fire and not be fired upon, but Jones knew it couldn't last. Even now *Coeur*'s stern seemed to be swinging to the west, and very soon the two ships would be parallel. Not good, but not unanticipated.

"Cut the cable!" he ordered, and a seaman stationed at the bow with an axe began chopping at the cable. The cable was massive, but the axe had been sharpened to a fine edge just for this moment, and at last the bitter end of the cable slipped into the water.

"Let tops'ls fall!" Jones ordered, and slowly the northeast breeze pushed *Renegade* backward. Next, Jones ordered the rudder hard a-starboard and back-winded the jib so that the frigate's bows would fall off and she would curl behind *Coeur*'s stern. The two ships were doing a little dance, and it would take excellent seamanship on Jones's part to drift backward with the frigate's stern swinging southward, eliminating *Coeur*'s firing angle while creating a new target for *Renegade*'s starboard guns: *Coeur*'s stern. The trick was to slip past the swinging *Coeur* before her larboard guns could get off a broadside. Even now the first-rate's gun ports were coming open, but it was too late. *Renegade* was past and had swung round!

"*Fire!*" yelled Jones, and *Renegade*'s great guns sent their deadly balls through the first-rate's giant stern gallery and on through the officer's quarters and beyond. The broadside obliterated bulkheads and furniture before coming to a rest halfway through *Coeur.* Any Frenchman in that broadside's path was probably, mercifully, dead in an instant.

"Courses!" yelled Jones, hoarse with excitement and lack of sleep, and slowly *Renegade*'s sternway was checked. The frigate gathered the strengthening breeze to her bosom and began to move forward.

Behind him, Jones could see the French *capitaine* shaking a fist at him, the other sleeve of his nightshirt empty and blowing about. He looked more aghast than angry, no doubt because his enormous ship had not fired a single shot.

THE BREEZE continued to strengthen as *Renegade* sailed out of the gulf and farther from land. Jones could at last breathe easily. Truth be told, he had never fought an engagement so thrilling— or frightening—and against a first-rate! And not a single casualty, except a seaman whose foot had been crushed by a recoiling gun. It had been a bold and daring plan, extraordinary in every respect, and he had to admit he could never have thought of it. His mind just didn't work that way, but how he admired a mind that did! And that mind belonged to Fallon.

Jones didn't expect *Coeur* to follow him to sea; there was too much on the ship to set right. He couldn't see all the damage during the battle, but he could imagine it was extensive, especially with the last broadside into her stern. He was on the point of collapse himself, having been awake all night waiting for a dawn that wouldn't come. He thought of Fallon, perhaps with the headlands of Cuba in sight now, on his way to carry out the second part of the plan. It had all the risks of what he'd just been through; more, if you considered that Fallon would be aboard a Spanish ship in a

French uniform and subject to capture as a spy. Then he could be hanged.

Jones shook off that thought and set *Renegade*'s course out of the gulf for Dame Marie. He had much to report to Davies, and he wanted to review his orders for the third act of the play. That is, if Fallon were still alive by then.

FIFTY-SEVEN

IT WAS coming on to evening when *Mistral* reached the entrance to Santiago after sailing for more than 24 hours and, rather than risk entering a strange harbor at night, Fallon decided to heave-to and await dawn. He had been obsessing all day about Jones's safety and the success of his battle with *Coeur*, but he had no way of knowing the outcome. It could easily have become a deadly fiasco if *Coeur* had gotten the upper hand, but it would be over by now, one way or the other. And the success of that battle did not affect what he had before him tomorrow.

Surprisingly, Fallon slept well. A dreamless sleep, thank God, that left him refreshed in the morning. He dressed in his *capitaine*'s uniform and moved a medal over his heart to hide the bullet hole Somers had put there. It was still quite early, and he took his time over breakfast, thinking about how the day's events would go, knowing full well that whatever he thought would happen, wouldn't happen that way.

At last, he stepped onto the deck to be met by Barclay and the rest of his so-called French crew. He smelled the air deeply and looked up to the French flag to gauge the wind.

"Mr. Barclay," he said, "let's be off to Santiago then."

"Aye, aye, sir!" replied Barclay. "It's a lovely day to see Cuba!"

Mistral fell off onto a course before the wind, bound for the entrance to the harbor of Santiago de Cuba. The harbor itself was long and narrow, stretching inland for nearly ten miles and dotted with coves and islands. Fallon had no idea of the exact location for the rendezvous with *Tigre*, but he was less worried about that than he was about his performance once she was found. Approaching the harbor, all hands saw the intimidating fort of El Morro—different from Havana's fort of the same name—glaring down at their tiny ship and, though Fallon had heard there was no garrison stationed there now, it certainly made him nervous. Any of those cannons, if manned, could easily blow them out of the water. He looked at the fort through his telescope and, indeed, saw no sign of life on the parapets.

Santiago was the largest town in Cuba after Havana, and James Wharton had said it played a major role in the importation of slaves. For thousands of kidnapped Africans, this was their first view of land after leaving their country. And their last view of the sea.

Mistral entered the harbor with the wind behind her and then promptly slowed as the ship fell under the lee of El Morro. The land was verdant on the starboard coastline, and islands dotted the harbor to their left. On they sailed, each sailor on alert, for God knew what was in store for them in this enemy harbor.

They passed several coastal fishing vessels beating their way out against the breeze, poor fishermen by the looks of them, with rusted faces aged by years of sun and wind. They looked up as they passed close by the French sloop, with eyes that appeared to have seen much and believed little, and then sailed past.

The sun was well up in the east, more or less directly behind *Mistral*. Fallon paced along the starboard railing as far as it went, and back again, deep in rehearsal for his meeting with the Spanish capitán. He had to convince a man to follow him who no doubt was already skeptical about meeting with a French ship in a French harbor.

The channel cut straight into Cuba, with no real twists and turns. The village of Santiago was ahead to starboard. Fallon raised his telescope and could see two large ships at a quay, perhaps unloading goods. Beyond them stood the village itself, pretty in the morning light, and Fallon could imagine shopkeepers shaking out their rugs and sweeping under tables and rearranging their goods to welcome the day's customers.

Another mile, and Barclay lowered his telescope just as Fallon was about to raise his again.

"Sir, I make the first ship with her stern to us as a slaver," reported Barclay. "I believe I can see the poor buggers on the quay. And the ship bow-on is a frigate. Spanish flag. And, sir, something is hanging in her rigging."

Fallon looked carefully at the frigate and saw it was a man hanging in the rigging. *What the devil?* he thought. He assumed the frigate was *Tigre*—the real *Tigre*. But as to the man hanging in the rigging, he had no idea. Perhaps a mutineer or other crewman who had committed a grievous offense punishable by hanging. It was a gruesome spectacle, barbaric and loathsome, but it was hard for Fallon to tear his eyes away. He thought at first that the body had been hanging there long enough to turn black. But as *Mistral* drew closer he could see that, no, it was a black man hanging there.

Fallon ordered the sloop to anchor, and Barclay brought her about and into the wind. At Fallon's cry of *"Allons y!"*—Let go!— the anchor dropped into six fathoms of water, and the ship drifted backward until the fluke bit into the soft mud below. The sails were furled, and Fallon's gig was dropped overboard. Fallon went down below to get one of the signal books he'd found on *Mistral* and then, returning to the deck, decided on a last word with Barclay.

"See here," he said, "if you see anything amiss on the frigate it likely means I've been discovered. You are to immediately weigh and sail for Dame Marie. Is that understood? Save yourself and save the men."

Barclay nodded that it was understood, and Fallon looked deep into the man's eyes to be sure he was clear on the point. Satisfied, he climbed down into the gig for the short row to *Tigre*. Barclay watched him go, and then he looked across the water at the dead man in the frigate's rigging. *What had he done that was so terrible?*

Fallon's gig clapped on and it was *Capitaine* Giroux who climbed the side of the frigate to be met by Capitán Ramos, *at your service, Señor*. Ramos did not invite his guest below to his cabin, which Fallon took as a sign the interview would be brief. Fallon took the opportunity to position himself with his back to the mainmast so as not to see the dead man in the rigging but, as it happened, the poor creature had swung in the breeze and now faced away.

"I see you have noticed our friend, eh?" said Ramos in fair French. "A pity, but runaways have to be taught a lesson, no?" He spread his hands in the universal gesture for *what can you do?* But he saw that it bothered Fallon, and their meeting was getting off to a poor start.

"Here, cut that man down!" ordered Ramos. He turned to Fallon. "He was a runaway brought here by the soldiers to be made an example of at the slave market. He was already dead, but we hanged him again anyway."

Seeing the distaste on Fallon's face he decided to change the subject completely, for clearly here was a man for whom égalité ran deep.

"What are your orders, *Capitaine* Giroux?" he said in his most conciliatory manner. "I am at your command."

Fallon began to breathe easier. Ramos seemed to be on the defensive, and no doubt as anxious for the meeting to be over as he was. Maybe this would work . . .

"I am to escort you to Port-au-Prince for a meeting on board *Coeur de France*, sir. A meeting between allies, ¿Aliados, sí? I have brought a signal book for you so we may communicate when necessary, and you may make the private signal when we arrive at Port-au-Prince. I am prepared to leave whenever it is convenient."

Ramos took the proffered signal book and looked at this French officer who was so driven by duty that he was prepared to immediately sail back where he'd come from without stepping foot on shore. It seemed odd, and he was mildly perturbed because *he*, Ramos, wanted to sample the delights of the town, and his orders said he had a day left to do it. But here was the sloop and the

French *capitaine* with the secret signal book, and perhaps the least he should do was show he was just as dedicated as a French officer.

"I am ready now, *Capitaine* Giroux," he said with a certain resignation and a slight bow. "Let me dispose of this body, and then I shall follow you out of the harbor."

"Excellent," said Fallon, hiding his relief. "I will burn a light off my stern at night so you may follow easily. If we become separated, I will wait at the southern entrance to the Gulf of Gonâve so that I might have the honor of escorting you inside."

Fallon bowed deeply and exhaled. But as he turned to leave he saw the slave's body sprawled on the deck, eyes open to the sky, and a wave of revulsion washed over him. The bile rose in his throat, and he feared he would vomit on deck, for he could see a black ring around the dead man's breast and a face that looked distorted in death but was still unmistakably Young David.

FIFTY-EIGHT

GET UNDERWAY immediately, Barclay," rasped Fallon as he stepped through the gangway, and the ship came alive. Within fifteen minutes the anchor was up and catted and *Mistral* fell off onto a larboard tack under all plain sail. Fallon watched to be sure *Tigre* followed and, when he was satisfied she was away from the quay, he went below to put cold water on his face. He had seen much in his life, too much of the baser side of man, but still he could be surprised.

After several hours spent tacking to and fro against the wind, the two ships at last cleared the headland upon which El Morro stood sentinel. The officers kept their uniforms on, of course, although Fallon longed to rip his from his body and throw it overboard.

Tigre ranged behind them, her sails reefed to keep station astern of *Mistral*. The big frigate appeared to be handled well enough. Certainly, in the brief moments Fallon was aboard, everything had seemed shipshape—apart from Young David in the rigging, of course. Ramos appeared to know his business and had seemed to accept "Giroux" as a genuine Frenchman, although Fallon cautioned himself against overconfidence. Well, Ramos had followed him out of the harbor instead of blowing him out of the harbor. So that was something.

The afternoon slowly crept into evening, the sky turning a brilliant red to the west. That was a good sign for sailors, for a red evening sky usually meant good weather the next day.

Mistral put her rails into the sea's rollers, and the miles ticked off with each hour. And with each hour Fallon retreated more and more within himself. The sight of Young David had affected him deeply, and he was conflicted about whether to tell Aja and Paloma. He wrestled with the decision in his cabin, standing by the stern windows looking out toward *Tigre*, not two miles behind, and beyond her the perfect red sky of the western world. In the end, he decided that the vision of Young David as a strong, free man needed to be kept alive. He needed to hold onto that vision himself.

As he so often did when lonely or sad, he got a glass of wine and wedged himself into the stern seats and wrote to Elinore, his pen scratching out a few lines of verse, or something like it.

> *You live in the space between my desires.*
> *In the miniscule space between*
> *heartbeats.*
> *Between blinks.*
> *Between breaths.*
> *You live in the unseen spaces of my body,*
> *invisible to everyone else.*
> *For my eyes only.*

It wasn't much; in fact, it was hardly worth writing to Elinore. But it was how he felt when he thought of her, and just then he needed to think of her.

FALLON AWOKE with a gentle nudge from his steward just before first bell in the morning watch, cramped and stiff from a night on the stern seats. He lay for a moment, in no real hurry to join the day. He craned his neck to look out the stern windows, saw the still-black sky, and noticed the ship was on the larboard tack, still thrashing along, the watches having noiselessly changed while he slept.

He rose to shave by the light of a candle, but the face he saw looked worn and old. In the weak light his eyes weren't green, nor bright, and he wasn't what you'd call handsome. *Well,* he thought, *damn the mirror.*

He finished shaving and dressing and, armed with a cup of coffee courtesy of his alert steward, he ascended the companionway steps. The light still burned at the stern, but it was too dark to see *Tigre* behind them.

"All's well, sir," came Barclay's voice out of the darkness. "We should see the western shore of Saint-Domingue in about eight hours if the wind holds."

"Thank you, Barclay," said Fallon. That would put them within sight of the Gulf of Gonâve and the beginning of the third act of this little play. It would be the end of the play, no matter how the act ended.

"How do you think it went with Captain Jones, sir?" asked Barclay. A question for which there was obviously no answer.

Fallon thought again of Jones and *Renegade* and wondered if he had escaped from *Coeur* or been obliterated by the first-rate's guns. If *Renegade* had never made it out of the gulf the entire plan was a fiasco. On the other hand . . .

He shook his head to rein in his optimism. Better to stay focused in the present here on the deck of a proud and brave little ship with a cup of steaming coffee in his hand.

"We will see what we see," he said. It was all he could think to say.

JONES WAS just getting dressed at that moment, feeling pretty good about himself and hoping it didn't show too much. He had been entrusted with a key part of the plan, and a tricky bit it was, what with anchoring just so under the eyes of a first-rate. And then cutting the anchor cable and drifting backward, for God's sake, back past *Coeur's* swinging stern so as to get off another broadside without taking a shot aboard!

Jones was born into nothing and grew up with less. His father died when he was young, and his mother took in laundry to put food on the table. He had a sister who struck out on her own for Ireland when she was sixteen. He himself left when he was twelve to join the Royal Navy as a ship's boy. He sent his mother what he could and wrote to her each month, and he pictured his mother's red hands opening his letters. They would not have been easy to read though, for his penmanship stayed a twelve-year-old's even as he grew older. Slowly, he had risen through the ranks of the navy, aided by the deaths of his seniors. And slowly, the birthright of inferiority he felt had given way to a greater confidence that maybe he could amount to something.

Of course, he had been matter-of-fact in the written report he'd given to Davies yesterday, and then solemn and straightforward when he'd given his verbal report. But inside he was jumping for joy. Obviously, it had all been Fallon's plan—but he'd executed it, by God!

With that little pat on his own back, Jones finished dressing and began to focus on the upcoming meeting with Davies, Kinis, and Beauty. It was meant to review the third act of the play—the players would need to be synchronized and well positioned. He thought of Fallon in Santiago de Cuba and wondered if he'd succeeded in fooling the capitán, or if the Spanish frigate had even been there. Without that, of course, there would be no third act. The thought of the danger Fallon had put himself in brought Jones down to earth and, frankly, humbled him. Well, he'd enjoyed feeling important, if only for a while. Now it was back to business.

FIFTY-NINE

THE GULF of Gonâve was shaped like a horseshoe, its open arms reaching toward Cuba as if offering an embrace. Port-au-Prince was at the back of the horseshoe, with Gonâve Island directly in front of the town. Beauty anchored off the northern coast of the island, well out of sight of any ship entering the bay from the southwest and, of course, out of sight of *Coeur*.

To the south of Gonâve Island, against the southern shore of the bay, lay Les Cayemites, two small islands of moderate height between which *Avenger* was anchored, close to invisible from east or west. And, finally, *Renegade*, disguised as *Tigre*, was idling out of sight to the northwest. Thus, the three British ships formed a triangle, and whatever battle occurred would happen somewhere inside it.

"Mr. Barclay," said Fallon, as the two stood by the binnacle and looked at the approaching green hillsides of the gulf's southern shore. "In very little time, perhaps two hours at most, we will be at the entrance to the gulf and soon after we will bid *adieu* to *Tigre*." He turned to look at the frigate not two miles astern, sailing on an imaginary leash.

"Aye, sir," said Barclay. "The hands are tense, sir, but I told them we would not be going far inside. They know about the first-rate, sir."

Yes, of course they would know. He had to admit he was nervous, too. Who knew what waited inside the gulf? They might well see the tips of *Renegade's* masts above the water, or her wreck upon the shore. Or some other horrible thing they couldn't imagine.

Barclay had *Mistral* on the starboard tack and intended, when they reached some invisible mark on the water, to come about for the final tack into the gulf. Fallon swept the sea with his telescope, but it was empty save for *Tigre*. That gave Fallon pause in spite of the fact that *Rascal, Renegade,* and *Avenger* were not exactly *supposed* to be seen—yet. He cursed himself for turning into a superstitious fool. What was happening to his confidence?

Well, his was a complicated plan with many moving parts. And this final bit depended on the French *capitaine's* temper and courage, which were unknowns. But surely the French wouldn't have sent a nincompoop on such an important mission in a first-rate! *Would they?* Fallon had to be careful here not to fall into the fatal trap of hubris, for the Royal Navy believed there were no captains on earth as smart and brave as their own. It had cost them many ships and was partially responsible for the loss of at least one war, that being with the United States.

In two hours they were inside the entrance to the gulf. It was time.

"Sir, we are ready to come about," said Barclay with confidence.

"Very well, Mr. Barclay," replied Fallon. "We're about to see what we see."

"Aye, sir!" said Barclay, a bit too loudly, for his own nerves were showing a bit.

Mistral went smoothly about on the larboard tack, the hands hauling on the sheets until the big booms swung across and the ship settled on her new course directly toward *Coeur's* last known position.

Mistral plunged into the Gulf of Gonâve just south of the centerline between its northern and southern coasts. Port-au-Prince was hidden by Gonâve Island by both distance and angle, as was *Coeur*. Well, hopefully she was still there. They sailed on for at least two more hours, seeing several small fishing boats about, but most were deeper inside the gulf and had not come farther out to fish.

Fallon exhaled, unaware that he had been holding his breath off and on for some time. The third act of the play was about to begin without him knowing how the second act had gone. He could now see *Coeur* as a faint image in his telescope, and presumably the French lookout could see *Mistral* as well. It was not a surprise to see the first-rate still there, although he would have liked to have seen some damage. Well, it was too far away; he could only hope. He ordered the ship to heave-to and await *Tigre*, who was coming up fast astern. Now if *Coeur's* *capitaine* was still angry . . .

As *Tigre* came up, Fallon took off his French *capitaine's* hat and doffed it to Ramos, who hesitated, and then doffed his back. No doubt he was a bit confused at *Mistral* stopping short of leading him all the way in, but there was the French ship ahead so perhaps Giroux felt he'd fulfilled his orders. And so *Tigre* sailed by, beautiful in the afternoon light, her Spanish flag standing out stiffly in the trade wind.

"Mr. Barclay, let's get underway for the far side of Gonâve Island, if you please," said Fallon, eagerness in his voice. "And Barclay, once *Tigre* is out of sight I believe we can take off these damn uniforms!"

BEAUTY HAD stationed a hand with a telescope on the island to look west, and at the first sighting of Fallon and the Spanish frigate he had climbed down from his rocky perch and rowed out to *Rascal* to report. When Beauty had judged the time right, *Rascal* weighed anchor and began to nose out from around the island—only to find *Mistral* sailing like thunder toward her.

That fucker, Beauty thought, *he pulled it off!*

Somers stood beside her, his wispy white hair blowing about, pistols in his waistband, and watched *Mistral* come closer. He, too, was smiling, and thinking exactly what Beauty was thinking.

"Aja," Beauty said to *Rascal's* new second mate, "I think we can now bring up powder and shot. And bring up some of those new fire arrows. You never know!"

"Powder and shot it is! And fire arrows!" said a laughing Aja. And then: "Fire arrows, Cully!"

"Look at that, now!" laughed Somers, and Beauty looked to see what he was pointing to. "But don't look too closely, Beauty!"

Fallon's crew seemed to be throwing their uniforms overboard! Laughter broke out as the Rascals momentarily stopped their duties and lined the railing to look at *Mistral*, her crew mostly naked now, laughing and waving at their old shipmates.

Beauty simply shook her head in wonder. *Fucking Fallon!*

SIXTY

Capitaine Ardoin was shaking his head in wonder as well, for no sane Spaniard could think the same trick would work twice! Yet *Mistral* had been reported in the offing, and here came a Spanish frigate, the private signal flying, and although it did not appear from this distance to be the same frigate that attacked *Coeur* before, it *might* be, for it had been dark then. Perhaps the capitán was returning, hoping to find a cripple to finish off. No matter, Ardoin would not be fooled by a Spaniard again.

Quickly, he ordered seamen with axes to be standing by to cut the anchor cable, thereby releasing bow and stern lines. He then ordered his marines to climb the rigging, and for cutlasses and pistols to be handed out to the sailors in case the fighting got close. Finally, he ordered the larboard guns to be loaded and run out. Ardoin would be ready this time.

Tigre sailed briskly past the western point of Gonâve Island, toward *Coeur*, and Capitán Ramos intended to round up in a flourish and drift to an anchorage close by. It was meant to be a show of Spanish seamanship, a little something to impress the French, yes?

At one-half mile he saw the marines climb *Coeur*'s rigging. This gave him pause, but perhaps it was to welcome their Spanish ally. Then, at two cables, *Coeur* opened her gun ports and, before Ramos could grasp what was happening, fifty guns erupted flame and smoke from the first-rate's larboard side and sent their balls hurtling toward his beloved *Tigre*, plunging into her hull and shattering her railing and cascading splinters into every man standing there. *Men who had been about to wave on his orders.*

"Come about!" Ramos shouted.

Tigre began to tack, bringing her bows through the eye of the wind and pointing to Gonâve Island, with not much room to spare before the coral shoals presented themselves, but Ramos wanted time to get his guns to bear. Then he could fall off and retreat. Fighting a first-rate beyond a single broadside for honor would never do.

As the frigate came about he ordered the starboard battery loaded and run out. He turned to look at *Coeur* just as smoke and flame erupted from the first-rate again. He felt *Tigre* shudder as the shots came aboard. Men screamed and collapsed in death. One of the helmsmen not ten feet from him went down in a bloody mess, and rigging snapped with a sound like musket shots. He looked the length of his ship and saw more dead seamen than he had time to count. But he saw his guns were ready at last.

"*Fire!*" he yelled, and now the thunder came from *his* ship! He saw with satisfaction at least some of the balls hit home, but he had no time to gloat as the island was close aboard.

"Fall off!" he ordered, and slowly, slowly the big frigate swung her bows west, each of her massive spars set in a controlled maneuver practiced thousands of times. But never under the guns of a first-rate, which made the discipline of the thing the more impressive.

"Cut the cable! Cut the cable!" ordered Ardoin. He was mad with rage at the insolent Spanish *alliés* and had all but forgotten Hedouville, who might be even now at the beach, expecting to board soon and watching in horror. Well, he could see for himself what an ally Spain was, thought Ardoin. This was an affront that would not go unanswered. The honor of France was at stake! Not to mention, his own.

The cable was cut and, moments later, the spring line was cast off, which let *Coeur*'s head fall off before the wind. The ship's topsails were let fall, and her courses set along with the jib and fore-topmast staysail, the fore staysail, and all of the myriad other sails—21 in all—seemingly all at once but not quite; eight hundred men who knew their jobs made it organized and orderly. The big ship gained speed with each yard through the water, her angry *capitaine* looking through his telescope at *Tigre*, which was less than a mile away. Ardoin wondered where she would go—Santiago, or up the coast of Cuba to Havana? Or perhaps she would sail to a port in Santo Domingo. He ordered more attention to the topgallants and then seethed in silence.

THE SITUATION aboard *Tigre* was serious but not dire. She still had her spars and rigging, though some of it would need to be spliced, and quickly. One gun had been upended by the last of *Coeur*'s broadsides and, as a consequence, four seamen had been added to the list of dead; all of them had been thrown overboard, along with what could be gathered up of the unfortunate helmsman. Many more sailors were below with the surgeon; perhaps some would live.

Ramos looked astern at *Coeur* trimming her topgallants and wondered how clean her bottom was for a long chase. She had just recently arrived from Europe, or so his orders said. But he didn't believe his orders anymore, so it didn't matter.

He thought rapidly of his options, Santiago or Havana, and decided on Santiago. He would have the wind on his quarter, which was a fast point of sail for his square-rigged ship. And, more important, Santiago was closer by far and, though he was comfortably ahead of *Coeur* now, that could change.

Ramos looked up and saw every inch of sail was drawing. It would be a race to safety now, and he felt he could win if nothing untoward happened.

SIXTY-ONE

RASCAL CLEARED the western tip of Gonâve Island and kicked up her heels like a colt out for a gallop. Fallon stood next to Beauty and reveled in the ship's speed and power. He had *Tigre* in sight ahead to the southwest, apparently making for Santiago as he'd hoped. The closeness of a friendly port was just too much to resist. Off to the west was *Renegade,* out of sight at that moment, but presumably dropping down farther south to intercept *Tigre.*

Now here came *Coeur,* looking like a massive, malevolent bully with every stitch of sail she possessed up and drawing. Through his telescope, Fallon could see that *Coeur's* bows were patched, if not handsomely, at least adequately, given the little time that had passed since *Renegade* had mauled her. *Rascal* was to the north of the big French ship, several miles away, appearing to innocently sail along without care. And behind *Rascal,* bearing along handsomely, was *Mistral* with Second Mate Ajani in command. Fallon smiled to himself, thinking this must be every parent's hold-your-breath moment: *Letting your child take that first step away from your hands.* He had given Aja a strict order to lay back and stay out of the fighting, however, for a sloop would have no chance under fire from much larger ships. He'd better obey that order, thought Fallon.

ONCE *TIGRE* had every sail drawing, it was clear that *Coeur* would not catch her, in spite of her greater press of sail. Ramos could breathe at last; he had no doubt *Coeur* would eventually see the chase was futile and, honor served, give up. Later, Ramos could try to understand what had happened, and why, but it had to have been a trick ordered by *Coeur's capitaine* and executed by Giroux. He wondered, not for the first time, if Spain and France were still allies. Or if they ever were.

Coeur was still several miles astern, but game enough, her big shoulders rolling in the following sea. Ramos could see a schooner off to windward of the first-rate—where the hell had she come from? And behind her was Giroux in the French sloop. Were they working together?

¡Madre de Dios!

He was about to turn back to the binnacle when the cry came from the lookout.

There was a frigate off the starboard bow! And she was Spanish!

ARDOIN GRITTED his teeth at the futility of the chase and forced himself to admit it was over. Or should be, for there was likely no way to catch *Tigre*. Barring a catastrophe aboard the Spanish frigate he stood no chance; the frigate was simply too fast and his own ship's bottom too foul. There was no dishonor in admitting that.

For some time, he had been aware of a schooner off his starboard bow, which was curious if nothing else. Certainly, it was no cause for concern, but he wondered at it.

"Deck! Ship ahead, *Capitaine!* A frigate! I think it's . . . it's *Tigre* also!"

What was this now? wondered Ardoin in alarm, slapping his forehead with his right hand. Another trap! How many *Tigres* were there?

"Deck! Another ship astern, *Capitaine!*" called the lookout.

Ardoin's head snapped around and he raised his telescope to balance it on the nub of his left arm. There, several miles to the southeast, was a ship-of-the-line flying British colors and an admiral's pendant.

Merde!

The British ship astern was sailing close-hauled to cut *Coeur* off from retreat—Ardoin could see it now! And the forward frigate, perhaps the forward two frigates, would soon come about to put the stopper in the bottle. Now the British and the Spanish were working together!

Ardoin's mind fought for clear air, and he found it: *Better to fight one ship than two.*

He ordered *Coeur* to tack and begin the retreat to Port-au-Prince. Slowly, ponderously, the massive ship began her turn. To have anything carry away would be disastrous, and every man on board knew it. Ardoin shuddered as he thought of sitting defenseless as Spanish and British ships battered his own ship from every direction. At last, *Coeur's* bows turned to the east, her larboard braces were hauled, and she began to pick up speed, every sail drawing on her new course back to Port-au-Prince.

Ardoin looked over his shoulder to see if the frigates would follow, but surprisingly they had not tacked yet. Off to larboard the schooner had tacked to mimic *Coeur* and was now beginning to edge down on her. And, he should have seen this immediately, she was *British!*

Ardoin's mind exploded. *What was happening?*

"Deck!" came the call from the lookout. "*Mistral* is behind the schooner!"

He raised his telescope and could see that *Mistral* had been hidden behind the schooner. She was now flying British colors, as well, and was sailing westward toward the frigates. Ardoin threw up his hand.

Sacré bleu! Where did all these ships come from? he thought. *I am surrounded!*

This was too much, too much by far to even begin to absorb. Ardoin had Spanish frigates to the west, a British ship cutting off his retreat to the east, and a British schooner and his own sloop— captured—doing who knew what.

"*Mon Dieu!*" he screamed. *My God!*

SIXTY-TWO

RENEGADE FELL off the breeze and sailed on a broad reach to intercept the Spanish *Tigre*, who was making excellent speed for Santiago. The frigates were still several miles apart, *Renegade* closing fast and still flying Spanish colors, and Jones could feel the perspiration running down his sides under his capitán's uniform. It was long odds that *Tigre*'s capitán had heard of *Doncella*'s sinking, even though she had called at Santiago. Havana and Santiago were at opposite ends of Cuba, and news travelled slowly overland. At this point, Jones was committed to his role in the little play and, he had to admit, things were going damned well so far. Now, if only *Tigre* thought *Doncella* was coming to help . . .

At a mile, Jones saw *Coeur* give up the chase and head for Port-au-Prince. Immediately *Renegade* hoisted a Spanish signal for *Tigre*: *Are you in distress?*

Tigre didn't hesitate in replying, asking for the frigate's private number.

Jones sent up: *Hold course*, and *Renegade* began to drop down on the Spaniard; soon enough only a half mile separated the two frigates.

Jones had not deigned to make *Doncella*'s private signal because he didn't know it, of course. But he knew telescopes were on him—thank God for the Antigua Sewing Circle's uniforms. On *Renegade* sailed, continuing to drop down slowly on *Tigre* . . . three cables apart . . . then less.

It was then, through instinct or suspicion, that the capitán of the real *Tigre* smelled a rat. He had been fooled already by the French sloop, who now was flying British colors. Could this be another trick?

He opened his gun ports to find out.

"Hoist the colors and run out!" yelled Jones in response, and *Renegade*'s well-trained crew jumped to their duties. The British ensign was hoisted, and a lusty cheer rose up from the men. The chance to die in a hail of iron was, ironically, what British seamen lived for.

"*Fire!*" ordered Jones, and *Renegade*'s great guns boomed out in chorus and sent a storm of iron across less than a cable's bit of water into *Tigre*'s starboard hull, a hull already battered by *Coeur*. *Tigre*'s guns replied, and Jones watched in stupid amazement as his men were flung backward at their stations, some completely across the deck. The frigates were evenly matched, and it seemed most of *Tigre*'s shots found their mark. *Renegade*'s hull was pockmarked and her deck was blotched in red.

"Again, lads!" Jones called, and in less than three minutes *Renegade*'s guns roared again, the smoke blowing over *Tigre* and making it hard to see the effects. But the fog cleared, and Jones could see dead Spaniards hanging over the starboard railing, some being thrown over the side by their shipmates. Now *Tigre*'s guns belched smoke and fire again, and again a withering broadside came aboard *Renegade*. Jones was thrown backward and landed on a dead seaman who had lost most of his head, his neck spurting blood into the air instead of his brain.

"Load with grape! Load with grape!" Jones yelled as he rose. "Prepare to board!"

This madness had to stop or there would be nothing left of either ship, and Jones wisely decided to risk it all on the main chance.

"Make right for them, helmsman!" he ordered, and *Renegade*'s bows swung south. Jones could see Spanish sailors standing on *Tigre*'s deck like wheat before the scythe. The ships were very close now, and Jones could see *Tigre*'s gun crews loading their guns again.

"Helmsman, lay her alongside," ordered Jones. "Ready the grappling hooks!"

The gunners signaled they were ready as the ship came alongside *Tigre*.

"*Fire!*" yelled Jones as the ships came together, just as *Tigre*'s crew prepared to fire their own broadside. Spaniards fell like wooden pins in a child's game. Men were down and bleeding as two-inch balls tore through their clothing and organs in a brutal spray of iron.

"Boarders away!" yelled Jones, trying to rally the men. He leapt onto *Renegade*'s railing and then down to *Tigre*'s deck, landing with both feet in a dead man's open chest.

The fighting was back and forth, each side gaining and losing ground, as more than three hundred sailors screamed in a riot of blood and fear. It seemed to last forever, and Jones thought at one moment the Renegades were losing more than they were gaining. But then a yell, a voice he knew, and Aja and fresh seamen climbed over *Tigre*'s larboard railing, firing into the Spaniards and hacking at the rear guard of the Spanish crewmen, forcing them back onto their own men who were fighting the Renegades. Now the Spaniards began to lose their spirit at this new onslaught, and Jones looked for the capitán to demand he strike. But Ramos would issue no more orders. He was down at the binnacle, a jagged splinter sticking into one eye, the other eye sightless in death.

Jones leapt to his side and stood over him. "*¡Rendición!* Surrender!" he screamed.

And slowly, like the dazed men they were, the Spanish sailors laid down their cutlasses and then they, too, lay down, too tired to stand.

SIXTY-THREE

KINIS HAD WATCHED *Coeur* complete her tack—that had taken a while—and saw that the big first-rate was now sailing more or less in his direction. She was sailing as close to the wind as possible, making considerable leeway, and her speed had dropped in consequence. Still, she was falling down toward *Avenger*, which was good.

He could see *Rascal* sailing hard and fast, and it seemed they might all intercept *Coeur* at the same spot. In spite of the admiral's orders, he never expected *Rascal* to stay out of the fight. Not with Fallon aboard.

"Captain Kinis, are you ready to take on a French first-rate?" asked Davies, who had been standing just behind Kinis with his telescope to his eye.

"We're ready, sir!" exclaimed the normally austere Kinis. He was a thoroughly competent British officer, and what he lacked in charm or personality he made up for with courage and a certain pragmatism. If he said the ship was ready for this battle, it was.

Kinis looked through his telescope at the oncoming *Coeur*. Her bows looked poxed; Jones had seen to that handsomely. But her jury-rigged bowsprit stood proudly raked at its upward angle, with the flying jib, jib, and fore staysail all set and drawing. Kinis stared a moment more and then reached a conclusion.

He would ask Davies for his approval, though in truth, as captain of the ship, he didn't need it.

✦ ✦ ✦

"Deck there!" *Rascal's* lookout called. "Signal from *Avenger*: *Crossing!*"

At the lookout's call, Fallon swung his telescope toward *Avenger* and he and Beauty both nodded instinctively. Kinis was going to attempt to cross *Coeur's* bows and loose a broadside into that most vulnerable part of the ship, doubly vulnerable since *Renegade* had attacked the bows already. But it meant *Avenger* would likely pay a heavy price because, after passing *Coeur*, her stern would be exposed to a broadside, or perhaps even two. And those were massive broadsides, indeed.

"Beauty!" called Fallon. "Lay a course to cross *Coeur's* stern but out of her angle of fire! Can you do that? Can *we* do that?"

"What are you thinking, Nico?" asked Beauty, looking closely at their sailing angle relative to *Coeur's* and working out the answer to Fallon's question in her own mind.

"I'm going to try to give the *capitaine* something else to think about to take his attention away from blowing *Avenger's* stern to hell," said Fallon. "Although I don't have much hope."

Beauty stared forward, her eyes on the shortening distance between *Rascal* and *Coeur*, and then she looked at the approaching *Avenger*, sailing with a bone in her teeth to cross *Coeur's* bows. Fallon kept quiet, knowing Beauty was better at sailing angles than he was.

"I believe we can bear off a bit about a half mile from *Coeur* and make up the ground with better speed toward her stern," said Barclay, reaching the exact conclusion that Beauty had already reached. "That should keep us outside her firing angle."

They sailed for perhaps another cable's distance, and Beauty ordered the schooner to drop down onto a beam reach. After she gave the order she turned to Fallon with a smile.

"Nico," she said, "I've got an idea that ought to get that fucker's attention."

✦ ✦ ✦

DAVIES WATCHED *Coeur* grow larger and larger in his telescope. She had run out her starboard guns in anticipation of *Avenger*'s arrival, but of course Kinis had no intention of coming under them. *Avenger* was close hauled and, unless a fluke of wind should alter things, they should just make it across the big ship's bows.

Kinis raised his telescope to look at *Rascal* again. She was making excellent speed and might intercept *Coeur*, but he wondered what Fallon's strategy was. Certainly, he should stay away from *Coeur*'s guns, but then what could he hope to accomplish? *Give him this,* Kinis thought, *he's a brave man.*

As he watched, *Rascal* seemed to bear off to the west slightly. At that angle, she would not intercept *Coeur* but rather cross somewhere behind her. Mystified, Kinis sighed and turned his attention back to his own ship.

"Load and run out larboard!" he yelled.

FALLON WATCHED Beauty stand by the helmsman, giving him subtle and barely audible direction as *Rascal* arched like an eyebrow to the west of *Coeur* and then hardened up to the east toward the first-rate's quarter. Here is where *Rascal*'s sailing qualities came to the fore, for she could point closer to the wind than any square-rigged ship and, even now, seemed to be sailing right up to *Coeur*'s stern. Would *Coeur*'s guns bear? The answer came almost immediately as the big ship's aft-most guns barked, and splashes exploded less than fifty yards from *Rascal*'s larboard railing.

Fallon smiled as Beauty shrugged.

"Cully!" she yelled. "Ready the larboard guns!"

Again, *Coeur*'s guns fired, but again the shots were wide. *Rascal* was going to reach *Coeur*'s stern before *Avenger* reached her bows, just as Beauty had planned. They were gaining ground with every surge forward, and the enormity of *Coeur*'s size stunned the entire crew. Most of the men had never seen a building that big.

Close. Very close, now. Suddenly they were up to the ship's stern, preparing to cross, *Coeur*'s huge size filling the sky.

"Fire!" yelled Beauty, and the damnedest thing happened: Flaming arrows shot out from *Rascal's* eight larboard guns! It was like Zeus hurling lightning into *Coeur's* open stern gallery! The arrows trailed smoke like an afterthought to mark their path up, up, and then into the big ship.

And then *Rascal* bore off quickly to protect her own stern as *Coeur* sailed on.

DAVIES LOOKED at Kinis and asked: "Did you see what I saw?"

Kinis smiled, giving the moment and *Rascal* their due, for he'd had the chance to bring fire arrows aboard but had scoffed, not seeing the sense of it when a cannonball did the real damage.

Now *Avenger* was almost up to *Coeur*, perhaps a cable away, and Kinis leaned into the binnacle as if to push his ship a bit higher to clear the oncoming first-rate. God, it was going to be close. As the ships drew closer he found himself holding his breath.

"Deck there!" the lookout called. "Smoke coming from *Coeur's* stern! She's on fire!"

"Goddammit, she's burning!" exclaimed Davies. "Look at that smoke!"

Coeur was trailing brown smoke against the sky now, and Davies could see the *capitaine*, who appeared to have one arm, waving frantically and giving orders to crewmen who were running here and there. Every seaman's greatest fear was fire aboard, and Davies knew there was real panic on that ship. And that was just the beginning, for *Avenger* was about to cross *Coeur's* bows and Kinis was taking a deep breath.

"Fire!" the flag captain yelled.

Gun after gun fired in succession, 37 explosions in all, and *Coeur's* bow opened like a daylily in sunshine, water pouring in as the big ship plowed on, gulping thirstily. When the last gun fired, *Avenger* was by! Kinis kept his course, sailing at a perpendicular angle away from *Coeur*, bracing for the expected hail from fifty guns into *Avenger's* stern.

But only the first-rate's forward guns fired, for smoke was now drifting from the aft gun ports as the stern of the ship was fully engulfed in flames. Davies felt the shot come aboard but could not see the damage. Quickly, Kinis called for a tack to bring *Avenger* onto larboard and sailing parallel to *Coeur*, though considerably behind her.

No matter. The first-rate was swallowing water even as her sails drove her bow deeper into the sea. Her stern was on fire, and there would be only one way to put out the flames.

Coeur de France had to sink.

Avenger hardened up to the east and *Rascal* moved away, fearful that *Coeur* could explode before she sank. Her bows down, the big ship slowly nosed deeper and deeper into the sea, her forward progress slowing, her downward progress increasing.

Wooden ships take a long time to sink. Wood, of course, doesn't want to sink, but the sheer weight of such a massive ship with its cannons and stores and humanity gives it no choice. It would take the better part of the remaining daylight for *Coeur*'s bows to slowly point directly at the bottom, the ship dropping deeper by degrees, groaning as she continued to sink below the surface.

At the last, *Coeur*'s massive stern stuck out from the sea, flames dancing from her timbers and sending sparks zigzagging upward, lighting the night sky like a giant torch.

SIXTY-FOUR

THE SUN rose into a pale sky, a somber yellow orb that bathed the world in light but not cheer. Certainly, there was little cheerfulness aboard *Rascal* as she prepared to leave Dame Marie for Antigua.

Rascal and *Avenger* had rescued every French sailor they could find; not surprisingly, the one-armed *capitaine* was not among them. Finally, darkness had put paid to the search; no doubt there were several hundred bodies floating ashore or out to sea. Most sailors didn't know how to swim, so survival was counted in minutes. British tars could gladly inflict maiming and death in a ship-to-ship battle, but seeing an enemy ship sink with all hands left the victors morose. The cries of drowning men were pitiful to hear and remained in memory long after they ended in a final, merciful silence.

Rascal and *Avenger* had anchored in Dame Marie after dark and had been joined before midnight by an exhausted but jubilant Jones bringing *Renegade* and the captured *Tigre* into the tiny harbor, followed by an equally elated Aja aboard *Mistral*. *Renegade* had lost sixteen men and had twenty-two wounded. The loss of life aboard *Tigre* had been spectacular, first from *Coeur's* pounding but especially from *Renegade's* last grape broadside. What prisoners there were had been locked below decks. The wounded had been transferred to *Renegade*, and her surgeon had done what he could, but he had his own shipmates to tend first.

Now, as *Rascal* and *Mistral* left Dame Marie, Davies and Jones were preparing to leave for Port-au-Prince to land the prisoners under a white flag. The French sailors would have quite a tale to tell about Spanish duplicity, a tale that might wend its way all the way to Paris.

Once in the open sea, Somers approached Fallon at the windward rail to have a word. He had observed the battle with *Coeur* as an amazed, if impotent, bystander.

"Nico, this whole thing, your whole plan to draw France and Spain into battle with each other, to make allies *distrust* each other, was the God-damnedest thing I've ever seen," he began. Fallon made to object but Somers cut him off. "No, I won't hear it. I know about luck and all that, but I'm telling you straight up that what happened these last few days was *art. Fucking art!* There's no other word for it. I know you feel bad about sinking *Coeur.* But, son, think of the hundreds or thousands of British lives that might have been saved over the rest of the war. Who knows where that ship might have gone next or what she might have done? It's not easy seeing death on that scale, I admit it. But better him than us. I, for one, am damn glad it was him!"

With that monologue, Somers went looking for Beauty to give her more or less the same speech, adding something about those *fucking fire arrows!* Damned if he would see long faces after a victory like that!

By two bells in the forenoon, a degree of happiness had returned to *Rascal,* the officers and crew having realized the role they played in sinking a first-rate. Cully, his good eye gleaming over his Irish smile, held up a fire arrow to the group of freedmen and described *how* it worked and *why* it worked. He didn't have to explain what it did, as every man had seen that for himself.

Beauty's mood had lightened somewhat as well. Yet, although her wound was not hurting, the same could not be said for her heart. She wanted to get to Antigua, welcome Elinore aboard, and depart for Bermuda as quickly as possible.

The day seemed brighter to Fallon now, and indeed the morning's haze had lifted wonderfully, and *Rascal* plunged along on a bow line. He looked astern and saw Aja wave; *Mistral* seemed to dance above the waves instead of sailing through them. Aja would be a brilliant captain one day, Fallon thought. He had let go of the toddler's hands, and the toddler had taken his first step.

Off to windward was Santo Domingo, lush and mountainous. And Spanish, unless Louverture was planning to conquer the whole of Hispaniola for France. Well, he was a determined leader, thought Fallon, at least as long as he could stay in power. Fallon hoped he had helped the general stay a bit longer.

He thought of Elinore now, no doubt looking out to the mouth of English Harbor throughout the day. Or walking with Paloma along the beach, the two of them becoming deeper friends: Paloma was a good influence on Elinore's recovery from such a devastating loss.

Fallon had felt the loss as well. But his mind had been forced to put it away, deep down, because there was a war to fight. He realized now it wasn't so deep down after all.

He thought about the baby—boy or girl? Was it Jack or Mary? He could picture himself playing with his baby, holding the pink-skinned fellow—*yes, Jack*—above his head and making him laugh and giggle and love his father. *Love his father.*

My God, he thought, *that was almost me.*

He walked the length of the ship, past cannons and crew, to stand at the bows and look to the east. The sea was an unimaginable blue, and dolphins surged alongside *Rascal* in a race to Antigua. The past was in his wake, he realized, but the future could be everything he wanted it to be.

AFTERWORD

*I*N 1802, Touissant Louverture was deported to France and imprisoned. He died soon after. Napoleon, as First Consul of France, revoked the decree abolishing slavery in all French territory the next year. France would not finally abolish the slave trade in her colonies until 1848, with a general and unconditional emancipation of all slaves.

green press
INITIATIVE

McBooks Press is committed to preserving ancient forests and natural resources. We elected to print this title on 30% post consumer recycled paper, processed chlorine free. As a result, for this printing, we have saved:

6.3 Trees (40' tall and 6-8" diameter)
500 Gallons of Wastewater
2.6 Million BTU's of Total Energy
20 Pounds of Solid Waste
2,700 Pounds of Greenhouse Gases

McBooks Press made this paper choice because our printer, Thomson-Shore, Inc., is a member of Green Press Initiative, a nonprofit program dedicated to supporting authors, publishers, and suppliers in their efforts to reduce their use of fiber obtained from endangered forests.

For more information, visit www.greenpressinitiative.org

Environmental impact estimates were made using the Environmental Defense Paper Calculator. For more information visit: www.papercalculator.org.